MW01713191

Mom & D

Thank you

your LOVE & support

~ Jon

Lani VanEck

Jon P. VanE

Jon

Peter Van Eck

The Odyssey of the Slingshot Man

The Odyssey of the SLINGSHOT MAN

Van Eck

PUBLISHING 3 MPH COMPANY

3 MPH Publishing Company, LLC
Dexter, Michigan

Printed in the United States of America

slingshotman.com
3mphpub@gmail.com

Published in 2018 by
3 MPH Publishing Company
Dexter, MI 48130

First Printing, 2018
10 9 8 7 6 5 4 3 2 1

Library of Congress Cataloging-in-Publication Data has been applied for.

ISBN 978-0-692-06645-4

Cover and book design by Kurt Parfitt

Printed and bound in Dexter, Michigan by Thomson-Shore Printing

ACKNOWLEDGEMENTS

This is the first novel any of us has written. We have needed a lot of help, and many wonderful people have contributed generously to the cause.

The creation of the work was made easier by Steve Fisher, who collaborated with Peter on the creation of Slingshot Man way back in 1973; by Karina Baylor, who helped build the original six-foot construction model of the kiva, which we started in the late 1990s; by Bill and Sue Griffin, who gave us detailed descriptions of the snowshoe class they took at Camp 33; by Bill Daniels, who made a special trip just to get a good photograph of a kachina; and by Ron Stafford, who provided spiritual, financial, and conceptual support. We also want to thank the many people who helped us by sharing local knowledge about the places on Ian's journey, whether by phone, email, or in person. Thank you all so much.

Once the manuscript was done, a whole new cast of supporters came on the scene. Twenty people volunteered—or were drafted—to read the book. We are deeply grateful for your time and for your thoughtful insights. Many of you caught errors we had missed or developed analytic frameworks we had not considered. Thank you a thousand times over! A special thanks to Christina Bych, our editor, who worked her fingers to the bone (using a pencil from Fingerle Lumber) to correct and amend the work. What a painstaking job it is to edit, to check every paragraph, every word, every punctuation mark, every fact. We marvel at her stamina and commitment—but we must admit we did not always follow her advice. Any errors are not to be laid at her door. Finally, the manuscript went to Kurt Parfitt, our graphic artist. To understand his challenges, you should know that the manuscript was composed on three different PCs, each one equipped with a different software package. These three parts were cobbled together into one manuscript and then had to be translated to a fourth and totally different layout program on an Apple computer. That was a Herculean task.

Finally, we would like to thank Barbara and Jean ("the Moms"), all our siblings, spouses, offspring, and the numerous other family members who have supported us in this endeavor over the past fifty years. We really couldn't have done it without you.

Dedicated to our future selves

Chapter 1

The stag watched steam billowing from his nostrils as he exhaled into the frigid winter air. His greenish-white glow reflected off deep snow creating a luminous boundary encircling the immediate area around him. He slowly turned and looked west. The thick deep blackness of night was descending quickly and only a thin sliver of the fire-red sunset shone on the horizon.

Below the swollen earth of Sour Creek Dome, a living, breathing beast was preparing to emerge. Millions of tons of molten rock had waited 640,000 years to make an appearance. And now, five miles beneath the stag's feet, the beast shook with anticipation.

Day 1

Gathering firewood from the woodshed, Ian Cameron paused a moment to take everything in. Large flakes of snow fell gently to the ground, a cold wind was blowing. The clean crisp smell of winter merged with the aroma of wood smoke, and bright red cardinals, in stark contrast to the snow, fought over black sunflower seeds in the bird feeder. The large red barn relaxed into each deep breath of wind that entered its body, and the white rolling hills and open farm fields boasted miles of winter splendor.

The sleigh bells hanging on the handle of the back door jingled as he carried wood into the house. The musty smell of the basement rose to combine with the cozy aroma of coffee and bacon wafting from the kitchen. His wife Theresa was standing at the stove stirring the potatoes.

"Hey, professor, do you want some help with that wood?"

"No, thanks. I've got it," Ian replied as he hesitated at the door waiting for their dog Arlo to come in.

He carried the wood to the box next to the woodstove, checked the fire, and went back into the kitchen to help with breakfast. Theresa handed him his coffee. He kissed her on the cheek and squeezed her butt.

"Aren't you ever satisfied?" She giggled. "I thought this morning would tide you over 'til you got back."

The cuckoo clock chirped while soft music played in the background. Theresa ran upstairs to wake the kids for breakfast. A few minutes later she came back into the kitchen and noticed that Ian seemed to be deep in thought.

"What's up?" Theresa asked.

Ian flipped the bacon as he thought about his response.

"Hmm, you name it. The house is cluttered, the studio's a mess, time seems to be speeding up.... I just feel like I'm spinning my wheels. Christmas is such a big letdown anymore. I don't know. Maybe I should get back into meditation or yoga or something."

"Time to reorganize the studio again?" Theresa suggested. "Maybe put away that six-foot painting? Spend some creative time alone with your potter's wheel? Working with clay always makes you happy and centered."

Ian smiled in quiet appreciation of her understanding. This was one of the benefits of marrying another artist.

They had met when they both attended the University of Colorado in Boulder. Theresa specialized in fiber arts and Ian was working on his MFA in ceramics. The couple married four years later. Within a few months, they found themselves in Michigan. Eastern Michigan University had offered Ian a tenure-track position in the art department's ceramics program.

In the spring of 1999, Theresa found out she was pregnant, and they decided to look for a more permanent housing situation. By August, they had moved into a beautiful old farmhouse near Dexter. They had 40 acres of gently rolling hills, barns, silos, and outbuildings. It was perfect! Four months after they moved into the farm, their son Gabriel was born. Two years later, their daughter Claire came into the world.

Claire sat down for breakfast as the skillet of sizzling potatoes was placed on the cast iron trivet in the middle of the table. After a few parental warnings were shouted up the steps, Gabe finally meandered into the room and took his seat.

"Are you excited about your trip, Dad?" asked Claire. Before he could answer, she quickly added, "We're going to miss you."

"Awww," Ian said, "I'm going to miss you guys too."

Ian's trip was going to provide a welcome break. Theresa knew how busy he had been this last year. In July, when the family was on vacation in Paradise, Michigan, they had visited Tahquamenon Falls. She noticed a posting outside one of the gift shops that advertised a snowshoe-making class to be held in November and December. She knew right then what Ian's Christmas present would be.

As they continued breakfast, Ian wove a colorful story about growing up in the country and learning everything he could about wild edibles, starting fires with a bow and drill, building survival structures, and making his own rope out of tall grasses from the field. He told the kids that their uncle had given him a survival manual called *Bushcraft* one Christmas, and every day after was an exciting adventure.

"One of the things I've always wanted to make was a pair of snowshoes," Ian told them. "And now, after all these years, I finally get to do it!" Then he added, "Plus, I can't wait to see northern Michigan in the winter."

With the conclusion of breakfast, the family worked together to clear the table. Gabe reminded Ian of his promise to go shooting when he got back from up north. Just before he died, Ian's father had given Ian an antique double-barreled shotgun. Gabe was excited to try it out. Ian assured his son that he had not forgotten, and that it would be a top priority when he returned.

Theresa finished cleaning up as Ian went upstairs to grab a few more things for his trip. A few minutes later Claire and Arlo came bounding up the steps and pounced on the bed next to Ian's suitcase.

"Dad, don't worry about us. Mom and I are going to head out to the store as soon as you leave and return all the gifts you gave us so we can get stuff we really want!" Ian looked over to see Claire lying on her back, pulling Arlo's ears out sideways and smiling. Ian and Claire laughed and talked until Theresa came up and announced that it was getting late and he really should be going.

At 1:00, Ian's family said their goodbyes. He promised to call when he got to the hotel. Gabe gave his dad a hug and Ian kissed him on his forehead.

"You're in charge while I'm gone, so be good!" Gabe smiled proudly and Ian patted him on the shoulder, then looked over at Theresa and gave her a wink. It was Claire's turn next. She hugged her dad and kissed him on the cheek.

"So, what if it snows too much in the UP and you can't leave, or your old truck breaks down?" Claire asked. Ian thought for a second, tweaked her nose, and replied,

"Then I'll just have to walk back, silly!"

Leaving Theresa with the Volvo station wagon and opting to drive his classic 1952 cherry-red Chevy pickup truck to the wilds of northern Michigan was not a hard decision. It was Ian's favorite mode of transportation. He unsnapped the custom cover, threw his bags into the back, snapped it back up, and was ready to roll. The dog chased the rumbling red monster part way down the driveway as the Camerons waved their goodbyes. Ian was finally on the road.

The snow had stopped falling and the sky was clearing. The sun was bright and reflected intensely off the white ground, making it hard to see without the aid of sunglasses. Ian drove US 23 North until it merged into I-75 near Flint.

Because southeast Michigan is so heavily populated, it never really begins to feel like "Up North" until somewhere near Standish. It's there that the cities disappear and the forests begin to take over. From this point north, the air smells fresher and time slows down.

Just before sunset Ian stopped for gas in Gaylord. The roads were in great shape and he had made good time, considering it was winter in Michigan. As Ian filled his tank the wind seemed to bite through his jacket and he did a little bobbing dance to stay warm. After filling up, he ran inside to use the bathroom and get a Coke. Northern Michigan's classic rock station, "The Bear," was being piped in over the speakers. While Ian was checking out at the register, a short news break announced that after weeks of trembling, the caldera in Yellowstone had erupted, spewing ash in a 20-mile radius around the park.

"Wow, that's gonna really screw with people's vacations this year!" Ian remarked to the clerk.

Back on the road, the sunset was a beautiful mix of intense colors that pierced through the black silhouetted trees, leaving long shadows on the snowy fields. Ian thought how the simplest things in life had always made him the happiest: sunsets, deer in the woods, heavy snow falling, and apple blossoms in the spring.

His mind wandered off, deep in thought. He recalled his teenage years, when he first observed the fast-paced insanity of the world. He began reading books like *Siddhartha* and *Be Here Now,* and he learned to meditate. As he journeyed inward, his outer life began to reflect the peace that he was feeling, and his perception of reality was altered.

Suddenly, Ian snapped back into this reality. It was dark, and he was passing the Indian River exit.

"Holy crap!" he thought. "I just traveled 30 miles and I don't even remember it!"

Five miles out of Mackinaw City, I-75 makes a series of curves. Rounding the final curve brings the 550-foot towers of the Mackinac Bridge into view. Travelers love this spot, because from here on, those magnificent towers seize the attention and anticipation increases with every mile.

At 6:30 he pulled the truck into the parking lot of the Super 8 Bridgeview hotel. Stepping out, he stretched and took a deep cleansing breath of the crisp northern air. He was excited to be up north in the winter and couldn't wait to see the sights. It was dark and the bridge's suspension cables were all lit up with festive lights. Their reflections danced playfully on the water below.

Ian checked into the hotel and took his bags to his room. The view of the Straits from his window was spectacular. He called Theresa and the kids to let them know that he had made it safely to the bridge. Then he headed out for dinner.

Famished from the trip, Ian was thankful that Audie's Restaurant was only four blocks from the hotel. He decided to go to the lounge first for some drinks and an appetizer. The news on the TV above the bar was showing aerial shots of the caldera in Yellowstone and interviewing people from around the area. Ian was too far away to hear what was being said. He headed over to the dining room for a whitefish dinner.

With little else to do after dinner, Ian decided to go for a walk down on the beach. Two large freighters, decorated for Christmas, were approaching the bridge. One had a tall tree with white lights on its bow. The other had its guy wires, antenna mast, and deck rails wrapped with multi-colored lights.

Waves crashed into the shoreline. Heavy wet snow started to fall as Ian watched the muffled movement of haloed headlights slowly crossing the bridge. A cold wind arose from the north as he leisurely walked back toward his hotel room. He stopped and turned to take one last look. The icy wind licked his face and he smiled, contented to be where he was.

Back inside, he looked over at the clock. It was only 10 p.m. Ian turned on the television and channel surfed until he found a live shot from Yellowstone. CNN was reporting that earthquakes continued in the surrounding region, but there had been no eruptions in the last four hours. The Red Cross, FEMA, and the National Guard were converging on the area to help with clean-up efforts and to assist evacuees and the injured. Ian shut off the TV in mid-sentence and thought to himself how every year there was some major catastrophe to shake up the human psyche.

"Never a dull moment!" he said out loud, as he switched off the light to go to sleep.

Chapter 2

Hazy evening sunlight painted the canyon wall across from where Ian sat in quiet contemplation. Leaning against the side of his stone hovel, he watched the dry burning scrub oak shower the air with glowing embers. His fire crackled and popped, echoing down the canyon. At first Ian only felt the kachina's presence, but then the shimmering aura gave its position away. For some time now it had been standing off in the shadows...observing.

Day 2

Startled, Ian awoke alone in a strange room. He lay there motionless until his pounding heart calmed down.

"Man, what is it with these hovel dreams?" he whispered to himself. "And why a kachina? Where the hell did that come from?"

He dressed for the weather and went out to watch the sunrise on the Straits. The early morning sun highlighted the towers of the bridge, and their ivory reflections were mirrored across the ice sheets that had formed near the shoreline. The sky was a wash of cerulean blue. With the exception of a few light clouds over the Upper Peninsula, it looked like the weather would be perfect.

Back in his room, Ian watched the news as he dressed for the day. Live reports were streaming in from Wyoming and Montana as the caldera continued to spew magma from its chambers. The intensity had escalated since last night, with a notable increase in the number of harmonic tremors being reported under Yellowstone. To avoid heavy casualties, officials in both states suspended travel within 100 miles of the eruption site. The National Weather Service reported a heavy plume of ash billowing to around 20,000 feet above sea level. The Federal Aviation Administration closed all airspace within a 200-mile radius of the caldera.

Ian slid into his black turtleneck and put a blue flannel shirt over it. As he slipped his socks on, he couldn't help responding to the ABC news reporter at the scene,

"You're right, buddy. It is like Mount St. Helens." Ian remembered how intense that disaster had seemed at the time, but how far away it all seemed too.

"I am so glad we don't have to deal with that around here," he mumbled to himself.

He gathered his things and called home to check in. Theresa answered and put the phone on speaker so that Claire could listen and talk as well. Gabe, however, was still asleep. Ian laid out his plan for continuing on to Paradise, spending the night and returning to Mackinaw City the next night.

"Dad, don't forget the Mackinac Island Fudge!" Claire burst out. "I want peanut butter." Ian promised he would pick up fudge, pasties, and whitefish, as well.

Ian rolled out of the hotel parking lot just before 10:00 and headed north to the bridge. He couldn't stand driving over that damned bridge: five miles long, 200 feet above the water, metal grates for the roadway exposing the choppy water 20 stories below. He always made Theresa drive that eternal five-mile stretch. Michiganders remember in 1989 when gale force winds roared through the open grates below and lifted a small Yugo up and off the roadway, over the three-foot outer rail. The car plunged 200 feet into the cold straits below. This terrifying incident always played through Ian's mind whenever he crossed the bridge.

I-75 continues north into the Upper Peninsula. Ian got off on Exit 352, where a brown National Park sign reads "Tahquamenon Falls." He continued north for approximately 65 miles until he reached Paradise. Deep snow covered the ground and thick tall pine trees lined both sides of the road for miles.

At 12:30 he arrived at his hotel. The place was packed with snowmobilers who were there to run the endless miles of nearby trails. He went to his room to unload his bags and check out the incredible view of Lake Superior from his balcony.

The truck was running low on gas, so Ian headed to the gas station across the street from the hardware store. Waiting in line, he counted 28 snowmobiles, all the newest makes and models, in double rows at each pump. The colorful machines and snowsuit attire splashed a bouquet of flamboyancy in juxtaposition to the snow-burdened surroundings. Ian watched the dragon's breath of steam escape from each person's nose and mouth. Machines pulled away from the pumps emitting small plumes of white smoke, and the air had a strong, sickening odor of burnt gasoline.

It was just about 1:30 now, and Ian was getting hungry. He drove fourteen miles west toward Tahquamenon Falls and arrived at the Camp 33 complex.

A group of rustic shops and a brewpub surrounded a large deck and outdoor fireplace. Cross-country skis and poles were sticking out of a snow bank by the buildings. He entered the Tahquamenon Falls Brewery, where the snowshoe class would take place in the morning. As he came through the door, the aroma of burgers made his stomach growl. The place was filled with snowmobilers and outdoor enthusiasts. All of the tables were taken, so he eagerly made his way to one of the last seats at the bar.

The food and beer were incredible! Ian relaxed into two more pints before paying the bill and heading outside to check out the falls. The snowy trails were alive with activity. Skiers, snowshoers, and even a group of six on mountain bikes with huge balloon tires passed Ian as he made his way down the path. The strong northern Michigan pine trees, tempered by decades of brutal winters, held a foot or more of snow in their outstretched branches without flinching.

At the observation area, Ian was in awe. Ice had formed around the face of the falls, and it resembled a wall of tightly molded stalagmites. Under the shade of the pines on the south bank, the small section of water still flowing appeared brownish-white. The sheer stone walls across the river were covered by columns of icicles that were easily twenty feet tall. The trees closest to the river were heavily coated with ice from the mist-laden air. Ian hung around for a while, but there were so many people coming and going that the solitude he sought just wasn't there. It was midafternoon and he still wanted to drive up to Whitefish Point before dark. He quickly hiked back to his truck and headed north toward the Point.

All ships entering or leaving Lake Superior must pass by Whitefish Point, which is known as the "Graveyard of the Great Lakes." Ian filled the half-hour trip with his out-of-tune version of Gordon Lightfoot's *The Wreck of the Edmund Fitzgerald*...verse after butchered verse.

Around 4:00, he arrived and walked down to the beach. Frozen wave shelves had formed on the shoreline. Looking like cliffs, some were taller than he was! Large crystalline shards of iridescent blue ice glowed in the fading sunlight. Eight-foot plumes of water shot straight into the air as waves crashed violently into the temporary ice wall. Superior seemed rough today. He stood watching a freighter heading south, trying to make Whitefish Point before nightfall. The cold north wind tortured his face, and he could only imagine what it must be like out on the lake in this weather.

Ominous clouds approached from the west, ostensibly ushering in the next winter storm. Ian paused to take one last look out across Lake Superior. Another distant freighter, also decked out in Christmas lights, had come into view. He smiled, turned, and headed back to the hotel.

It was dark when Ian arrived back in Paradise. He stopped to have dinner. Many of the conversations he overheard at nearby tables centered on the worsening situation at the caldera. One couple even talked about packing up and heading home in the morning.

Ian finished his meal and returned to his room. He called his wife to see how things were going back home. Theresa immediately started talking about the volcano. She was worried.

"What if it gets worse, Ian? Why don't you just come home now? Don't worry about the money."

Ian assured her that there was nothing to worry about. He reminded her of Mount St. Helens and how everyone was afraid of what would happen back then.

"Nothing happened then and nothing is going to happen now. Everything is going to be fine. Promise me you'll just turn off the TV and go to bed."

After saying goodnight to everyone, he watched the news reports for a while, then called it a night around 9:00. He could hardly wait for his snowshoe class in the morning.

Two hours later, Ian was fast asleep when the caldera at Yellowstone erupted. The moderate sized blast threw an ash plume 50,000 feet into the air, where it entered the jet stream and headed east at 100 miles an hour.

Chapter 3

Day 3

Ian awoke and turned on the news. He walked down to the lobby, grabbed a quick cup of coffee, and returned to his room to get ready for the day. After showering, he watched the latest information about the volcanic eruption. Interstate 90 had been shut down across South Dakota by 4 a.m. The first dusting of ash hit Minneapolis and Duluth in the early morning hours. Most of the trucking companies based in Minneapolis tried to move their trucks out of the area before the roads became too hazardous to navigate. However, the ash descended too fast. Trucks jackknifed, causing major blockages on both I-35 and I-94. The governor of Minnesota declared a state of emergency.

At the local news break, the meteorologist predicted that the ash would probably not travel as far east as the Upper Peninsula. If it did, though, only a light dusting would hit Tahquamenon by 11 a.m.

Theresa hadn't called, so Ian assumed she was still asleep. Trying to fend off the panic attack he knew was coming, he texted that he would call her when his class broke for lunch. He packed his clothes and headed to Camp 33. Arriving at 9:00, he signed in at the door and made his way over to the coffee and donuts.

The snowshoe-making workshop was not scheduled to begin until 10:00. The unprecedented events 1300 miles to the west had assured the early arrival of all sixteen participants. Most had been up for hours watching national coverage of the ash plume moving east at 100 miles an hour toward the Upper Peninsula.

The dusting of electrically charged ash was causing more problems than just slick roads and automobile accidents. It short-circuited electrical substations, transformers, power lines, and cell phone towers. Most communications ceased behind the rolling ash plume. Massive widespread power outages cascaded out from the caldera, heading east. Social media exploded with rumors, then speculation, then panic.

The sixteen workshop participants and the two Department of Natural Resources instructors convened in the dining room to decide whether to continue or cancel the class. Most had travelled over 250 miles to get to Tahquamenon, at considerable cost and effort. The DNR offered refunds to anyone who wanted to leave due to these unusual circumstances.

An elderly couple from Grand Rapids were the first to cancel. The woman could not risk an exacerbation of her mild emphysema so far from a hospital. Three people from northern Ohio, a 50-ish couple and their 25-year-old daughter, were also becoming uncomfortable with the unfolding events. They had come 400 miles and in the end did not have faith in the predictive power of experts. They would take a partial refund and finish their snowshoes at home. Everyone else voted to continue with the class. The teachers agreed to stop the class immediately if atmospheric conditions deteriorated further.

One instructor led the five departing workshop participants to the window seating on the far side of the dining room. Ian glanced at them across the makeshift classroom. The dining tables were strewn with the wooden skeletons of unborn snowshoes. Momentary panic seized him. Within minutes these five fleeing refugees would be processed, credited, and gone. Had he made the right decision? Was this his last chance? Should he get the hell out now, while he still could—just in case?

Then, beyond the windows, his eye captured the white birch trees bathed in dazzling winter morning light. When his thoughts returned, the fleeing five were gone.

Shortly before 10:00, the instructors passed out the materials and equipment needed to make the snowshoes. The eleven remaining participants each received a pair of finished wooden frames, over 110 feet of lacing, rulers, pencils, and complete directions with diagrams.

Ian had chosen the Ojibwa-style snowshoe, which narrowed down at both the front toe and the rear tail. This allowed the toes of the snowshoes to cut through the snow like the bow of a boat through a wave. That would work well in the brush and deep snow around his farm in Dexter. The frames and the super-strong lacing would also easily hold his 250 pounds. Ian was finally about to handcraft the snowshoes he had always wanted.

Despite the volcanic eruption preoccupying the world, a wave of excitement surged through the workshop participants. Amidst laughter and smiles, cameras emerged. Panoramic pictures and selfies documented the start of this creative experience. The class instructor disrupted the conviviality with a cautionary statement:

"Take all your pictures now, because you aren't going to be smiling in a while."

When they opened the instruction packet, everyone understood immediately why: the packet included over 50 pages of detailed lacing diagrams. Each shoe required 38 stations where knots were tied to the frame. Slip knots, square knots, clove hitches, lark's knots, and saddle cinch knots were required at precise locations. Then there were all those "crossover" lacing rules: right lacing crosses over lefts and under horizontals; lefts cross over horizontals but under rights; horizontals cross over rights but under lefts. This was all pretty damned confusing!

"It's a good thing you didn't send me this before the course," someone blurted out in frustration. "I wouldn't have come!" Everyone burst into laughter.

The instructors reassured the class that while it might be a bit frustrating and confusing at first, within a couple of hours they would begin to see the patterns. Lacing would then become dramatically easier and quicker. Virtually all those taking the course in the past had completed their snowshoes. The pep talk worked.

The next hour and a half brought great embarrassment to Ian. Here he was, a university art professor, for God's sake; but he struggled with the diagrams and he struggled with the knots. The lacing constantly rolled off the table and became tangled under the chairs. He had to follow the crossover weaving patterns exactly, working with three separate laces. If he lost his focus for just one second, he didn't know if he was even pulling the correct lace. He had to call the instructors to his table frequently.

The insides of his thighs and legs hurt from bracing the snowshoes against his body. His knuckles were sore from tying knots. Would the instructors make him start over if he wove too tight or too loose? This was not the fun project he thought it would be. It was mentally exhausting.

No one was making much progress. Well, except the four basket weavers from Houghton: they weren't having any problems. The instructors were rarely called to their table for help. One of the basket weavers already had most of her lacing finished. Maybe if everyone else persisted for just another hour or so, the smiles might return.

That was never to be. At 11:30, the first dusting from the ash plume arrived. It would continue passing through for hours. Shortly thereafter, people started wandering into Camp 33 to report the effects. The local roads quickly became ash-covered and slippery, resulting in multiple accidents.

At this point, not a lot of work was getting done on the snowshoes. Everyone in class shifted their focus to the reports on highway conditions. Many, like Ian, had a long treacherous drive ahead of them.

The light dusting had shorted out power and communications all the way west to Wyoming. At 11:45, the instructors officially cancelled the remainder of the workshop. The basket weavers from Houghton could not reach anyone at home by phone or text. They immediately packed up and headed out into the teeth of the ash plume. Ian gathered his materials and the unfinished snowshoes, then ordered a beer and headed for his favorite table over by the windows. By noon he was watching the latest CNN volcano updates with everyone else.

Where they were, 1300 miles east of the Yellowstone caldera, the situation was improving. Although ash dusting continued here, it was not yet heavy enough to short-circuit phone or electrical service. Driving, however, would be dicey and slow on the glazed highways. It might take Ian four hours to travel the 80 miles to the bridge; but once he made it to the Lower Peninsula, I-75 should be plowed all the way to the Ohio border. If he left by 1:00, he should be home by early evening. About 12:10 Ian called his wife to let her know he was leaving Camp 33 within the next hour.

Settling in with his beer, Ian noticed three large, hand-carved wooden kachinas on the fireplace mantel. How could he have missed these before? They had sat there unobserved in plain view.

With a trained artist's eye he examined the intricate details of each carving. The two-foot-tall kachinas were exceptionally rare and expensive and they engendered feelings of great spiritual significance. They were not for tourists. Ian read the brass plaque on one of the carvings: “Hopi Great Spirit Eagle Dancer. The eagle is the messenger between the people and their spirit guides.” He flashed on that dream—the kachina, the hovel. A shiver ran up his spine.

A burst of greenish-white light suddenly engulfed the Eagle Dancer Kachina. The glow lasted for two seconds, then everything returned to normal. Everyone else had left the dining room to watch TV at the bar, so Ian was the only witness to this supernatural event. He sat spooked and speechless for the next several minutes, trying to comprehend. Despite all of his prior consciousness experience, Ian could not decipher its meaning. Loud voices at the bar jolted him out of his thoughts.

“Damn it,” someone yelled, “it just blew! For God’s sake! Yellowstone just blew up!”

At 12:15, CNN announced that seismometers throughout the region recorded multiple catastrophic earthquakes within the Yellowstone caldera. Satellite and ground imaging confirmed that over half of the 50-mile-wide volcano had violently erupted, sending ash plumes 70,000 feet into the air.

Now it was getting really strange. At the very moment that eerie green-white glow had burst forth from the kachina, the massive volcano at Yellowstone exploded. There were no words or questions appropriate to encompass this kind of synchronicity.

Pondering his dilemma, Ian wandered into the bar. CNN interrupted with another “Breaking News Alert.” Reports confirmed that the explosion had instantly vaporized a large portion of Yellowstone Park. Within seconds the town of Cody, on the eastern edge of Yellowstone, was buried under 100 feet of molten pyroclastic ash. The wall of ash was now traveling due east, riding the jet stream at 100 miles an hour toward Minneapolis. It would arrive there in eight hours.

Everyone at the bar stood in stunned silence. Scenes from past Yellowstone vacations played in their heads. Old Faithful, the falls, the buffalo...gone...vaporized.

"Shit, man," someone shouted. "It's coming right at us! We're only five hours east of Minneapolis. Camp 33 will be buried, like Pompeii. I've got to get the hell out of here!" Several others followed him out the door.

Moments later, CNN issued another "Breaking News Alert." The eastern United States and Canada should prepare for a sonic blast caused by the exploding volcano. A reporter pedantically explained that, historically, these types of sound blasts from volcanoes travel at 600 miles per hour and can shatter ear drums and break windows. They can be heard as far away as 3000 miles. The 1883 eruption of Krakatoa was heard in Perth, Australia, 2300 miles away.

Everyone left at Camp 33 stood at the bar and tried to figure out what to do next. This had already been a geologically challenged day. At 11:30 the light dusting from last night's minor eruption arrived, causing slippery roads. Then, at 12:15, Yellowstone was obliterated. At 2:30 the large sonic blast from the explosion would hit them, and within thirteen hours Camp 33 would be buried in ash.

Someone at the bar changed the channel. CBS news reporters were interviewing scientists who monitored volcanic eruptions. They explained that this was an imperfect science. They could not determine what would happen next. Sometimes there was a single large eruption and it was over. Other times large eruptions lasted for years. Ash depths could not be predicted. The size of an eruption, the direction of the spray pattern, and wind speeds all affect ashfall depth. A prior Yellowstone eruption dumped 10 feet of ash on Illinois.

Given the grim news reports, the manager decided to close up and evacuate. If the power went out, the food in his refrigerators would soon spoil. Besides, his customers would need sustenance on the road. He brought out platters of ham and cheese, bread, and buckets of smoked whitefish. Free beer and food for everyone. They all stood at the bar and raised their glasses in a final farewell toast to the community center that was Camp 33.

Ian had no problem deciding what to do. He was only 80 miles north of the bridge and could be in the Lower Peninsula before dark. He'd be back home with his family in Dexter long before the wall of ash reached Michigan. But what about these other people? If we all evacuate now, could we really outrun the ash? What if everybody left and clogged the slippery highways? Would we all die parked in our cars, buried under six feet of ash? Panic washed over Ian. There were so many terrifying questions left unanswered. So many potential outcomes to consider.

With a sudden sense of urgency, Ian raced to his truck. He tried to call his wife to tell her he was on his way home. Unable to get through, he sent a text. He slid out of the parking lot at exactly 1:15 p.m. with his snowshoes, a Tahquamenon Falls T-shirt, three huge sandwiches, and a ten-pound bag of smoked whitefish.

Driving to Paradise, Ian had his first introduction to the belching behemoth 1300 miles to the west. Less than half an inch of dry fine ash had been deposited from the first minor eruption. That dusting was coming to an end, but strong winds whipping off Lake Superior had stirred up the earlier deposits. Clouds of ash billowed in front of Ian's truck, making it difficult to see more than a few yards. Lanes on the highway were completely obscured by a monochromatic gray coating. Only the plowed snow piled along the shoulders gave the road any definition. Ian reduced his speed to ten miles an hour and steered a course up the middle of the roadway. He prayed that no one would suddenly emerge out of the ash cloud.

Ian passed in and out of several of these ash clouds on the road from Tahquamenon to Paradise. The road was slick, worse than black ice. The old rear-wheel-drive truck fishtailed countless times and once almost spun totally out of control.

He hunched forward, white knuckles firmly grasping the steering wheel. His eyes and whole body strained from hyperfocus. He was already in desperate need of his chiropractor and a stiff double scotch, and he'd gone just five miles in half an hour. Only 350 miles left to go.

Minutes later a "Moose Crossing" sign appeared out of the ash cloud. What he did not need today, of all days, was to have a 1500-pound moose lumber out onto the highway in front of him. Braking on the glazed road was not possible. Such encounters usually resulted in the annihilation of all concerned.

Fortunately for Ian, the moose were occupied elsewhere. Unfortunately for them, the four-leggeds and the trees would not find shelter today.

Just before 2:30 p.m. the truck pulled into the dark, deserted gas station in Paradise. The snowmobilers were gone. The townsfolk had fled. He was alone in Paradise. While he was humorously pondering that ontological thought, an explosion shook the truck and blew out the front window of the gas station. Rattled, Ian lost focus. His nerves were shot. He shook from the overload of today's assault on the senses. And it just kept on coming. In eleven hours this gas station would be buried under ash. He had to keep moving. He could not stop. He needed to get south below the bridge, south below Flint. Focus and reason slowly returned as he reviewed his survival plan.

Then he remembered: the sonic blast from the obliteration of Yellowstone. That's what caused the explosion and blew out the gas station window. He ventured out of the truck to stretch his legs and noticed several six packs of bottled water dangling through the broken glass. In the excitement of hauling away ten pounds of smoked whitefish from Camp 33, he had forgotten to bring any water. If he maintained his ten-mile-an-hour pace, he would need it. But how could he pay for it? Clearly, everyone had fled hours ago. Five dollars thrown onto the counter covered the water and a big bag of Doritos. Ian was not a looter, stealing from a catastrophe-damaged store. He was a professor, a pillar of society. Pillars did not pillage.

Pillars, however, did pee outdoors. Ian spelled his name defiantly in the newly fallen ash. Only 75 minutes and fourteen miles later, Ian had already developed a disdain for volcanic ash.

After another failed attempt to call his wife, Ian sent a second text. He pulled out of Paradise on Michigan Highway 123 headed south toward the Mackinac Bridge. Those billowing ash clouds, driven by gusts off Lake Superior, diminished the farther south he travelled.

Increased visibility was offset by the challenge of climbing and descending minor hills. Ian had learned to drive on icy mountain roads in Colorado. If he kept his tires on the right shoulder, he could climb up the slippery roadway at five miles an hour. Downhill, he used the right shoulder to slow his descent.

In the gathering gloom, four crashed vehicles had become out-of-control toboggans. Now they sat at the bottom of the first hill. Ian crept around them on the right shoulder, stopped, and examined each vehicle for occupants. All were empty; but one car with Ohio plates had snowshoe supplies and frames strewn about the backseat. These were the Ohio people who left the snowshoe class early! Where were they? The scene held no clues.

Around 4:30 he was still southbound, headed toward the bridge. Other than those wrecked cars, he had not seen any other vehicles. That changed once he got to east–west Highway 28. Refugee traffic from both directions turned south at this intersection, fleeing toward the bridge. Now he encountered even slower travel—the exodus out of Pompeii.

A weird, eerie darkness smothered the roadway ahead of him. As if entering a black hole, light from his own headlights grew fainter in the enveloping ash void. He became confused and disoriented, but he couldn't just stop. There wasn't room to pull over on the shoulder. Someone coming from behind wouldn't see his brake lights in time. And what if he encountered another hill? His journey home might end here.

Frantic, he just needed to hear another human voice. Ian phoned his wife. No answer. No texts. He had kept the radio off to keep his hyperfocus. Now he turned it on. Only FM static. He switched to AM and picked up WJR out of Detroit.

The news wasn't good. At 4 p.m. EST a 100-mile-an-hour wall of ash had blasted Rapid City, South Dakota, near Mt. Rushmore. Two feet of heavy pumice ash fell on top of twelve inches of snow. Driving and walking ceased. The ash was too heavy to move. Dry ash was ten times heavier than fresh snow. Roofs collapsed. Buildings collapsed. From Yellowstone to Rapid City, nothing was expected to survive. And the caldera continued to erupt. The ash was now headed directly toward Minneapolis and Duluth, with an estimated time of arrival of 8:30 p.m. EST. By then, Ian figured, he should be south of the bridge.

WJR reported that the initial light dusting this morning had coated roads from Lake Superior south to Toledo. Motorists were advised to travel only when necessary. Until further notice, speeds were restricted to a maximum of fifteen miles an hour on all highways statewide. For the thousands of vehicles evacuating northern Michigan, snowplows were leading long slow-moving convoys to the south along I-75. Ian just needed to get to the bridge.

First, he had to get focused. For a while, red taillights seemed to flicker, then disappear into the swirling ash. Other cars were definitely out there. Just ahead of him, they slowly picked their way through the apocalyptic blackness. Suddenly, a burst of red brake lights ahead crossed left into the northbound lane. Ian instinctively followed. Dim headlights in his rearview mirror confirmed he was now part of an unintended convoy. Off to the right they passed the first of many broken-down vehicles. The convoy slowly slithered back into the southbound lane. Within the next few miles they weaved around several more breakdowns. If your vehicle died here, you died here. No one could stop for you.

"But why are they all breaking down now?" Ian wondered.

A FEMA report at 5:15 provided the answer. Volcanic ash is drawn into the air filter of the vehicle. Within 50 miles, the air filter can become clogged, allowing abrasive ash to enter the engine. Moving parts become damaged, leading to overheating and engine failure. The same applies to lungs. Wear a mask and clean it often!

"Damn it," Ian thought. "How in God's name was I supposed to know that? I don't know anything at all about volcanic ash. Hell, I didn't even know there was a supervolcano at Yellowstone until recently."

He was only 50 miles south of Camp 33 and had been driving for over four hours without cleaning his air filter. There were no idiot lights on these old Chevy trucks, but the analog temperature gauge read 200°F, just twelve degrees below boiling. Ian needed to pull over, let the truck cool down, and clean the air filter.

"If this truck boils over now, I'm dead," Ian thought.

Two miles south of Trout Lake he pulled off onto a road heading west. For several minutes he watched the departing convoy pass him by. An illuminated snake over two miles long wove through the night—and then, foreboding lonely darkness. He shuddered.

Ian found his tools and flashlight inside the cab and popped the hood. He removed the air filter and thumped it against his leg. Ash deposits had also built up inside the throat of the carburetor. Within minutes he had a clean carburetor and a semi-clean air filter. Hearing that FEMA report had saved his engine and probably his life.

While the engine cooled, he paused to eat. Large pieces of smoked whitefish and a huge ham and cheese sandwich calmed his nerves; bottled water and Doritos completed the meal. Ian called Theresa again, and this time he got through. He told her his plan to get south of the bridge by 8:30, join a National Guard convoy, and head for home along I-75. Even at fifteen miles an hour, he would be well toward the southern edge of the spray pattern when the ash wall struck in eight hours. Suddenly, he realized he was talking to dead air. The call had dropped. He didn't know how much she had heard. He would have to try again later.

Only one car had passed in the last few minutes. Probably not many more would make it out. With only twelve hours of evacuation warning and road speeds at less than ten miles an hour, most people could get no more than 100 miles. The Upper Peninsula of Michigan is several hundred miles wide. Only those near the bridge would get out alive.

Loading up the truck, he noticed that the wind had died down with nightfall. Swirling ash, stirred up by the lake squalls and the convoy traffic, had settled down. Some stars and a crescent moon occasionally peeked through the dust. The black shroud was lifting. Visibility was returning to the roadway. After the half-hour engine-cooling hiatus, Ian was on the road again, headed out alone with no convoy.

The farther south he travelled, the more visibility increased and ash coating decreased. Sometimes he could exceed 15 miles an hour. A continuous line of abandoned cars sat stranded along the roadway. Clearly, these people hadn't heard the FEMA warning in time.

By 7:00, he was about fifteen miles from the bridge. Almost imperceptibly, his breathing had become uncomfortable. His nose started to run, and his eyes and throat became irritated. Then he remembered the FEMA warning, "Wear a mask, clean it often." Oh God, he didn't have any masks in the truck. Repeated opening of the truck door had let ash into the cab. The residual ash recirculated into his throat and lungs. The FEMA report had suggested that if no mask were available, one could be improvised using clothing that would filter out most particles. Moistening the fabric would further improve filtration. Ian stopped and poured some bottled water on his Tahquamenon Falls T-shirt. Problem solved.

At 7:30 Ian was about ten miles out of St. Ignace, going toward the big, sweeping curve just west of I-75. A squall coming off Lake Huron kicked up swirling ash in front of him. The road felt slick and ash glazed. He slowed to below 10 miles an hour.

His concentrated gaze focused on the edge of the road. He gripped the wheel, desperately willing the truck around the curve. The moment seemed to stretch forever. Then Ian became aware of a light farther along the curve ahead of him, a light that shouldn't be there.

His foot instinctively lifted off the gas pedal. He reached for the gearshift mounted on the steering column and dropped it into neutral. The truck slowly drifted farther into the curve as Ian squinted intently, searching for the source of the light.

Then he saw it. There, completely blocking the road directly in front of Ian, was a gigantic stag with a magnificent rack of antlers.

AND IT WAS GLOWING!!

The light radiating from the stag was the same eerie greenish-white glow that had emanated from the kachina on the mantel at Camp 33.

In shock, Ian slammed on his brakes. The truck spun out on the ash, slid into a tree, and bounced back onto the highway. The old 1952 truck had no restraints. Ian was thrown forward, hitting his head hard on the steering wheel.

Everything went black.

Chapter 4

Veronica Forteau

Day 3

7:30 p.m.: Veronica Forteau steered her Subaru carefully down Highway 123. At just over five feet tall, Veronica found herself peering through the steering wheel, rather than over it. The swirling gray ash fell like snow in the beams of her headlights. Even four-wheel-drive made no difference. It was like driving on a sheet of ice. Narrowing her eyes, she squinted through her tri-focals at what little she could see of the road ahead. Damned kids, anyway! If her daughter and son-in-law weren't such old hens, she'd be safe at home in her own living room. Instead, she was trying to get to St. Ignace so they could "take care" of her. As if she needed to be taken care of!

She was coming up on that god-awful long curve. With almost no traction, she was worried she might slide off the road, so she eased up on the gas pedal. In a soft monotone, Veronica began to swear with steady creativity and a lack of repetition. Eventually, she ran out of obscenities, blasphemies, and scatology in English. She then switched seamlessly to the Canadian French of her childhood and kept right on swearing.

What was that?

Just ahead, around the curve, there was a sudden flash of light. Veronica felt her heart rate increase, and her breath came just a bit faster. It wasn't lightning, she swiftly decided. Lightning didn't have that greenish glow to it—nor did it fade as slowly as this. In fact, it didn't look like anything natural.

"Oh, my God," she thought. "Am I about to have a close encounter of the third kind?" Somehow, the thought was not as amusing as she had hoped. If anything, she felt more apprehensive. Veronica eased up even further on the gas pedal and crept forward.

Her headlights inched their way around the curve, briefly illuminating the vague shapes of trees dimly visible through the swirling ash. The greenish-white glow had faded completely now.

She hoped fervently that whatever had caused it was gone. Inexplicably, though, there was more light ahead of her. Veronica peered over the dashboard, trying desperately to penetrate the curtain of gray dust roiling through her headlights.

There it was! Another set of headlights cut through the night; but these were pointed in the wrong direction, and they weren't moving at all.

"Oh, Lord," Veronica thought. Some fool had tried to take the curve too fast and ran into a tree. She sighed as she took her foot completely off the gas. Her car drifted slowly to a stop just a few feet behind a wrecked pickup truck. Sometimes being a retired nurse was a real pain in the butt. Now she'd have to waste time dealing with some drunk who shouldn't have been on the road in the first place.

Grumbling, she opened the car door and hoisted herself out into the storm. A blast of ash-laden wind nearly knocked her off her feet. She blinked rapidly to clear her vision. Head down and eyes carefully focused on the ground, she shuffled toward the truck. Her 70-year-old bones wouldn't take kindly to a fall.

She expected the driver to be moving by now, but the form she could see remained slumped over the steering wheel. "Oh, great. So what do we have here?" Unfortunately, there was only one way to find out. With another prodigious sigh, Veronica reached for the door handle with one hand while she rapped her knuckles against the window. When there was no response, she opened the truck door.

"Hey," she called. "Wake up, you." Nothing. She gingerly reached into the truck and sought the carotid artery pulse. It was there, beating slow and strong. Well, at least he wasn't dead. She analyzed the situation. The guy was out cold and showed no signs of regaining consciousness anytime soon. He wasn't going to be any help in assessing his injuries. A quick visual scan showed no external bleeding. The body appeared to be slumped forward at normal angles. Nothing was obviously pointing in the wrong direction. His head was leaning against the steering wheel and his breathing was normal. So far, so good.

Veronica had lived in the UP her entire life. Seventy winters had ingrained habits that now would serve her well. She turned away from the truck, carefully closing the door behind her. In the trunk of her own vehicle, a full emergency kit awaited her. Muttering to herself, she rummaged through her supplies. She probably wouldn't need the kitty litter or rock salt, and it was doubtful that the tow chain would be of any help either. The sleeping bag was a keeper, though. The snap-and-heat hand warmers might come in handy later. She closed the trunk and shuffled back toward the truck.

Once she had tucked the sleeping bag around the unconscious man, Veronica returned to her car. Without taking her eyes off her patient, she hit the On Star button.

"I need an ambulance," she told the operator. "It's about ten degrees out here, and I have an unconscious man who's just wrapped his truck around a tree."

"We have your location, ma'am," replied the operator. "But I'm afraid it may take a while to get a response unit to you. We've been really slammed with distress calls from your area."

Veronica looked skeptically at the unconscious figure in the truck.

"Listen, if I could do this on my own, I wouldn't have called you," she said. "I'm five feet tall on my tiptoes, and I weigh a hundred pounds soaking wet. This guy is huge. He's well over six feet tall and he's got to outweigh me about three to one. Oh, and did I mention I'm 70 years old? I don't think that dog's gonna hunt."

"I'll do my best, ma'am. Please stay on the line. Let me see what I can do for you."

It wasn't easy waiting. The stranger in the truck was still and silent. The unrelieved darkness surrounded her. Swirling ash drowned her headlights' feeble glow after just a few feet. The wind howled and drove harsh abrasives against her windshield. It sounded and felt as if a massive hand were scrubbing her car with sandpaper. She wondered what it would do to her unprotected skin. Veronica shivered, not just from the cold.

A very long fifteen minutes later the On Star operator came back on line.

"I'm so sorry it's taken so long," she said, "and I wish I had better news. It looks as if every emergency vehicle in a fifty-mile radius is already out on call. There've been multi-car pileups everywhere. Nobody is predicting when, or even if, they could get to you. It's a real mess out there."

"Hmm." Veronica's mouth pursed in frustration. "Any suggestions?"

"Is there anyone else who could help you? I could get a call through for you if your cell isn't working."

Veronica thought about it. Well, if the kids were so determined to take care of her, let's see how far that would go.

"Try my son-in-law, Ben. Tell him to bring a carry board to help stabilize this guy until we can see if he has any spinal injuries. Just tell him to bring the leaf from the dining room table. And tell him it's damned cold out here, so get a move on it." She recited her daughter's phone number. Five minutes later, the On Star operator came back on the line to report she had succeeded in contacting Ben. He was on his way. Veronica thanked her and settled back to wait some more.

Twice during the next hour, she made her way over to the truck to check on her patient. He still hadn't moved.

It was 9:30 when Ben's truck came into view, creeping along the road toward her. Veronica breathed a thankful sigh of relief.

"Thank God you made it. I almost froze my ass off waiting," she commented when her wiry son-in-law stepped out of his vehicle.

"You have no idea what it's like on the road, Verna," he replied. Then he stopped himself and apologized. "Well, I guess you do. So, what now?"

"Now we get this guy to the hospital," she replied.

"That isn't going to be easy," said Ben. "I was listening to the radio when On Star called. About an hour ago, a wall of ash hit

Minneapolis. There's over two feet of ash and snow on the ground, and everything is getting buried. It's headed straight toward St. Ignace at a hundred miles an hour. We don't have much time to get the hell out of here. If we don't get to shelter in the next couple of hours, we're done for."

"Damn," Veronica breathed. "I was hoping it wouldn't get any worse." Then she gave herself a brisk shake. "Well, we'd better get moving, then."

With that, she led the way over to the disabled truck and its still-unconscious driver. She carefully opened the door and stood back so Ben could see the problem they faced.

"What the hell? No way! This guy's huge, Verna. I'm gonna get a hernia if I try to lift him!"

Ben was average in height, weight, and muscle power. The guy in the truck was about half again his size. Ben was right. It was going to be next to impossible for the two of them to move the stranger. But what could they do? They couldn't just abandon him. He'd die here. Veronica met Ben's troubled gaze with her own hopeless eyes.

"Can we wake him up?" Ben asked.

"No. I've been trying," she replied.

"Okay. So, he's not going to wake up any time soon, or at least we can't count on it. He's too big for us to lift; and he may have something wrong we can't see, so hauling him around probably isn't a good idea anyway. We don't want to kill the guy. His truck is trashed, so we can't just move him over and drive it in to town. There's no other traffic, so we aren't going to be able to flag anybody down to help, and from what On Star told me, the cavalry ain't coming to the rescue. We can't just leave him here, either. Geez, Verna, this is a real pisser."

Veronica had nothing to add. They stood in silence for a moment, until a gust of wind nearly knocked them both off their feet.

"Let's talk about it in the truck," Ben suggested. When they had settled into the warmth of the cab, Veronica began talking.

"We need to get him out of his truck and into the back of yours. You brought the dining room table leaf, didn't you?" Ben nodded. "Okay, then, we can shift him onto that and slide him across the seat. If we make a draw sheet out of the sleeping bag, we can haul him into your truck bed, and off we go."

"Just a couple of problems there, Verna. We can't fit everybody through the cap together, so pulling him in is going to mean taking the cap off my truck first. But that's the easy one. The big problem is his truck's door. We can't get it open far enough for me to back my truck up close enough." Ben paused to think. Then his face lit up. "I've got an idea. Remember that demolition derby in Traverse City back in October?"

Veronica sighed. She would never understand Ben's fascination with driving in those things. What was so great about deliberately smashing into someone else's car? But she held her tongue and just nodded.

"Remember how I got Ted Deschamps disqualified? I popped his driver's side door and rammed it off. As soon as he was exposed like that, he was out of the derby. I could do the same thing here. We can pad this guy in so he doesn't get hurt, and I can just take the door right off!" His eyes gleamed with excitement. Veronica gave him a moment to savor the thought.

"Yeah, you could," she replied slowly. "Just one thing, though. We can't afford to risk your truck. It's our best bet to get out of here, and my car's not heavy enough to pop his door. That's an old Chevy truck, and they built those things like tanks." Ben's face fell.

"Would the winch work?" Veronica asked, and Ben's face lit up again. "Men and their toys," she thought with an inward chuckle. Sometimes, though…those toys can be really useful.

"Okay," he said. "That'll work. But let's try On Star again. Maybe we'll get lucky."

Reluctantly, they left the warm cab of Ben's truck and shuffled to Veronica's car. It was 10:15 by the time they got a response. The news was not what they had hoped to hear. Instead of an operator, a recorded message came on.

"As of 10 p.m., a Federal State of Emergency has been declared for all of the upper Midwest, covering North and South Dakota, Minnesota, Wisconsin, and Michigan. The state of emergency is in response to a volcanic eruption in Yellowstone National Park that took place earlier today. Wyoming, North Dakota, South Dakota, and Montana are now buried under 30 inches of snow and ash. Initial estimates are two million or more dead in the upper Midwest."

Ben and Veronica looked at each other in horror. Two million people dead? My God!

"Houses and buildings continue to collapse," the recording went on. "Only emergency and police vehicles should be on the road. All others are advised to seek shelter immediately. Please hold for information specific to your area." The recording ended in silence.

"Seek shelter where?" Ben asked. "If everything's collapsing, where can anyone go?" Veronica glanced at Ben's shocked face and felt a knot of fear in the pit of her stomach.

A new recorded voice broke in.

"A state of emergency is in effect for all of upper Michigan due to a volcanic explosion taking place earlier today in Yellowstone National Park. The eruption has resulted in a 70,000-foot-tall wall of ash traveling eastward on winds estimated at 100 miles an hour. This has affected widespread areas of the upper Midwest.

"All people in this area are urged to take cover immediately. The estimated time of arrival in specific locations follows now." Ben and Veronica held their breath as the voice began listing times for places to their west. Finally, the voice listed St. Ignace: "ETA 1:30 a.m."

Veronica breathed out a prayer. "Dear God, we have only three hours." Ben sat frozen in place, his eyes glazed and staring wildly into the green glow of the dashboard lights.

"Ben, we have to move, now!" She reached across the seat and shook his shoulder hard. He jolted out of his horrified trance and nodded jerkily.

Veronica opened the car door and stepped back into the nightmare outside. She headed toward the damaged truck with Ben stumbling along behind her. "Please, please, let this guy wake up," she prayed; but there was no stirring of the unconscious man. She pulled open the truck's driver-side door again to examine her patient. Her eye was caught by the front of the door.

"Ben," she said with a lilt of hope in her voice. "Look at the door! It just has hinges! The whole thing is held on with six bolts! Get a wrench, damn it! And some WD-40 while you're at it. We can just pop this baby right off."

Ten minutes later it was done. Both of them were sweating and breathing hard, but the heavy door now lay on the ground. Ben gave an abrupt, satisfied nod and took off for his truck.

"Keep your flashlight on the door so I can see to back up," he called over his shoulder. Veronica bathed the unconscious man in light and held steady as Ben cautiously maneuvered the tailgate toward its goal. He stopped about three feet short of the other truck.

"Okay," he breathed, shuffling back to Veronica's side. "Now we have to get the cap off my truck so we can move him in. You take the left side, I'll take the right. Just slide it back, then we'll lift it off." He grinned. "At least it's lighter than that door, Verna."

More sweating, more heavy breathing, and a whole lot of cursing followed. Finally, Ben's truck cap sat on the ground next to the stranger's truck door. Ben dropped the tailgate and backed his vehicle flush with the door of the damaged truck. He scrambled into his truck bed and helped Veronica up.

"Your turn, nurse Verna. How do we get him over here?"

Veronica eyed the unconscious man slumped over the steering wheel.

"Well, first we have to stabilize his neck and spine. If we break his back, he'll never walk again. Having to move him isn't good, but we'll do the best we can. Let's see what we have to make a neck support for him." She rummaged around in the back end of Ben's truck.

"Oh, good. You thought to bring blankets and towels. Well done, Ben!" She grabbed a bath towel and began twisting it into a cylinder. Then she wrapped the cylinder around her patient's neck and held out her hand toward her son-in-law.

"Duct tape, please."

After she had taped the improvised neck brace in place, Veronica turned her attention to the dining room table leaf. This sturdy board measured about three-and-a-half feet by a foot and a half. It would support Ian from the top of his head to the base of his spine. She wrapped his torso and arms tightly in a blanket and duct taped him to the makeshift carrying board.

Ben had been busy as well. The bed of Ben's truck was roughly six inches lower than the seat of the damaged truck. Anticipating that they would slide their patient from one location to the other, he had created a slope using the bags of kitty litter he kept over his axles as ballast. Veronica smiled her approval.

"Now for the fun part," she said. "I'll get in the other side and rotate him around so we can slide him into your truck. Keep your fingers crossed."

The passenger door opened without protest, allowing her to climb in beside Ian. She wrapped the sleeping bag around his back, turning him so he lay supine on the seat. Ben moved the stranger's legs out the driver's side door and grasped the bottom corners of the sleeping bag. He began pulling slowly as Veronica guided and steered from inside. The sleeping bag slid down the kitty litter slope, carrying its burden safely from one vehicle to the other. The unconscious man lay still and safe in his cocoon as Veronica scrambled back into the bed of Ben's truck.

The kitty litter bags now became stabilizers, packed close around the body on its carrying board. Veronica and Ben replaced the cap and closed the tailgate. They stood panting and disheveled, looking at each other in triumph.

"We did it! Now let's get the hell out of here!"

"I'll drive," said Ben. "You want to sit up front with me or stay back here with him?"

"I'd better stick with him," Veronica replied. "If he wakes up now, he could panic and hurt himself even more."

"Hang on a minute, let me get my stuff out of the car," Veronica called. She hauled her suitcase out of the back seat, then locked the door. "Hope I can get back to you, Little Sure Foot," she murmured, patting the car hood affectionately. She crawled back into the rear of Ben's truck.

"What time is it?" she called to Ben.

"It's ten after eleven," he called back.

"Dear God, get moving! We've only got until 1:30!"

Two hair-raising, white-knuckled hours later Ben eased up to the emergency room entrance at the St. Ignace hospital with twenty minutes to spare. When he unbent his body from behind the steering wheel, Ben looked about a decade older than when he had started driving ten miles earlier. As he helped Veronica down from the tailgate and made way for the ER team with its gurney, he shook his head in exhaustion.

"Wow. No demolition derby is ever going to match that!"

Chapter 5

Day 4

Ian's inert form was transferred with gentle efficiency to the gurney and he was whisked away through the emergency room entrance.

"I'll go park the truck, then I'm going to try to find Becca," Ben said wearily. Veronica just nodded and turned briskly toward the emergency room, following her new patient.

Inside the doors, Veronica skidded to a stop and stared in shock. The waiting room was wall-to-wall people, so tightly packed they could barely mill around. Though everyone spoke softly, the volume of so many voices in such a small space hit her ears like the roar of a sports arena. Life teemed here, while death stalked in the inhuman silence of the ash-laden world outside. It was overwhelming.

She searched through the confusion for any sign of the emergency team who had preceded her into this mess. Alas, a five-foot-tall woman is at a distinct disadvantage in these circumstances. All she could see was a wall of torsos. She gave up and elbowed her way to the counter.

"Excuse me," she said to the exhausted-looking woman behind the desk. "I'm with the patient who was just brought in on the gurney. Can you tell me where they took him?"

"The unconscious guy?" the intake nurse asked. Veronica nodded. The nurse waved an arm to her right. "We've run out of room, so right now we're doing triage in that hallway. Good luck!"

The hallway wasn't much better than the waiting room when it came to overcrowding. Patients and their anxious families lined both walls. Those patients who could sit up were slumped in chairs or sat on the floor. Others lay on improvised pallets along one wall. Three or four gurneys stood in a line farther down the corridor. Hospital staff moved quickly up and down the passageway, taking vital signs and dispensing blankets, medications, and comforting words as they went. Veronica's practiced eye picked out categories of patient: coronary, pulmonary, wounds, breaks, possible concussion. The nurse in her nodded in approval at the efficient way they had been grouped together by type of medical need, making it easier to attend to them.

Her patient would be at the end of the hall, near the Radiology Department. She picked her way through the crowd until she spotted him, still strapped to the dining room table plank. A young resident was bending over the unconscious form as Veronica approached.

"Are you with him?" the doctor asked. Veronica nodded. "Nice improvising with the towel and duct tape."

"Thanks. I worked here as an ER nurse for 35 years," she said, "and my daughter is in pediatrics. She's around here somewhere right now."

"What can you tell me about him?"

"Very little," she answered professionally, nurse to doctor. "I found him unconscious in the driver's seat of his truck. He'd just had a close encounter of the worst kind with a tree. He was unconscious then and he's never opened his eyes. His vitals are good, no evidence of broken bones, no sign of bleeding. We transferred him as carefully as possible and got him here as fast as we could. I'd say concussion, but I stabilized his neck in case it's worse than that."

The young doc nodded soberly. "Thanks. We'll run a quick CT-scan. Can you stay with him? We're kind of short on staffing. We could use the help."

"I sort of expected that," Veronica sighed. "What the heck. There's nothing on TV, and I don't have any other plans."

Day 5

The CT-scan results had held no surprises. Fortunately, there appeared to be no damage to the spine, no fractures, and no internal bleeding. Veronica and two orderlies had shifted the heavy body to a pallet against the wall, taking advantage of the move to empty his pockets.

"All right! Who do we have here, anyway?" She flipped open the wallet and examined the driver's license. "Ian Duncan Cameron of Dexter, Michigan. You're a long way from home, pal."

Moving on to the cell phone, Veronica checked for an ICE (In Case of Emergency) number. Sure enough, there was a listing for Theresa Cameron. She hit the call button. All circuits were busy. By this time, it was after 3:00 in the morning. Veronica commandeered a chair and settled against the wall to wait out the few remaining hours of the night.

She dozed, coming alert whenever a staff member stopped by to take Ian's vital signs. They continued to be strong and stable, but he did not regain consciousness. Finally, at about 6 a.m., Veronica stood and stretched her tired back. She decided to try the cell phone again. Surprisingly, the call went through. She heard one buzz before a frantic voice exclaimed,

"Ian! Thank God! Where are you? Are you okay? I've been so worried!"

"Mrs. Cameron, this is Veronica Forteau. You don't know me, but I'm here with your husband, Ian. There's been an accident, but he's going to be all right—"

"What? Who are you? Is he hurt? What happened? Where are you?"

Hearing the beginnings of panic in the other woman's voice, Veronica immediately decided to blur some of the facts. She switched to her most soothing voice.

"I'm a nurse, Mrs. Cameron. We're in St. Ignace at the hospital. Your husband had an accident on the road and was brought here. He's unconscious at the moment, but his vital signs are all good and he does not appear to be in any danger. I found his cell phone in his pocket and called because I figured you'd be worried. I repeat—he's in no danger. Everything is going to be all right."

The breathing on the other end of the line was close to hyperventilation. Veronica continued to offer soothing noises until the woman calmed a bit. Then she repeated her explanation. This time Theresa appeared to comprehend and was able to respond more rationally. Her first impulse, of course, was to head for the car and start driving north; but Veronica needed little time to discourage that idea. She suggested instead that they try to keep in touch by phone despite the uncertain phone service. Finally, to Veronica's great relief, they ended the call.

Retirement certainly had spoiled her, she realized. She had always hated contacting next of kin, even under the best of circumstances. Coffee…now, that sounded like something she could handle. She headed for the cafeteria at top speed. After coffee and a sandwich, Veronica went hunting for her daughter and son-in-law, finally tracking them down in the atrium.

"Do I look as tired as you two?" she asked, gazing with concern at their exhausted faces. Rebecca focused bloodshot eyes on her mother and simply nodded in reply. Veronica sank onto a bench next to them.

"This is a bitch, ain't it? Did either of you hear what's going on outside?"

Ben roused himself enough to answer. He had been following the news in the waiting room, first on television and then, when the satellite signal died, on radio.

"It's pretty bad, Verna. Most everything between here and Yellowstone is in a black hole. We haven't heard a peep out of the Dakotas or Minnesota or western Wisconsin. Everybody's scared that it's just gone, buried under the ash. Hell, there's half a foot of it right outside the door. A bunch of us who can't do anything else to help have been up on the roof, shoveling it off so the whole place doesn't collapse. Let me tell you, that shit is heavy!"

The three of them fell silent, lost in exhausted musing. A few days ago, everything had been normal. The difference could hardly have felt more extreme. They were strong and sturdy people, but everyone has limits.

"Well, I'd better get back and check on Mr. Cameron," Veronica grunted as she pushed herself up from the bench. "Oh, I didn't tell you, did I, Ben? The guy we found is named Ian Cameron. He's from Dexter, Down Below." Veronica used the old term to describe people from the southern peninsula of Michigan.

Determined not to look as old as she felt, Veronica strode back toward the makeshift emergency room. Ian still lay quiet, but the involuntary twitches were becoming more frequent. Maybe he'd wake up soon. She settled down in what had become "her" chair and resumed her patient wait.

It was several hours later that Ian's eyes fluttered open. Veronica waved her arm to attract the attention of one of the medical staff. She leaned over so Ian could see her.

"Oh, my head," he croaked. "What happened? Where am I?"

As Veronica opened her mouth to reply, a frazzled nurse bustled up and began checking Ian's vital signs. Veronica signaled that she'd answer when the nurse had finished.

"You're certainly looking better, Mr. Cameron," the nurse said. "Your vital signs are all good. Just stay quiet for a while, and I'll get you something for your pain. You should begin to feel better shortly." She turned to Veronica. "Can you stay with him for a bit longer?"

"Of course," Veronica replied. "I've waited quite a long time to talk to this guy. I'm not leaving now." She settled back more comfortably in her chair as the nurse moved on to the next patient. "So, Mr. Cameron. What do you remember?"

Ian frowned in concentration. "I was driving," he began tentatively. "Oh, right! The volcano! Is everybody okay?"

"So far, so good," said Veronica philosophically. "It's still raining ash out there, and we have about a foot of accumulation on the roof. My son-in-law has been up there shoveling like crazy, so we should still have a roof over our heads for a while. What happened to you?"

"Well, I was going slow when I came around the curve, and…" he hesitated, suddenly looking apprehensive. "Um. I skidded. I saw a tree coming right at me, and that's the last I remember. How did I get here?"

"I was right behind you. I saw this weird green glow up around the curve, and I slowed down even more coming around it. Good thing I did. You were right there, and if I'd been going any faster, neither one of us would be here."

"You saw it, then? I'm not crazy. I wasn't hallucinating! Okay!"

"Saw what?" Veronica asked curiously.

"That big-assed glowing green deer!" Ian replied eagerly. "Oh, I'm sorry about the language. It was just so strange."

"Honey, I've heard a lot worse than that. But no, I didn't see any deer, big-assed, glowing, green, or otherwise. Just the light. When I came around the curve, there was nothing there but your truck. You were out cold, so I called my son-in-law for help. We got you here just before the ash hit."

"How long was I unconscious?"

"Couple of days."

Ian's jaw dropped in consternation. "Couple of days? Oh, my God, Theresa will be frantic! I've got to call my wife."

"Relax. I called her for you. She knows what happened and where you are. She was pretty freaked out at first, but she calmed down eventually. In fact, she should be trying to call shortly. Why don't you get some rest? I'll wake you up when she calls."

A few hours later, the cell phone began chirping. The noise stirred Ian awake. Veronica held the phone out to him, and he grabbed it eagerly, hitting the talk button. She discreetly moved away to give him what little privacy she could. She could still hear, though.

"Theresa? No, sweetheart, it's okay.…I'm all right, just a little banged up.…Well, I skidded on the ash and ran into a tree, so the truck's probably a mess.…Yes, I'm still in the hospital.…No, I don't know when I'll be coming home. I just woke up, so I haven't even talked to a doctor yet. How are the kids?…Honey, don't cry. It's going to be all right, I promise.…"

"Mr. Cameron! I see you've rejoined us," a cheerful voice rang out. "Let me take a quick look at you, hmm?"

It was the young resident who had treated Ian two nights ago. Veronica had never been so happy to see anyone.

"Give me the phone, Ian. I'll fill Theresa in while you get checked out." A few crisp sentences later she pushed the "off" button and turned her attention back to her patient.

"How are you feeling?" the young doctor asked. "Is everything tracking all right? Any odd sounds, smells, lights?"

"Pretty good, doc, except for the headache," Ian responded.

"And the glowing, gigantic stag," Veronica joked. The doctor shot her a quizzical look.

"The what?"

"Nothing, doctor, really," Ian protested. "Just something I thought I saw before my accident. Probably just a trick of the headlights in the ash, or something…" he trailed off.

"I think we'll keep you here for a little while. Concussions like yours are nothing to take lightly." The doctor gave another meaningful look to Veronica. "Can you keep going? We're still overwhelmed around here, and I can't tell you how much help you've been with Mr. Cameron."

"Sure." Veronica shrugged. "Even if I wanted to go home, I doubt I could get there at this point. Might as well stick around and keep Ian company. That okay with you?" she asked her patient.

"I'd be happy to have you here," Ian replied with a smile. "Thank you, doctor," he called to the retreating back of the young resident. An over-the-head, backward wave was his response as the doctor moved purposefully toward the next in line.

Days 6–7

Ian and Veronica settled into a comfortable pattern over the next two days. They talked, shared meals, and played cribbage with a board and cards Veronica liberated from the gift shop. Ian slept a good portion of the time, leaving Veronica free to seek out her daughter and son-in-law. The young resident came by at least twice a day, now announcing himself by asking Ian in a loud voice whether he'd seen any glowing deer lately. Ian winced every time this happened. He noticed that he was getting some odd looks from the other staff members and patients, but there was nothing he could do to counteract it.

Theresa called whenever she could get a free circuit, which was less and less often, given the high call volume and the ash accumulation in the air. Several times their calls were terminated with no warning, so they spoke quickly and urgently.

Ian and Theresa discussed the ongoing situation with considerable concern. She was particularly worried about Gabe, whose asthma was really starting to react to the ash-laden air. And there was no sign of a letup in the volcano's activity. Ash was accumulating at an alarming rate, with well over two inches on the ground in Dexter already. Travel had come to a virtual standstill, making Ian's return home more problematic every day. After several of these conversations, Ian came to a decision.

"Take the kids and head for your parents' place," he forced himself to say, not admitting even to himself how abandoned that would make him feel. "I can follow as soon as I'm cleared to leave the hospital. But the kids have to come first. Gabe can't hold his breath until I get back. Go now, Theresa."

He was a little dismayed at how easy it was to convince her. There was something very like relief in her voice as she promised to leave tomorrow, before it got any worse. She'd wait for him in Albuquerque. Meanwhile, Theresa said, she would leave a cache of food and water for him with their smaller valuables in the tornado shelter, just in case he needed supplies. People were starting to hoard, she told him, so getting groceries might be difficult. In fact, she sounded so well organized that Ian couldn't help wondering if she had already thought this through and had just been waiting for a chance to tell him what she planned to do. Ian agreed with the plans. Then, swallowing hard, he said goodbye to Gabe, to Claire, to Theresa.

"Be safe. I'll see you soon," he ended the conversation. His eyes brimmed with tears as he clicked off the phone. Veronica, just returning from a brief break, smiled gently and laid her hand on his shoulder in comfort. Wisely, she said nothing.

Day 8

Ian was anxious and depressed the next day, worrying about his family. He mentally counted down their preparations, their departure from their home, and then he started tracking their progress southward. Veronica listened patiently as Ian recreated their nail-biting trek down to I-94, then east to US 23, then south to the Ohio border. When his imaginary journey finally reached I-75, her patience ran out.

"Enough, already!" she exclaimed. "You're making yourself sick, and you're driving me crazy! Let's assume they're wending their way happily southward with no problems. Everything is going to be just fine. How about a game of cribbage?"

She dedicated herself to distracting him for the rest of the day. That was an exhausting proposition, and she came to understand Ian's single-mindedness. Once he sank his teeth into something, he was almost impossible to move. What a bulldog! By the time he finally fell asleep, she was worn out completely. Even on a makeshift pallet on the floor, even with her old, aching bones, she slept deeply and without dreams.

Day 9

They woke to a subtle shift in the atmosphere. People moved through the area with a sense of urgency that had not been there the night before. Ian was now allowed to get up and walk for short distances, so he and Veronica went to investigate.

The hospital seemed to be even more populated than the night before, and many of the newcomers wore National Guard uniforms. Suddenly the PA system came to life with a small crackle.

"Can I have your attention, please?" said a pleasant voice. "All staff and ambulatory patients, please come to the cafeteria. The Michigan National Guard has an update for us."

Like spawning salmon, everyone leaped forward, battling upstream toward the cafeteria in a surging wave of curious humans. Anxious hopefulness shone on every face.

The cafeteria was already crowded when Ian and Veronica arrived. They elbowed their way to Ben and Becca, and Veronica performed quick introductions.

A sonic shriek announced an active microphone on the lectern set up at the front of the cafeteria. Every head swiveled in that direction as an immediate silence swept through the room. At the lectern, a woman in uniform looked embarrassed at the uncouth noise.

"Sorry," she mumbled. "Ladies and gentlemen, I am Major Reeves of the Michigan National Guard. We've called you here for a very serious reason." She paused while the audience members looked at each other and murmured anxiously.

"As you know, the ash fallout from this Yellowstone eruption continues to move eastward, and we have gotten our share. There's over eight inches of ash on the ground outside right now, and it's still coming. Eight inches of ash is ten times heavier than regular snow. Roofs in the area are beginning to collapse.

"We don't know when it's going to stop. Hell, we don't even know *if* it's going to stop. After careful deliberation, the governor's office has decided to evacuate this area. You-all have been particularly hard hit, but we can still get you to safety if we start now.

"So," she raised her voice as the people around her began to talk excitedly, "we are going to begin running convoys down to the southern part of the state, starting tomorrow. We have several heavy plows to clear the roadways ahead of us. We have brought trucks to transport those who don't have their own vehicles available. Those who do have vehicles are invited to join us. We'll lead the way and bring up the rear to help anyone who runs into trouble.

"Over at the tables on your left we have people waiting to sign you up and answer your questions." People eagerly moved toward the tables as she continued, "If you can't go this time, for whatever reason, do not worry. We will be back." With that final reassurance, she clicked off the microphone.

Veronica stood close to Ian, using his bulk to keep herself from being swept away. The two of them watched quietly for a couple of minutes as people swarmed the tables.

"Well, what do you think?" Veronica asked. "Should we join the other lemmings?"

Ian looked thoughtful.

"I think I'll wait," he said finally. "My family's already on their way to higher ground. Theresa will get the kids to Albuquerque. I'm sure of it. A few days one way or the other won't make much difference for me. Besides, I haven't been released yet. You go ahead."

Veronica shook her head.

"I'm in no hurry either," she said. "If a lot of people head out, they're still going to need help around here. I can wait, too. Coffee?"

They collected plastic cups of the life-giving elixir and wandered out of the cafeteria, back to "their" little corner of the hallway. The cribbage board came out, and they settled into a friendly game. About two hours later, Ian glanced up to see Ben and Rebecca hurrying down the hallway toward them.

"Verna! There you are," called Ben. Beside him, Rebecca beamed with delight. "I got us into the convoy! We're getting out of here," he hollered enthusiastically. Veronica looked up from her cards, startled.

"We leave at 6 a.m. tomorrow," Ben announced triumphantly. "We're outta here!"

"Great!" responded Ian. "Congratulations!"

Veronica remained silent. Ben looked at her, puzzled.

"What's wrong?" he asked. "I thought you'd be glad to get away from this."

"Well," she answered slowly, "I probably would be happier if we were taking everybody. You see, I was planning to stay here and help for a while, and Ian still can't leave. They haven't released him yet. I can't leave him here alone!"

Ben's embarrassed glance at Ian spoke volumes. He'd been so proud of winning their freedom, he hadn't even thought of anyone other than himself, his wife, and his mother-in-law.

"No, Veronica, Ben is right," Ian said. "You need to get safe as soon as possible. I'd never forgive myself if you stayed here and then got hurt."

"Are you all going to gang up on me?" Veronica exclaimed in exasperation.

"Yep," said Ben. Rebecca, who still hadn't said a word, nodded vigorously.

"Really, Mama, it's time to go. I called Uncle Phil in Florida, and he said to come on down, he's got plenty of room." Rebecca seemed particularly proud of herself for thinking ahead.

Veronica blew out an explosive breath.

"You people will be the death of me yet," she muttered with a scowl.

"But not today," said Ian gently. "And not tomorrow, either. You get yourself down into that warm sunshine. I'll be along shortly, and when this is all over I'm going to come looking for you, Veronica Forteau. I owe you big time, and I'm going to find a way to pay you back. Besides, I try to hold on to my friends." With that, he smiled and drew her into a warm hug.

Day 10

Ian and Veronica had sat talking late into the night. Neither one was, as a result, in top form at 5:30 the next morning, when Ben and Rebecca came to collect their reluctant fellow traveler. Veronica grouched and grumbled all the way to the hospital's main entrance. Once there, she burst into tears and whirled around to clutch Ian tightly.

"I don't want to go," she wailed. "This is my home!"

Ian held her for a moment, then disengaged her arms from their grip around his waist. Veronica was so small and Ian so large that her arms reached only half way; it wasn't hard to loosen her hold on him, at least physically.

"You have to go, Veronica," he said around the lump in his throat. "I need to know you're safe. Please."

She nodded and followed her daughter, head hanging and footsteps dragging like a child headed for her first day of kindergarten. Outside, she turned once and waved, forcing a smile in Ian's direction. He returned both gestures and watched until her tiny figure was out of sight.

"God go with you," he murmured. Then he trudged back into the suddenly quiet hospital.

Day 11

With the sudden drop in population, accommodations in the hospital became a bit more comfortable. Ian was transferred from his pallet on the floor to a cot in a room with only three other people crammed into its corners.

It was lonely, though. He hadn't realized how much he had come to depend on Veronica's company. Now he had no one to talk to, no opponent for cribbage, no sense of another caring presence. Ian wandered the halls aimlessly.

Late in the afternoon, the young doctor breezed in, looking as if he had actually managed to get a little sleep. He cheerfully examined Ian, checking his vital signs one more time.

"You're doing better, Mr. Cameron!" he declared. "However, given the severity of your head injury, I would feel uncomfortable releasing you at this time."

Ian smiled wryly. "Oh, well. This place kind of grows on you. Guess I'll stick around for a while." He paused, thoughtful, then offered hesitantly, "Is there anything I can do to help out around here? You still have a full house, and I'm about to go crazy from sheer boredom."

The younger man pursed his lips. "I don't know what we're doing about volunteers. And I still don't want you exerting yourself too much. Let me check with my superiors."

Day 12

The young doctor came through early the next morning. His superiors were concerned that any additional stress could result in serious complications, like vertigo, double vision, or even amnesia. He offered Ian light-duty options. Ian chose to help the sick and injured.

For the next several hours, he was very busy. He kept watch over a patient in the recovery area after surgery. He answered call signals for the nursing staff, adjusting bed heights and fetching fresh blankets. He unkinked the tubing on the oxygen feed for a pulmonary patient. Ian certainly wasn't bored.

When lunchtime came around, he grabbed a sub and a cola and sagged against the hallway wall. Even after so little exertion, he was tired. Still, it felt good to be doing something. He tore into his sandwich with real appetite.

Ian was about to take his last bite when he suddenly realized he was being watched. Warily, he scanned the hallway. His observer was not trying to be particularly subtle. Leaning casually against the opposite wall was a brown-skinned man in a National Guard uniform. When he saw that Ian had become aware of him, the man pushed away from the wall and sauntered over.

"You Ian Cameron?" he asked. Ian nodded in the affirmative. "Cool. I've been looking for you. Hear you had an interesting experience recently, and I wanted to talk to you about it."

Ian looked puzzled for a moment. Everybody had had an interesting experience recently. Who was this guy, and what did he mean?

So Ian asked him.

"Oh. I'm Oscar Windrunner. And I heard you had a run in with a spirit stag. That true?"

"Oh, shit," thought Ian. "Not that again." But wait. This guy looked Native. Maybe he'd know something that could help Ian understand what had happened. It was worth a shot, anyway; so Ian began to tell the story of his attempt to return from Paradise. Oscar Windrunner listened with an intense, unwavering focus that increased Ian's confidence with every sentence. Finally, he reached the end of his narrative.

"So, that's what happened. What do you think?"

Windrunner gazed at the floor for a minute, apparently deep in thought. Then he looked up with a faint smile on his face and said,

"Not bad—for a white guy." And without another word, he walked away.

Ian was not accustomed to being treated with condescension. After all, he had spent a large portion of his life becoming Professor Cameron, and he felt he was entitled to respect. Yet he had just been casually and contemptuously dismissed as just another "white guy." It rankled—a lot. Hell, who was this guy to judge his experience? Why did so many natives consider all whites to be spiritual "wannabes"? Out west, some Lakota still call the white man "Waisichu" and spit on the ground. Whites are considered violent, greedy, and spiritually bankrupt. It would probably be a long time before white men were welcome at the spiritual table.

He found himself returning to this experience over and over as the day continued. Ian was no stranger to higher states of consciousness. In Boulder, he had had the opportunity to learn from Hindu swamis, Buddhist lamas, and powerful native shamans. His slow burning anger turned to dark brooding, then eventually to bitter acceptance. Ian decided he would keep his mouth shut about the stag episode in the future. He could do without that kind of reaction from others. He couldn't change attitudes forged by 500 years of experience. Ian was glad he didn't have to be the one to reconcile these views.

Somewhere, the Fates shared a quiet laugh.

Days 13–20

For the next week, Ian fell into the routine of the hospital. He worked increasingly longer shifts, doing grunt work with a willing cheerfulness that was much appreciated by staff and patients alike. He got on good terms with the squads of National Guardsmen who shifted through, shepherding groups of patients and UP residents southward to safety. The Guardsmen were a breath of fresh air, bringing new faces and fresh information about the outside world on a regular basis.

The Guard also brought food supplies in the form of MREs (Meals Ready to Eat). Commercial deliveries of food had stopped, and hospital cooks, as nonessential personnel, had already been evacuated. There was no more nabbing a quick sandwich in the cafeteria.

Every night he tried to call Theresa. Every night the call failed to go through. Otherwise, everything went according to schedule. Well, except for the snow. An additional eight inches of the stuff fell, adding to the foot of mixed snow and ash already on the hospital roof. The teams shoveling the roof looked more and more exhausted and worried every day.

Ian was pushing a cart full of dirty laundry down the hall when one of his National Guard pals hailed him.

"Hey, Ian, hope you haven't unpacked," he said with a wink.

"I don't even have my own toothbrush," Ian replied.

"Well, here." The Guardsman reached into his bag, pulling out a gas mask and throwing it to Ian. "Now you have your own Personal Breathing Apparatus, courtesy of the United States government. Thanks for all the help you've given us."

"Thanks, man," Ian responded in surprise, "but am I really going to need this? What's going on out there?"

His friend blew out a puff of air and shook his head.

"It's insane. Everybody's fleeing south and east. The southern states are getting slammed with refugees. We can't keep the roads clear, and that's adding to the mess—more accidents, more injuries—and then it gets even more congested with the smashed cars blocking the roadways. The people who can't get out of the cities are starting to panic. Cincinnati is in lockdown. Three days of rioting about leveled the city, and it's just a question of time until it blows up again. Man, if you were planning to head south out of Michigan, I'd seriously consider an alternate route!"

"Holy shit," Ian replied soberly, "I was planning to head for Cinci."

It really wasn't a surprise, then, when the hospital administrator announced later that day that a final evacuation of all movable patients and all remaining nonessential personnel would take place as soon as possible. The structural integrity of the hospital building was becoming questionable, and there was still no sign of letup. Ian spent the remainder of his time at the hospital helping to organize the evacuation and loading the National Guard trucks.

Chapter 6

A Long Ride Home

Day 21

At 6 a.m. the convoy, fully loaded with patients, staff, and equipment, slowly pulled around the circle drive of the hospital. A skeleton crew of medical staff remained to care for those who were too sick to be moved and to provide services for any others who stayed behind. From the passenger seat of the large military transport vehicle Ian noticed one of the nurses waving goodbye from under the awning. He could see the frightened look in her eyes and knew exactly what was going through her mind as the convoy turned south, headed for the bridge.

Leading the convoy were a couple of 2½-ton trucks equipped with large V-shaped snow plows. The desert-colored, ten-wheeled trucks parted the snow and ash like Moses parted the Red Sea. Even so, travel was slow, no faster than 25 miles an hour. The fine ash particles and wet snow made the road very slippery.

Ian worried about crossing the Mackinac Bridge with all of the heavy ash piled on the road surface, and he mentioned it to the driver, Sergeant Timothy Oaks. Oaks reminded Ian that the bridge had a grate system instead of pavement running down the center two lanes, and any snow-ash mixture, which he called "snash," would simply fall through the grates into the water below.

"Plus," he added, "the bridge was engineered to stand for 400 years or more. I think we'll be fine."

It was frightening how dark it was. "We're all so used to street lights, and house lights and light pollution," Ian thought. "I bet it hasn't been this dark since before the light bulb was invented."

The toll gates sit on the north side of the bridge. As the trucks rolled through without stopping to pay, Ian looked around at all of the empty booths and thought about how surreal all of this seemed. It felt like a dream, as if at any moment it would all just stop because he would wake up and everything would be normal again. He looked over at Oaks, who seemed intently focused on his driving.

"I'm glad you're driving," Ian commented. "I hate driving over this bridge on a good day, let alone during a catastrophe!" The sergeant just laughed, his hands at ten and two, his eyes fixed on the road ahead.

Near the center of the bridge Ian looked out the window. The blowing snow and ash obscured everything but the road and sides of the bridge. Only the first twenty feet or so of the large towers were visible as they passed under them. Ian wondered what the long-term effects of the ash would be on the Great Lakes.

The radio chatter seemed continuous as members of the convoy, as well as support teams from various command centers, relayed information back and forth. Ian was amazed at the professionalism these troops displayed in the face of disaster and how comfortable this made him feel.

"Man, how do you do this?" Ian asked. "I mean, you guys don't seem to be affected by what's going on, you just do your jobs like professionals!"

"We don't have time to be afraid," Sergeant Oaks replied. "We just stay focused on the task at hand and hope that it will be okay in the end." Ian watched out the window as their vehicle made slow progress. He thought about the sergeant's response, *"We just stay focused on the task at hand and hope that it will be okay in the end."* These words were optimistic, filled with hope and determination. They did not deny what was happening but merely looked at it differently.

It usually takes less than an hour to travel from Mackinaw City to Gaylord. At a slow and steady pace of 25 miles an hour, however, it took them just under two-and-a-half hours. While the convoy stopped for a rest, reports squawked over the radio about vehicle accidents, collapsed houses and buildings, and injured civilians. I-75 was shut down in numerous places due to car accidents and jackknifed or overturned trucks. The bridge at Zilwaukee was impassable. A decision was made that the convoy would divert just outside of Grayling and travel south toward Lansing on US 127.

The convoy pulled back on the road. The dim gray light exposed the depressing realities of this environmental disaster. Buildings, billboards, and trees all lay crushed or collapsed under the weight of the heavy snow-ash mixture. Ian wondered if the people had gotten out of the structures safely. Cars and trucks lay scattered along the sides of the road. Some were flipped over completely, some had their emergency lights still flashing. They spotted only one moving vehicle after they left Mackinaw City, and it was a heavy 4x4 truck merging south in front of the convoy onto the expressway. No signs of life existed otherwise.

Three-and-a-half hours later, the convoy decided to take a ten-minute stretch-and-pee stop at the Michigan Welcome Center in Clare. Four vehicles sat broken down in the parking lot. Three men who stood around the hood of a large passenger van looked surprised when the convoy pulled in and parked. One of the men quickly headed over to the building and moments later appeared with three women and multiple children in tow behind him. All climbed into the van and closed the door.

Once all vehicles had come to a full stop the commander pulled his men aside. A few minutes later four of the soldiers split off and approached the men at the van while another four headed over to the building to check things out. After what seemed like an eternity of investigating the premises and questioning the families, the Guardsmen loaded back into the vehicles and the convoy was on the road again. Ian asked what had happened. Sergeant Oaks explained that the families were traveling south together yesterday to escape the ash fall.

"They pulled into the rest area because their cars were acting up. Once they turned the cars off, they couldn't get them started again. They had little children and no provisions. They broke into the welcome center for water and to use the bathroom facilities. They also broke into the vending machines for food and sodas. Our guys gathered information and other guard units in the area were contacted to come to the families' aid. We couldn't take them. This convoy is already filled to its limit with people. They're lucky that another Guard unit is close by that can help them. Good thing we stopped when we did."

Approaching Ithaca, visibility was still under half a mile. Ian remarked at how unusual it was to drive through the area and not see the 500-foot-tall windmills that stretch as far as the eye can see on both sides of the highway. He could just barely make out the Ithaca High School football stadium that parallels US 127.

After miles of silence, a report suddenly came over the CB. I-96 was completely shut down at Fowlerville and there was also an overturned semi blocking all southbound lanes of US 23 near Lee Road in Brighton. The commander came over the radio a few minutes later and announced an alternative route. The convoy would now continue south on US 127 until they hit Jackson, then head east on I-94.

"Sweet," Ian said. "Now I can get off at Zeeb Road. I can hitch a ride from my neighbor who works at the road commission offices just off the expressway!"

Ian sat adjusting the straps on the gas mask that he had been issued in St. Ignace. The convoy slowly pulled off the highway onto Lake Lansing Road. They would take a short break before continuing the journey. Standing around with some of the soldiers, Ian asked why the military vehicles didn't seem to be affected by the ash like the other vehicles stranded on the sides of the road.

"During the first Iraq war, they had a lot of problems with the fine sand particles breaking down the engines," a Guardsman responded. "The military went to work on designing vehicles that could withstand that kind of abuse and more."

A few minutes later and a mile or so down the road, they passed the Frandor Shopping Center. Many of the roofs had collapsed under the excessive weight and a few buildings had burned to the ground, probably due to power lines snapping and igniting broken gas lines. It looked like a war zone. Ian started worrying about his farmhouse and barns. And what about Dexter or Ann Arbor? And what about his job?

At Jackson, the convoy headed east on I-94 but had to maneuver slowly around multiple vehicles that had broken down on the expressway. At one point the large snowplow trucks had to ram through a tangled mess of cars that were partially blocking the road. It was now 6:00 and it was pitch black again. It had taken twelve hours to get to Jackson. It would still be some time before they got to Ann Arbor. The commander contacted the Washtenaw County Road Commission offices on Zeeb Road and managed to talk to Ian's neighbor who worked there.

"Man, I lucked out," Ian thought. "That would have been one long, dark, cold walk."

At 7:54 the convoy pulled off the road under the Zeeb Road viaduct. Ian jumped out, gathered his things, said his goodbyes, and expressed his thanks.

Ian watched the convoy slowly pull away. The muffled sound of the engines gradually disappeared into the distance. This was the second time a convoy had abandoned him in the dark. And standing alone he realized how truly dark it was. A primal fear overcame him. He started the quarter-mile walk north to the road commission offices. Unaccustomed to walking on the slippery ash mixture, Ian shuffled slowly toward his destination. His neighbor sat waiting in a snowplow truck, his headlights illuminating the end of the parking lot. Ian hopped in and greeted his friend. They slowly turned up Zeeb Road on the final stretch of a long ride home.

Chapter 7

How to Abandon Your Life

The beautiful sunny day was picturesque and breezy, the skies were blue, and fat fluffy clouds leisurely drifted by as if migrating back from the south to their warm summer encampments in the north. Ian and Gabe played catch in the side yard while Theresa and Claire, sipping lemonade, watched from the comfort of their lounge chairs under the shade of the large sycamore trees. Suddenly everything went black. Ian could no longer see his surroundings; the air became thick and it was difficult to breathe. His family cried out to him, but their screams were so muted that he could not make out what they were trying to say. He attempted to reach them but his feet kept slipping and he could not advance without falling. Panic engulfed every fiber of his being as he reached out to them, screaming.

Day 22

And then he was awake.

Lying in bed he looked around and suddenly remembered where he was. Reggie C. Green, his neighbor from the road commission, had picked him up and suggested that Ian spend the night. Reggie had food and heat.

"You might as well eat and have a warm place to sleep tonight. We can go over to your place tomorrow and check things out after you've rested."

Reggie's house was the only one around to have electricity. He had hooked the power-takeoff on his tractor to an old road commission generator, and this powered his whole house in case of emergencies. Reggie was a great neighbor and a true Midwestern farm boy. He had grown up on this farm, which he had inherited from his mother. Even though he didn't farm any more, he still had that old-fashioned farming mentality.

Ian sat up on the side of the bed, remembering the dark, eerie ride back from the road commission offices last night. The falling ash made it impossible to see the road surface. There were no signs of habitation and the absence of any light made the five-mile drive north on Zeeb Road daunting, to say the least.

Now he wondered what he would find when he returned to his house. Had it been looted? Had the roof collapsed? Were there squatters living there? His wife had fed and watered the chickens just before she left and asked that he do the same when he returned.

"Hopefully the chickens are still alive," he whispered to himself.

Making his way downstairs Ian could smell coffee and hear the news on the radio playing in the kitchen. Reggie was busy preparing breakfast and was startled when Ian rounded the corner, boisterously bidding, "Good morning, sir!"

"Good morning!" retorted Reggie. "How'd ya sleep?" Ian thanked him for the comfortable accommodations and the great night's sleep and then brought up his dream from this morning. Reggie laughed,

"Yeah, I've been having my share of 'ash-mares' too…must just be our way of coping with the situation, I guess."

At breakfast the two men talked about their wives' departures and their plans to reunite with them in the near future. Reggie told Ian how he and his wife Lynn had helped Theresa and the kids pack up the car before seeing them off. Reggie thought it was counterintuitive for Theresa to be heading anywhere toward the west, but Theresa was not to be dissuaded.

"Well," Ian laughed, "Theresa's the kind of gal that if she's sick or if something's wrong, she wants her Mom."

Reggie went on to say that Lynn left shortly after Theresa. She headed to Virginia to stay with her relatives and wait for him to join her. He had remained to keep the roads clear and open, but the county trucks started breaking down quickly and now there were only two working trucks left in the whole fleet.

"Supposedly, the National Guard will soon be taking over the responsibilities for the roadways, and that's when I'm out of here! I keep trying to call Lynn to let her know I'm coming, but I can't ever get through. The phones are useless."

Ian discussed his plans of catching rides when he could and walking when he had to.

"Shouldn't be too bad. There are plenty of people heading south out of the ash. Maybe I can hook up with another National Guard unit."

"Sounds like a rough way to go," Reggie sympathized. "Are you sure about this?" Ian responded that his options were pretty limited.

"It's not like I can hop on a plane or take the bus. I mean, what would you do?" Reggie drank his last sip of coffee, stood up and started clearing the table.

"I will take you as far south as I can, but then I'm heading east. Hopefully that'll get you south of the ash and started off on the right foot."

After breakfast, Reggie grabbed his gun and the two headed to Ian's house to check things out. The six inches of snow and ash made driving up the hill into the farm impossible, so they had to walk in from the road. The lack of noticeable tracks in the driveway was an indication that there weren't any unwanted visitors lurking about, but the two men cautiously walked around the buildings, inside and out, to make sure. While policing the area they also checked for any problems with the structures and found nothing wrong. Everything was intact and appeared to be structurally sound, despite a heavy coating of snash. There was, however, one problem: dead chickens—lumps under the snow-ash mixture. The food still in their feeders made it apparent that ash inhalation must have been their downfall.

Reggie stayed long enough to help Ian make the temporarily uninhabitable situation habitable once more. The two brought wood into the house and got a fire going before Reggie decided to head over to the road commission offices.

"I'll be in touch with you as soon as the Guard moves in to take over the roads," Reggie said, reaching out to shake Ian's hand. "Shouldn't be more than a week or so, and then we'll head south. How's that sound?"

"Sounds good!" Ian responded. "Thanks again for picking me up and all your generosity. I really appreciate it!"

Alone, Ian began the task of assessing what he needed to survive the days and nights to come. He gathered together supplies from the basement, then went out to the tornado shelter to retrieve the food and water that Theresa had left for him. He placed everything on the dining room table for easy access.

Ian looked for the shotgun and ammo, but they were nowhere to be found. He laughed and said out loud,

"Well, knowing Gabe, that was the first thing he grabbed when they left!" The thought of this made him both proud and pleased that his son was capable of protecting the family in Ian's absence.

The house was so quiet. The lack of people, animals, music, clocks—life!—the total lack of everyday life! None of this seemed real. It seemed like any second the back door would fly open and the kids would be fighting and the dog would be barking and Theresa would be calling Ian for help with the groceries, and it would be a bright and sunny day again.

"Perhaps the volcano will stop and I won't have to leave!" These thoughts ran through Ian's mind as he stood with his back against the kitchen sink, staring at the floor.

Working well into the late afternoon, Ian realized he hadn't eaten since breakfast and it was getting dark. He switched gears and focused his attention on making dinner.

"Hmmmm, I think I'm going to start dinner the proper way!" He headed down the cellar steps to retrieve a bottle of wine. It was their shared passion for good wines that convinced the Camerons they should establish a proper cellar. Now with over 500 bottles, their selection reflected not only their love for wines, but their love for travel as well. Ian selected a 2010 zinfandel and eagerly dashed up the steps to indulge in his abundance. Finding the aerator, he poured a generous glass and commenced making a delightful beef stew which cooked on top of the wood stove and filled the house with the smell of home once again.

The oil lamps, candles, and woodstove made for a cozy atmosphere that seemed to defy the cruel punishment Mother Nature was inflicting outside. The wind had increased and the blowing snash whipped the house as it groaned with discomfort and uncertainty. The creaking made Ian uncomfortable as he sat quietly contemplating his options.

"It is what it is," he declared to the house. With that he stood up, walked around and blew out the candles and the oil lamps. He settled into his makeshift bed in front of the woodstove.

Near midnight, Ian was startled awake. It took him a few disoriented moments before he could comprehend what had just happened. The crashing sound seemed to come from outside, and the first thought that ran through his head was *"Looters!"* A sudden burst of fear and adrenaline surged through his body as he sprang up into a sitting position. Peering wide-eyed into the darkness, all he could think was that someone was in the house. He sat quietly listening, trying to control his breathing. Then it happened again. A second loud crash shattered the silence, only this time it was obvious. The barn had collapsed. Grabbing his flashlight, he jumped up, slipped on his shoes, and ran to the back door to assess the damage. The falling snow and the settling dust from the barn made it impossible to see. His inspection would have to wait until the morning light.

Ian stoked the fire and sat looking into the woodstove as the hungry flames eagerly began to consume the fresh supply of fuel. The collapse of the barn only served to introduce more fear and panic into the situation. Ian's mind raced with multiple scenarios, which ended with the house collapsing and either crushing him to death or leaving him exposed to the elements. A new sense of urgency washed over him, and he realized he had some busy days of preparation ahead. He loaded a few more logs into the fire, closed the stove down, and climbed back into bed. Sleep, however, would prove to be elusive, as every sound, at least in Ian's mind, was an indicator of imminent collapse and probable death.

Days 23–24

Groggy from lack of sleep, Ian slowly rose out of bed to start his day. He stoked the coals in the woodstove and added the necessary ingredients to start a new life-sustaining blaze before getting dressed to head out to the barn.

The morning seemed colder than yesterday as Ian stepped out into the wind and adjusted the collar of his coat. From where he stood at the back door the barn was in full view. The center of the roof had given way under the weight of the snow-ash, causing the roof ridge to buckle like the broken spine on a four-legged animal, pulling both sides of the barn walls inward as it collapsed. The left side wall was almost completely demolished, having snapped at the section between the first and second floors. It now lay resting on the roof below it. The right side wall leaned at a sharp forty-five degree angle, precariously hinged between the same floor sections. It reminded Ian of a ship sinking into the ocean.

Standing at the barn door, Ian could see that the lawn mower, with the snow blower still attached, had narrowly escaped being crushed by a huge, twelve-inch square beam. The same could not be said about the farm tractor. The roof had collapsed directly on top of it, crushing the engine cover and ripping the exhaust pipe, seat, and rear fenders off completely. It was too unstable to venture inside to check for anything that could be recovered. That would have to wait until the barn was taken down later. He was shocked and overwhelmed by what he saw.

"Will my insurance cover this?" Ian wondered.

The next two days were spent assessing and sorting his family's belongings, a depressing and remorseful task. Frustrated, Ian began talking out loud.

"Now I know what people deal with during floods or fires."

In an effort to make the task less depressing, Ian got organized and created three categories: (1) things to Abandon, (2) things to Store, and (3) things to Take.

The tornado shelter seemed like the most logical place to keep the items he wanted to stash. They would be locked up underground and hidden from sight. The ash and snow would bury the door and no one would ever find it.

"Perfect!" Ian thought.

Sorting his belongings into three piles, cleaning out the shelter, and packing it full of his family's treasures made for two days of solid work. This kept his time filled and his mind busy. He had to fight the urge to sit and waste time reading, or worse, looking at every photograph that passed through his hands. His "Things to Abandon" pile was quite large. Unfortunately, so was his "Things to Store" pile, which meant he had to pack things into the shelter more efficiently. By late afternoon Monday, the tornado shelter was almost full and Ian was exhausted.

With his mind on what to make for dinner, Ian opened the back door heading for the shelter with another load. Suddenly, a crashing sound from inside the house made him jump. He rapidly set the items down and returned to investigate. Looking past the kitchen, Ian could see dust in the air. He grabbed the flashlight on the counter next to the stove and cautiously approached the dining room. A quick scan revealed nothing but the floating dust. He opened the door to the adjacent room. There was only sky where the ceiling had once been. The house was no longer safe.

Days 25–26

The fatigue Ian felt was sickening. Sleep was sporadic. Fear had replaced it, and all he could think about was getting out of the house before it became his permanent resting place. He would have to switch gears now and just prepare for his departure. There was no time to store anything else. Ian headed out to padlock the shelter. As he was covering the doors with snow he heard a high-pitched scream or whistle coming from down the street.

The wind-whipped snow and temperatures in the teens made walking down the road fairly unpleasant, but Ian needed to make sure that no one was hurt or in need of help. The high-pitched noise would sound off every minute or so. It sounded as though it was coming from the Brenner farm, about a quarter mile or so to the west.

"Bob! Pat! Hello!" Ian started calling out as he approached the house. But there was no reply.

In the barn, he discovered that a section of the roof had collapsed into the grain storage area. Peering into the room, Ian jumped back as the sound screeched directly in front of him. A dislodged section of the corrugated roof blew in the wind and dragged across a metal fence pole, producing the horrid noise. Relieved to discover that it wasn't his neighbors, Ian laughed nervously as the sound pierced the air again. Since he was already out, he decided to do a quick survey of other houses in the area.

Ian had been gone from his house about an hour when Reggie pulled up. Since his departure, the wind gusts had blown the snash, covering his tracks and leaving no indication that Ian had ventured away from the farm. Reggie searched and waited for about 45 minutes, but when Ian did not return, Reggie decided to leave a note which read:

Ian,

I looked everywhere for you... where the hell are you? I'm not waiting any longer. My roof has collapsed! I waited around for about an hour but I can't find you and can't wait around any longer. I'm sorry.

Good Luck—Reggie

Four out of the six houses Ian checked had either collapsed or been damaged. Thankfully, he did not find any bodies. He had left his house a little over three hours earlier; hunger now guided his footsteps home.

The multiple stalls, corrals, and outbuildings behind his barn, not visible from the back porch of the house, were in full view from the western edge of the property. Ian stopped at the fence to examine the damage. Several outbuildings had collapsed just this morning; a grain store and two interconnecting horse sheds lay in ruin. His beautiful farm was slowly dying. Added to everything else, it was just too much.

So many emotions were churning inside of him; anger, fear, panic, betrayal, loss. Ian sat staring at the fire, brooding, while he ate. The image of Reggie's note tucked in between the screen door and the jamb was burned into his mind. He couldn't believe that Reggie would just leave him behind. Now Ian felt truly stranded and alone.

"I've gotta get the hell out of here," he quietly muttered, shaking his head and biting his lower lip.

He cleared the table, gathered a couple of oil lamps, and grabbed his box of maps. He would spend the rest of the night and part of the next day going over his travel plans. He tore pages out of an old atlas, which unfortunately lacked many of the states he needed, and highlighted the routes he wanted to take. He avoided major cities and highways to be less conspicuous, and in an effort to avoid the riots in Ohio he diverted his route into eastern Indiana and decided to cross the Ohio River at Louisville.

Ian sat visualizing how he would travel. Hopeful that he could use his riding mower the whole way out west, he made a list of what he would need to make that happen: panty hose, extra gas cans, oil, his trailer attachment. Would he need the snow blade as well? He knew the possibilities of using a vehicle were limited, but he held to the notion that if all else failed there would still be military vehicles willing to help. The one option he did not want to consider was the idea of walking the whole distance. This was Ian's last resort, worst-case scenario, but it was the idea that occupied his thoughts constantly.

By late Wednesday afternoon, Ian had gathered all of the items he would need to take on his journey. He had recently purchased an internal frame, large capacity backpack to go on Scout outings with Gabe. Some of the essentials were still inside: sleeping bag, compass, rope, knife, whistle, fire starter, and first-aid kit. For defensive purposes, he included his great-great grandfather's Civil War sword and his Russian bayonet. The maps he had worked on for the last two days fit nicely in the upper compartment behind his head. He packed some trail mix and grabbed the protein bars that were left over from the last Scout outing. He was now ready to leave in the morning.

Day 27

The image of the barn on the day he left for the UP flashed into his thoughts. It was quickly erased as a gust of wind caused the large red barn to groan with great discomfort. It shuddered and choked with each frozen breath through its empty broken carcass.

Ian carefully pulled the riding mower out of the barn and stopped to say goodbye to his farm. As he looked around, grief, sadness, and guilt overtook him. He cried for the loss and devastation of his home, his life, and his family. He felt somehow responsible, as if he had let them all down, as if it were his fault the farm was destroyed and their lives were thrown into chaos. Abandoning it all just seemed to compound those feelings. With one last tearful goodbye, he strapped on his gas mask, mounted the mower, and headed down the road toward Dexter.

Approaching town, Ian had to stop because a large oak tree had collapsed across the road. He got off and cleared some branches away so he could get around it. When he put the mower into gear, his foot slipped off the clutch, sending him speeding toward the tree trunk. Ian turned the wheels to avoid the tree, but the tires just slid sideways and the impact snapped the front axle. In total disbelief Ian got off the mower and started kicking the back tire and swearing profusely.

Pissed off, he unloaded his backpack, abandoned his mower, and headed into town on foot. A mile from the accident site he reached the emergency shelter that had been set up at the Dexter police station. Although it was early still, Ian decided it was probably safer to stay here and continue on in the morning. Besides, he wasn't ready to leave…not just yet.

Chapter 8

Leaving Dexter

Day 28

Today Ian would leave Dexter. He stood outside the doors to the police station, dreading the long cold walk to Chelsea. His back hurt from trying to sleep on the cot that was provided, and he was hungry. The supply of MREs had been exhausted due to the large influx of refugees pouring into the station. Ian snagged two bottles of water before he walked out the door, but he would have been more comforted if there were food and he didn't have to break into his personal stash.

Dexter was deserted. Businesses were closed and boarded up. He headed toward the old A&W Drive-In, which sat overlooking the town from the west. Its metal awning had collapsed under the heavy ash.

From the A&W, Ian traveled southwest on Dexter–Chelsea Road. The ground beneath his feet was like ice, and he knew he would have to walk slowly and deliberately to avoid injury. The road had not been plowed for some time and the gray snow-ash mixture had accumulated to about six inches or more. Walking the seven-and-a-half miles to Chelsea would not be fun.

Ian found himself gasping for air. The straps of the gas mask had loosened, causing the interior of the heavy respirator to rest on the brim of his nose, making it difficult to breathe. He stopped for a few minutes to slow his breathing down and make adjustments. This helped dramatically.

Getting used to the mask was going to take some time. The constant, hollow, Darth Vader-esque sound of his own breathing was distracting and made him feel apprehensive. His natural senses felt restricted. His peripheral vision was now limited, and he had to rely on breathing through a filter, which reduced his ability to detect smells.

Resuming his slow shuffle down the road, Ian stopped frequently to see if he was being followed. His mind incessantly played tricks on him. The wind hitting his mask made it sound as if cars were approaching from behind. He started to worry about being ambushed. This distraction was becoming obsessive, and the constant turning to stay on guard made for slow progress. In an attempt to refocus his mind, he started singing songs and shuffling his feet in tempo.

It's nature's way of telling you something's wrong
It's nature's way of telling you in a song....

Ian stopped dead in his tracks. His eyes panned over the lifeless pallor of the frozen landscape. Death was now in command. His mind grappled with the words he had just sung. Devastation of the environment and its resources, political corruption and greed, putting profits before people, and the apathetic populus whose only concern was when the next iPhone upgrade was going to be released: was this finally "Nature's way" of ridding herself of the parasitic human species?

He pondered this idea as he continued down the road. His pace seemed to quicken ever so slightly. Ian's internal philosophical rant had refocused his mind. His personal predicament seemed to wane the more he thought about the human scourge that ravaged the Earth and his own role in it. He always recycled, ate organic foods, and protested against chemical companies. But so what? He was still a consumer! He still wanted the newest electronics, he still wanted gas in his old truck that got horrible mileage. The fact was that he was one of the willing participants, no matter how much he disguised it with buying "green" products or talking about "reducing his carbon footprint." No matter his good intentions, he still played the game. He still participated in destroying the Earth.

The wind started to pick up and Ian noticed the sky to the west was darker. A storm was approaching, but there were still easily four or five miles to go before he arrived in Chelsea.

"This really sucks!" he yelled. As fear set in, he attempted to shuffle faster. Being caught in a storm could be fatal and he was determined to not be taken so easily.

Ian had advanced a few miles with head-down determination before the snow began to fall. The wind blew the snow and ash horizontally, causing almost whiteout conditions. Approaching the small industrial buildings that stood a few miles outside of Chelsea, Ian forgot about the railroad tracks that crossed the road. As soon as his foot hit the slippery track, he found himself painfully sprawled out, looking up at the sky.

He was already in agony before the fall. Walking on the slippery surface was causing muscle pain and fatigue. Since he was fifty pounds overweight, his thighs now chafed against his pants. Ash had entered into his clothing and his shoes, creating abrasions and blisters.

When he fell, he landed hard on his left hip and elbow. The impact jarred his neck and his spine. He was also cold and tired. He rested on the tracks for a few minutes as he gathered the energy to stand. Rising gingerly, he brushed himself off, stretched, checked his things and continued on his way. Only now he winced in pain with every step.

The final two miles into town took another hour. He had been warned at the Dexter police station that the Chelsea high school's roof had collapsed and the refugee center had moved to the hospital. He headed there, hoping the rumors were correct.

A very kind elderly woman greeted Ian at the door of the hospital as he arrived. She directed him to where he could place his things and hang his coat. The hospital's generators kept the building warm, and after six hours of walking in the bitter cold, warmth was a welcome relief. Another volunteer took Ian to a registration table, where he was issued a pillow and blanket and shown to his cot. Forty-six people had registered before him, and the noise as he entered the holding area was a welcome change from the unnatural silence of late.

Warm food and hot coffee seemingly compelled many of the refugees to share their stories.

"I was in my house when it collapsed..."
"My father had COPD and was overcome by the ash..."
"We tried to escape, but our car died and..."
"I thought it was going to stop!"

For six hours Ian listened to one story after another of hardship and suffering, pain and escape. Everyone's story was different, but they were all connected, and they shared in the providence that had brought them together now.

At lights out, Ian lay in his cot looking up at the ceiling. "It took six hours to go seven miles," he thought. "I've got to get faster." The chafing between his legs burned. He had blisters on his feet and abrasions on his face where the mask rubbed. His hip was in pain and now bruised from the fall. He had been given some zinc oxide cream for his legs and face and a roll of moleskin to apply to his blisters. Ian took three ibuprofen and closed his eyes. The next day's itinerary ran through his thoughts, but exhaustion overpowered his ability to stay awake.

Day 29

Ian awoke to a commotion that reminded him of camping in a state park. Children, the first to awaken, started playing and making noise. Babies began crying because their diapers were wet and they needed to be fed. Soon the adults were up, and there was conversation and the smell of coffee and breakfast. Parents started yelling at their kids, and there was banging and clatter. He lay there not wanting to be awake but forced out of bed by the motion of life.

Ian groaned as he sat up. Every inch of his body hurt. He quickly lay back down.

"Ten more minutes," he whispered to himself. But it was already too late. He was awake, and he felt like he had been hit by a bus. His mind raced with anxiety, and the idea of walking another eight miles to Manchester only made him more anxious.

"I gotta get moving." He grunted, as he willed his body to sit up again.

There are certain sounds that only old men make when they attempt to stand from a seated position. These were the sounds that emanated from Ian with each step he took as he hobbled toward the bathroom.

Ian examined his inner thighs in the bathroom mirror. The burning sensation made walking problematic, and now he could see why. He exited the bathroom and went straight to the nurses' triage area in search of relief.

He checked in and was asked numerous questions before being placed in a room to wait. About twenty minutes later a nurse practitioner walked in. She bandaged his chafed thighs with gauze and told him to keep the area covered until it was no longer irritated. She suggested he could use gauze, tape, or even clean cloth to prevent further abrasions on his thighs or where the gas mask rubbed against his face. If he tied or duct taped his pant legs at the bottom, it would keep ash from getting into his pants and shoes. This should help with the blistering and irritation on his feet.

Returning to his bunk, Ian stashed the medical supplies and headed over to the breakfast line. Most of the hospital patients had been evacuated, and the influx of refugees was dwindling quickly. The hospital was trying to use up its food supplies so the facility could be shut down. Breakfast was generous: eggs, bacon, potatoes, toast, cold cereal, hot coffee, milk, juices, and water.

He took his time eating as he watched the room. There were families gathering together to strategize their next moves. There were people packing, people arguing, babies crying. There were individuals attempting to team up with others to travel together, and there were couples walking out the door. Ian knew where he was going next: to his friends' A-frame near Manchester.

"I can't wait to see them," Ian thought. "Once I get out there, they can help me figure this whole thing out."

The eight mile walk was painful and cold. Luckily it was a straight shot from Chelsea, but the route was exposed. Flat farm fields on both sides of the road assured that the freezing wind would lick your body with its razor tongue. Ian had pushed himself hard today, and managed to walk the distance in six hours.

"A little better than yesterday!" he thought, but this made his already stressed muscles feel even more pain. He lethargically limped up the long driveway to the house. "Wonder which A-frame I'll get today?" Ian thought. The place had always had a split personality. There was the peaceful, calm resort, a focal point for pipe ceremonies, large drumming circles, and group meditations. Then there was the other side of the double-edged sword. The extradimensional flavor of the place was forever cemented back on New Year's Eve of 1969. Ian's brother had gone into a deep trance state in the last hours of the 1960s. From the stories Ian had heard, a water pipe burst in the bathroom and his brother zapped the torrent of water with his extended right hand.

That powerful burst of energy, of *intent,* sealed the pipe but created a permanent hole in the fabric of space-time at this location. Ever since that moment, voices and music frequently entered from some other adjoining dimension. The site where this happened could not be repaired, despite repeated remodeling. The hole in the floor always returned. The voices always returned.

Not seeing anyone, Ian knocked on the sliding glass door and waited. He peered through the glass, but there was no sign of anyone at home. Retrieving the key from its hiding place, he opened the door.

"Hello!" Nothing. "Where are you guys?" A sudden flash of fear washed over Ian as he thought the worst.

"Oh shit, what if someone else is here? What if they're dead?" He grabbed the fire poker next to the wood stove and cautiously proceeded to search each room. Finally satisfied that the house was empty, he lit some oil lamps and candles. Though the well didn't work, he found bottled water and poured himself a scotch. Then he worked on starting a fire.

Where could his friends have gone? They left no notes and hadn't left any messages with Theresa. Over the many years, they had all agreed to meet here in the event of an apocalypse to set up a defensive perimeter. So, where the hell was everybody? Ian looked around and shrugged ironically. Well, maybe next apocalypse!

After dinner, Ian sat and reflected on his situation. Walking was way worse than he had expected, but he couldn't think of another option. He had walked only two days so far and he felt like he was going to die. What if he had to walk all the way out west? Overwhelmed by this prospect as well as his sore muscles, abrasions and blisters, Ian decided to lay low for the next couple of days. He would need the time to figure out his route south, give his body a rest, and hopefully give his friends time to return. Rest was definitely what he needed now.

Day 30

Today was Sunday, the thirtieth day of this volcanic ordeal. Ian sat lost in the memories of the many peaceful mornings he had spent here. On his first visit, when he was just seven years old, an unexpected blizzard blew in, trapping them in a wooded wintery fairyland for two days. That was his most favorite memory of all.

But that was also a long time ago. This morning he would rest his weary feet and body. He had heard that ash was ten to twenty times denser than snow, and after walking through five inches of the stuff, he could believe it. Every muscle ached. Soon, though, a roaring fire in the woodstove helped to ease the pain.

After breakfast Ian listened to the old battery-powered radio he had found in the bathroom last night. Sunday radio sermons were building fervor among fundamentalist Christians regarding an impending apocalypse. Sermons began with the more traditional "Sunday is the Lord's Day of Rest" and transitioned into the familiar Psalm 23: "Yea, though I walk through the valley of the shadow of death." Then most burst into a full blown hell-fire-and-brimstone harangue. Incessant ash fueled their certainty that the end times were upon us.

At 10:00, FEMA reported that refugees were continuing to create problems in the eastern part of Indiana. Civil unrest had spread west along the Ohio River from Cincinnati to Louisville.

Ian could no longer travel to the east of Indianapolis but needed to go farther west and come down the west side of Indiana. This was becoming more complicated. He would now need a new route.

His friends frequently vacationed all over the U.S. and Canada in their RV, but he could find no maps or atlases anywhere in the house. Finally he located a ten-year-old AAA road atlas in a broken-down van out in the pole barn.

It was near dark and lighting was poor in the house, so he deferred poring over the maps until tomorrow. Sitting by the warm crackling woodstove in the living room, thinking about "the Lord's Day of Rest," he fell into an exhausted sleep in the large, comfortable recliner rocker.

Day 31

The 9 a.m. FEMA report updated the continued civil unrest in eastern Indiana and Indianapolis. By day's end he would need an exit strategy that included both a route south out of the ash and a survival plan for food, water, and overnight shelter.

The newly revised exit plan would have to include two major factors stressed by FEMA. First, stay away from population centers. Avoid people! The riots and civil unrest had become too deadly. Second, avoid bridges across medium to larger rivers. Bandits were seizing food, water, guns, and ammo from roadway refugees. Shootouts ensued. Many died protecting their valuables.

The outdated road atlas still offered a bounty of information. Ian first marked the major population centers with yellow markers. Then he marked the medium and larger rivers. Weirdly, the exit path revealed itself immediately. He realized he could enter Indiana, head west below Kendallville, then stay just north of the Tippecanoe River and west of the Wabash all the way down to Terre Haute. For almost 300 miles he would never cross a single river or bridge in Indiana. This route would give a wide berth to every major population center. If he could walk ten miles a day, he would be out of the ash in thirty days. Setting up his next ten-mile increment each night would establish his goal for the following day.

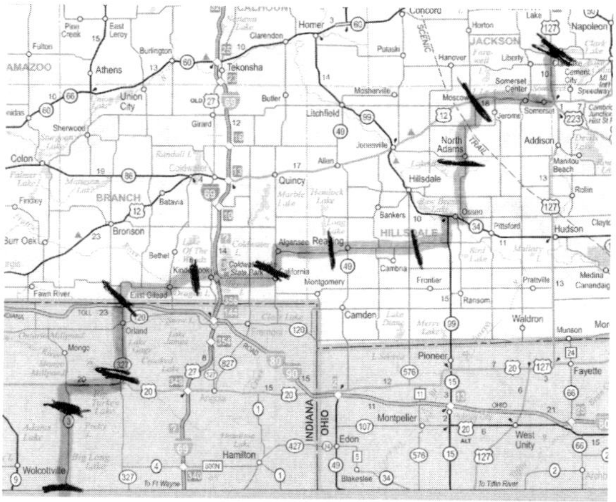

There would be no ash below I-70 and his speed could increase. Nothing stood in his path all the way down to Evansville. Then he could cross the Ohio River into Kentucky. This plan would work!

What he needed now was a plan to survive the ashfall that covered the ground clear down to Terre Haute. Below I-70, he would probably find hotels, restaurants, and stores. He might even be able to rent a car or hitchhike.

His immediate problem would be getting potable water. Billions of people around the world had heard daily FEMA advisories regarding the lethal effect of volcanic ash on rivers, lakes, and drinking water. They were told that particulates in ash-contaminated water stimulate excessive bacterial growth. Boiling and disinfectants are rendered ineffective. To overcome these obstacles, he would take enough bottled water to last a few days. He'd have to hope there was a refugee center in Hillsdale.

He also had to eat for the next thirty days. From his early teens, he had read survival books and had taken wilderness survival classes. The next month would be filled with those outdoor skills. He would hunt and fish and build snares for food and construct secluded shelters in the woods to avoid people. Ian had been preparing for a catastrophe for thirty-five years. He was ready!

Ian went to bed early on his last night at the A-frame. The walk from Dexter had been through familiar territory that he had traveled hundreds of times. Tomorrow the journey into the unknown would begin.

Chapter 9

Day 32

There were no soldiers, no police, no hospital staff. From now on, he would have no back up. This was the first day he was on his own in unfamiliar, unprotected territory. "Now I start my real journey," he thought. He gripped the walking stick he had found in the pole barn and carefully picked his way down the driveway out onto the dirt road headed south.

The once vibrant fields and woods in this rural farming area were now shrouded in gray. Ash continued to swirl all around him, making it hard to see even the road. Ian's steps were cautious.

He had wanted to walk ten miles a day, but in this slippery ash, ten miles would take six or seven hours, and that was all the daylight there was. He resolved to force himself to walk about ten miles a day to keep to his original schedule, meaning he would have to use every minute of daylight, from when he got up to when it got dark around 4:00.

Throughout the day, the gas mask continued to bother him, restricting his hearing and vision. Without the mask, though, he couldn't breathe. Until he got free of the ash, it was a necessary evil.

After ten miles of walking, he was at the point of exhaustion. He would not be able to cut timbers and build a survival camp tonight. He would need shelter, but he couldn't bring himself to break into a house. When he stopped for the night, he found an unlocked garage. He wouldn't have to break and enter. He could not see himself as a criminal.

Ian ran a quick assessment of his situation. He had painful blisters from today's walk. His cramped body ached. He was hungry and thirsty, but he had only the food and water he had brought with him. Ash had slipped through any tiny gap in his clothing, irritating his skin wherever it came in contact with his body. He desperately needed a bath, but he couldn't wash up in the garage. He was cold and tired and thoroughly miserable.

Ian worried about local residents spotting him and thinking he was breaking and entering. He was afraid of being caught trespassing or shot as a looter. All night he listened tensely for sounds and got little sleep. Prolonged lack of sleep, though, could cause him to lose focus and attention—and could get him killed.

It was late January and winter. Ian pondered whether his survival outweighed society's perceptions of looting.

Day 33

After the poor night's sleep, he was groggy. He poked his head out of his sleeping bag and immediately started to shiver.

"Damn, it's cold in here!" Ian snaked an arm out to grab his shirt. The shirt was cold too. Getting dressed was not going to be a pleasant experience. He gritted his teeth and started moving at top speed. It was the fastest he'd ever gotten dressed.

"I'd kill for a cup of hot coffee," he muttered; but the only source of heat here was his own body. "Never again. I am not going to have another night like this. I *will* have a fire, and I *will* have hot coffee in the morning. Whatever it takes!"

Unhappily, he ate cold food and drank cold water. Then he headed out onto the road to get his ten miles in.

Late in the afternoon, he approached Clark Lake. There he found a summer cottage with a storage shed and a portable metal fire pit with firewood stacked outside. He built a fire at the entrance to the shed for warmth and to keep animals away.

Though the house and shed sat on a back road, sheltered from view, he still wouldn't break into the house to get warm and stay safe. He worried all night that someone would see his fire and shoot him. His water and supplies continued to dwindle, but at least he was warm.

Day 34

Fortified with a warm breakfast and a hot cup of tea, Ian set off southward. He had about half a day to go before he would hit US 12, Michigan Avenue, where he would turn west. He was very cold and running low on water, but the ice on local lakes and rivers was thick with ash. The water did not look safe to drink. He was worn down by the ash, the gloominess, his hunger and thirst, and the pain of his blistered feet. He was not focused.

About five miles down US 12 he found a house with a storage shed and a wood pile. He was ready to spend another night in a shed, but as he rounded the corner of the house he came to an abrupt halt. Across the yard were four dogs. When they saw him, their lips drew back in snarls and they slowly moved toward him, growling menacingly.

Ian ran up onto the back porch with the dogs closing in. He smashed in the door glass with his elbow and barely got inside. They were snapping at him through the broken window and throwing themselves against the door.

These dogs were a feral pack. He couldn't go back outside. Even if they didn't tear him apart, he couldn't risk rabies. Ian was still reluctant to become a home-invading looter, but he didn't have any other choice.

The dogs continued to attack the door. He had to get them away from that broken window. Ian rummaged through his backpack and found his last remaining length of sausage. Moving to the kitchen window, he yelled loudly to attract the dogs' attention, then threw the sausage into the yard. The snarling pack raced to fight over the meat. Ian upended the kitchen table and shoved it up against the door. This bought him time to find a hammer and nails. Nailing the table to the doorframe would keep out the wild dogs.

"Are we always only one broken window away from feral animal attacks?" he wondered.

The electricity was off in the house, so the well pump couldn't run; but the three-gallon tank on the back of the toilet was full of water. The house temperature was about 50 degrees, much warmer than the outside 27 degrees with its wind and ash.

In the pantry, he found a bag of oats that was probably too bulky for the homeowners to take. After digging through the cabinets, he also found candles and a pot. It took a lot of patience, but eventually the candles provided enough heat to boil the toilet water. He made tea and oatmeal.

Ian warmed water for a sponge bath and washed the ash out of his hair. He felt much better. Next, he cleaned and treated his blisters. Then he began to wonder what he would do about dirty clothes. His underwear was going to have to be washed at some point, but it would never dry at these temperatures. The cumulative effect of everything he had been through was getting irritating. He'd be really glad to get out of this ash.

He couldn't even start a fire to keep warm. He was still worried about attracting attention. Ian found several heavy quilts in a small first-floor bedroom, which, along with his sleeping bag, would at least make a comfortable, warm bed.

The dogs left around dusk. Ian secured all the doors and windows. He began to feel safe inside the house.

His sleep was disturbed throughout the night by weird house settling sounds due to the weight of ash on the roof. Would it collapse? Was that sound the owner returning home? Was it the dogs? The sheriff? Zombies from *Night of the Living Dead*? His imagination worked overtime.

Day 35

Not really rested, Ian stumbled into the kitchen and boiled water to make sugary tea and oatmeal. His spirits had been lifted by having a decent meal and sleeping in a warm bed.

This momentary respite was offset by terrifying images of the feral dog pack replaying in his mind. This startling turn of events was a game changer. Were they still lurking outside the house, waiting? Or would they lie in ambush along an open, deserted back road? Frantically, he went from window to window, searching for any movement. There were no signs of life anywhere. Apparently, the dog pack had departed in search of an easier meal.

It was time to get back on the road. He started out walking, and as he walked he realized that if he had been out in the shed last night, he would have been killed by the wild dogs. That strategy was fatally flawed. Throughout the day his feral dog antennae were on high alert as he pondered this realization.

Slowly over the next ash-laden ten miles a new strategy began to form. He needed to spend each night in a house, safely protected from wandering threats. He was not stealing or looting jewelry or riches, he argued to himself. He was only seeking overnight survival shelter in a world gone mad. He wasn't asking for much. He needed only a few things: a little warmth—he wouldn't even build a fire in the fireplace; a little food, abandoned by the fleeing homeowners; water; and a warm, secure bed. He rationalized that he wouldn't be a looter but simply an uninvited overnight guest, gone by morning.

That line from the Bob Seeger song, "A perfect lodger, a perfect guest": Ian sang the song lines over several times as the concept resonated and was embedded in his brain. He realized he had become "The Beautiful Looter."

In the early afternoon, he began to assess each house he passed for overnight safety and survivability. He saw big farm houses, small ranch houses, summer lake houses, McMansions. He found himself evaluating each for its defensibility. What would it take to make that house safe? What amenities does it have to offer?

He was still reluctant, not quite certain of his moral justifications. This was all new to Ian, but he needed a new shelter procurement plan immediately.

He determined that before nightfall he would need a house that was smaller and easier to defend, with fewer windows and doors; preferably single story. The house must be off the main road. This would reduce the chance of encountering vigilantes. It should have an outside propane or charcoal grill, so he could boil the water he would find in the toilet tank. Hopefully, there would be some good quality food in the pantry. Candles would be nice, to be used in bedrooms with covered windows. Candles create warmth and light.

Within twenty minutes he detoured off the main road just south of North Adams and quickly found a house that met these requirements. He broke the glass on the back door and entered. He set up the outside propane grill on the back porch, got a couple of gallons of water from the toilet tank, and set it to boil.

When he picked up the pot of bubbling water to go inside, a small movement caught his eye. In the gathering dusk thirty feet away, the slinking bodies of feral dogs appeared. Could it be the same pack? Could they have been following him? There were now six dogs, and they were silently stalking him as prey. "Thank God I'm not out in a shed tonight," he thought.

He quickly brought the water into the house and slammed and locked the back door. Next he boarded up the broken glass and went to work to secure and fortify all of the windows. Knowing that he was temporarily safe and secure from the dog pack, he scavenged a meager dinner from the pantry. Then he warmed up the small interior bedroom with candles and body heat and fell into an exhausted sleep under ancient handsewn quilts.

Overnight the house creaked and strained under the weight of the ash. He woke up many times, worrying that the roof might collapse.

Day 36

Bad dreams filled the night. Dogs. They were still outside. They had been stalking him for days. They wouldn't give up. He'd have to kill all of them. It was either him or them. Otherwise, he would never be able to leave this house. In fact, it was urgent that he develop defensive weapons against *all* feral animals, including humans.

But first, he thought, I need some breakfast and to get cleaned up for the day. Ian was struggling to reestablish his normal morning routine. If that meant boiling water in a pot with a candle and scavenging other people's food, so be it.

After breakfast, he searched the house and found flares in the basement. The only gun case was empty, but there was a loaded

.22 rifle in the back of the bedroom closet. The owners must have taken the higher-powered guns when they fled.

Now he needed to develop other weapons. When he left Dexter, he had not been thinking about defending himself from wild animals. He had brought with him his family's Civil War sword and a Russian bayonet he had purchased last year with his son. He paused to remember that afternoon filled with sunshine and civilization, shopping for Russian sniper rifles and bayonets and boots. He'd give anything to be back there, in that other world.

My God. How was Gabe now? Where was he? Where were Theresa and Claire? Were they safe? Did dogs hold them hostage, threatening their lives? A flood of memories washed over him, mind videos from just last month. "Damn, it's only January 31st. These bastard dogs will not keep me from finding my family! I have to get out of here alive!"

He gathered his weapons onto the living room carpet. It was noon. It was clear he wouldn't be traveling today. He realized that there were just going to have to be "Stop" days, other than Sunday, that would allow him to deal with what was happening.

With renewed optimism, he determined that his six-foot staff could serve as a club. If he carved out grooves, he could permanently attach the bayonet and use it as an eight-foot spear. He honed the Civil War sword back to its original perfection.

It was now late afternoon. Ian needed to reclaim the back porch and the propane grill. It looked as though he would have to kill some dogs. He eased the .22 rifle through the kitchen window and expertly toppled the first dog out in the yard. The others scattered, afraid of the sudden noise. Within a few minutes of long silence, some of the dogs came back to sniff their fallen comrade.

"Man, I wish I had that Russian sniper rifle now!"

He killed a second dog and severely wounded a third. The remaining three dogs descended on the wounded dog, further reducing the threat. They would feast tonight.

As darkness enveloped the world, he shot two more of the desperate dogs gorging on the blood of their compatriots. The last remaining dog slunk back into the darkness, alone and fearful. A feral pack of one against one feral human.

He had now reclaimed his porch. The threat had diminished. Small victories can be the sweetest.

More water from the toilet tank was boiling on the grill. Soon there would be dinner. He considered dog stew but decided against it; it would be too dangerous to retrieve the bodies from the dark yard.

This "stop" day had been highly productive. If only the creaking and cracking walls and roof could hold up for twelve more hours, he would be gone.

Chapter 10

Day 37

Ian had a restless night filled with bad dreams he couldn't remember. He woke covered in sweat and feeling uneasy.

"Where am I? Oh, the Night of the Living Dog House. Damn those feral dogs. Are there more of them out there today for me to face in mortal combat? I've got to put some distance between me and this house and those damned dogs."

At least the roof hadn't collapsed overnight in the impenetrable darkness. He got up and washed, then went out to the back porch grill to make breakfast and boil water. It was the first day of February and bitter cold. The temperature on the thermometer was ten below zero. Was this ashfall going to bring on a new ice age, as some were predicting? He had to get further south…fast!

At breakfast, he remembered it was Sunday again. Just a week ago he was at the A-frame, ready to begin his journey. He remembered the preacher's radio sermon advocating a Sunday "Day of Rest." He would love another day off, but how could he waste another day at this house? He had been here since Friday. In one whole week he had walked only forty miles. Hell, just five weeks ago he could have driven that same distance in under an hour. Unfortunately, a car wouldn't go very far through six inches of frozen volcanic ash.

But a tractor will go easily through six inches of ash.

If he could just steal a tractor every Sunday, he wouldn't have to walk one day a week. He could then go ten to twenty miles and still get his day of rest. He realized that this could also help him make up time for other "lost" days.

Through the picture window, he could see a large farmhouse down the road. Maybe he could find a tractor there. He packed his gear and left the scene of the canine massacre.

The first farmhouse had no tractor, no cars. The windows were broken and the back door hung open. He struggled south through the howling, bitter wind. The wind chill must be minus thirty degrees. Death could come quickly here.

After slip-sliding along for another half mile, to the east he noticed a truck farm with a vegetable stand out front. "Marsh's Corner," the sign read. Just a few months ago this stand had overflowed with succulent tomatoes, juicy peaches, melons, and countless other bountiful delights of a Michigan harvest. Surely, Marsh must have a fine tractor to steal.

An old orange Allis Chalmers tractor waited patiently to go on a journey. Ian hoped that the battery could turn the engine over in the bitter cold and that there would be a key left in the ignition. His luck held: the key was there. He choked the carburetor, and the tractor jumped to life.

"Bless you, Marsh's! I'll be back next fall to buy tons of veggies and fruit! I promise," the grateful thief vowed silently.

Along slippery, treacherous roads, through ash-blasted wind, Marsh's tractor labored on for the next three hours. Ian skirted the eastern and then the southern edge of Hillsdale, trying to keep a cautious three-mile distance from any urban feral humans. He was now coming into Michigan militia country.

About six miles southwest of Hillsdale along Reading Road, the pistons on Marsh's tractor literally ground to a halt. Ian realized he had forgotten to put a filter over the carburetor; but, on the verge of frostbite, he also could go no farther. The tractor came to rest at the driveway of a picturesque old farmhouse with huge ancient trees and weathered barns. It was one of those farms where the eldest son had built a ranch-style home a few hundred feet from the big house.

Barely able to close his frozen fingers, he stumbled up to the farmhouse desperate to thaw his hands and body. He climbed onto the back porch; but he felt a weird, uneasy sensation that something was wrong. He readied his .22 rifle, knocked on the door, and entered the kitchen cautiously. Suddenly, a huge Rottweiler snarled and lunged at him.

Bloody human body parts and the fur of at least two cats were strewn across the kitchen floor. There was a stinking smell of death. Ian yanked the door shut as the dog slammed into it, breaking the window. That was close! The now-feral former pet lunged at him through the broken glass, wanting to rip him to shreds.

Adrenaline pumping, Ian thought his racing heart would burst. One more lunge and the seventy-pound Rottweiler would explode through the broken door glass out onto the back porch. Ian fired point blank through the window glass. The dog yelped but kept snarling. Ian had wounded the animal in the hip. He fired two more shots into the dark kitchen. The dog yelped once more but kept growling and barking.

"Now what do I do?" Ian thought. "I sure as hell can't go in there. The dog would rip me to shreds. I can't let him out, either; he'd attack me. Should I just leave him in the house to die? Or should I just kill him? But I've already fired three shots. That will likely draw someone's attention. Thank God it's getting dark."

A light snow mixed with ash began to fall as he stepped off the back porch. The son's ranch house next door would be his Motel 6 for the night. He needed time to ponder what to do about the dog.

Half frozen and hungry, Ian started grumbling to himself. He realized there would be no fires tonight on the back porch to get warm or to boil water or to cook food. The smell of smoke would draw attention. He'd have to clean up in cold toilet water, in the dark.

Exhausted, Ian huddled under piles of blankets, trying to thaw from today's excursion. He thought about the three gunshots he had fired at the Rottweiler. He would decide about the dog in the morning, when his mind was clear.

Would neighbors have heard the shots and investigate? Were there Michigan militia encampments nearby? Would he be besieged by twenty vigilantes with automatic weapons waiting to blast anything that moved? Those armed crazies could simply follow the big tire tracks right up to the driveway. For the past ten years he had heard stories about the militias. He would have to get out of here pretty quickly in the morning. Would they follow his tracks as he headed south?

Day 38

Overnight the temperature slowly increased as a storm front moved in, dropping three inches of snow and ash. By 4 a.m. his tracks from the farm porch to the ranch house had disappeared.

Ian awoke to the angelic sound of wind chimes. For quite some time the earth had smothered all sounds. There had been no birds; they all died in the ash. No people sounds, no vehicle sounds, no planes overhead, no animal sounds. The world had the muffled eternal quiet of a bardo hell.

Now, at 5:00, a brisk warm wind thawed and released the wind chimes from their frozen grip. The heavenly sounds reminded him of civilization.

As the wind intensified, the chimes responded and sprang to life in a cacophony of sound. He remembered the Sunday morning he awoke two blocks from the cathedral in Cologne to the fury of the bells. Lost in his memories, he began to get ready to set out while fresh snow would cover his tracks.

He had decided last night to put a notch on his walking stick for every Sunday on his journey. Before he left this farm this morning, he would have to notch his stick. Ian had left his family and begun this journey over five weeks ago. He whittled five notches in the middle of the walking stick, wondering just how long this quest would last.

Suddenly, the loud crack of a rifle shot reverberated through the wind chime symphony. Ian heard yelling, loud barking, and yelping. Two more high powered shots rang out, accompanied by a scream of intense human pain and muffled dog yelps. There were two more shots, then silence.

The wind chimes faded into a decrescendo. After weeks of oppressive silence, Ian had just witnessed an overwhelming symphony of sounds: human fear, human pain, dog fear, dog pain, rifle shots, wind chimes—all ripping open the fabric of this silent frozen hell.

Next door at the big farmhouse, Ian could see two militiamen in uniforms. One was on the ground writhing in pain and bleeding profusely. The other was trying to stop the bleeding from his companion's mangled thigh. Near them lay the dead Rottweiler with most of its head blown off.

The storm had deposited enough snow and ash to cover Ian's tracks next door; but the uninjured militiaman looked around, saw the tractor and realized there must be somebody nearby. He told his injured buddy they had to get back to camp for medical help. But he would come back in a couple of hours with a team to ferret out and terminate this intruder. He loaded the injured man onto the ATV and headed out to the south.

Ian panicked. He had to get out of here before a team of vigilantes returned. Thank goodness it was still snowing pretty hard. With luck his tracks would be covered as he fled. The militia had driven south, so he had to go west along the road toward Reading. He set out in the drifting snow, slowly headed west.

After about four miles he was exhausted, cold, and hungry again. The rapidly falling ash and snow drifted and covered his tracks well. He found a nice barn with plenty of hay in the loft and decided to spend the night here. Like a bear hibernating in a winter cave during a blizzard, Ian watched his tracks disappear in the blowing snow. Unless they searched every house within ten miles with bloodhounds, he was safe here momentarily.

In a nice, warm, enclosed nest of hay, Ian rested and thought about his friend who had run the regional census. The friend had warned about the militia groups he had encountered south and west of Hillsdale all the way over through Branch County. They shot at census takers and other outsiders even in normal times. Now Ian was being hunted like a dog, and they intended to kill him on sight.

The militia had automatic weapons. He had an old .22 rifle with one round left. The odds were not in his favor.

"But I've got my great-great grandfather's sharp Civil War sword. I will not go down without a fight."

Day 39

Ian awoke in pitch dark buried under several feet of loose hay. He dug himself out, still immersed in the remnants of a very pleasant dream. He could vividly see and feel the warmth and quiet of a small hovel nestled among the mounds of a well-tended garden. Deep peace and centered energy permeated the solitude of that secluded space.

Refreshed by this pleasant burst of good energy, Ian hauled his cache down from the loft and girded himself for today's journey. He had little food or water, but he could rest and eat tonight.

Today the snow had stopped, so he would leave tracks for his pursuers to follow. They couldn't be far behind. He needed to get to the small village of Reading, a couple of miles to the west, where he hoped to walk on plowed and traveled streets. If there was anyone left, his tracks would blend in and they would lose his trail.

The strategy worked, and by late afternoon Ian had gone six miles further west, having passed through Reading. Ten miles now separated him from the militia. His trail could not be seen.

Ian spotted a small house nestled back from the road. His arms, legs, and neck were sore. He decided to spend the night and take an extra day to recover from his terrifying experience. The propane grill on the back deck meant hot water and a chance to wash up. There would be coffee tonight! And there was even food in the pantry.

Enjoying his first cup of coffee in a while, Ian reflected that all had returned to normal. "Normal? Is this my new normal? Please, God, make it stop! Stop that damn volcano. Let me be with my wife and kids!"

Day 40

Ian awoke in a comfortable bed. He felt rested but sore. "I do need to stop here and rest my weary soul," he thought. Last night he had another very strange dream, filled with heavy snow and ash and old people being loaded onto railroad cattle cars. They sobbed and wailed in the freezing cold. Where were they being taken? Images of Nazi death camps and Hurricane Katrina nursing homes haunted him. What would they do with the frail ones who couldn't get out? Who would make that decision? He shuddered.

When he stood up, his pants fell down to the floor. He looked over at the full length mirror in the bedroom. "My God," he thought in astonishment, "I've lost so much weight my pants don't fit any more."

He went to the closet and grabbed a terry cloth belt from a bathrobe and cinched it up around his shrinking waist. Ian decided right then that he needed to eat more and reduce his baggage. That .22 rifle was old, heavy, and almost out of bullets. It was slowing him down. The rifle would remain at its new home.

Days 41–42

After his day of rest, Ian travelled without incident and without running into another Michigan militiaman. Going west and south around Coldwater Lake, he crossed I-69. There were no cars, but the road was plowed. Still, with all the militia out there, Ian worried that it was too dangerous to walk down the expressway. He continued west and south and spent the night at the Michigan border just north of Orland, Indiana.

Chapter 11

Day 43

As he crossed into Indiana, he reflected on the first hundred miles and how hard it had been—feral dogs, militia, the cold, walking, finding shelter. He worried about the rest of the trip, and he worried about how his family were handling the difficulties.

It was dark, like constant dusk, only with an eerie light and feel to it, which made it difficult to figure the direction that he was traveling. Without the luxury of seeing the sun's position or the North Star at night, he had to rely on his compass, his maps, and street signs.

His focus and awareness had become extremely heightened. He was now hyper-vigilant against attacks from humans and animals, constantly looking behind and around himself, straining to hear over the rasp of his own breathing.

Ian was realizing his place in the food chain had changed. He couldn't just call animal control when he had a run in with a skunk or a raccoon or a feral dog. He was now vulnerable to being killed and eaten by animals that had once been viewed as pets. Now he lived in nature, not culture.

Pondering these things, he lost focus, tripped, and fell. He saw that he had tripped on a dead pit-bull. Maybe it had been overcome by the ash. Maybe his problems with feral dogs were over.

Just outside of the little town of Brushy Prairie, Indiana, Ian began using the criteria he had developed for finding overnight accommodations. He found a long driveway leading back to a house and outbuildings nestled in a small wooded area. This house was perfect, as it was a couple of hundred feet off the road. It was mostly hidden in the woods and it had everything he needed. He found a gas grill with propane, firepit with wood, available food, and water in the toilet tank.

He settled into the evening routine. Out of curiosity he opened the chest freezer and discovered that the food was still semi-frozen. He was able to prepare a meal of grilled chicken and boiled broccoli and corn.

After dinner, he plundered the bathroom cabinets and found new first-aid materials to replenish his supplies. He then cleaned up with warm water and soap, but his clothes were filthy. Thinking about the effort and time it would take to wash them, he had an epiphany. Why not take clothes from the houses that he visited? It would save both valuable time and energy. As he went through the dressers to find what he could, it became evident that this home belonged exclusively to a female. Reluctant at first, he finally gave in and put on her clean panties. He managed to find a pair of long underwear, undershirt, flannel shirt, socks and a pair of bib overalls that were slightly too big. Grinning, he started to sing, "I'm a lumberjack, and I'm okay…."

As he lay in bed, he again thought of his family and how hard it must be for them. He felt guilty and angry that he was unable to be there for them.

Days 44–45

Last night, his second night in Indiana, he had stayed without incident in a farmhouse just south of the town of South Milford. Since yesterday was Sunday, he had tried to steal a tractor, but the damned thing died after only a few hundred feet. This meant that he was forced to walk on his day of rest.

Today, as he walked, he started to see McMansions everywhere. Ian concluded that the only problem was that the sheer size of these houses would make them difficult to defend. Perhaps they would just be a place to stop for lunch or pick up extra supplies; he would have to weigh the situation as it arose.

He was now seeing more and more animals that had apparently died from breathing the ash: farm animals, birds, deer, and dogs. This only made him worry about his family even more, especially his son, who suffered from asthma.

The plan for today was to bypass Kendallville. He would go around the northwestern edge of the city. But plans are made to be changed. Hearing gunshots and screaming ahead on the route he intended to follow, Ian immediately decided to head east, hoping to catch the next southerly road. He skirted the town heading south. In a lakeside subdivision he discovered a large house that was perfect. Front windows faced the lake with a farm field to the east. It sat far back in the subdivision, so he hoped he would not be disturbed.

This mighty fortress had two kitchens, the main one upstairs and another in the basement area. There was a fully stocked bar. The pantry was loaded down with pre-packaged processed foods. Not only did they have two refrigerator-freezers in the kitchens, but there was also an upright freezer in the four-car garage. A four-wheeled ATV with three-quarters of a tank of gas was parked in the garage as well. Since he had arrived about midday and had decided to park here for the night, he knew he would have to make up the extra miles lost. The ATV would surely help in that regard—if it stayed running.

He fixed himself a stiff drink and went about the business of repairing the door. He found a cornucopia of high-end food: grilled kobe steaks, lobster tails, bags of frozen edamame and "root vegetables." He even found a box of Godiva chocolates. Ian ate like a king. Later, he opened a bottle of wine and sat in the living room looking out over the lake. This was a good day! He thought about a saying of Buddha's, "It is your mind that creates this world." He wondered if this was really his manifestation or just plain luck.

Day 46

In the morning, he looked at a map and decided to stay north along the Tippecanoe river and use the river as his guide. If he went south of the river, he would run into the problems of crossing bodies of water or major towns.

He loaded supplies—snack food, first-aid stuff—into a nice gym bag he had found, got on the ATV, and headed across the field. He passed the Mid-American Windmill Museum and continued south until he ran into Route 8 heading west.

The ATV sputtered to a stop after about fifteen miles, so he had to walk. He crossed Route 9 to find a "Comfort Inn," as he now referred to the McMansions. It was at this house that he realized he had become comfortable with the idea of being an uninvited guest. He found a radio with batteries and listened to an AM station out of Tennessee. He got news, weather, ashfall totals, and even music. This would become one of his survival routines from here on out.

Day 47

All of this traveling had caught up with Ian. His last rest day had been a full week ago, back in Michigan. He forgot to set the alarm on his watch and slept in until 10:00, giving him a late start. He headed northwest, for Lake Wawasee. By the time he stopped for the night, it was around 6:00. It was so dark Ian turned on his flashlight to break into the farmhouse he had chosen for the night. Thirst drove him to the bathroom looking for water, but a partial roof collapse created considerable resistance to opening the door. The toilet was smashed into pieces.

Desperate for water, he headed to the basement to look for canned goods. All canned vegetables are packed in water.

The steep, narrow stairs creaked under his weight as he descended cautiously. A cobweb brushed his face. He dodged a peanut-butter-baited rat trap at the base of the stairs.

"Wonderful," he thought. "Spiders and rats!"

The basement was cluttered and filthy. Ian quickly scanned the area with his flashlight beam, checking for critters. On the far wall of the basement, his light illuminated Mason jars stacked on a shelving unit. While inspecting the canned goods, he heard a dripping sound. Looking for the source, Ian discovered water dripping from the blow-off valve on the water heater.

"How did I miss this?" Ian exclaimed. "Forty gallons of potable water, and all along I've been drinking out of the damned toilet!".

Day 48

Stocked up and ready to go, he headed out early. For the first few miles the rural Indiana landscape rolled gently in front of him. Ian's thoughts kept wandering back to that water heater dripping in the basement. Every house in the country had a large tank full of fresh water. Simply blow off the sediment, and it was good to go. That was a game changer.

At the bottom of Lake Wawasee, Ian was jolted out of his rural daydream. Directly in front of him sat an eight-story highrise, flanked by upscale shops and restaurants. It was an opulent ghost town in the middle of nowhere.

"Unreal," Ian thought. "Where did this come from? It looks like an abandoned movie set." He moved through the spooky resort as quickly as possible.

As evening approached, he found a farmhouse for the night. At the back of the house there was a small screened porch leading to the back door. As Ian entered the kitchen, he saw a pistol on the floor in the hallway. Excited, he went to pick it up and as he did he saw the body of an elderly man in the living room, lying in a frozen pool of blood. Out of sheer fear and panic, he grabbed the gun and ran out the back door.

He didn't stop running until he was a few hundred yards from the house. Then he stopped to gather his wits and realized that the treasure in his hand needed bullets. Ian took a few moments to think things through and headed back into the house to find them. Avoiding the body, he found a box of bullets on the end table, beside the lamp, next to the old recliner.

The man must have taken his own life out of desperation. Maybe this was the only option left for those who have run out of options. Ian took the bullets and the gun and left to find another place to stay for the night, the image of the old man burned into his mind.

Chapter 12

Marcie Baldwin

Day 1

The first eruption occurred on Saturday, December 27. Marcie Baldwin learned about it from the evening news as she was fixing dinner for her two children in their small home in Beloit, Wisconsin. Deeply alarmed, she burned the hamburgers, setting off complaints from the kids.

Since her husband had been called up for duty in Syria, Marcie was barely able to hold things together. Dave had been her rock since she was a sophomore in high school, and without him she was often paralyzed by indecision. The kids took advantage, acting like brats without the firm hand of their father to rein them in.

She managed to get through that evening, but sleep was elusive. She worried about the volcanic eruption until the early hours of the morning.

Day 2

Dave called on Sunday, his regular time, and calmed her down. "Wait and see," he told her. He'd keep an eye on things from Syria and let her know if she needed to do anything. Meanwhile, he told her to stock up on canned goods and bottled water, just in case. Then fill up the four-wheel drive Jeep with gas. Marcie was good at following directions, so she did everything he told her to do. She waited as ash began to darken the sky.

Day 7

The ash had continued to accumulate, first just a fine layer of dust on the ground, then a grimy, two-inch coating on all the surfaces outside. It overlay the snow, creating increasingly hazardous driving conditions. She kept the lights on throughout the day now. There had been no sunshine since Christmas Day. Her nerves were shot, and she snapped at the kids whenever they raised their voices. They picked up on her mood and whined constantly. The news on TV was unrelentingly bad. With the eruption spreading a blanket of ash across the north central states, people were beginning to panic. Those with health problems were being advised to evacuate.

Dave called again in the late afternoon. He had been following the news and told her it was time to "get out of Dodge." She should call her parents, who had retired to northern Florida, and tell them she and the kids were on their way. Dave was a mechanic, so he told her about the effects of dust on engines. He had heard about a trick to help keep the air intake clear: use pantyhose to cover the air filter, then clean the accumulated grit off every hour or so.

Marcie swallowed her fear and took notes as he told her what to pack in the Grand Cherokee: food, water, blankets, flashlight, medical kit, cell phone and charger, warm clothes. He outlined the route she should take to get to her parents as quickly as possible. It was all by interstate: south to Bloomington, Illinois; east to Cincinnati, Ohio; then I-75 south to Florida. She was to call him from the road every day until she reached her parents' house.

Day 8

The next morning, by the time she packed the Jeep and got the kids settled, it was 10:00. She backed out of the driveway through four inches of slushy ash and fishtailed when she tried to turn on to the street. Already shaking, she put the car into four-wheel drive and set off slowly, skidding at every stop sign. At first there was no traffic at all; but as she got closer to the expressway, the volume increased dramatically. Everyone was headed the same way—out of town. She started to notice gas stations that were closed, some with signs posted: "No Gas." She was grateful for the big tank on the Jeep; it should get them past this.

It took an hour to get on the highway—bumper to bumper, one car at a time merging into traffic that was crawling forward. All headlights were on, but it was still hard to see. The stop-and-go driving gave the ash time to accumulate on the windshield, and there was no time when she could speed up enough to blow it off. She turned on the wipers to clear the windshield. It worked, but there was a terrible grinding sound and she noticed that the wipers were scratching the glass. After that, she used the wipers as little as possible, and when she stopped to clean the air filter, she also cleaned the glass. The windshield continued to score and pit, though, and vision became more difficult.

The fifteen miles to Rockford, Illinois, normally took less than half an hour. Today it took over an hour to reach the northern outskirts. The kids started whining for lunch. Marcie passed sandwiches and juice boxes over the back seat and kept driving. More lines of traffic jammed the entrance ramps. Marcie was clinging to the right lane of the freeway, so she was further slowed by the car-at-a-time merging pattern. One driver tried to enter too fast and fishtailed wildly, almost hitting cars ahead of her. Horns blared from all directions.

There were four entrance ramps leading out of Rockford, each crammed with vehicles heading south. It took two hours to reach the south end of the town. They had left home four hours ago and had now covered only about twenty-five miles. Bloomington was still 120 miles away. At this rate, it would be tomorrow by the time they got there.

Off to her right, Marcie could see flashing red tail lights where several cars had gone off the road. Skid marks snaked down to the ditch, where one SUV lay, drunkenly lopsided. Others sat with frantically blinking lights at the side of the road. People were trying to hitchhike away from those disabled vehicles. When traffic jammed to a stop, some of them pounded on the windows and shouted for help. Marcie stared straight ahead, avoiding eye contact with the doomed.

"Go away," she muttered under her breath. Then she screamed, "Please, just leave us alone!"

The kids stopped squabbling in the back seat. Now they were very quiet. In the rearview mirror, she saw them holding each other, wide-eyed with fear.

Hours passed. It got even darker as they neared Bloomington. By this time Marcie was exhausted and in real pain. She had been clenching the steering wheel for almost twelve hours, hunched forward with her shoulders tensed, peering through the ash-fogged and-scarred windshield. Everything hurt, her eyes were tired and gritty, and she was beginning to get a pounding headache. She passed the kids more sandwiches and juice and grabbed a sandwich for herself. It tasted like warm, sawdust-filled cardboard.

At Bloomington, I-39 merged with freeways out of Chicago and Peoria. This was a true nightmare. Traffic was at a near standstill. It was only six miles to the south end of the city, but it took another two hours to get there. By the time she turned east on I-74, it was after midnight. The kids had fallen asleep, still holding each other. Marcie decided to try to go a little farther. She was now about 150 miles south of Beloit, and the ash on the roadway was only about an inch deep. Maybe she could get to bare pavement by morning if she just kept going.

Less than ten miles later, she encountered ash fog. A wall of fog moving northwest from the Wabash River had collided with the wall of ash moving southeast. The combination resulted in a terrifying black, impenetrable void across the road ahead of her. Her headlights stopped dead, as if they had been swallowed by a black hole. Incredulous, she stared for a moment, wondering if she had literally reached the end of the world. If she went forward, would they just fall off?

But her luck held good, for once. There was an exit ramp immediately ahead. She pulled off the exit and parked at the edge of the ramp. The ash fog surrounded the Jeep. No farther tonight, at least. Suddenly, as the tension eased in her body, she realized she had to pee. She turned off the overhead light. Don't wake the kids, she told herself. She got out and squatted right by the door, with one hand still on the car. It was so dark that if she took a step away she might not find her way back.

She dozed through the night. When the interior of the car got too cold, she turned on the engine for a few minutes. Emily and Jacob slept restlessly. Emily cried out, "No!" Then she whimpered and quieted again. Marcie heard every rustle of the blankets, every change of breathing pattern. She heard the whisper of a breeze in the early morning hours and vaguely hoped for a clear day. Finally, exhaustion overcame her and she slept.

Day 9

Marcie woke to find she had left the engine running. She was down to a quarter tank of gas, about 100 miles worth at the rate they had been traveling. Quickly, she turned off the ignition. She woke the children and got them out of the car to use the roadside as a bathroom. Emily was modest and refused to do anything until Marcie set an example. They all brushed their teeth using bottled water, and Marcie washed faces with the remainder. She brushed out their tangled hair, trying to make everything seem as normal as possible. There were power bars for breakfast with more of the inevitable juice boxes. When the kids had eaten, she realized she had forgotten to call Dave all day yesterday. She pulled out her cell phone and turned it on. All she got was a "No Signal" message. The call would have to wait. She hoped Dave wouldn't be too worried about them.

Jacob ran around and around the Jeep for a couple of minutes, then started coughing as the ash clouds he had kicked up began to reach his lungs. Marcie pounded his back and a blob of dark mucus shot out onto the ground.

Even though it was still gray and dark, the ash fog had dissipated. Marcie got everyone back into the car and started back to the highway feeling hopeful. She turned the radio on, looking for news. There was a lot of static, but nothing else until she realized she had it set on FM. She switched to AM and searched until she found WLS in Chicago. The news was unrelievedly bad. There had been no reduction in the amount of ash from the eruption, and it continued to head east in a widening cone. Minneapolis was completely cut off; no radio, TV, or phone service. Chicago had three inches of ash on the ground, and a mass exodus had begun. That explained the traffic jam around Bloomington, she thought. All those people from Chicago heading for St. Louis and points south.

"Here are some tips for getting out," the announcer said. "Take side roads if possible. They are faster and less crowded than expressways. Don't waste gas. If you sleep in the car, turn off the ignition. Stay out of the right lane, especially around towns where people are entering the highway. If you run out of gas, stay with your vehicle. State police emergency patrols are out with gas cans to rescue stranded motorists." Marcie's cheeks burned with humiliation. She had done everything wrong.

She kept driving east. Well, at least there was no sun in her eyes. That was one positive thing, but gas was becoming a serious concern. She passed Le Roy, Farmer City, Mansfield. All the roadside gas stations were closed except one in Mahomet, and they were just selling bottled water—at $5.00 per pint. By the time she passed Champaign and Urbana, there was about an eighth of a tank left. Marcie was getting desperate. St. Joseph, Ogden, Oakwood, Tilton, Danville—no gas. Then she crossed into Indiana. Surely there must be gas in Indiana! At the first exit, she decided to take the radio announcer's advice and get off the Interstate. She turned south on Route 63. The idiot light had been on at least since Danville. She didn't have much gas left. There was no other choice. Marcie flipped the right turn signal and headed south toward Cayuga.

The area was very open. As she drove, even though the ash-laden air clouded her vision, she could see for great distances. Unfortunately, there was little to see: open fields, a few patches of trees. There were very few buildings, and all appeared deserted. The gas gauge slipped below E and she began to panic.

Finally, ahead on the right, she saw a large building—with cars parked near it. She scanned anxiously across the open fields and noted that the entrance was off a side road to her right. Marcie turned into the circle entrance of North Vermillion Elementary School. She parked just as a man appeared at the front door of the school. Marcie expelled a breath she had been holding far too long and collapsed with her head against the steering wheel. Safety, at last!

Chapter 13

Day 49

Ian had been lucky. Millions of people had died, and until last night he had not seen a corpse. He lay in bed watching his warm breath rise toward the ceiling. The thought of the old man putting a gun to his head and pulling the trigger played out as some film noir scene. Cut to the smoke rising from the barrel.

He headed west. Another farmhouse loomed on his right and he found himself edging to the other side of the road. Were there bodies in that house, too? How many of the houses he had passed on his journey were actually tombs? He had assumed they were abandoned, but now....

Near Leesburg, the road made a big left turn and headed south. As he walked past the first farmhouse, he heard a woman frantically crying out for help. He waded down the drifted driveway yelling,

"Hello! Hello!"

Ian entered the farmyard between the house and barn. This area had been plowed out. A tiny yappy dog started nipping at his feet and growling. He found an old woman outside of a red metal outbuilding. The roof had partially collapsed and she was standing there, one hand up to her face and the other hand grasping her bunched up apron. She turned to see Ian and cried out desperately,

"Please help! My husband's trapped in there!"

Ian began pulling away the debris until he reached an old man. He dragged the husband to safety. The woman hysterically danced around them asking anxiously,

"Is he okay? Oh, Lord. Is he okay?"

The man was shaken up but none the worse for wear.

"Knock off the hysterics," he growled. "Jesus Christ! The God damned Chinese couldn't kill me. Do you think a woodshed's gonna do it?"

Ian got the old man into the house and set him at the kitchen table. The man explained that he had gone out to collect firewood for the cook stove when the roof collapsed. As he continued to talk, Ian looked over to see an ornate antique wood cook stove with tarnished yellow enamel paint.

Everything about this place reminded him of his grandparents' farm: the house, the outbuildings and barns, the wood stove, the cows, the antiques. Even the back porch had that same musty smell, a mixture of mildew, the cream separator, a bushel of wintered-over apples, and the faint smell of kerosene from the oil lamps in the window.

And then there was the elderly couple themselves. They were the timeless embodiment of the family farm, giving off the same kind of energy his grandparents always had. There was a strength and a level of self-respect he hadn't experienced in the past forty years. Ian realized that these family farms were the final bastion of a moral and ethical system that would be missed. Even without the volcano, these two old people represented the last of their kind.

Ian's thoughts wandered back to the kitchen table as the old man finished talking. Having helped out at his grandparents' farm, he remembered the work was seemingly endless. Given the age of these people, he decided right then and there that he was going help in any way he could. Ian offered to get wood and start the fire. Then he told the man he would reinforce the wood shed and volunteered to do whatever else needed to be done.

Ian worked until the old woman called him in for supper. He came in to a potpourri of the incredible smells of fresh biscuits, ham, and beans. He wondered aloud if he had worked all day long.

"Why heavens no, dear," she laughed. "It's just time for the mid-day meal." Ian remembered his grandmother also calling lunch "supper" and remembered it being a fairly big meal.

The couple started out the meal by saying grace. As they ate, Ian told them about how he had been separated from his family and was trying to find them. He regaled them with his exploits thus far. He confessed his guilt, not only about his family, but also about looting and being an uninvited house guest. The couple assured him that he seemed like a good man, and he was staying at houses simply to survive. Their earnest concern made him feel protective, and Ian decided not to tell them about their neighbor up the road, the one who had killed himself.

After a few sips of coffee, the old man started to talk. The farm had been in his family for generations, he said.

"Hell, I grew up here! My family has owned this farm since 1898. These cows are all we have. I owe my livelihood to them. We should've probably moved on like everyone else, but I just can't see leaving them here to die. Plus, we have no other place to go, really. The thought of leaving our land is just too much. I can't accept this. That God damned volcano will not drive me away from my farm."

But it was getting harder to stay. The farmhands had fled, leaving the couple behind to fend for themselves. All but five cows had died, but the remaining cows still had to be milked. Now it was being done by hand, twice a day. Ian inquired about where the milk was being stored.

"We use what we can," the farmer said. "We give the rest of it back to the cows. They love their own milk."

Listening to their plight, Ian offered to stay on for a few days. He would help them milk, feed, and water the cattle. Being proud old farmers, they protested. This problem would not last much longer. They only needed to survive the hardship for a few more weeks. He shouldn't stay to help them. He should go to find his family. Eventually, however, they "reluctantly" gave in.

After lunch Ian finished shoring up the woodshed. He then went about the task of clearing the ash off the roof of the house. Next, he worked with the farmer to start the generator to pump water into a 1200-gallon plastic container. The old man said it took about ten hours to fill one of these tanks. Ian took a second hose and filled the water troughs for the cows. He also got fresh hay to feed them.

While the cows ate, the couple taught Ian how to milk. Ian tried hard not to be intimidated by the massive animal looming over him as he sat on the low milking stool. His trepidation increased when the old woman warned, “Don’t touch those udders with cold hands, or you’ll get kicked to Kansas.”

Having survived the milking experience, Ian shoveled the manure out of the stalls and put clean straw down for bedding. This would be the last chore of the day. They turned off the generator and came in to clean up for dinner.

Grace was said. Dinner was fairly small, consisting of sandwiches and soup. After dinner the woman made coffee and served up a slice of pie. The old man pointed over at the windowsill and said to his wife, “Could you get my desserts?”

Confused, Ian looked up wondering what he was talking about. She had just put the pie in front of them a few seconds ago. Grabbing the three pill bottles off of the sill, she took a pill out of each and handed them to her husband. He, having spilled coffee in his saucer earlier, set the cup on the table, put the pills in his mouth, and slurped the coffee from the saucer.

“These are my just desserts,” he said with an impish smile. This same ritual would play itself out each night after dinner.

Ian truly enjoyed the food and the couple’s company. Today had been the first positive interaction with people since he left Michigan. With candles and oil lamps lit, they listened to music on an AM station out of Tennessee. The old man told story after story about his days in the Korean War. As the stories progressed, raw emotions of anger and hurt surfaced. He told how, when he came back from the war, the VFW wouldn’t allow Korean War vets to join.

“They said it was a police action, not a real war at all. Took nearly fifteen years before we were even allowed in.” He laughed. “Musta killed the ‘Greatest Generation’ when I became commander of their post.”

This was one stubborn man, Ian realized. He’d defend his farm as if it were Pork Chop Hill, or he’d die trying.

The old woman had prepared a bed for Ian earlier in the day. He drifted off to sleep as the Westminster clock chimed 9:00.

Day 50

Ian awoke abruptly from being shaken. It was the farmer with a flashlight. His gravelly morning voice announced that it was 4 a.m. and time to milk the cows. To Ian, it felt as if he had just fallen asleep. He got dressed and met the couple downstairs. The dog barked at him as he entered the kitchen.

After chores and breakfast, the farmer took Ian out to the barn and explained that the food was getting low in the house. The barn door slid open to reveal the hanging, frozen carcasses of several cows. The old man and Ian spent the rest of the day butchering. Their hands cramped with cold as they separated out the different cuts. Most of the meat was cut into strips and hand ground, some for hamburger and some for sausage.

The woman hung up rib sections and strips of meat to be smoked. She made fresh hamburgers and grilled them for the evening meal.

Finally, they settled down to relax. They had dessert and coffee, then played dominos while they listened to music on the radio. It was a quiet close to a grueling day.

Day 51

Eggs for breakfast! The perfect reward for completed morning chores. He had almost forgotten the joy a fresh egg could bring. And with fresh sausage and potatoes, the day couldn't get any better in Ian's mind.

They spent the rest of the morning preparing the smokehouse. This venerable brick structure dated back to the original settling of the farm. When he opened the door, Ian's nose was assailed by the spirits of smokings past, a haunting, pungent aroma of hickory and apple wood and meats of all kinds. This smoking would add another layer of history to the walls of the old building.

Once a good bed of coals was established, they hung up the meat. They would tend the fire with wood that was soaked in water until the process was completed.

After lunch, Ian asked to borrow a tractor and one of the hay wagons so he could replenish their supplies from the neighboring farms. The old couple found themselves in a moral crisis. Their elation at the thought of having more food was quickly followed by anger and fear. After all, Ian would be taking food from their neighbors. And if they got caught, they could be put in jail and lose the farm. Finally, there was sin. They would go to hell for stealing.

He reminded them of what they had said to him on the first day. They were good people, just trying to survive and keep their animals alive. Besides, they could square this with their neighbors once things returned to normal. Survival takes moral flexibility. After more discussion, the couple came around to Ian's point of view.

Ian moved from farm to farm, collecting everything he thought the old couple could use. In a little over three hours he was loaded and ready to head back.

It was now pretty dark, so he drove with the headlights on. As he approached the farm where the old man had killed himself, he thought he saw a man standing by the side of the road. Just then the tractor lights flickered off. When they came back on, the figure was gone. A chill ran up Ian's spine. He wished he could get away from there a little faster. Spooked, he kept looking back over his shoulder all the way home.

When he arrived back at the farm the old couple rushed out to greet him. They were concerned, relieved and a little angry. They had thought he was either dead, injured, or had taken off with their only tractor.

Soup, bread, and a couple glasses of milk, combined with the hard work Ian had done that day, made him dead tired. He decided to head to bed. He resolved not to tell the old people about the apparition he had seen because he didn't want to frighten them. He figured if anyone came around, the little dog would surely sound the alarm.

Day 52

After chores and breakfast, he spent the morning helping the couple package the smoked meat. That afternoon, when he unloaded the wagon, he discovered that the tailgate was missing. He must have left it behind at one of the farms.

Ian retraced the path he had followed yesterday. The blasted tailgate was, of course, at the last farm he had visited.

He hoped to be back before dark. As he approached the suicide farm again, he definitely saw a man rocking in a chair on the front porch. When he got closer and looked down the driveway, however, the man was gone—but the chair was still rocking.

That did it! It was time to be moving on. He had helped the farmers to a place where they could ride out the storm for at least a month. Who knows? Everything could be back to normal by then.

The hard part was to tell the couple of his decision to go in the morning. He waited until after dinner. They acted happy for him. He would be on his way again to find his family. The old woman said she would pack some provisions for him to take. While the men had dessert and coffee, she put together a care package of jerky, flat bread, and homemade soap.

They sat around listening to the radio one last time. Roofs were collapsing throughout the Midwest region. The old woman broke down, remembering how just a few days ago the roof had collapsed on her husband. And now Ian was leaving them. The old man tried to comfort her, saying that the volcano problem wouldn't last much longer and soon everything would be back to normal.

Ian told the couple how much they reminded him of his grandparents. He had felt honored to help them. He thanked them for all that they had taught him. He promised that when all of this was over he would stop back with his wife and kids to spend some time with them, maybe over the coming summer. They agreed that would be wonderful, and they looked forward to meeting his family.

Day 57

It had been five days since he left the Leesburg farm. He thought a lot about the old couple. On his last day there, he had gotten up at 4:30 and helped feed, water, and milk the cows. Then he had breakfast with the couple and said his goodbyes.

Since then, Ian had followed a path which kept him just north of the Tippecanoe River, avoiding any towns and keeping to the back roads. The landscape along the way was mostly flat, with farms, lakes, and woods. Skirting the town of Culver last night, he ended up in a house just north of the city. It had a long driveway and a swimming pool in the back yard. He felt safe that far back from the road.

He left the next morning heading west. The sun was starting to make its presence known. The gloomy days were a little brighter and sunlight peeked near the horizon in the morning and evening. Maybe the caldera had finished erupting and life could get back to normal.

It was 2:30 when he arrived at Bass Lake. He found a house just south of where the road started to make a bend westward. The house had a long driveway and was directly on the lake. Ian had always wanted lakefront property. This would be a pleasant place to spend the night.

Chapter 14

Day 58

These wonderful hosts had left him pricey, high-end Ethiopian Harrar coffee beans. Without electricity, though, he couldn't run the coffee grinder. He looked all over and eventually found a hammer. He put the beans in a dish towel, smashed them, and threw them into a pot with some boiled water. He let this sit for a while, and voila—camp coffee! He took the rest of the water and did a pretty thorough sponge bath.

Upstairs he found good clean clothes and refreshed his wardrobe. It was nice to go "shopping" for clothes each morning at the "mall" in the upstairs closet.

By the time he came back downstairs, he was ready for a nice breakfast of cookies, dried meat, and strong rich coffee. It was Sunday, time to notch his walking stick. Eight weeks had passed since that first eruption, eight weeks of never-ending hell. Ian added three more notches to the five already on the staff. Eight notches, eight weeks; two whole damn months—and he was still just in northern Indiana. Today he would steal a tractor, head south, and put on some miles.

He headed out into the bitter cold, amplified by a gale force wind coming from the west off Bass Lake. From a farm just south of Bass Lake near Route 35, Ian appropriated a tractor. He decided not to follow the road south toward Winamac. He remembered the militia in Michigan and Marsh's tractor.

Heading west a couple of miles, he then turned south and traveled about ten miles through desolate country. It was cold, windy, bitter. Thank God he was not walking this stretch. There were very few houses, but large, numbered parking lots lined this remote dirt road for miles. What was this? Overflow parking for Notre Dame football games? He snickered. Finally, just west of Winamac, the tractor began to sputter. It managed another two miles before it ran out of gas near an abandoned farmhouse, where Ian spent an uneventful night.

Days 59–60

His crude map of Indiana lacked detail, so he continued to stay a few miles west of the Tippecanoe as it meandered southwest toward its marriage with the Wabash. Although the atlas helped him avoid towns, it frequently dumped him into tree-barren, windswept, ash-blasted, God-forsaken, Russian-steppes landscapes. That stretch of Indiana 39 running straight down to the Tippecanoe just about did him in. Thoroughly exhausted, Ian began to hallucinate that he was Dr. Zhivago, lurching through the blizzard, his face crusted with snow. Later he envisioned himself as an ancient Greek, trudging through a monochromatic Hades, headed back toward the River Styx, seeking the impossible passage from its ferryman. Back, back across the river to the land of the living, his family, light and color.

"Stop this," Ian screamed. "I'm an artist! The palette of my life is color. This sucks." On some horribly black and white days he was certain that God had mistaken him for Ansel Adams.

Suddenly in an unconscious act of circumstantial defiance, he burst forth into his best Paul Robeson impression, singing:

Oh, I get weary
And sick of tryin'
I'm tired of livin'
And scared of dyin'
But Old Man River,
He just keeps rollin' along.

Although he may not have gotten the lyrics right, Ian felt much better.

Finally, as night began to fall on the second day, he found an abandoned farm just outside Monon, Indiana. The house was a little too close to the road, but ash snowdrifts indicated there had been no traffic for quite some time. There was no propane grill on the back porch. Tonight would be cold wash-up and a light dinner.

Charcoal and clean barbecue tools hanging in the utility room, however, alerted him to the presence of a charcoal grill. It lurked in the adjacent garage, waiting to spring into service for humanity. Exhaustion forced the encounter into the next morning.

Day 61

Ian got up early. The roof had creaked and moaned all night, making it hard to sleep. He dragged himself into the kitchen, wishing he'd brought that strong Ethiopian coffee with him. Searching for food, he found two things that wouldn't spoil: smoked bacon and bagels in the recently unpowered freezer.

"I wish there were some eggs! I miss eggs." The only eggs he had eaten in the last month were at Leesburg.

Ian went to the garage and hauled the grill out onto the concrete apron. There was no starter fluid, so he used paper and wood. This created lots of smoke, but it worked. Since the sky was densely overcast, he hoped no one could see or smell the smoke.

He made a big pot of hot tea and prepared water for his morning wash-up. Bacon fried in a pan and bagels toasted at the edge of the grill. When he sat down to eat, he tuned the radio to an AM station from Indianapolis. This would be a civilized breakfast with entertainment, listening to a pleasant mix of rock and country music and thoroughly satiated with good food.

His thoughts wandered back to the A-frame and the start of this epic hike across America. Just thirty days ago he had envisioned a very different journey, one filled with outdoor survival skills. He had planned for hunting, fishing, and constructing shelters in the woods.

There would be no hunting or fishing here. Some wildlife had died drinking the ash-contaminated pond and river water. Most had just vanished. He had survived only by becoming a professional looter, a consummate uninvited overnight guest. He drank out of toilet tanks and hot water heaters, foraging foodstuffs from the pantries of the McMansions. What would happen to him if things changed quickly again? The journey had already morphed from difficult to near impossible.

And just where had all the people gone? He had encountered only a handful of humans. He hadn't even seen any military or police. He had expected to battle hordes of refugees and crazed armed looters. Where in the hell was everybody?

Ian had not foreseen the continued damage to Mother Earth. Now shrouded over vast distances in oppressive darkness and bitter cold, she was devoid of life, yet strangely still not dead. With focused intention, she had assumed a mantle of undead consciousness. Perhaps the human obsession with zombies had been a foreshadowing of Gaia's impending apocalyptic event.

Angry, angry ghosts. Hundreds of millions of life forms had been extinguished. Many refused to transition. The living cohabited with the angry ghosts, the undead, and the empty carcasses strewn along the highways. Multiple dimensions merged at this tear in the fabric of space-time. What was real? Whose rules of reality applied here?

A sudden emergency signal squawking from the radio abruptly ended the pleasant music and his jumbled meandering thoughts.

"This is the Indiana Emergency Broadcast Network.

"As of 7:00 this morning, posse comitatus is in effect for the following counties: Newton, Jasper, White, Benton, Warren, Fountain, Montgomery, and Tippecanoe. Under this law, sheriffs in these counties can now summon all able-bodied citizens to assist in the enforcement of the law and the restoration of peace and order. Additional emergency powers have been granted by the governor for the duration of this crisis."

The broadcast was repeated twice. Then, after ten long seconds of dead air, the announcer abruptly stated, "That ends the emergency broadcast from the Indiana Emergency Broadcast Network. We now return you to your local station."

Ian sat stunned. After a few seconds, the Indianapolis newscaster began to recap the situation. As the system began to unravel, Ian found himself fascinated by the clash of federal law, states' rights, individual rights, and emergency management.

The governor of Kentucky started the whole thing at 6 a.m. by ordering the National Guard to close all Ohio River bridges crossing from Illinois and Indiana. The governor declared that millions of refugees pouring into Kentucky had overwhelmed the state's resources. Kentucky was no longer able to provide food, shelter, or police protection to its own inhabitants. He suggested that the flow of refugees be moved farther east along the Ohio River toward Ohio.

"Jeez, what an asshole," Ian thought. "He's forcing them all back into the riots in Cincinnati. What gives him the right to close down interstate bridges? Isn't that federal? Who is in charge here anyway?"

A heavy flow of refugees from Chicago, northern Illinois, and Wisconsin continued to pour into west and northwest Indiana. Widespread looting had been reported. Sheriffs of the northwest counties were considering using some of the extraordinary powers granted to them by the governor to close all access roads from the north and northwest. The eight southwestern counties near the Ohio River had also just declared posse comitatus. The additional emergency powers would allow them to control the movement of refugees swarming in from the north.

Ian reached over and turned off the radio. He needed time to think through this broadcast. Some of it was good news. They were organizing food, medical assistance, emergency housing, and evacuation assistance.

Most of it was troubling, though. The governor and local law enforcement now had the right to commandeer property and control the occupancy of premises. They could also restrict travel and movement into, out of, and through western Indiana. Would refugees be arrested? Could he be detained? Indefinitely?

The implications were scary. Some power-crazed local sheriff, intent on permanently suspending habeas corpus, could conscript work gangs under posse comitatus. "Looters" could be impressed into "prolonged" service to the local tyrant. Or they could just be shot. Late night radio was filled with reports of "vigilante" sheriffs south of Chicago who "terminated" looters and nailed their "carcasses" to trees. Troubling thoughts, indeed.

What should he do now? When his wife had phoned him in St. Ignace, they had agreed that she would drive south through Ohio, Kentucky, and Tennessee to Interstate 40; then west to her parents' home in Albuquerque. Although she would probably encounter hordes of refugees, she would not have to travel into the teeth of the ashfall. Ian had agreed to take the same route, arriving in Albuquerque about four weeks later.

Michigan National Guard troops at the hospital in St. Ignace had alerted him to refugee problems developing at the Ohio River around Cincinnati. Reports from FEMA indicated much lighter traffic crossing the Ohio River at the far southwest corner of Indiana around Evansville. A month ago, at the A-frame, he had revised his exit strategy to travel along the Wabash river through western Indiana and on into Kentucky.

Now the damned governor of Kentucky had closed all bridges over the Ohio River. Plan "C" was immediately required; or was it Plan "D" or "E"? How many more revised exit strategies would he need? He would have to travel farther west now, into the wind and unceasing ashfall; across Illinois, across the Mississippi River and into Missouri. God, he *was* traveling through Hades, and he *would* have to cross the River Styx!

The government never closed the bridges across the Mississippi. They remained the major escape routes headed east out of the apocalypse. Most days volcanic pumice, blasting at 60 miles an hour, deterred the westbound; but at least he wouldn't need a ferryman to cross that mile-wide Old Man River.

The threat of posse comitatus or worse yet, impending martial law, motivated him to get out of western Indiana and into Illinois. Detention or conscription here could delay his journey considerably. He needed to pick up the pace and get south, where there was less ash and he could travel faster.

Ian pulled out his map and realized he was about to have his first major encounter with refugees streaming out of Chicago. At this moment he was only twenty-five miles northwest of Interstate 65, which dumped straight out of greater Chicagoland.

The freeway would be filled with limping, travel-worn refugees with weapons—trigger-happy and with little patience. They would be fanning out for miles from the freeway searching for food or water. Most homes within five miles either side of I-65 would be ransacked and not safe at night. As of this morning, if the looters didn't get you, the local sheriff might just shoot you dead and call it "just-ti-fi-able de-fense." Wonderful, just wonderful. This next thirty miles would be very, very dangerous.

As Ian finished his last swig of hot tea he sighed; all of this anxiety, grief, pain, fear, and exhaustion brought about just because he chose not to buy an $89 pair of snowshoes. The decision to build handmade snowshoes at a workshop in northern Michigan had forever transformed his life and altered his probability line.

Lost in thought, Ian quickly inventoried all of his defensive weapons. He still had the pistol from the dead guy, with the box of seventeen bullets; his Civil War sword; and his walking stick with its fixed bayonet.

He pulled the sword out of the scabbard, feeling its balance and killing efficiency. He recalled how the sword had accompanied his wounded great-great grandfather from the bloody killing fields at Gettysburg to the recovery hospitals in New York and later by train through Cleveland and on to Indianapolis. Exactly 150 years ago, this sword was at the side of a distant grandfather who marched through Indiana. Now 150 years later and eighty miles to the north, this sword accompanied Ian, marching across Indiana through the ruins of a very different national tragedy.

Ian quickly donned his winter coat and boots. He wished he still had the double-layered soft winter scarf his wife had knitted for him so many years ago. "I miss her so much! Please, make this stop!"

He threw his pack over his shoulder, closed and locked the back door, and bounded down the steps. The consummate overnight uninvited lodger had only to put the grill back in the garage and he would be on his way to slay the dragons along I-65.

He drew his sword out of the scabbard, pointed it to the heavens above, and started singing the *Battle Hymn of the Republic*—

> *Mine eyes have seen the glory of the coming of the Lord*
> *He is tramping out the vintage where the grapes of wrath are stored*
> *He hath* something, something, something *of his terrible swift sword....*

Ian charged around the back corner of the house toward the garage with sword raised on high. He suddenly noticed two sets of fresh tire tracks running up to the smoking charcoal grill. These tracks were not there when he brought in the bacon and bagels forty minutes ago. His bounding, sword-wielding charge stopped abruptly.

He froze in place, not breathing, staring straight ahead at the charcoal grill. Three soft clicks broke the dead silence, three safeties clicking off. Off to his left at the edge of his peripheral vision sat a police SUV and a pickup truck. Near the SUV, three men stood with rifles fixed on him.

"Put down your weapon, son! Drop it!" Ian loosened his fingers from the hilt of his prized family heirloom. The sword fell to the ground, point sticking in the snow. Then it toppled over into a snow-ash drift.

"Don't move a muscle, son, or we'll shoot your thievin' ass full of holes. Dale here is gonna search ya. Don't move."

One deputy searched his body but found nothing. When they searched his pack, they found the gun and the bullets from the dead guy's house. They took his walking stick with its bayonet and his sword with its scabbard.

"Son, we're gonna keep the weapons you stole, as evidence."

They also threw the pack and walking stick into the back of the pickup truck. Then they handcuffed Ian and took pictures of the arrest.

"That is an old family heirloom," Ian protested.

"Son, we caught you red-handed, breaking and entering a house. Don't lie to me and tell me this sword belongs to you. I could just shoot you dead, right here. My posse would confirm what the photographs prove. You are a thief. This morning we finally declared war on you looters. The governor extended the state of emergency, and the sheriff of White County has declared posse comitatus. I sure as hell don't have to read you your Miranda rights. You're my puppy now, son. The judges all pussy-tailed it to Indianapolis. Goodbye hab-e-us cor-pus. I am your judge, your jury, and your executioner. Get in the car and shut the hell up."

Thirty minutes later, Ian was sitting handcuffed on the floor in the gym of the high school in Monon, Indiana, with twelve other unfortunates caught "looting" by the sheriff and his posse. It was cold in there, about 50 degrees. An electric cord ran from a gas generator outside to one small electric heater inside the gym. Twelve floor mats were placed around the heater. Each prisoner had a floor mat and two blankets. The mat was their bed and prison cell. Huddled under blankets, handcuffed and shivering, were nine men and three women. Some had been prisoners for a couple of weeks.

City water and sewer had been shut down due to volcanic ash. Several five gallon jugs of water had been pumped by gas generator from a well on a nearby farm. A guard explained the rules to Ian. He had to request a drink of water. Food was provided twice a day—at 10 a.m. and 5 p.m. A camp toilet was located outside the back door exit, in the snow. Prisoners were not to leave their mats except for toilet trips. When they went outside, they must be accompanied by a guard. Any prisoner trying to escape would be shot.

Other prisoners told Ian they all had been moved from the Monon police station to the high school gym a couple of days ago in anticipation of a huge influx of new detainees. The local Monon chief of police, Officer Obie, was assisting the White County sheriff by providing temporary emergency shelter for the newly captured. Ian hadn't yet become acquainted with Officer Obie of Monon.

Hours passed. The handcuffs chafed. Ian was cold. He huddled in a blanket because the heater was not turned on yet. Other prisoners said the small heater was turned on only during late night, between 11 p.m. and 5 a.m.

Around three o'clock, Officer Obie arrived. He stood at the front of the gym, legs firmly planted and hands clasped behind his back. The razor-sharp creases in his trousers and his mirrored sunglasses almost made up for the fact that he was only 5'4".

"Gentlemen and ladies. You are here in handcuffs because you have been caught in the act of looting. Now you're a prisoner in this gym and we don't know what to do with you. We can't just let you go. We also can't just let you stay here. We can't just shoot you. We need time to ponder this dilemma. In the morning we will decide what to do with you."

Suddenly Ian's mind flashed back to that wounded Rottweiler in the farmhouse in southern Michigan. The Michigan militia had solved his problem. Who would solve Officer Obie's problem?

Disconsolate, Ian felt his life cascading downward. He had morphed into the damned dog, resorting to lapping water out of toilets to survive. The shoe was now on the other paw, waiting for the vigilantes to finish him off.

A 5 p.m. meal of bread, water, and venison broke the monotony. Prisoners huddled under blankets and told stories of their own epic journeys to this gym, this nexus point. Lights were turned low after 9 p.m.

One of the evening guards came over. He had been listening to Ian talk about being a professor at EMU, being separated from his wife and kids, and getting trapped by the volcano at a hospital in northern Michigan.

The guard turned out to be Officer Obie's nephew, back home to help his parents after Indiana University closed. He and Ian talked about university life, family, the great cultural diaspora, and the good old days—just two months ago. Good kid! Ian felt better. The heater came on at 11 p.m. and Ian quickly fell asleep.

While Ian slept, Officer Obie of Monon and his county sheriff sat deliberating about what to do with their prisoners and how to move some stranded elderly people to the hospital in Monticello.

Day 62

Officer Obie came in at 10:30 a.m. to update everyone. Yesterday the White County sheriff got the right to commandeer railroad trains and freight cars to transport food, water, and injured patients. For now, until the moving exposed train parts seized up, the trains could plow the tracks from Monticello to Monon. The vital lifeline could be maintained temporarily.

A makeshift urgent care center had been set up at a church to treat the frail elderly who were difficult to transport, had no local family, or had not been evacuated before the roads became impassable. Obie needed a work detail of six prisoners to move six elderly patients from the church in Monon to the emergency room at the hospital in Monticello, ten miles away by train. The hospital was still fully functional: lights, water, and all the comforts of civilization.

One prisoner asked why not drive them to Monticello? It's only ten miles.

"There's fifteen-inch drifts in most of the county," Obie answered. "They're so heavy we can't plow them any more. The ash can't be moved."

He went on to explain that now only four-wheel-drive vehicles could plow through the crusty, pumice-laden snow. The two police SUVs and the deputized posse vehicles could still get around the small town of Monon, but with increasing difficulty. After sixty days vehicle engines and exposed parts were failing. Time was running out, fast. Every day the damned volcano spewed more ash. It never let up. Eventually the entire county could be buried under six feet of snow-ash like Minnesota and Nebraska. Everyone else might then need to be evacuated farther south and east.

"We're in trouble, folks. We need to work together."

Obie proceeded to pick his team: one prisoner and one deputy per patient. His nephew had reappeared and made sure Ian got picked as his work partner. Obie would be going on the train; the White County sheriff would stay in Monon.

At the church they collected the elderly in a modified school bus. This was a one shot operation. Everybody must fit into the bus on the first trip.

Obie, Ian, and the kid headed for an elderly woman wearing a red sweatshirt over her coat. The shirt asked in big letters: "Hoosier Granny?" She greeted Obie as "son." Ian asked about the sweatshirt.

"My grandson, here, gave it to me. I'm so proud of him."

The kid said, "Yeah, those shirts are everywhere—Hoosier mama, Hoosier daddy, you name it."

At the loading dock, Ian saw the train and remembered his dream about sobbing, wailing old people being loaded into boxcars in the cold. There sat an engine connected to three boxcars, with another engine at the end facing the opposite direction. One boxcar was lined with bales of straw as insulators. Inside was a pile of down sleeping bags "commandeered" by the White County sheriff from a local store. Ian thought, "If I took one of these, they'd shoot me. Guess it depends who does the commandeering."

The wheelchairs were lowered from the bus and loaded into the boxcar. Sleeping bags were placed over the shivering old people to protect them from the cold. The third wheelchair got stuck on the platform and the passenger started wailing,

"Help me! Help me!" It was just like Ian's dream. These precognitions were starting to get a little weird.

On the train all went well until Grandma Obie had a COPD exacerbation, reacting to the cold and the ash. She had forgotten to take her medicine in the rush to get out. After years of dealing with his son's asthma, Ian recognized the symptoms: breathlessness, coughing, tightness in the chest. He confirmed this with her and told Obie, who walkie-talkied ahead for an ambulance.

The farm supply store had the only loading platform in Monticello. An ambulance and assisted living van were waiting. Ian and the kid rode with Grandma.

At the hospital, it was decided that Grandma would need overnight monitoring. Ian and her grandson volunteered to stay with her. Officer Obie took the other prisoners back on the train, now loaded with supplies for Monon.

The hospital provided a reminder of how life had been: lights, water, hot food, coffee, real bathrooms. Ian was welcomed by the overworked hospital staff. He sat watch all night, drinking lots of good, strong coffee. He reflected back to St. Ignace and remembered that the night shift nurses always made the best strong coffee.

Day 63

A nurse came by around 3 a.m. She was at the end of a 36-hour shift and headed for bed. She told Ian she lived here now: ate here, slept here, showered here.

"Shower?" said Ian. "You've got running water? How?" The nurse told him about the emergency system set up after the tornado of 1974. Ian told her it had been weeks since he had a shower. The nurse took pity on him and sent him down the hall to have a blasting hot shower while she watched his patient.

He felt like a new man, and the day kept getting better. A breakfast cart came around with orange juice, toast, oatmeal, hot coffee, bacon—and eggs! Grandmother, grandson, and Ian shared a feast. A nurse came to check Grandma's vitals. She was declared well enough to move in with other Monon patients.

Right after lunch, Officer Obie appeared. The kid told him how Ian had sat up with Obie's mother all night, then helped the others all day with no sleep. Grandma chimed in on the chorus—she loved Ian, such a nice young man.

"How did you find him?" she asked her son. Obie was embarrassed.

"I volunteered, ma'am," Ian said.

Obie shot Ian a grateful look and said, "Time for us to get back to Monon."

The kid decided to stay with his grandmother until she was completely out of the woods. He and Ian said goodbye.

"Don't forget I promised to help you get into grad school at Michigan," Ian reminded him. Obie was hearing all of this. The kid turned to his uncle.

"Uncle Obie, you take good care of Ian. He's a good man."

The train had been reloaded with water, food, gas, supplies, and Ian. Obie was very quiet until a few minutes out of Monon. Then he told Ian he wouldn't be taking him back to the gym. Instead, Ian would go to Obie's office, spend the night there, get his things, and be free to go in the morning.

The White County sheriff was waiting on the Monon platform with several bags and boxes at his feet. Obie and Ian debarked and the sheriff started loading boxes on the train, declaring that he was going back to Monticello.

At Obie's office, there was only one deputy. As soon as they came in, he rushed to Obie to complain about the White County sheriff.

"That dude's crazy, Obie. He shot two prisoners dead when they tried to run. Started 'commandeering' anything that caught his eye. He's trouble, Obie!"

Obie went into his office and noticed that things were missing. Ian spotted his pack and walking stick with its bayonet, but the sword and the dead man's gun were gone. Obie promised to get them back and return them to Ian when this was all over. Ian, numb with fatigue, just nodded. They said their farewells. Obie headed for home, and Ian stumbled to a cot in an open jail cell.

Chapter 15

Ring Around the Rosy

Day 64

Ian headed west out of Monon, then turned south at a rapid pace. The more distance he put between himself and that trigger-happy sheriff, the happier he would be. He was really apprehensive, though. The threats were heightened. Looters were actually in the area. And his only weapons now were his bayonet and staff.

After ten miles he stopped for the night at a one-story ranch house. The house had seen better days, but it was the only one in sight. The grill in the back yard was rusted. The screen door was torn. Linoleum on the kitchen floor was worn away in spots, cracked in others, and there were kids' toys everywhere. So much for the McMansion lifestyle: there was little comfort or luxury here.

The kitchen cupboards didn't offer much in the way of food, just some canned jalapeno beans and moldy Ritz crackers. It didn't help his mood. Still, there was water in the water heater and he had some of the jerky and a little of his flatbread from Leesburg. He made dinner, finished his evening rituals, and went to bed in the parents' room.

Day 65

Ian was now only a day away from the time he would have to cross I-65. This was the first major freeway he would encounter that was an escape route from a big city. He was seriously worried about the potential for meeting real problems here. What if the highway had been taken over? It would be like the old days in England when roving bandits robbed and killed travelers.

Sunday was his usual day to steal a vehicle, but the experience in Monon was still too fresh. That meant he had to walk, and he felt vulnerable to attack. He was aware again of the restrictions the gas mask imposed, including paranoia. He found himself looking behind frequently. Today's highwaymen were desperate and well-armed. It made for an uncomfortable day.

Most of his travel today was straight south through miles of barren, windswept fields. The ghostly silhouettes of gigantic windmills stretched in all directions as far as the eye could see. Row after row, rank upon rank, they stood as silent, immobile sentinels, ground to a halt by tiny particles of ash.

Before dark, he turned west and found a driveway leading to an abandoned farmhouse. The bed was more comfortable than yesterday; but his proximity to I-65 kept him awake most of the night, worrying about who else would discover his refuge before dawn.

Day 66

Today was the day. He looked out across the flat, open landscape and wondered how he could get to I-65 without being seen. Did this farmer have a set of binoculars, maybe? He hunted through the house, but no luck. Guess I'll have to keep a low profile, he thought as he started walking.

The expressway was visible for almost a mile, even in the gray ash landscape. He lay along the bank of a creek and scanned the road. There was no movement. No traffic passed by as he watched, not a single car. No bicycles, no pedestrians—nothing. Unable to believe his eyes, he continued to lie in the cold ash, staring at the empty freeway. Finally, he stood up cautiously and continued on his way. There would be no dragons today, and he couldn't even tilt at the windmills. What a fucking anticlimax!

As he was standing on the overpass looking down on the freeway, it hit him. The government was going to close the access roads from the northwest. My God, they must have done it. He could sleep soundly tonight.

Days 67–68

For the next two days, he kept moving south and west, skirting the small towns of Otterbein and Pine Village. He was trying to stay north of the Wabash River and west of W. Lafayette, where Purdue University was located.

In the afternoon of the second day, he noticed changes beginning. The area was still mostly bare farmland, but there were more trees. The ash in the air seemed to be getting thicker, as well.

He stopped for the night at a brick Cape Cod. It didn't belong in Indiana, and neither did he. Inside, he found a large battery-powered radio and turned it on. Bad news awaited him.

A second massive eruption had shaken the Yellowstone caldera late last night. Even more ash was expected to rain down on Indiana in the next few days. People were being urged to take precautions and leave the area as soon as possible.

He didn't sleep well that night. Just how bad was this going to get? Everyone thought the small daily eruptions were tapering off and everything would get back to normal soon. No chance of that now.

Day 69

Today was even darker than usual. Ian groped through his morning routine and set out, feeling uneasy. He walked south for the rest of the morning. Then the absolutely flat Indiana farmland abruptly morphed into a heavily forested, high hilly area.

The dramatic change brought Ian to a sudden confused stop. This detail didn't show up on his map. Of course, when all of Indiana was crammed onto one page, a lot of detail got lost. He still wanted to avoid all the towns that sat straight south of him along the Wabash. If he took the county roads due west, within five miles he'd hit a big state highway running north and south. The hills might also offer a little protection against that wind.

Decision made, Ian turned west and started around Hog Back Hill. Within a short time, the pavement ended. The road turned to dirt, narrowed, and disappeared into a dark forest. Ian hesitated. Something didn't feel right here. But retracing his steps would consume valuable time and energy. He kept going. The road twisted and turned until he lost his sense of direction. The wind had died down temporarily, but swirling ash made visibility very low. Ian's feelings of unease intensified.

A sudden burst of energy froze him in his tracks. It was fearsome, primal; but somehow, familiar. He had felt this before. When he was in England, on the moors, he had had this same sense of being unwanted, being an intruder in the realm of something ancient and powerful. Whatever it was, it did not want him here. He pushed ahead anyway. Fear hadn't stopped him yet.

Then the road forked. One fork descended steeply into a gorge. The other went straight ahead, along a ridge. Neither had a road sign. He couldn't decide which way to go. All he was sure of was that he needed to follow the river, but he couldn't tell where it was.

He continued along the wider ridge road, thinking he was going west. The energy focused on him intently, feeding off his fear and confusion. Had he gone the wrong way? He had a moment of sheer panic. In all this time, he had never really been lost before. Now, everything around him was eerily still and ominous. He didn't know where he was, and the terror made him want to run, just run. Instead, he stopped cold and sat down in the middle of the road. Holding still, he centered himself. The adrenaline surge eventually passed. He pushed himself back up on quivering legs that protested the idea of standing again. Almost as a final insult, a strong gust of wind came out of nowhere and knocked him back on his ass.

"Well," he laughed to himself, "at least I know which way is west."

He staggered back north against the renewed wind and turned left at the intersection. Quickly he dropped down into the protection of the gorge. He fell repeatedly on the slippery, ash-covered road.

"God damned worthless map! This sure doesn't look like flat farmland to me."

The energy was a continued presence, but in Ian's centered state, it had little effect. He hadn't panicked, hadn't thrown himself off the nearby cliff into the ravine. The energy seemed content to let him pass.

The next few miles brought him out of the ravine and back to the old familiar flat farmland. The wind pushed against him every foot of the way. Ash stung against every inch of exposed skin. The cold was bitter. He wore down quickly. Soon every step was an effort and he began to think longingly of curling up under a tree to rest—just for a minute. That "minute" would kill him, however, and he knew it. He floundered on, one hard-fought foot at a time.

When he finally found a roadside house for the night, he was so drained he almost couldn't force himself to fix food or go through his evening bathing routine. Being a stubborn man could, on certain rare occasions, be an advantage, though. He made himself eat and clean up before he fell into bed.

Days 70–71

Two days later, Ian reached I-74. There were cars eastbound as far as he could see. Even the westbound lanes were filled with traffic headed east. That last eruption must have convinced even the diehards to make a run for it. The freeway was clogged with cars, bumper to bumper, moving slowly but unceasingly.

The drivers all looked truly desperate, totally focused on the road ahead. He stood on the overpass of the freeway for a while, marveling at the sheer number of cars. Who would ever have thought to see the day when all of Chicago emptied out in a controlled, civilized panic?

It was almost dark by the time he left I-74. Traveling south along Indiana Route 63, he made it only another two miles before stopping for the night.

Day 72

Another drab, gray Sunday. It was time to steal a vehicle, but this household had left nothing behind except a riding mower with no gas. He sighed and started walking south. Then his luck changed: there was an abandoned car pulled off the road near a drainage ditch. The keys were even in the ignition! He got in and tried to start it. The car started right up. Ian drove off, wondering why anyone would desert a vehicle that still had half a tank of gas. With this car and an empty road ahead, he could really make some distance today.

Or not. Five miles down the road, the red temperature light came on. He coasted to an intersection just before the car died. Steam was pouring out from under the hood. He got out to check the radiator. It was the hose. Where's Red Green and his duct tape when you need him?

Frustrated, he looked back the way he came; nothing there. Nothing east, but in the distance to the west sat a large farm. To the south, though, there was a large building with several cars in the parking lot. The sky was darkening again and the wind had picked up. He set off down the road toward the most promising shelter in sight.

Movement ahead. He stopped cold, heart thudding wildly, and strained to hear over the wind. Voices? No, one voice. It was a woman and she was—singing? He peered through the blowing ash. There, about thirty feet ahead of him, he saw a woman and two children, all holding hands. They were moving around in a circle.

The woman had dark hair. Wild strands blew around her face. The wind whipped at the skirt of a dark green dress that was far too lightweight for this weather. She held the hand of a young girl with long brown hair in two ponytails. The girl wore jeans and a dark blue sweatshirt with "Beloit College" lettered in gold across the front. The second child was a blond toddler in Oshkosh overalls and a red jacket.

The girl was looking desperately at the woman as they circled, her eyes filled with fear. The little boy was clearly confused and unhappy. The woman's eyes were wide and vacant. What in better times might be called a smile was pasted to her face as she pulled the children around and around, singing—

Ring around the rosy
Pocket full of posy

Ashes, ashes
We all fall down!

She pulled the children to the ground, giggling in a high, nerve-stretched voice. Then she jumped to her feet and started again.

He watched this bizarre scene from the road for several identical performances. What on earth was she doing? No answer occurred to him. Finally, he walked toward the play group. The little girl saw him first and froze. Then the woman turned toward him. Her terrified scream ripped through the air as she snatched up the toddler and began to flee toward the building, dragging the girl behind her.

"No, wait!" he called. "I won't hurt you! Please stop!" There was no answer and he was left alone with the wind and the ash.

"Oh, great," he thought. "I feel terrible. I scared the crap out of them. I've got to explain." He started toward the building, only to be met at the door by an older, gray-haired man in slacks and a sweater.

"Welcome to North Vermillion Elementary School shelter," he said. "I'm Reverend Vertelli." After introducing himself, Ian explained about the woman and children and asked if he could see her to apologize. The minister gently shook his head.

"Oh, that would be Marcie Baldwin," he said. "She got here about the fifth of January, when her car ran out of gas right on the circular drive out front. Her husband was away in Syria when the first eruption happened, and poor Marcie just couldn't cope with the whole thing. Others have gone on since, but Marcie won't leave. She claims that Dave, her husband, will come for her, but he won't know where to find her if she doesn't stay put. Best just to leave her alone."

Ian's thoughts flashed to his own wife and children. He spent a night full of bad dreams at the shelter, but he never saw Marcie Baldwin or her children again.

Day 73

The next morning he said goodbye to Reverend Vertelli and started south again. As he was leaving, the minister called after him.

"When you get down around Newport, don't worry about the mutants. They're harmless." Then he laughed. "That's a joke, son. The Newport Chemical Depot is the old army nerve-gas storage dump. Far as I know, it's all clear south of here."

Ian veered west to avoid going through Newport, so he never did see the depot—or any mutants. Then he skirted the little town of Dana. About a half mile south, he came to US 36. That's the road we used to take from Boulder to Estes Park, he thought. I could just start walking west from here and end up back in Colorado.

He spent the night near the highway for old times' sake, but he had trouble getting to sleep. His mind replayed memories of college, meeting his wife, their wedding, the children. Finally he cried himself to sleep.

Day 74

His last day in Indiana was uneventful. He passed by St. Bernice and spent the night west of Blanford near the Illinois border.

Chapter 16

Ashmore

Days 75–76

Ian's first two days in Illinois were uneventful. The land continued to be very flat and open with few trees. A fierce wind blew out of the west. Ian was almost underneath the jet stream. A new frontal boundary had set up along the 100,000-foot-high wall of the ashdome, slowly moving south. It was a desolate, dark day with a bitter cold wind freezing his body. This route could be lethal. He had second thoughts about continuing west. In roughly thirty miles he would reach Interstate 57. Maybe he should go south on I-57 and get out of the sandblasting ash.

Day 77

On his third day in Illinois, Ian stopped at 4:00 just outside of Ashmore. Because the ash totals were lower here and electricity had only recently gone out, many of the houses were still occupied. A week earlier there was less than an inch of ash on the ground. After the second major eruption, two more inches of ash had accumulated. It took a while, but he finally found an abandoned place just east of town.

Day 78

Ian walked half a mile before he saw the "Welcome to Ashmore" sign. He smiled at the irony as he continued west. Just past the town was a farmhouse with rambling additions and an open porch. The front door was handmade with a ship's porthole serving as a window. A small barn sat behind the house, near a tractor shed. A picket fence ran around the front of the house.

In the yard was a four-foot-tall bronze statue of a Giacometti-esque chicken. A privacy fence ran parallel to the house in the side yard, and various bits of found-object art were suspended from it. Other art work dotted the yard, including two stone Buddhas, a Shiva, and a five-foot-tall Scottish touching-stone. Ian stopped at the fence and watched as an older woman concentrated on clearing the ground around her statuary.

"I like your Giacometti chicken sculpture!"

The woman jumped, startled. She whirled around toward Ian. "Shit!"

Immediately from the side of the house came a big golden dog barking and baring its canines. The woman gave a shrill whistle through her teeth.

"Down, Cedar," she commanded. The dog stopped dead in its tracks but continued a low growl. "We don't get many art professor types walking past here."

"How did you know I was an art professor?" Ian asked in surprise. The woman laughed and replied,

"You just told me. You don't see many refugees who know Giacometti."

The woman explained that she was startled because the dog usually let her know when someone was coming. She had been getting a lot of refugee traffic passing her house of late. She said that the radio stations were telling people to stay off of the main roads and to take the back routes. Ian noticed that her hand had never left the pistol holstered on her hip.

Ian introduced himself and said he was a ceramics professor He told her about a show he did annually with his students, based on "outsider" and "found object" art. He laughed and said he enjoyed this show every year because some students started questioning their reasons for being in art school. They each had their epiphanies and realized that art school was doing damage to their creativity.

"They were already artists the whole time, and they were the only ones who didn't know it."

He heaped praise on her yard art. She told Ian that she was stimulated during her travels. The chicken sculpture was in fact inspired by Giacometti's ideas of alienation and remoteness from others. The touching stone she carved after her travels in the Celtic realms; she purchased the Buddhas and Shivas in India and Asia.

She explained that the found objects on the fence began when she started walking for exercise every night after her divorce. Eventually the fence took on a look of organized chaos and nostalgia, which seemed to parallel her existence.

At this point, the atmosphere between them was much less strained.

"What do you do besides art?" she asked.

"Well, I'm married and have two kids. I was out of town when the volcano erupted. All I know is they're heading to New Mexico, and I'm trying to catch up."

The conversation continued until sometime around noon. As Ian talked, she watched him closely. Finally, she reached a decision. She was now comfortable enough to invite him in for lunch.

"I'm Ellen, by the way," she offered. "Are you hungry?"

Entering the house was like entering an eclectic museum. There was a Victrola in the living room. She had a record and book collection that reminded Ian of his brother's. Her records ranged from *The Incredible String Band* to *Music for Zen Meditation*. Her bookshelves were filled with Castaneda, Hesse, and other thought-provoking authors. Ian approved. He had learned years ago to know people by their record and book collections.

There was artwork everywhere. Ian saw ceramic bowls, sculptures, paintings, and handcrafted furniture from China.

Ellen set a plate of sandwiches on a hand-planed dining room table with a deep rich reddish-brown oiled finish. She served tea from a cherry red Xia Xing teapot with an intricately carved dragon spout. It took them two hours to finish lunch.

It was the first real, cultured conversation he'd had since the eruptions began seventy-eight days ago. No thought was given to anything outside the house, except when the dog had to go out.

Eventually, Ellen opened up about her background. She earned a Bachelor of Fine Arts degree from the University of Kansas, then spent six months at the Haystack National School of Crafts in Maine. Later she married an anthropologist who took her to China in the 1980s. They were married for thirty years.

Then he had an affair with a grad student and she left. She bought the property here where she could do her art without his criticism. The freedom was exhilarating.

After cookies and more tea, Ian talked about missing his family and about Dexter and Ann Arbor. Ellen remembered that her sister Katie lived in Ann Arbor in the 1970s, and that she had visited her there for a couple of weeks. It was a nice college town

They were startled to notice that it was getting dark. Their stimulating conversation had lasted the whole afternoon. Since Ellen had no electricity, she lit candles and oil lamps.

Ellen's house was equipped with a propane gas stove and oven. Her electric water heater and furnace no longer worked, so she heated water and her entire house with a #8 Jøtul wood stove.

Thankfully, she still had water. Ellen had not removed the working antique well pump from the sink in her recently remodeled kitchen. That meant that, unlike some, she did not have to abandon her home.

She had plenty of good food in the freezer, so they prepared a special dinner of chicken breast with marinated vegetables and Jarlsburg cheese. They drank wine and shared laughter as they prepared the food. Their tiny oasis of warmth and light sparked a spontaneous celebration.

"When you visited Ann Arbor in the '70s, did you and your sister ever go down to Farmers' Market and Kerrytown?" Ian asked. "My brother owned a gallery in Kerrytown called Jacob's Ladder."

Ellen replied, "You know, the name sounds familiar, but it's been so long, over forty years ago. I can't really remember." She laughed. "After all, I am an old woman."

After dinner they cleaned up the dishes. Ellen asked Ian if he would like to stay the night and continue their "civilized" talk and try to act as if everything in the world was somewhat normal again. Ian agreed gratefully. It was cold outside. They settled down with candles and a roaring fire in the wood stove. Ellen served port wine in European glasses and they listened to music on the wind-up Victrola.

"So back to your brother and my era," said Ellen. "Did being exposed to your brother's art gallery at an early age influence your decision to become an artist?"

Ian smiled. "I was absolutely captivated by the mélange of colors and textures and forms. Six foot bronze sculptures, oil paintings, watercolors, and ceramics." Ian paused. "They all wove a pattern with colorful books, ink lithographs, and intricate textured fabric art. So, yes. It was a visual and tactile feast. It dramatically influenced my emerging right-brained awareness.

"Later, I came to understand that it was much more. Jacob's Ladder was in fact a consciousness art gallery. You know, it was like an embryo. The first vestiges of a still evolving consciousness school. 'Prophets not profits' was the prime directive."

Silence. Lost in thought, Ellen was struggling with Ian's last comments. As an art student in the '60s, Ellen had existed for years at the intersection where drugs, altered consciousness, and art converged. Countless nights, late into the night, had been spent trying to untangle meaning from experience. Her profound insights had always melted by noon.

"But it didn't happen 'til I got to India in the '80s," Ellen blurted out, shattering the prolonged silence. "In a monastery in the Himalayas, I had a powerful experience that didn't involve drugs. Why was that? Why didn't it happen here? In the '60s, when I was taking drugs?" Embarrassed, she realized her sudden outburst had made no sense to Ian. "I'm so sorry. I've been isolated here for so long. Sometimes my thoughts just come tumbling out. Obsessing about that damn volcano is driving me crazy. I'm sorry."

Ian nodded in understanding. "I know. Since the eruption, I've spent every second in a hyper-focused survival mode. One misstep, one bad fall meant that I could freeze to death. Alone, in that damned dark silence. Or worse yet, lying there helpless, being ripped apart by a pack of wild dogs—alone."

Ian sat overwhelmed, recalling the horror of the past weeks. Then tears suddenly welled up, as repressed fear and anger cascaded out. After months of feral survival, Ian had just now understood how far he had descended back down into the mammalian and limbic worlds.

"Ellen, when you're hunted and tracked by desperate wild animals, you're bumped down the food chain. You are tonight's dinner. As a species, we don't remember that. We have no words to describe it." Ian continued, "Civilization has come a great distance in the last millennium. Hardscrabble existence has given way to leisure time. Now we have professional thinkers who ponder the great questions of mankind.

"My life has been spent searching for meaning. Humanity has had the precious opportunity to wax philosophic for hours each day, to create a free space to think. Unfortunately, for those of us caught under the ashdome, all of that ended abruptly eighty days ago. That monster sent us reeling a thousand years backward in time. We're trapped now in a world of primal fear and unholy raw survival, with millions dying all around us. But Kurtz understood. 'The horror…the horror.' This is the Heart of Darkness."

Ellen smiled; then tears of overwhelming exhaustion filled her eyes. "You are absolutely right. We haven't spent much time waxing philosophic, slip-sliding through this ash. There are no right-brained thoughts, no creativity, no artistic moments. Today is the first normal conversation I've had since the first eruption. We must do something about this! When I listen to what we both are expressing, it is apparent that post-traumatic stress 'figures largely in our lives.' But the 'post' isn't 'post'. It's continuing. Yes, it's Continuing Never Ending God Damned Traumatic Stress Syndrome. And I can't take it any more!"

Despite Ian's desperate need to keep moving and find his family, Ellen's impassioned cry for help resonated clear to the center of his being. The volcano had almost destroyed him. Ian suddenly flashed back on the woman with the wild look in her eyes, insanely dancing in circles with her kids, singing *Ring around the Rosy:* "Ashes, ashes, we all fall down." Did she realize that she had slipped far over the edge? The volcano had defeated her.

Ian wouldn't let the volcano win here, and Ellen was in complete agreement. In the dwindling firelight, Ellen and Ian made a pact to stop, regroup, and rest for a few days. They needed to take back their right-brained creative lives for the sake of their continued sanity. They needed to build more fires, sip more port, and try to restore the luxury of spiritual and artistic reflection in their lives. Failure to comply would surely lead to insanity.

Ellen paused to freshen their glasses with more of the fine port. Then she let Cedar out the front door. She returned shortly with the grateful dog, wound up the antique Victrola, and added several hunks of scrap lumber to the wood stove. Flickering light from the fire merged with the flickering candlelight in a dance across the darkened living room walls. The old wooden needle on the wind-up Victrola crackled in harmony with the burning scrap pine. The healing had begun.

The fire worked its magic. Through the welcome soothing silence, an idea began to emerge. A renewal of a reflective, philosophical space was needed, where creativity and free thought replaced the caldera's destruction and fear. The mantel clock chimed eight times. With wineglasses raised on high, Ellen and Ian toasted the start of the First Annual Ashmore Sanity Chautauqua. Playfully, Ellen stood up, as though addressing a large gathering.

"Dog and gentleman," she announced to those assembled. Cedar, who had not been the center of attention for hours, perked up, shook his head, and gave her that priceless inquisitive doggie look. Ellen and Ian exploded in laughter. Cedar responded with licks and fiercely wagging tail all around. Everyone was feeling much more normal, happy, and sane. Ellen regained her composure and continued.

"I propose that tonight's discussion explore a mystery that has perplexed me for almost fifty years. Perhaps now, at the most unlikely of times, the fates have brought you to my door bearing large missing pieces of my puzzle. God, that sounds so dramatic, but this really is important. It sounds like you spent a lot of time around people who had experienced altered states of consciousness. Like at your brother's gallery in Ann Arbor. You haven't said anything about your own experiences, but hopefully you understand enough to help me sort through mine." Ian nodded tentatively, not knowing where this was going.

"Well, I'll do my best," he said.

Ellen began fifty years earlier, in the fall of 1966, when a cultural earthquake rumbled through American universities. Swiss drug companies were legally distributing LSD to academics and their graduate students at major research institutions across the U.S. Everyone, even the U.S. military, was trying to determine how this powerful psychedelic could be used. LSD was not banned federally in the U.S. until late 1968.

Early on, only the wealthy elites, academics, rock stars, or Hollywood actors had access to this drug. Eventually, LSD began to filter down to radical undergraduate students, mostly on the coasts. Soon the potent consciousness altering drugs would flow out into the expanding hippie counterculture along Haight-Ashbury during the 1967 "Summer of Love" in San Francisco.

"But nooo, not to Kansas. I was trapped in art school in Kansas, out on the vast prairie, far from civilization. Midwest undergraduate students were so socially obtuse that just a few of us were beginning to experiment with pot and hash. Everybody else in the Midwest was bingeing on booze, the drug of choice.

"Then came Owsley, the 'LSD cook'. I heard he made more than two million hits around 1966. His acid was primo shit, man. It was sooo good and sooo pure, and he put the Owsley 'mark' on each tab, so you knew you could trust it. There were rumors that he supplied LSD to the Grateful Dead and to the Beatles. You know, Ian, I think I met that man once in Denver. It was the Summer of Love in 1967 and my friend Amy and I were headed out west to San Francisco, with flowers in our hair. We were young Midwest college art students on a quest to get laid and get high, not necessarily in that order.

"Amy knew people with good dope in Denver. I kind of remember a house across from the Denver Zoo. We met some people and wound up in Nederland, 4000 feet above Denver, dropping acid for the next week. By God, Rocky Mountain high. I swear I saw God, and I think I met Owsley."

Fifty years of confusion settled into her face.

"Ian, no one saw this coming. We were not prepared for this. We were handed the most powerful mind-altering drugs on the planet and sent out to explore the multiple universes and separate realities that exist within the mind of God. For some, it was an exotic hippie high; another way to get wasted and blow your mind. For others, curiosity would lead them on a mystical journey down the rabbit hole. Everyone who blasted out into inner space immediately discovered how woefully unprepared they were for this head trip. Nothing was based on past experiences or assumptions. And no one could tell you what to expect. There were no reference points, no road maps, no time, no space, no landmarks. Proportions were…different."

Ellen paused for a moment, collecting her thoughts, centering her mind. She continued, "Can you imagine landing back into this reality after such a mind-blowing experience? First comes the confusion. What the hell was that all about? Am I sane? Was it real? How do I describe this, even to myself? There are no words for it. So, how would you go out and explain this to others? Among ourselves we tried to understand. We tried to reconcile these experiences with ordinary reality. We spent many a night late into the night, but none of our questions could be answered from the linear, rational, intellectual mind."

At that time, science rigidly rejected any beliefs not upheld by the scientific method. Academics piled on and called the experience "delusional," "catatonic," or "schizophrenic." Western religious leaders considered "oneness with God" as blasphemy or heresy. It became painfully clear that these pillars of Western culture were hostile to mystical experiences. They seemed to be operating on a very narrow bandwidth, completely unaware of surrounding wavelengths. Many cultural mentors were clueless and bull-headed. To function within the separate realities, an alternative description of the universe would be needed.

"But where could we get help? We would now need new and different mentors. Where would we find them?" In the dim firelight Ellen could see that her compadres were fading rapidly.

"Okay, listen up everyone," Ellen blurted out, not willing to put everyone to sleep with her monologue. "You've probably been wondering where I was going with this story. Believe me, this story is very relevant! Look outside. The ash is piling up out there. Every May, for hundreds of miles in any direction, grains are planted in these fields. It's now the middle of March, and we're only six weeks away from spring planting. It's ten degrees outside right now. The ash is turning into a concrete crust. Do you really think that crops will be planted here this year? We're headed for a famine. How long do you think it will be before the liquor and beer producers run out of grain and have to shut down? What effect will that have on this culture of alcoholics?

"The entire history of Western civilization has been one continuous drunken bacchanalia. From the Greek and Roman orgies, clear through to Superbowl Sunday, alcohol was the intoxicant of choice. It drove the engine of the culture. For millennia we have been binge drunk bullies. We've plundered the world and terrorized and pissed everyone off. What's going to happen to us when our booze is cut off? We are baaad, nasty drunks. You will see riots. Cities will burn. Even if you could make alcohol at home, there wouldn't be any supplies: no grains, no sugar, no fruit."

Ellen finally stopped. She raced for the door, exclaiming over her shoulder,

"I've got to pee, Cedar's got to pee, we need more wood, and I need a double Scotch real bad." Ian burst out laughing. Five minutes later she returned with a smile on her face and two big triple scotches in hand.

"Now I'm going to just sit here and enjoy this warm wonderful fire." Ian silently nodded in agreement, and soon all were huddled deep in sleep around the life giving warmth of the old woodstove.

Day 79

"Happy Ides of March," Ellen noted, as she assembled a pot of coffee to put on the wood stove. "How did you sleep last night?"

Ian furrowed his brow. "I had that strange dream again." He then told her of his recurring dream about a small hovel nestled among the mounds of a well-tended garden. He could vividly feel the deep peace that permeated this quiet, secluded space. "I don't know what it means…but I've had this same dream before."

"Do you think it has anything to do with what we talked about last night?" Ellen asked. She was very curious about what Ian thought of their discussion. Ian hesitated. He realized these discussions could run nonstop for days.

"Maybe we should limit the Chautauqua to evenings after dinner," he suggested. Ellen reluctantly agreed.

They shared a lazy morning with coffee. The sun peeped through for five minutes, and they both rejoiced. That reminded him of how he met his wife in Boulder in 1993. With a reminiscent smile, he told Ellen how it all came about.

His wife was a freshman at the University of Colorado that fall; Ian was just entering the Master of Fine Arts program. Both attended a large gathering of Native American artists and dancers on the Pearl Street mall in October. A fierce early afternoon storm moved in, and heavy rain began. Aztec dancers, led by a powerful Aztec shaman, performed a sun dance. The shaman stomped his feet and the downpour immediately stopped. Miraculously, the heavy dark clouds parted as hundreds watched in wonder. The sun was out for the rest of the afternoon. When the dancers drove the storm away, Ian was amazed and delighted. He turned to share that with the girl standing next to him. Their relationship sprouted in the magic of that moment.

Near 11:30, Ian and Ellen decided to concoct a late breakfast and get into this peaceful warm Sunday. There were reasons to feel hopeful. Eleven weeks had passed since the first eruption. This was the first time the sun had broken through. Maybe the weather would get warmer. Maybe the eruptions would stop. After brunch, Ian notched his walking stick for the eleventh time.

On cue, the sun reappeared and stayed out for the rest of the afternoon. "Ah! The energy of the Aztec dancers blesses us," Ian thought.

Taking advantage of the natural light, they headed outside to do chores. The outdoor thermometer read 35. They stayed out for hours, enjoying the sunshine. Maybe things really would get better now.

Or maybe not.

Waning sunlight drove them reluctantly back inside, back into the confined darkness. They hurriedly stoked the fire and lit the lamps in an effort to dispel the gloom; but darkness comes in many forms.

The 6 p.m. FEMA broadcast out of Nashville reported that an estimated fifteen million were now presumed dead in the Midwest. Over fifty million had been evacuated to the south below I-40 or to the east of I-75.

Now, seventy-nine days after the first eruption, it was estimated there was six feet of snow and ash covering South Dakota and Minnesota. As the ash crept south, FEMA ordered a mandatory evacuation for everyone north of I-80, from Ohio to Utah.

The FEMA report was followed by a presidential address. It was already mid-March and the volcano had erupted continuously for almost eighty days with no end in sight. The government was concerned that spring planting of grain crops might not occur in areas around the world affected by the ashfall, There could be serious food shortages. World surpluses of last year's grain crop would be depleted by late July.

"It's just what I said last night," Ellen reminded Ian. "And if the famine goes worldwide, there'll be no one who can come to our rescue."

Exhausted from an afternoon spent outside in the ash and depressed by the radio reports, neither had much energy to cook and little energy left to eat. They ate the remnants of last night's wonderful meal along with some homemade bread Ellen had retrieved from her car, which was now a refrigerator.

After the light dinner they stoked up the stove and settled in for their nightly sanity discussion. Ian started a small pot of tea, pondering Ellen's dilemma.

"So what you are saying is that a perfect storm came together around the fall of 1966. Sounds like you had millions of students at the front wave of the Baby Boom colliding with millions of hits of mind-altering psychedelics, producing millions of indescribable altered states of consciousness. Western civilization had no clue that these realms of awareness even existed. This was new territory.

"Interesting. You remember the Chinese movie, *Crouching Tiger, Hidden Dragon*? The spiritual student discovered the 'Endless Sorrow of Heaven' and realized his teacher was unaware that this place existed. Disconsolate, the student abandoned his intense spiritual practice. So, after you discovered that your mentors had no clue, you too must have been pretty pissed off!"

Ellen responded, "And we felt betrayed, then alienated. After 2500 years, how could Western culture not know this information? How could we miss something this big? There weren't even any books to read.* This is beyond clueless. It bordered on a conspiracy to suppress the nature of reality."

Stirring his pot of tea, Ian listened to her frustration and thought about how very differently his life had unfolded. It had been almost mythological. Since early childhood good consciousness teachers around him shifted his life toward a more right-brained, Eastern, indigenous model of existence. He was led down an experiential path that explored the inner workings of the mind.

---

*See Appendix A

Through mindfulness and meditation he learned techniques to control quantum conscious energy—and that rascal, ego.

"I'm sorry your struggle has been so intense with so few answers. Yesterday you said that after these experiences in 1966, you needed new and different mentors and you wondered where you could possibly find them. Those statements surprised me. What about the other 70% of humanity not in the Western world? For the past 4000 years they took a strikingly different path. Their cultures promoted consciousness. They learned to get high and then perfected it. Ancient Eastern religions and native peoples worldwide explored the inner workings of the mind. Their holy men and women figured out how to shut off the nonstop chatter of the ego. They became quiet, calm, and centered. Then they 'stopped the world'. From this calm place they experienced the many separate realities. They developed advanced meditation techniques to expand their awareness even more. Best of all, they mapped it out for all of us to see. They created a new, alternative, right-brained description of reality. Why the hell didn't you go there? That was exactly what you were looking for!"

Ellen scoffed. "Back then, we knew virtually nothing about the mysterious Orient and even less about the world's tribal people. After all, we lived in the 'occidental' world, where logical thought prevailed over superstitious tribal mumbo jumbo. For God's sake, for centuries we were told it was our duty, the 'White Man's Burden', to tame the savages, wherever they might slothfully lay about. And we did just that.

"Just look at the devastation the Spanish inflicted on the native peoples in the Americas. Who knows what information was lost in the Roman destruction of the Great Library at Alexandria? The Belgians, French, and Dutch enslaved the ancient kingdoms of Africa. Endless native massacres figured largely in the U.S. Manifest Destiny. Australian aborigines, who had held the thought pattern of the Dream World for 40,000 years, were killed for bounty. We've been such assholes!

"And don't get me started on the Inquisition! The Catholics. The Protestants. The burning of the witches. The message here was real clear:

'Live within the narrow left-brained bandwidth or you will be terminated!'"

"I spent some time in India with my husband. Did you know that England occupied India for 350 years? In all that time the Western world never heard about those ancient consciousness road maps created by both the Hindus and Buddhists. The English were too damned busy pillaging the countryside. Have you ever been to the British Museum? Greed blinded them, so they portrayed the people of India as dirty snake charmers who slept on beds of nails. 'A totally unimproveable race.' The keepers of those 4000-year-old consciousness maps would not be coming to our aid anytime soon!"

"Then who did come riding to your rescue?" Ian asked.

"Well, mostly we just muddled through. Then our English-major cohorts shared the writings of an earlier lost generation who had been alienated by Western excesses and the horrors of World War I. Reaching out from fifty years in our past, these writers mirrored our spiritual quests. Hesse, Tolkien, and Maugham became wildly popular in the late 1960s.

"They introduced us to Hinduism, Buddhism, India, China meditation, and spiritual seeking. *The Razor's Edge* showed us life in a Himalayan monastery. They opened up a whole new culture to us, one we never knew existed. Hesse used Western words to help us understand Eastern culture and thought. Slowly we became fellow travelers on the *Journey to the East.*

"Then in early 1968, the Beatles made a real Journey to the East to study meditation in India. Millions of people suddenly became interested in Eastern spirituality. These new/ancient belief systems did not allow the use of drugs to get high and offered us a path to move to higher consciousness."

Ian raised one eyebrow, clearly in confused disbelief. "It takes at least eight years of rigorous daily practices to become somewhat proficient in the use of conscious energy." He leaned forward. "But we're all so bored and addicted that we constantly hop from one thing to another. ADHD reigns supreme. I can't imagine anyone I know remaining focused on anything for more than a few minutes at a time, no matter what the reward. How did the practice of meditation work out for all these people?"

"You're right, it didn't work at all," she said. "We are an undisciplined lot. Virtually everyone I knew dropped out. They were too damned impatient. The process took too long. Hell, I've tried to understand this for fifty years. Apparently, you can only understand spirituality through experience. This is a real dilemma. If you can't logically understand the process—and you're unable to have the experience—how can you ever become a spiritual being?"

"Yeah." Ian shook his head. "It only looks like we've painted ourselves into a corner. However, maybe it's not logic or experience. Maybe it's genetic wiring burried in our junk DNA. Catastrophe can level the playing field. The puzzle pieces can then be reassembled around the junk DNA left waiting patiently. If I were a gambling man, I would always bet on the least obvious of the unintended solutions. I would always bet on junk DNA."

Ian paused; then he continued. "I forgot to tell you about the stag, didn't I?"

"What stag? Where did you see a stag?" Ellen asked.

"Well, on the day the volcano erupted I left my snowshoe class early and was trying to get south of the Mackinac Bridge, back into the Lower Peninsula. It got dark, ash was falling, the road was like a sheet of ice. I was only nine miles out from the bridge when I rounded a big sweeping curve—and there it was, standing in the roadway in front of me. The translucent apparition of a huge, eight-foot-tall, white-and-green-glowing stag. I hit the brakes and began to spin on the slippery ash. I slid into some trees by the side of the road and everything went black. I woke up in the hospital in St. Ignace with a severe concussion. The lady who took me to the hospital said she saw the whole curve bathed in greenish-white light, but she didn't see the stag. So what the hell was it? A ghost?"

Ian sat trance-fixed, eyes staring off beyond space-time, lost out there on that light-bathed Michigan curve. Ellen waited until Ian gradually came back to Illinois.

"Wow, what a great story! Thank you so much for sharing that with me. Clearly, that was a really weird thing to experience. I can't even imagine what the stag is, where it comes from, or what it wants.

"For what it's worth, I've noticed over the years that Spirit sometimes places seemingly unrelated images into our minds, hoping that we can rummage through the clutter and connect the dots. I'm not connecting the dots very well, because I'm a tired old woman halfway to bed.

"But it instantly struck me that at the very moment you were waxing philosophic about genetic unintended solutions and junk DNA, the story of the stag popped into your mind. If I were a gambling woman, I would place my bet on the stag.

"Ian, follow the stag."

Chapter 17

Day 80

Once again they slept huddled around the old woodstove. Ian awoke with sore lungs from coughing throughout the night. One day of working outside without the gas mask had seriously affected his breathing.

He thought about his son Gabe suffering with asthma in this wretched ash. But they were probably out of the ashfall within a couple of hours after leaving Dexter. Gabe would breathe much easier the farther south they drove.

Lost in thought about his family, Ian perked up at the smell of good, strong coffee permeating the air from the top of the woodstove. The sun came out, bathing the house once again with warmth and light. Ellen went around opening all the curtains. This was cause for great celebration. Two days in a row of glorious sunshine! Perhaps it's all over! Perhaps this is the end of this nightmare!

They turned on the radio to try to pick up a weather forecast. Would the sun stay out? Was this the end of the eruptions? But when the morning FEMA broadcast came on, the National Weather Service confirmed that the volcano continued to erupt, with no end in sight. A new frontal boundary had set up along the ashdome. This wall varied in height from ten to twenty miles, depending on the strength of the daily volcanic output. Scientists were uncertain of the dynamics of this boundary. From the beginning, aircraft had not been able to fly into or over the ash-dome, and the dense ash clouds obscured any satellite images of the ground.

The jet stream winds, blowing at 240 miles an hour, would dip to the ground at unpredictable intervals, inflicting historic devastation. When this happened, temperatures could plummet to 120 degrees below zero. For the last ten days the frontal boundary ran from Hannibal, Missouri, across Illinois toward Dansville. Scientists expressed concern that the cold jet-stream winds might collide with warm, moisture-laden air flowing north out of the

Gulf of Mexico. This collision of fronts would create an epic blizzard, depositing twenty to thirty feet of snow and ash, with hundred-foot drifts possible along the frontal boundary.

The FEMA report reiterated last night's depressing update of fifteen million dead and fifty million refugees evacuated below I-40. An estimated ten million people might still be trapped inside a fourteen-state bubble. FEMA appealed to citizens outside the bubble to assist the unfortunate shell-shocked survivors still trickling out. Ellen reached over and turned off the radio.

A heaviness hung in the air. Ellen stood up.

"Fifteen million people may have died all around us," she said, "but it is incumbent upon the living, we the unlucky ten million souls still trapped within the bubble, to enjoy this glorious sunshine while we can!"

They bundled up, went outside, and walked around slowly in the sunshine, trying to imbibe the last vestiges of "normal experience." Something so simple as the sight of shadows cast upon the ground. Shadows cast from sunshine! Something so simple as sunshine!

Ellen and Ian wandered, each lost in thought, reframing reality. Slowly time moved toward noon. Dark ominous snow clouds overcame the life-affirming sunshine. The temperature dropped precipitously. Light snow with a mix of ash began to fall.

They retreated inside to recreate the calm of another peaceful "civilized" afternoon. In the flurry created by the morning's bad news, they had forgotten to eat breakfast and now had no appetite for lunch. Ellen built a fire and they sat by the fireplace pushing away overwhelming thoughts of death. Impending death. That incessant behemoth continued its projectile vomiting of lethal ash, purging the parasites from the surface of the planet.

"Let's have some music!"

Ellen dug through her CD collection and found Mozart's Piano Concerto no. 21. She especially loved this piece, recalling her days as an art student watching foreign films with English subtitles.

The Swedish movie *Elvira Madigan* featured this concerto, and she had been strangely drawn to that movie. Thoughts of the tragic plight of the characters brought her back to her own reality.

"We aren't going to make it out of this alive, are we?" she blurted out suddenly.

The resigned acceptance of those who are doomed hung in the air for an eternity. She finally tried again: "I think we're gonna need some cookies and tea!"

Soon the soothing sounds of Mozart flowed through the room. Civilization returned. Ellen made a big pot of hot tea and brought out a large tin of wonderful Danish butter cookies left over from Christmas. An intricately knitted tea cozy and hand-thrown tea cups added the final touch.

Ian and Ellen sat quiet and absorbed, sliding through the drowsy mid-afternoon biologic lull. They did not notice the music had ended some time ago.

Late afternoon, Ian was startled awake by the chorus of his loud growling stomach and Ellen's explosive snoring. Except for the handful of butter cookies, they hadn't eaten anything all day. Ian moved quietly, trying not to disturb Ellen. After letting Cedar out the front door, he retrieved a package of sausage from the freezer and wrapped a couple of large potatoes in aluminum foil. He stoked up the dying fire and buried the potatoes in the glowing embers. Dinner would be ready soon.

Returning from outside, Cedar hastened past Ian and past a sleeping Ellen to his food dish. Growing darkness and the signs of food prep in a candlelit kitchen cued Cedar that his dinnertime was imminent. Ian entered the room to the sound of Cedar's loudly clicking toenails tapping out the ancient doggie food anticipation dance. Ian chuckled, remembering Arlo, his dog extraordinaire, dancing that same dance. Suddenly Ellen burst into the kitchen to retrieve Cedar's dish. Pavlov's clicking had sounded, and the groggy but trainable human had immediately responded. Cedar—human whisperer extraordinaire.

Two hours passed. They had shaken off the snow and ash and death and hunger of the day. Everyone was sated yet alert. Nice combination of carbs, protein, and sleep. The sanity session for the evening could now commence.

Two nights ago Ian had agreed to help Ellen make sense of her confusing consciousness experience. Now he began the discussion.

"These conversations have helped me recall some important experiences. For thirty years I've been trying to connect the dots within this vast hodgepodge called spirituality. It covers everything from Yogananda to Ouija boards. There's a lot going on here, but I think we can piece together some answers to your questions.

"Let's enter this maze where you are most perplexed. From what I understand, you ingested weapons-grade, mind-altering drugs and skyrocketed out into deep inner space. You didn't know where you were...how you got there...or how to get back home. When you landed back in this reality, you faced total confusion.

"Denial of those separate realities was not an option for you. The hippie-doped-up-freak path would leave you wasted and burned out, devoid of answers. No, these glimpses into multiple universes demanded exploration and answers. You wanted answers that could be replicated and explained. But how? Your repeated explorations with mind-altering drugs created even more confusion. And your failure to comprehend this journey has haunted you for fifty years. So here's the first clue."

Though Ian had only briefly discussed the extent of his spiritual training, Ellen had surmised there was more, much more. She scooched forward to the edge of her seat in eager anticipation.

Ian smiled and began his story. In early 1967 his brother's repeated forays into altered consciousness were also dependent on potent drugs. While he could blast out into other realms, he was not in control of the journey. Like Ellen, he could not replicate the experience without drugs.

Then one night the fates intervened. He arrived two hours late at a weekly "consciousness exploration gathering." The others were well along on their journeys to separate realities. His brother decided just to sit this one out, to observe.

The warm glow of a single large candle floated in the midst of the pitch-black room. The familiar comforting smell of jasmine incense blended with the fading hint of someone's reefer madness. *Surrealistic Pillow* played in the background. Within this subcultural womb the embryonic journey had begun.

Ian's brother slowly drifted off into right brain. The squirrel-cage din of ego grew fainter and fainter. Silence, empty peaceful silence. From that space the candle came into hyperfocus, enveloped in nimbus. The center of his forehead tingled, bringing the candle into even sharper focus. Then a fierce, concentrated, vibrating cone of energy filled his forehead. The world stopped. Hours later he returned to a near-empty room.

Ian paused for a moment to reach over and grab a handful of cookies. Ellen seized that moment to ask a question.

"When your brother came back from his high, did he know where he had been, or how he had gotten there?" Then she added, "He probably experienced a contact high, and how is that any different from a drug-induced high?"

Ian chomped down on his cookies and continued.

"No, it wasn't a contact high. At first my brother didn't understand what had happened. But these guys were all Explorers of a new frontier.* He told them what he'd experienced. It was just fragments, bits and pieces; but using what we now understand to be mindfulness, they began to assemble the clues.

"Clearly, the first clue was that...*you did not need drugs to get high.* And this high was very different from anything he'd ever seen or experienced. It was not ingested; it came from within him. It moved out into right brain, shut down the ego, and opened up a fierce, blasting, unknown energy. It didn't make sense. What in bloody hell caused this?

"Trying for any kind of correlation, the Explorers treated this like data. They listed every type of high they knew about. People

*See Appendix B

called anything that wasn't normal waking consciousness a high. Getting drunk or huffing airplane glue was considered getting high.

"The stronger psychedelics, like LSD and peyote, blasted you out of left brain ego up into the ego-based astral plane. Ellen, that's where you went to—just another nearby hell zone. There's nothing spiritual or mystical about those highs, because *you are still trapped in another version of left brain ego.* Getting shit-faced, fucked up, wasted or addicted to meth, painkillers, opiates, whatever, is not getting high."

Ellen got up, poured some tea water, and let Cedar out for a potty break. When she returned, she asked Ian, "So what makes a spiritual high different? I still don't understand."

Ian responded, "It's a relaxation high that shifts to a super-focused meditation high. It takes place over in right brain. Probably the most important thing my brother and the Explorers realized was that all those other drug and alcohol trips began in left brain and stayed linked to left brain. This was different! All the real consciousness action is in right brain and beyond. It doesn't involve hanging out with all that drama in left-brained ego.

"Think about it. Two nights ago you condemned Western civilization and its left-brain culture. Well, this linear, logical culture is run by accountant types who can't even get into right brain. The greed, the drama, the hopelessness, they all fester in this culture. It's all Ego. And it gets worse. **The Operating System for <u>All of Creation</u> Is Ego**."

Ellen interrupted, "So you mean like when Lucifer was cast out of heaven? Heaven is part of creation, right? That was an ego war, right?"

"Yes, that's true. The 'Stairway to Heaven' passes right through those astral zones. Although the One permeates all, you won't find God sitting on a throne in heaven.

"But, there is a way to find God," Ian said. "The ego operating system is difficult, but not impossible, to overcome. Unfortunately, Western folks don't even know the operating system exists. Even sadder, they don't know it's just the *default* system. But without ego, we mere mortals wouldn't even bother to feed ourselves or our young, or defend the nest from intruders.

"Thousands of years ago the Hindus and Buddhists discovered techniques to override the operating system. Those guys were the *first cosmic hackers.* If you could transcend the operating system, you could transcend all of creation. Were we imprinted with the ability to hack this system—and the desire to use it?" Ian paused to ponder this new idea.

"In fact, that's just what happened to you in India," he continued. "When you took all those potent drugs in the '60s, your entire trip stayed within the ego astral boundaries. You would not meet God there. But in India, the rotating mandalas and the sounds of the Tibetan bowls, without drugs, moved your point of consciousness into far right brain where ego does not venture. The endless chatter and the constant whirling ideas stopped. Egoless, the **God Gates*** in very far right brain could now open…to accept you home."

Silence enveloped the room. Ellen did not quite know how to respond to that last statement. Consternation filled her face.

"Okay, okay, time out. Too much bewildering information. Let me see if I heard you correctly.

"I was sort of with you through that left brain stuff—and not being able to get to God through all that ego–astral crap. But, then you talked about 'moving my point of consciousness' into far right brain. What in the hell does that mean? How does that happen? And what the hell are 'God Gates'?"

Ian took a moment to gather his thoughts. Finally, he responded.

"Well, you've asked me several questions here. Let's sort through them. Through intense meditation and concentration you can draw your consciousness together into one single focused point. That single focused point is what Castaneda called the 'Assemblage Point.' Zen Buddhists call it 'Point of Consciousness.' A disciplined practitioner can move this assemblage point anywhere

*See Appendix C

inside the body, on this planet, out of this dimension, or beyond. It's amazing!

"If you want to see an incredible demonstration of this, watch the 1993 Bill Moyer's video on Chinese medicine. There's a segment on martial arts where a Chinese Chi master moves his point of consciousness six feet beyond the end of his hand. He then sends a blast of Chi out to this assemblage point, knocking down several advanced students. Throughout this event, Bill Moyers protests vigorously that this just can't be. Humans don't emit blasts of energy. This defies all the known Western laws of energy." Ian paused and sadly shook his head.

Ellen observed, "Okay, this is easy if you are a Zen master, but what about the rest of us undisciplined folks?"

"Good point. You've probably noticed that I've repeatedly expressed disdain for ego. The ego is a very strong and harmful adversary, causing great suffering for all of humanity. Buddha was so concerned with ego and suffering that the effort to free all human beings from endless suffering became the primary goal of Buddhist practice.

"That three-volume set of *A Course in Miracles* sitting over there on your bookshelf was divinely downloaded into Western civilization. It also teaches us about the pervasive nature of ego and how to overcome its stranglehold grip. Just think, a manual that teaches Westerners how to override the operating system!"

Sheepishly, she admitted, "Yeah, but those books are so confusing. I get bogged down. It just doesn't make sense. Sometimes it takes me an hour to read one paragraph."

"Whenever that happens to you, it's always because your assemblage point is far over into left brain. Look, you are an artistic right-brain creative person. I know, I'm an artist, too. It's almost painful to be in left brain. And so slow, like wading through molasses. No, the *Course* was not meant to be read from left brain, even if that's how the educational system trained us to read. *A Course in Miracles* downloads were not just for the authors. Shift over to right brain and you will get downloads. Some that last almost an hour. Believe me, everything will be quite clear, not confusing at all."

Ellen abruptly stood up and headed for the kitchen, toward the call of the "sanity discussion happy hour." Soon she would not feel quite so overwhelmed. While pouring her scotch, she shouted from the kitchen, "You keep talking about downloads. What are downloads?"

"Oh. A direct communication from the Universe. Sometimes it comes down as a complete package—sight, sound, smell, the whole bit. Sometimes it's just a phrase, a message for someone else. And sometimes it's a total understanding of something you never knew before—an epiphany, a revelation."

Ellen wandered back into the room and handed him a scotch.

"Thanks. I think I get it," she said uncertainly. "Now, where were we?"

"You wondered how undisciplined folks could go about learning to shift their Point of Consciousness. After all, getting past the endless brain chatter is difficult. Do you remember the sudden popularity of those biofeedback machines in the early 1970s? The ones with all the different types of brain waves and their hertz frequencies? Understanding those frequencies is key to helping you understand how to shift your assemblage point.

"I can't remember the brain wave frequencies, but if you're in the normal daily living mode, your brain is operating at about 60 hertz. You gradually move from there, through creativity down to heavy relaxation. Deep meditation occurs at a really low rate, like under 10 hertz. Oh, yeah, here's something interesting. The frequency of the Earth's magnetic field is around the same as deep meditation.*

"There's a huge drop in brain wave activity between a normal waking state and a deep meditative state. Whenever artists become creative they move their assemblage points into the creativity parts of right brain. You should see the work the *National Geographic* channel did on this! Large portions of the

*See Appendix D

brain actually shut down. As an art student engrossed in creativity, your brain waves probably fell to around 25 hertz. From there it would be very easy to drop down into the deep meditation zone. You were almost home! Instead, you did the opposite. You used potent drugs that shot you back over into left brain ego and way up into the higher hertz range. That wasn't where you wanted to go!

"However, when you were in India in the ancient monastery, that powerful experience was actually your artistic right brain kicking in—absorbing colors, shapes, and sounds. Your hertz rate was dropping. Then, at the right moment, those Hindu hackers flooded you with 4000-year-old intonation chanting that resonated at a deep meditation level. That created your 'peak experience.'

"Tones and sounds and music can create various hertz frequencies. Ancient languages like Sanskrit even had words that could alter your state of consciousness.* If I played the Pachelbel Canon when you were in a normal waking state, the slow moving but sequential music would be soothing and peaceful. But if I played that same music when you were in a meditative state, you would come after me screaming in pain and begging me to stop. Try it sometime. Be a consciousness Explorer. Explore moving your point of consciousness."

Ian apologized for the extended monologue. Enthusiastically, he joined Ellen in the "sanity discussion happy hour." Soon the single malt would work its magic. He would close out the nightly discussion with one more quick—and he promised it would be quick—story about his brother using his point of consciousness to travel to Machu Picchu.

In February, 1974, a woman his brother met at his gallery had traveled to South America to visit Machu Picchu. Late one Saturday afternoon, after closing the gallery at 4 p.m., he took a six-foot painting of the *Grape Woman of the Andes* and set it up in front of him. Within minutes he had disappeared into the picture. When he returned to his body, it was only 4:30. But it was totally dark and deserted outside, which he thought strange. Then he realized

*See Appendix E

it was 4:30 a.m. He had been "gone" over twelve hours. He remembered being in Machu Picchu and consciously "joining" with his friend all night. Within a week, she sent a letter confirming his presence that night. He was stunned.

His point of consciousness had traveled thousands of miles and had "joined" with another person for many hours.

Ellen's eyes opened wide and she exclaimed, "I've heard that story before! That exact story! From my younger sister Katie. Over forty years ago, she was in Ann Arbor, met this gallery owner and later, while she was down in South America, joined with him all night across space and time. She even wrote me a letter about all of this from Peru. I've still got the letter in the attic. I've got to find it. Oh, my God! Your brother knew my sister!"

Day 81

Ellen had rummaged in the attic until after 1 a.m. Unsuccessful, she moved the search for Katie's letter down to the second-floor storage area. Cold and exhaustion ended her search around 3 a.m., and she collapsed under a pile of blankets between the dog and the woodstove.

Ian was up, coffee in hand, by 7 a.m. He had not yet told Ellen about his plans to finish their sanity discussions and get back on the road. Somewhere out there beyond the ashdome his family was waiting for him. Ellen's late night search and her probable late morning awakening would provide the quiet he needed to figure out what to do next. He pored over his maps.

About a week ago he had entered Illinois on Route 16. Miles of flat open land offered no shelter from the bitter cold, sandblasting wind. He was having second thoughts about heading directly west into the teeth of the jet stream. I-57 was only about fifteen miles west of Ellen's farm in Ashmore. If he headed south, within a hundred miles there would be only a light dusting of ash on the ground. His pace could quicken to twenty-five miles a day. Within two weeks he could be crossing into Missouri, 120 miles from Memphis and I-40. The goal was to get to I-40 and head west toward New Mexico.

Although he desperately wanted to find his family, he dreaded returning to his dangerous slippery trek. The last few days had transported him back to life before the volcano. Now Ian just wanted things to return to normal. He thought about praying for a ride on a bus all the way to New Mexico. Cedar interrupted that thought with a petition for a potty run.

While Ian stood on the porch watching the dog and thinking about the bus, sunlight momentarily engulfed Ellen's car.

"Yes. Ellen's car. We can take her car to New Mexico." He would not have to walk the 200 miles down I-57 to Missouri. They could drive! Startled by Ian's sudden exclamation, Cedar started barking. Ian calmed the dog down and continued working through this idea.

His mind was racing. Ellen needed to get out of here anyway. If the volcano continued to erupt, the roads would drift over and become totally impassable. She would die here. She needed to evacuate with Cedar. Ian needed a ride. The bridges into Missouri were still open. Driving at 20 miles an hour, they could be out of the ash within five hours. Then they could travel at 50 miles an hour. Ellen had two five-gallon cans of gas in the barn. Her car got good gas mileage. With the gas left in the car plus the two gas cans, they could make it to Oklahoma.

Ellen and Cedar could stay with his family in New Mexico until all this blew over. That settled that! By nightfall they could be in Missouri. No matter what happened next, he refused to continue walking west. He was finished with that damned volcano.

Cedar bounded back into the house straight to Ellen, who was sitting next to the woodstove nursing a cup of coffee. The shouting and barking had jolted her into the morning.

"What was going on out there? Is something wrong? More refugees?"

Ian laughed. "No, Cedar and I were just talking and got a bit too exuberant," he replied.

Ellen had spotted the maps on the couch and hesitantly asked, "This is about you leaving us, isn't it?" A deafening silence filled the room. Tears welled up in Ellen's eyes. "Please don't leave me here. Take me with you." As strong as she was, she was still terrified of being abandoned, trapped in this house, left to die alone. For a second, Ian flashed back to when he left the elderly couple on the farm in Leesburg. No, he would not let Ellen perish here.

"It's going to be all right. Cedar and I have really good news! We came up with a solution this morning out in the yard." Ian repeated the entire newly-minted plan to use her car to drive all of them to New Mexico. They would wait out the eruption there.

"Ellen, ten days ago there was only one inch of ash on the ground here in Ashmore. Just a hundred miles south of here, right now, there is no ash on the ground. The time has come for you and Cedar and me to evacuate, head south and get the hell out of the path of this crazy volcano! Are you okay with that?"

"I'm okay," Ellen replied. "But I kept hoping this was going to be over. I waited too long. I should have left a couple of months ago with Katie." She gasped. "Oh, my sister Katie! We have to pick up my sister. It's her sixty-fifth birthday tomorrow, and she's all alone at the family homestead just south of Mattoon. There's plenty of room for her to come with us. I haven't seen her in a month, but I can guarantee you she'll come. Especially when she learns about you and your brother. Our families have known each other for over forty years. This plan will work! We're getting out of here. We're finally getting out of here." Now Ellen was excited.

Ian didn't have the heart to interrupt her sudden ecstasy. He would have liked to tell her that this is how it feels to shift your assemblage point suddenly. Just three minutes ago she was distraught, inconsolable, gasping for air. Now, her brain was lighting up in the "happy place." She had shifted her consciousness to a totally different location in a split second. Western people unknowingly do this every day. He just couldn't tell her that now.

For the next hour the two ecstatic evacuees sat around the woodstove drinking coffee and planning their imminent escape.

Earlier owners of Ellen's farm had built a secure waterproof tornado shelter under the floor of the tractor shed. Virtually all of her smaller valuable belongings had already been neatly packed in the shelter. Looters would not bother with the larger antique pieces. Ian explained that "overnight uninvited guests" only wanted food, ammo, and water. No one wanted to lug around heavy items for hundreds of miles. The more plywood and barricades she put up at doors and windows, the more damage looters would inflict on her house. Ian, after all, was offering the advice of a professional looter, once arrested. Ian and Ellen worked through all the last-minute evacuation details, then ate a hearty lunch.

Ellen was hell-bent on finding Katie's letter from Machu Picchu before she left. After lunch she went back upstairs to continue her search. About 2 p.m. a yelp of success pierced the air, followed by Ellen bounding down the stairs clutching two envelopes. In one hand, the letter from Katie; in the other, a copy of *The Periodical Lunch.*

She read Ian the letter from Katie. The letter confirmed exactly what Ian had described, but from the Machu Picchu end of the experience. She described the arrival of his brother's energy field, and the twelve-hour merging of energy at that holy Peruvian power spot. But the letter went on. Walking down the trail out of Machu Picchu, she "accidentally" encountered a local native with blazing eyes and fierce personal power. Further down the steep trail he suggested they take an easier route. He touched the rock wall bordering the trail and the rock opened. Clearly, he was a shaman with great power. They entered a series of ancient, well-traveled tunnels that led down the mountain. Later they came back out through the rock to the trail. She then noticed a dog standing on the trail behind them. When she turned back around the shaman had disappeared. She whipped back to look at the dog but it, too, had disappeared. What an amazing 24 hours. The letter ended there.

Ian responded, "Wow, I've never heard that part of the story, about the shaman and the tunnels. You know, it makes perfect sense, though. The natives in that region have always told stories about those tunnels, but nobody in Western civilization would believe them."

Ellen said, "I know. It's really strange. Katie swore repeatedly it actually happened. We have to get to her house so you can meet her. My God, you're practically family. I can't believe this! Oh, look what else I found upstairs. *The Periodical Lunch.* Inside is a full-page ad for your brother's art gallery, Jacob's Ladder Gallery in Kerrytown. What the hell is this guy with the slingshot?"

"Okay, that guy is *Slingshot Man.* The original drawing hung in the gallery for quite a while before they decided to use it in an ad. Today, probably, most Western folk would recognize the eye in the drawing as the third eye, even if they don't have a clue what that means. But rewind back to the late '60s, before the Beatles went to India. Had you ever heard of the third eye or chakras?"

"No, never," she replied.

"Well, neither had my brother. You probably know now that there are seven major energy portals, called chakras, located along the spine. Each of the upper chakras serves as a vortex to focus energy coming into or flowing out of the body.

"The fourth, or heart chakra, sits on the spine near the heart. The sixth chakra, or the third eye, is in the center of the forehead above the eyes. The seventh chakra is in the crown of the head. It is through the seventh chakra that we move beyond time, space and creation and merge with the one. All personal awareness is gone. The separation is gone. I saw your copy of the Moody Blues *In Search of the Lost Chord.* That painting on the cover depicts a seventh-chakra energy burst. The mandala on the inside of the album helps to accelerate your focus.

"*Slingshot Man,* on the other hand, shows the moment just before a sixth-chakra energy flow. After fierce tingling in the forehead, a blast of pure cosmic energy is emitted out of the third eye. Two people with eyes locked would be joined as one, intertwined yet still separate."

Over the next couple of hours Ian discussed chakras, Jacob's Ladder Gallery, and *Slingshot Man* with Ellen. He told her about the many successful "joinings" the Explorers had experienced using the fourth, sixth, and seventh chakras. And how finally, by 1974, the Explorers wanted to cast out a cosmic net to see who would appear. They placed that *Slingshot Man* ad in *The Periodical Lunch* as bait.*

Suspicions were quickly confirmed. Others were out there waiting, patiently. Others not from here.

By 4 p.m. Ian had become so focused explaining these experiences that his eyes no longer blinked. His words had begun to take on a kind of power. He recognized the aroused energy of kundalini. Breathing stilled. Heart rates dropped. Hertz rates plummeted. Soon both felt the fierce tingle in the center of their foreheads. Conversation ceased. Ellen's eyes came into sharp focus, her head enveloped in a divine, foggy nimbus. Then the slingshot was released.

The cosmic circuit opened between them. A palpable concentrated blast of cosmic energy blew out from both of their foreheads. Pure white light, brighter than a billion suns, poured freely from the heavens into their heads. Their merged energy fields intertwined in the dance of joining. They touched the Oneness of God, felt the great bliss, the ineffable flood of peace that came with the unexpected release from the prison of separation. Words could not describe this great, prolonged, cosmic orgasm of God love. Ian and Ellen sat motionless for three hours, locked in this powerful gaze. They focused on some invisible point halfway between them and infinity. They would not blink for hours.**

Cedar needed desperately to go out but would not interrupt them. Slowly, the Kundalini loosened its grip. Slowly, Ian and Ellen disentangled from the joining…emerging out of the light into a very cold and very dark living room.

There would not be much sleep again tonight.

---

*See Appendix F
**See Appendix G

Chapter 18

Day 82

Ellen's venerable but dependable four-wheel-drive "Snow Snuffy" fishtailed down her driveway, slid sideways across Route 16, and came to rest with one wheel hanging suspended over the ditch. The greatly anticipated cross-country journey to New Mexico had almost ended immediately in an out-of-control collision with her cement mailbox.

Within minutes Ian had righted the teetering vehicle and was headed west toward Katie's. The expedition was underway.

For hours after last night's quantum energy flow, left-brained planning was not on the table. Preparations for the hastily thrown together evacuation plan had begun early today, around first light. By 9:30, the car was filled with personal belongings, two five-gallon containers of gas, canned food, water, dog food, and some frozen meat to share at Katie's. An assortment of tasty leftovers provided an ample breakfast and on-the-road snacks. Within one hundred miles down I-57 they could shop at grocery stores and gas stations. They could withdraw money from their bank accounts. He might even be able to telephone or text his wife to let her know company was coming. Life just might return to near normal. Soon!

Two weeks had passed since the second major eruption of the Yellowstone volcano. The spray pattern of the volcano was enlarging, moving farther south as eruptions continued. Ashmore sat several hundred miles south of Minneapolis. The ashfall had taken a couple of months to work its way down to the middle of Illinois. County road crews here were just now learning to cope with the multiplicity of problems engendered by volcanic ash.

Constant 40-mile-an-hour winds from the jet stream merged with incessant ashfall to glaze the road. Well-intentioned daily plowing had only made matters worse: Route 16 was Zamboni slick. Ian, however, offered the skills and experience of a veteran volcanic ash driver, only once hospitalized. He guided the car down the center of the road toward Charleston. They encountered no traffic this morning, but road conditions warranted speeds well below ten miles an hour. The twenty-five mile trip to Katie's would probably take four hours.

About a half hour into the white-knuckle journey, the scenery offered more rolling hills and trees. The abnormal endless monochromatic expanses, combined with the abnormally slow speed, had disrupted Ellen's spatial memory. Nothing looked familiar. She finally realized they were approaching the Embarras River and remembered the steep hill rising up on the other side. That hill would be too treacherous to climb, even with her four-wheel-drive. They might forever be stranded on the bridge at the bottom of the river valley.

She suggested they detour north and use a more gently sloping nearby bridge. Within minutes large "Road Closed" signs confirmed Ellen's excellent observation. They detoured north, crossed that bridge when they came to it, and traveled down through the center of Charleston, rejoining Route 16. One car-dodging, fishtailing hour later, they passed the Coles County airport. Now they were only one mile from I-57. Ellen recommended a shortcut out around Mattoon to the old family homestead near Lake Paradise.

I-57 was one of the last remaining evacuation routes southbound out of Chicago. After they picked up Katie, this would also be their escape route south into Missouri and beyond. Ian stopped Ellen's car on the viaduct passing over I-57 to reconnoiter driving conditions on the freeway below. Despite a cleanly plowed roadway, they observed only one vehicle fleeing south. Ian had expected more. He used this pit stop to raise the hood and clean out built-up ash in the air filter. Ellen and Cedar relieved themselves at the rear of the car. Fresh water and snacks all around improved the mood. The expedition could now continue on toward Katie.

Just before three o'clock they sideslipped into the driveway of the old homestead. Ellen reached over and put her hand on the horn.

"I've got to honk my signal to Katie. We have a special honk we use to identify ourselves. Mine is two longs, a pause, then one quick short." She honked the message. "It's Morse code," she added quite proudly. "It means 'me'. We had to come up with something, with all these refuges afoot, and all."

They were barely out of the car when Katie came bounding down the front steps. Today was her sixty-fifth birthday. She knew her sister would come. Her big sister would never forget, even if the ash had cut off all communication.

Ellen and Katie flew into each other's arms.

"Katie, you're alive!"

"Ellen, you're alive! Thank God!"

They hugged each other, sobbing.

Ian was suddenly immersed in the scene last summer of a female cardinal lying dead on the dirt road in front of his house. It was one of the female cardinals from the nine mating pairs he had fed throughout that devastating polar vortex winter. Now, she lay dead along the road. Somewhere out there in the trees, the mate waited as it gradually got darker and darker, not knowing if his loved one had suffered some cruel death. Never to return. Not knowing. Waiting. He called for her for days. Dying changes everything.

That was how fiercely the two sisters hugged. That was how these times had devolved into the primal. Not knowing who would return this time. No telegrams. No calls. No texts. Never finding out.

Holding Katie, knowing she was still alive, allowed Ellen to loosen her desperate grip on her sister.

Pent-up terror from today's twenty-five mile ash trip finally released. Dammed up thoughts cascaded down the spillway and out her mouth.

"Oh, Katie, this is Ian. You knew his brother. The guy at Machu Picchu. You know, Jacob's Ladder Gallery? Ann Arbor. He's practically family! We've had sanity discussions. We brought food. We're all going to New Mexico to stay with his wife and kids. We brought booze! Happy birthday, sweetie! Happy sixty-fifth birthday!"

Ellen stopped, confused by the bewildered look on Katie's face.

"What?" Katie asked. "We need to slow down here. Let's get you unloaded and get back inside. Then we can sort through all of this."

The second eruption had increased ashfall and diminished daylight. Temperatures decreased further. By 3:30, brutal polar darkness had descended on the last Sherpas schlepping boxes through the front door.

Certain that her sister would be coming today, Katie had kept the usual obligatory pot of coffee warm on the wood stove. For a few minutes they all stood around the stove warming their insides and outsides, discussing the harsh life-threatening climate changes. When they all began to feel a little warmer and more comfortable, Ian introduced himself.

"Well, first things first. After hearing about you for decades, I want to introduce myself properly. I'm Ian Cameron. I've been slogging through this ash from my home near Ann Arbor for the last seven weeks. I ran into Ellen by accident, while she was out cleaning sculptures in her yard. I'm an art professor and a refugee trying to get to my family in New Mexico. We started talking about art, which led to scotch—which led to the nature of consciousness. Ellen wanted to come here for your birthday, so here we are. Happy birthday!"

Katie thanked them profusely for risking life and limb to get to her on this day. The greatest present of all was their company. Alone twenty-four hours a day for the past several weeks, she had been almost paralyzed by fear. Anticipation of the roof collapsing or a late-night home invasion overrode all normal sleep patterns. You can only stay awake so long. Her nerves were frayed. Now there were three adults and a large barking watchdog to guard the fortress. Tonight she would sleep. But first, the party.

Ellen had packed all of her frozen steaks, a bag of potatoes, canned asparagus, several bottles of wine, three bottles of scotch, and a box of brownie mix. After dinner, though, they would not feast on Katie's infamous brownies. The volcano had disrupted the supply chain for the "magic." Regular brownies would have to do.

Ellen broke out the wine. Serious food prep could now commence. Two glasses of wine in, the birthday girl finally broached the subject of Ian's brother.

"Ellen mentioned Ann Arbor and Jacob's Ladder Gallery and your brother and Machu Picchu. Yes, I do remember that night at Machu Picchu, but, you know, that was so long ago, over forty years ago. And I do remember him and the Gallery. It's strange what we keep in our memories, but I remember that weird picture of the guy with the third eye, and that six-foot-tall life-sized painting of the grape lady. So, he's your brother, huh? Isn't it strange that fate would bring you to our door after all these years?"

Potatoes and meat were nearing perfection in the wood stove. The wine flowed freely. Ellen brought out Katie's forty-year-old letter describing that night in Machu Picchu. Katie recounted the longer version of the story, complete with the disappearing shaman and the dog. She swore once again this story was absolutely true.

These old memories melded with more wine, then steaks, to obscure time and space momentarily behind Katie's barred door. The living room at the old homestead began to change, assuming the energy of a portal to earlier, more conscious times. Foreheads tingled all around. Images of a long ago afternoon in Findhorn wavered in and out of view, seeking sanctuary within this space-time. Findhorn? Why? Was their conjoined energy attracting attention from somewhere, somewhen, someone, or something? But what?

Tingling intensified in all three foreheads. Images of some future afternoon at the Great Kiva came sharply into focus. Three women sat immersed in the joining energy of the 300-foot kiva. The full sensory hologram then faded from view.

Two discrete moments in time escaped the bonds of their space-time...and sought refuge in that moment in Katie's living room. Ian's mind could only record this for later analysis. Katie looked inquisitively at Ellen.

"Did you see that?" she asked. "Who were those three women?"

"I don't know, but damn, that was weird. I don't have a clue. Ian, did you see that? They looked like they were sitting on the floor of a huge amphitheater. It's like here merged with there. You could see here and yet you could see there at the same time. What's going on?"

Ian paused to collect his thoughts, then cautiously proceeded.

"I know what just happened, but I have no idea why or what it meant. I've experienced the blended sensory screen several times before, but always when I was with my brother. So I just figured it was him being his usual weird. Weird things happen around that dude all the time. But this is different. He isn't here.

"But those three women? I don't know who they are, or when they are, but that has to be the Great Kiva we've been trying to build for years. Through some very wondrous strange circumstances my brother was downloaded with the plans for a huge, 300-foot-wide meditation kiva. I was at his home in Boulder in June of 1999 when we started construction on the six-foot circular scale model of the kiva. Months later we discovered that the very evening we glued the first two layers together, a crop circle was laid down in Morcott, England. It was 300 feet wide with the exact same seating dimensions. It was full scale! For three years, each June, the kiva was laid out at Morcott with additions and ingenious designs, like a 300-foot suspended roof.* Somebody out there wanted this built.

"I recognize the layout! The three women we saw

*See Appendix H

were sitting on the main performance floor of the kiva, near the sipapu…the place of emergence. Holy Jesus! The kiva got built! Somewhere out there in the future!"

Ian could hardly contain himself. He paced back and forth across Katie's living room, in a good way.

"It got built! You guys saw it! It got built!"

He paused to pace again. Ellen used this interlude to let Cedar out the front door, and to reload her wine glass.

"Okay," Ian eventually continued. "I've got to quiet myself down and think about this. You both wondered what just happened here. Overriding the operating system changes everything. If you move beyond space and time, beyond the linear and the sequential, then pasts, presents, and futures can all overlap and merge.

"When the old forehead begins to tingle, it's not strange to see energies begin to flock together. It's not strange to have the conjoined energy of those women in the kiva seek out empathetic energies. To be drawn here. After all, Katie joined with my brother at Machu Picchu. And Ellen, I joined with you in a third-eye energy flow. Despite our circumstances buried under the ashdome—the joining power is strong here. Power stalks us."

Ian stopped reluctantly. What else could be said? Despite his urge to explore their cosmic holographic experiences, they needed to get the hell out of here—now! Back to left-brain downer reality.

Ian and Ellen then laid out their proposed exit strategy down I-57 and beyond to New Mexico, seeking safe harbor in the desert. By now Katie did not want to spend one more hour alone. There was safety in numbers, and she was ready to leave with them tomorrow morning.

Unfortunately, there might be one small problem to work out in this evacuation plan. Every morning Katie listened to briefings from the Missouri Emergency Broadcast Network. She was unsure, but she thought the governor of Missouri had closed all the bridges across the Mississippi about four days ago. That would dramatically alter their evacuation route. So tomorrow morning they would listen to the broadcast. She hoped she was wrong.

Ian prayed she was wrong. He could not trek one more mile through this ash.

Day 83

The daily Missouri Emergency Broadcast began precisely at 9 a.m. The date, time, and day of the week were announced at the beginning of each broadcast. For many this "time stamp" represented the only consistent order amidst continuing chaos and social disintegration, not unlike the BBC World Service, still persistently broadcasting to the far-flung reaches of the empire.

The announcer updated the civil unrest at the I-57 bridge crossing into Missouri. Citing public safety concerns, the governor of Missouri had closed all bridges across the Mississippi south of St. Louis. Thousands of cars, fleeing Chicago in the mandatory evacuation, were still trapped in a traffic jam at the I-57 bridge. Most of the cars had run out of gas. There was no gasoline to be had within a hundred miles of the bridge. Although there was no ash below I-64, the cold was brutal. People had run their cars to stay warm. Many froze to death when the gas ran out.

National Guard troops were spread too thin across Illinois to get there quickly. Thousands of vehicles now needed to be towed off the road. For two days FEMA had advised evacuees of the unfolding crisis, saying they should head east and avoid all southbound routes.

Desperate curses exploded out of Ian.

"Damn it! God fucking damn it! Stop it! I fucking can't take this any more. I can't go back out hiking in that God-damned ash!"

Katie shut off the radio. Ian paced, and not the good kind.

"Ellen, how did we miss this? This happened after I came to Ashmore. How? What happened?"

Ellen grimaced. "Well, we only ever listened to the very beginning of each FEMA broadcast. After they told us how many more millions had died, and how many more millions were still missing, and how we could get covered by hundred-foot snow drifts, we always turned off the radio. We never knew."

Ian added, "And that's why we didn't see a mass exodus on I-57 when we stopped on the viaduct. Everybody else knew not to go south."

"Well, crap. What do we do now?" Ellen asked.

"Damned if I know. I think first we need to pay better attention to these broadcasts. Like listening all the way through, for starters. We are at a critical juncture right now. We need good information and clearheaded thinking. Let's look at the maps."

Katie volunteered information. "For these last few weeks there was nothing to do, so I started gathering information to keep from feeling lonely. I figured that when Ellen got here we'd make a break for it, head south out of the ash, and get to a safe place where we could weather out the volcano. I figured we'd need to know things like ashfall totals, gas, food, banking, and where we can use our cell phones. It all needs to be organized yet, but I've got the information."

Ian and Ellen were ecstatic at this piece of good fortune. After hugs and high fives all around, Katie added, "Hey, I was bored. This kept me busy."

Katie brought out a large artist sketch pad and easel. For the next two hours, they tried to formulate a working battle plan.

It became obvious they were getting trapped here. They needed to get out now. North or west would keep them under the ashdome. After that hair-raising drive from Ashmore, they knew what the roads were like to the east. And south, the bridges were closed. Much debate later, they decided that the only route still open was to get south another hundred miles. Get below the ash line. Then they could travel east, skimming along the bottom of Illinois, Indiana, and Ohio.

Katie pointed out the only problem with this strategy. For roughly 200 miles around the ashdome there was an area now called the "Marginal Zone." It ran along the Appalachian

Mountains to the east and followed I-40 to the south. Although there was no ground ash in the zone, most grocery stores and gas stations were closed. Heavy airborne ash had affected phone and electrical lines, cell phone towers, and the internet. Credit and debit cards could not be electronically processed. And most banks were closed, so no cash was available. Sporadic food riots and marauding looters popped up throughout the area.

"Why don't we all go to Aunt Evelyn's farm in Virginia?" Ellen suggested. "It's getting hard for her to walk and she would probably welcome the help and the company. Besides, her farm is far enough east that we would never be in the volcano spray pattern. Ian, you could wait there with us and maybe contact your wife when things improve."

"That gets my vote," Katie exclaimed.

They both looked over at Ian, awaiting his excited approval. That was not forthcoming.

"I need to look at something," he said. Ian picked up Katie's road atlas to check out the east end of Kentucky, where it joins Ohio, West Virginia, and Virginia. And there he spotted north/south US 23. Ian had started his trek from Dexter, only five miles from US 23. Now he would have to go back east hundreds of miles, just to start at US 23 all over again. All that wasted time and effort. He needed time to think. He retreated to the kitchen table with Katie's maps, sketch pad, and collected information.

Palpable silence permeated the old homestead. The focus of Ian's intense deliberations was not readily apparent. After all, he had repeatedly and vehemently opposed any further trek through that "damned ash." The women had offered him an alliterative alternative exit strategy out of the ashdome, riding in the comfort of the "slip-sliding Snow Snuffy," clear to higher ground. Instead, he had grown sullen and morose. This just didn't make sense. They waited.

Near noon Ian emerged from the much colder kitchen.

"If you listened to my hostile rants about walking through this God-damned ash, you would assume I would welcome evacuation by car. That would be absolutely true, if it were possible to head south or west toward New Mexico. It's too late for that. Our options are closing down around us. The only possible evacuation route is south and east toward Virginia. When I saw US 23 on Katie's road atlas, something snapped. I realized it was only a few miles from where you indicated Aunt Evelyn's farm was. I started my journey at US 23 in Michigan. This whole experience has gone too far. I'm screwed no matter which way things turn out.

"I would love nothing more than to ride out of here in style. But if I went with you back east, there are no guarantees. We have enough gas to make it to Virginia, assuming the car and we survive the journey. But there are gas and food shortages in the Marginal Zone all around Aunt Evelyn's farm. We could be stuck there for years with no escape route except by foot. Then it's 500 miles back to Memphis and the Mississippi, all through dangerous territory teeming with refugees and more food shortages. From Katie's data it looks like people along the length of I-40 are getting desperate. Looters are becoming threatening and dangerous. There are now different rules of conduct within the Marginal Zone, and I don't know those new rules. As it gets more chaotic, I might lose track of my family and never be able to find them again."

Concerned, Ellen interrupted. "Then what would you do? Continue to walk through deeper and deeper ash?"

"Ellen, you know, more than anyone, how much I hate this ash. But as I sat there thinking, I realized the path east is fraught with too much danger and uncertainty. The wild card in the east is the millions of hungry, displaced refugees. An entire class of emerging roadside bandits, willing to cut your throat if you walk through their territory. You also know I need to find my wife and kids. You know I would leave Virginia within a month. I just couldn't stay. Travelling through the bandits would place my life in great jeopardy.

"The path west through the deepening ash sounds improbable and insane. Yet strangely, after almost 500 miles of hiking, I have had no negative encounters with refugees. You would have to be crazy to hike into forty-mile-an-hour sandblasting wind. Without the gas mask I would have died within a week. Those National Guard soldiers in Michigan gave me the mask that kept me alive. Under the ashdome millions of homes have been abandoned with some food and full hot water tanks. Most of these homes to the west provide warmth and shelter and sustenance. However, most of the homes in the Marginal Zone to the east are still-occupied fortresses, defending against refugees.

"No, I have developed a weird working relationship with my adversary, the volcano. It's not my enemy. It is not cunning and does not personally direct attacks toward me. Walking through the deepening ash has its own set of survival rules to follow. I have learned to cope with that situation.

"If we can't drive west, then I must continue walking west. Within 120 miles I can reach the Mississippi. The bridge at Alton, Illinois, just above St. Louis, is still open. Once I cross the river and turn south, within thirty miles I am out of the ash for good. That would take only two weeks. It is the only real option left open to me if I ever want to find my family."

Silent reflection overcame the living room for the next while. Ian would miss the consciousness conversations, the sanity discussions with Ellen. Their third-eye energy flow had reactivated his consciousness wiring and brought a fierce cosmic intent back into his life. He couldn't wait to tell his brother about meeting Katie. Now, however, after this extended respite he needed to get back on the road. Extended respite? How long had he been here? Time assumed a plasticity. Some weeks were fifteen days long; other weeks, three days long. He had been with Ellen less than a week, but it felt like a fortnight.

Ellen's entire worldview and cosmic outlook had changed dramatically since their blasting third-eye flow. She now recognized herself as a free-spirited cosmic Explorer, guiding her consciousness beyond the limited astral ego planes. In a few short days many lingering questions had been resolved, but they were just getting started. Ellen would mourn Ian's departure. Deep in her memory, Vera Lynn sang that old World War II song:

We'll meet again
Don't know where
Don't know when....

Momentary sanity was one more time rent asunder by the damnable exigencies of a chaotic world.

Katie had expressed great enthusiasm at meeting Ian and enjoyed the Jacob's Ladder conversations about her youth, but all she really wanted was to get the hell out of here. She did not want to get stranded at the old homestead in two-foot ash drifts that could not be shoveled—left to die a cruel death. Going west into the accumulating ash was not an option for her. She was already planning for her arrival in Virginia.

Evacuation plans came together quickly. Ian would head southwest, walking along Route 16 to the Alton, Illinois, bridge. Katie and Ellen would drive south then east toward Virginia. Ian gave them pointers for navigating through the ash, including a hands-on, bone-chilling outdoor demonstration on how to keep the air filter free from ash.

"Clean that filter every 25 miles while passing through accumulating ash. Failure to remember could result in fatal consequences. In the event of a breakdown, just how far could you walk through 40-mile-an-hour winds at ten degrees without a gas mask?"

Ian helped them assemble the cargo for their journey on the living room floor near the front door. Once they were packed, they offered to help Ian prepare for his grueling trek.

"All that time you stood in my yard talking," Ellen observed, "I kept watching your staff with the bayonet attached. I thought then that the bayonet on your stick needed a small flag. Something signifying truce or that you come in peace. Grandma's old foot-powered treadle sewing machine is sitting right over there by the parlor. We could come up with a really cool design. After all, each of us is a professional artist. And the machine still works well. Together we could create your flag in a couple of hours."

Ian thought it was a great idea, wondering why this had never occurred to him before. They set up the easel and the giant sketch pad and put their three right brains together. Ideas flowed profusely. Months of untapped creativity sought almost orgasmic release. The refugee artists perhaps lingered a bit longer than necessary, bathing in the creative afterglow.

Finally, Ian made a choice. The winged Hermes "peace out" design. The artistic signature that had followed him from art school: spread flying wings attached to a peace sign, visually depicting "I come in peace."

Ian sketched the design onto both sides of the flag's fabric. Indelible ink markers created the permanent banner that would accompany Ian throughout the rest of his journey.

The antique sewing machine now sat away from the parlor wall. Both women smiled fondly, remembering their first fumbling attempts to sew on this machine. Soon the two muslin pieces were sewn together sandwiching three ties at one end. The ties were triple-stitched, reinforced to insure they were sturdy enough to survive the entire trip. Ian secured the ties to the ash-dulled bayonet.

"There! That's better!" Ellen declared with great satisfaction. Katie poured wine and offered a toast to their creative handiwork. Ian was now ready for the open road.

Darkness set in early once again, bringing a somber mood into Katie's living room. They realized their time together was coming to an end. They shared the remaining fresh meat and a couple of bottles of wine for their last supper. Tomorrow morning early, they would abandon ship, jumping into a cold uncertain fate.

Day 84

Anxious anticipation rousted them out of bed before dawn. Katie made a big pot of coffee and a big iron skillet of high-protein Johnny cake, as it used to be made, on the wood stove. Emergency provisions for lean times on the road.

Ian and Ellen assembled an eclectic breakfast of leftover food that could not be easily transported. By 8 a.m. Cedar was a nervous wreck, bouncing around, whining and barking—aware that something was afoot. Ian helped Ellen pack most of the car. Katie and Ellen wanted to hear the 9:00 Emergency Broadcast before they packed the last of their belongings. Impending bad weather or other alerts might delay their departure until tomorrow.

But Ian needed to leave today. Now. Ellen offered to drive him the three miles to Route 16, but he vehemently declined. He did not want to wonder if Ellen made it back alive to Katie's house after dropping him off. No, he would resume his journey from Katie's house.

Ian said his goodbyes to Katie in the living room, promising to pass on her best wishes to his brother. Ellen walked Ian out into the front yard. Sobbing, they said their goodbyes. She would miss him. Their daily discussions had brought her back to sanity. Each had dramatically evolved from their energy work. This would allow him to complete the next perilous part of his damned fool mission. They hugged, promising to keep in touch, to find each other "some sunny day." Cedar sat in the open front seat of the car waiting patiently to go for a "R-I-D-E." Ian patted his head, turned, and disappeared down the driveway, flag fluttering in the wind.

The wind blasted strong today. Travel would be slow on the unplowed side roads. Ian had not hiked for about a week. Unexercised muscles protested under the strain. That three miles to Route 16 took three hours. Ian was depressed. He already missed Ellen and Katie and Cedar, and good conversation, and the warmth of the wood stove, and not having to go outside in the blasting cold, and the energy exchanges—and happy hour.

But he slogged on. When he emerged onto Route 16, the pavement was recently plowed but slick. Ian could pick up some speed if he stayed along the shoulder of the road. Within an hour he entered the small town of Gays, Illinois, whose major claim to fame was a historical 1872 two-story outhouse. He couldn't take the time to check it out, but that concept was so intriguing it diverted his attention for the rest of the day, as he imagined all the potential combinations and permutations.

Days 85–87

Ian zombied grudgingly along Route 16, every step one step closer to the Mississippi. Many of the homes through Shelbyville and Tower Hill were already vacant and looted. The emergency Johnny cake provisions dwindled. The continued cold and hunger and loneliness was pretty damned depressing. He trudged on in a mind fog toward the city of Pana that loomed ahead. Later he would find a note he had scribbled during a hurricane blast of ash.

The winter was long that year...
Blown ash unsheathed
Rent wounds immedicable to sap.

Chapter 19

Day 88

Church bells woke Ian from a dream about his wife. She was sitting in Ellen's living room, wearing that little black velvet dress he loved so well, and she was laughing—not just giggling, but head-thrown-back, full-throated laughing. He woke smiling in response to her delight. When realization of reality set in, the smile faded and tears filled his eyes.

He hadn't dreamed so vividly of Theresa for a long time. Why now? In his head, he started counting the days. Oh, crap, it was her birthday! Not just any birthday, either; she turned 40 today. He had such plans to celebrate this milestone. Dinner at the Gandy Dancer; a concert at Hill Auditorium; late night dancing; flowers and a pair of earrings she had been coveting. Instead....

Thoroughly depressed, Ian slipped out of the house where he had spent the night and wandered toward Pana. After his experiences with Ellen and Katie, he was terribly lonely. He needed human contact, but the dream held him in its brooding embrace. He walked slowly along the edge of the road, trying to analyze his feelings. God knew he missed his wife, but it wasn't just that. He felt guilty for ever having left her and the kids. If only he'd been home when this happened! He was gut-wrenchingly worried about them. He knew Theresa was smart and strong and capable. If anyone could get them all to safety, she'd do it. But he should be there with her. They needed him. He had failed his family.

Now absolutely despondent, Ian trudged along the road as it entered the small city of Pana. He hardly noticed his surroundings, but it gradually penetrated his awareness that there was movement here. The place wasn't exactly bustling, but there were people on the streets.

His attention was caught by a large sign strung over the roadway:

Travelers' Rest Stop
Pana Fire Department
Free Food
Straight Ahead

His stomach rumbled a loud approval.

The fire station was a low, brick-faced building with four glass bays, on a corner next to City Hall. It was a pleasant looking building, almost cozy. The church bells that had woken him sounded again, ringing ten times. Interesting, he thought. They must be using the church bells to broadcast the time.

Ian entered the building to find a hive of activity. There were small groups of people in comfortable conversation, holding coffee cups and sandwiches. Near the street door was a card table staffed by a middle-aged woman with cropped, iron-gray hair. She smiled warmly at Ian and welcomed him to Pana. He smiled in return, thinking of Monon. What a different greeting this was!

The woman asked him if he'd like to sign their guest register. She explained that FEMA was keeping a record of those traveling through.

"Quite often," she said, "people have gotten separated and are looking for each other. Sometimes we can help, if their family or friends came through here." Ian's heart leapt.

"Oh, yeah!" He explained that he was looking for his wife and son and daughter. Theresa, Gabriel, and Claire.

"Let's see if they're in the ledger," the woman offered. But an extensive search of the guest register proved futile.

"Still," said the woman, "if you sign in and they come through later, we can let them know where you were headed." Ian had little hope of this, but he signed the register anyway.

He talked to the woman about what was happening here. She explained that Pana had become a search-and-rescue center. Volunteers from Catholic Social Services used the local church as a base camp. From there, they sent out rescue missions into the surrounding area to bring in people who had been stranded by the volcanic ash.

"You know, farmers who won't leave their cows," she said. Ian flashed on Leesburg.

The local church, St. Patrick's, had become the new seat of the diocese. An "End of the World" riot in Springfield had resulted in the burning of the church there.

"Funny," she laughed. "When things were being set up, Pana and Springfield were in competition to be the seat of the diocese. Pana was so confident that they'd win, they built a church grand enough to house it. It took almost a hundred years, but in the end—here we are."

The woman asked if Ian had a place to spend the night. He admitted he didn't. She told him that St. Patrick's had donated its school to serve as refugee housing. He was welcome to a bed for the night. And Ian would be happy for the company of others tonight.

Ian told the woman about a recent conversation he had in Ashmore about social institutions in times of disaster. The economic system, education, and the political system were all fragile and vulnerable. Family and religion, however, were rock solid. Families would pull together, while churches would provide hope and a sense of community.

"Absolutely," the woman agreed. "Even if this *is* the end of the world, I can't think of any better way to go than while I'm helping others."

Though he was reluctant to leave his new friend, Ian wanted to get settled before all the beds were gone. The woman directed him to the church.

"Go left at the corner and down about three blocks. You really can't miss it."

She was right. As Ian walked down the street, his attention was captured by the looming complex that came into view.

"My God, it's a cathedral!" he breathed to himself. Massive, domed, majestic, awe-inspiring. Nothing he would ever have expected to find in a small town in the middle of Illinois. There was something comforting in the sheer bulk of the building, a reassurance of permanence and safety.

When he got closer, he saw the soft glow of the stained glass windows, lit from within. Even from a block away, he could tell they were works of art in and of themselves. A large rose window presided over the massive double doors at the entry to the church. There was even a dome behind the bell tower. It was truly magnificent.

There were three men standing near the church steps. He asked them about the location of the school, and they directed him to a simple, rectangular building behind and to the left of the church. Ian entered.

Inside, people bustled in all directions, intent on purposes Ian could only guess. He stood in the entryway, uncertain of how to proceed. Finally, a woman hurrying down a hallway with an armload of linens noticed him. She walked quickly toward him, smiling warmly. The woman was small and slender with very red hair and luminous gray eyes.

"Need some help?" she asked. Ian explained his presence, and the woman nodded briskly. "Follow me," she said. "Oh, by the way, I'm Jeanette."

Their first stop was a storage area. Here Jeanette asked Ian to leave his walking stick.

"We can't have anything like a weapon in the shared areas. I'll attach a label to it," she added, eyeing the bayonet and the peace banner, "but I don't think you'll have any trouble finding it again." She led him to a classroom that had been converted to a dormitory. Cots sat in neat, precise rows. "Take your pick," she offered. "Get settled in, then come and find me. I'll show you around and fill you in on the routine, okay?"

Ian dropped his backpack on a cot. He sat down heavily, suddenly exhausted. This was so different from other towns. Here, he was simply welcome, accepted—an invited guest for a change.

A few minutes later he went searching for Jeanette and quickly spotted her. That flaming head of hair was a dead giveaway. She was talking to two younger women, who were nodding emphatically as she gestured. The two women gave a final nod and split apart, marching decisively in opposite directions, like two soldiers who had just gotten their orders. Jeanette saw Ian and waved him over.

"I'm about finished for today, so I can spend whatever time you'd like. What would you like to know?"

"Wow," said Ian, "Where do I start?"

Jeanette laughed. "How about a quick tour?"

She led Ian around the school building, pointing out the bathrooms and the auditorium, which was now a dining hall and general purpose meeting room. She explained mealtimes and curfews.

"Yep. We lock up at night for everyone's safety. If you're outside after ten o'clock, you're on your own. I don't think I have to tell you this," she noted apologetically, "but we expect everyone here to behave with courtesy and consideration for others." Ian nodded agreement.

"Have you seen the church yet?"

"Only the outside," he replied. "It's fantastic! I'm an art professor, you see. This church is wonderful!" He went on in this vein, letting his enthusiasm have full rein. Jeanette's smile grew even warmer.

"Wait until you see the inside, then," she said.

They walked across the playground to the back door of the church, entering through the vestry. Ian's first sight of the interior was the same as that of the priest entering to conduct a service.

He stopped cold, impressed by what he saw. Before him was a vast open space filled with neat rows of polished oaken pews. The church soared upward to a high vaulted ceiling. At the farthest point from him sat the choir loft with a magnificent pipe organ and the beautiful rose window he had seen from the outside. Marble columns lined the aisles at the sides of the church, and glorious stained glass windows depicted various Bible scenes. The stations of the cross were set into the outer walls, and statuary saints stood watch over the flock. The dome, clad in bright gold leaf, glowed high overhead.

Ian's artist eye drank in the color, the symmetry, the perfect arrangement of all these components. It was majestic and distant, but somehow it created in him a feeling of deep peace and comfort.

"Oh…" he barely breathed the word. Jeanette nodded in satisfaction at his response.

"My uncle painted most of the paintings along the walls. We're very proud of our church, and I think we've maintained it quite well."

"That's an understatement," Ian replied.

"Let me show you the sanctuary," Jeanette offered, and Ian followed her through the expanse of pews to the main entry of the church. Turning left, Jeanette gestured to a stairway that led to the choir loft. "If you want a bird's-eye view, we can go up there later." She pointed ahead to a stand holding rows of lit votive candles. "These are always here for those wanting to offer a prayer for someone," she noted.

Then she turned left again and stood aside. Ian looked down the marble colonnade to the sanctuary. He could not believe his eyes. A large sculpted grotto embraced the figure of the Virgin. The stone was purest white, but rather than being polished smooth, it was roughened to a soft, light absorbing texture. The outer edges blended organically with its surroundings.

Next to the grotto was a statue of St. Bernadette. Jeanette explained that she was the patron saint of miners, here because the original congregation all worked in the local coal mines.

An impulse surged forward in Ian. "Jeanette," he said, "I need to spend some time here." He explained about the journey he had undertaken, his feelings of responsibility for the old couple now buried under feet of ash in Leesburg, the loneliness of separation from his family, Theresa's birthday. Her eyes softened.

"I'll leave you here, then."

Ian spent several hours sitting on the floor in the grotto. He lit a candle in honor of Theresa's birthday and simply sat quietly, bathing his senses in the beauty of his surroundings. The flowing lines, the color, the peace, the loveliness of it all was such a welcome change from the harsh, monotonous gray of the outside world.

Eventually his attention focused on the grotto and the graceful figure of Mary. He let his mind wander free. In this contemplative state, he began a silent conversation with the alabaster figure. Ian sat, musing to himself and the pure work of spiritual art facing him. He offered a heartfelt prayer. "Let all be one," he prayed.

Then everything changed. First, Mary looked into his eyes and smiled serenely. Her skin warmed to a soft brown, her eyes darkened to a deep, liquid chocolate. She bent her head gently toward the woman lying on a pile of straw in Ian's hovel, then looked upward to the face of the eagle kachina. Ian felt a mild astonishment at this transformation, muted by wonder as his attention focused on the woman. "She's giving birth!" he realized. Mary and the kachina watched intently as something holy struggled to enter this world.

Ian felt his own abstraction growing, felt himself slip away from the scene of this nativity and return to the grotto with a sense of awe, the confused feeling that he had just witnessed a miracle. Head spinning, he sat staring at the alabaster statue, trying to understand. Was that a dream? A vision? It had the taste of prophecy, but to his waking mind it made no sense.

It was well after dark when he returned to his assigned cot. Ian lay down and, despite the turmoil in his mind, fell deeply asleep.

Day 89

Breakfast was hot and plentiful, served by cheerful volunteers to a handful of grateful travelers. Ian had bacon, scrambled eggs, hotcakes, and coffee.

As he was finishing a leisurely second cup, a group of people arrived. It was clear they had just come in from the road. They were covered with ash and obviously exhausted. There were four men who seemed to be familiar with their surroundings as well as an older couple, a woman, and a young boy.

One of the breakfast workers grabbed a cup of coffee and rushed to a black man in his thirties who was lowering a backpack to the floor.

"Father Adrian! You're back. And you've brought us new guests," she exclaimed. The man straightened up slowly, fatigue written in every line on his face, and broke into a beautiful smile.

"Yes, Marie, we were blessed to find this family. Thank you for the coffee—you're a saint." Marie, all 200-plus pounds of her, giggled like a schoolgirl and blushed to the roots of her hair. Ian watched as the other three men shepherded the family to the breakfast line, watched the desperate hunger in their eyes as they were handed loaded plates of food, watched as they tried to show restraint and give proper thanks, watched as they fell on the food like people who have been without a good meal for a long time. He certainly knew how they felt, and his face settled into an expression of compassion.

When he looked up, Father Adrian was watching him watch the newcomers. The priest nodded, and Ian raised his cup in an invitation. Father Adrian moved over to sit next to Ian.

"You've been there, haven't you?" he asked. "On both sides of the equation, from the look on your face."

Ian grinned wryly. "Didn't know it showed so clearly."

Father Adrian chuckled. "I'm a priest," he said. "I read faces for a living."

Ian noticed a musical lilt to the priest's speech.

"You aren't from these parts, are you?" he asked. Adrian laughed and admitted that his parish was in Haiti. Ian's eyes widened at this.

"Don't look so surprised," the priest said. "When we suffered our earthquake disaster back in 2010, you all came charging to the rescue. Did you think we'd forgotten? When the volcano erupted, the Church leaped into action and sent in emergency rescue teams from all over the world. We've had a lot of experience over the past couple of millennia dealing with this kind of thing, you know. I volunteered and was chosen to come here.

"We're fighting a losing battle, though. That ash just keeps coming. We used to be able to get as far north as Decatur, about 35 miles. But those days are gone. Chicago now has almost two feet of ash and snow on the ground, and if you get more than about 25 miles north of here, it starts getting bad; drifts between two and three feet deep." Ian's heart sank. That meant Monon was gone, and Monticello, too. He sent a quick prayer that the Obie family had made it out safely.

"We're going to have to pull back pretty soon, relocate our base camp," the priest continued. "I'll be sorry to abandon Pana, but when the Church says 'move', we'll move." The Father paused. "Where are you headed?"

Ian repeated his story. He told the priest he planned to head west from here along Route 16 and eventually cross the Mississippi at Alton. Father Adrian shook his head.

"That won't work," he said. "All the bridges around East St. Louis and St. Louis are now closed due to civil unrest and local martial law. In fact, almost all the other bridges across the Mississippi within 40 miles of St. Louis are impassable. The only bridges I know of that can still be crossed are the two bridges to the north around Hannibal. Avoid I-72 and any major freeway bridges. It's like the Wild West out there. Refugee problems and bandits. Too many tragic incidents. I would recommend that you first cross the Illinois River at the drawbridge at Florence. That bridge is still open. Then go 30 miles west and cross the river at Pike. There's less foot traffic and it's safer. That would, however, require you to go a little north of here." Ian was pissed. "One step forward, ten miles back," he thought bitterly.

The observant priest became quiet and thoughtful. "Listen," he said at last, "I may have a way to help. Hey, Lars!" he called loudly. Across the room a blond man who had been leaning over a map on a table raised his head and looked at Father Adrian. He came over to join them. "Aren't you headed out toward Taylorville this afternoon?" asked Father Adrian. Lars nodded. "Do you think you could take a passenger that far?"

"Sure, Father," he said with just the slightest hint of a Swedish accent. "We'll have plenty of room on the way out." The smile on Ian's face was all the thanks the others needed.

Lars' used Army truck was scheduled to leave around noon. That gave Ian more than enough time to collect his belongings and say hasty farewells. Well before the appointed time, he found himself standing by the ash-pitted vehicle, nervously shuffling his feet as he waited. He tried desperately to stay out of the way of the three men loading supplies. When they were finally satisfied with their preparations, Lars climbed into the driver's seat. Ian clambered aboard eagerly. The other two men settled into the back of the truck and began talking quietly to each other.

A little maneuvering through the streets of Pana carried them out to Route 29, the most direct route to their destination. The truck lumbered slowly forward, slipping and skidding its way northwest out of town.

"How far do you think we'll get today?" Ian found himself shouting to be heard above the heavy wind and grinding of the engine.

"Well, we're going up north of Taylorville," Lars shouted back. "But you won't want to go that far. I think you'll want to get off at Owaneco. Your road is pretty much straight west from there. Besides, we can even offer you a place to stay in Owaneco. We have a transitional house there for the families we rescue. Hot food, a warm fire, a soft bed—all the comforts of home. Take advantage of it! You won't find anything like it for a while."

Unhappily, Ian believed that to be true. The road ahead looked awfully bleak. There was little to relieve the gray flatness that stretched in front of them. Even the highway disappeared under the blanket of ash.

Lars kept his attention on the demanding task of wrestling the unwilling truck down the invisible highway. Ian, tense beside him in the passenger seat, found himself automatically steering and braking with every shift of the vehicle. It took over two hours to cover the eight or so miles between Pana and the tiny town of Owaneco, and by the time they arrived Ian was exhausted from his phantom driving. Lars pulled into a driveway a short distance up Mill Street and stopped the truck.

Everybody piled out and stretched. They now stood next to a small, clapboard ranch house, probably built sixty years ago. It looked as weary as Ian felt.

"Home sweet home," Lars declared cheerfully. "It may not look like much, but it'll be warm and dry for the night." He started for the front door, keys in hand.

Inside, the darkness was relieved quickly when Lars opened the drapes on the living room windows. He bustled about, setting a fire in the small wood-burning stove and lighting a kerosene lantern. He beckoned Ian into the kitchen and showed him the food and cooking supplies. A five-gallon water jug sat on the counter.

"Bathroom's through here," he said, pointing off to his right, "and the bedroom is the only door off the living room. You'll have the place to yourself tonight. In fact, you'll have the whole town to yourself. We've evacuated everyone from here."

Before leaving, Lars outlined what to expect the next day when crossing Taylorville Lake. There was almost a mile long causeway across the lake. The crowned two-lane road was very narrow. It had only low guardrails. The wind howled across the lake and the road was always slippery. He wouldn't drive it again. The truck almost skidded off last time.

"You don't have a lot of options here. If you try to avoid the causeway, you'll have to go all the way around the lake. The farther north you go, the deeper the ash. North of Taylorville, it's almost impassable, even for us. So the best route is still across the causeway.

"But be very, very careful!" Lars warned.

Day 90

Ian woke to yet another lonely gray morning. What he wouldn't give to see the sun. He bet himself that seasonal affective disorder was now an epidemic in this area. There wasn't anyone keeping track at the moment, but the suicide rate was bound to be way up.

Yet, he reminded himself, he was still alive, still moving west. This morning he would even have coffee and a hot breakfast before starting out. It could be a lot worse. Hell, it had been a lot worse just last week.

Having filled his stomach to the bursting point, Ian restocked his backpack from the supplies Lars had generously provided for his journey. He started humming to himself as he set out once again. "Pack up your troubles in your old kit bag" sounded muffled and tinny through the gas mask.

It was still late morning when he reached the shores of Taylorville Lake. The road ran straight ahead, out over the water itself. Ian stared at it apprehensively and shuddered. Just as Lars had described it, the narrow ribbon of pavement was bounded only by a low metal guardrail. It stretched across the lake for almost a mile. The high wind had scoured the surface of the road to a clean, gunmetal gray and polished the frozen lake surface to an obsidian gleam. He would truly be walking the razor's edge. One gust of wind at the wrong time, one slip on the icy crown of the road could end everything. Who could tell if the ice was strong enough to hold his weight? He took a deep breath and closed his eyes. Then he squared his shoulders and set out to conquer his latest demon.

He fixed his eyes on the pavement about three feet ahead and began walking slowly and deliberately, focusing on keeping his breathing even. As long as he didn't look left or right, he'd be okay.

An eternity later he reached solid land again. Ian made sure he was a good distance inland before he paused to catch his breath. His body sagged in relief and he lifted his gas mask to wipe a thin sheen of sweat from his face. It wasn't even noon yet, but Ian was exhausted. Wooden thighs and rubbery knees made any further progress out of the question. A tree had fallen halfway across the road. It offered a much-appreciated place to sit while he recovered. Ian allowed himself time to muse gently, letting his thoughts ramble as he munched a packet of cheese crackers.

When his legs worked again, he set out westward once more. If he walked steadily, he could easily make it to Clarksdale in time to find a place to sleep.

Ian's walk progressed through a wooded area, then out onto flat, open land as far as the eye could see. He continued generally west, curving north as the road curved, then back west again. Finally the small village of Clarksdale came into view.

If there was a commercial district, Ian couldn't see it. Clarksdale appeared to be a neighborhood without a town attached. Small single-story houses lined its few streets. It looked as if he could have his pick of accommodations for the night. The streets seemed to be completely deserted. He picked out a small house on the north side of town and settled in for the night.

Days 91–92

For the next two days Ian continued to travel west with two short jogs north. It was endless prairie, monochromatic gray under a lowering sky that weighed heavily on his head. No movement broke the dreariness, no sound relieved the deadly boredom.

He plodded on. The days passed in a dull, indifferent blur. He ate when he remembered to and slept leadenly in whatever cold, deserted shelter he could find. The second day out he crossed an interstate highway, I-55, without registering anything other than the emptiness of the roadway.

Ian brooded. He felt himself slipping further and further into depression. Everything was hopeless. He began to feel he would walk forever through this colorless hell, sweating and straining futilely to return to his own world of light and warmth and laughter. Desperately, he clung to his memories of his family and the more recent, even more important,* connection to Ellen.

*See Appendix I

Chapter 20

Captain Monty

Day 92

From the prow of his small riverboat, "Captain Monty" Montgomery gloomily surveyed the four inches of ash that had settled over Hannibal, Missouri. A short, stocky man in his 50s, with grizzled hair and a luxuriant moustache of which he was very proud, he had worked on boats for decades while saving to buy his own riverboat. The boat was his life.

Captain Monty was an independent operator based out of St. Louis. This year, though, he had stayed in Hannibal over the winter because his boat needed repairs before next season.

Monty was supremely proud of the boat. It measured 60 feet by 24 feet, not counting the sidewheels. While his sidewheeler was wider than a sternwheeler, it was more maneuverable. Its paddles could move at different rates and in different directions, one forward, one back. This gave it rapid turning ability.

The boat boasted ornate port and starboard smokestacks as well as four decks. The engine occupied the bottom deck. Above that sat two passenger decks. One was for dining, complete with a galley; and one was for observing, entertainment, and dancing. A pilothouse sat on the top deck. The riverboat was white with black and gold detailing. Painted proudly on the side was the name, *Ms Duchess*. Monty always explained that the "Ms" didn't stand for "Miz" but for "Mississippi."

Ms Duchess offered trips for tourists. There were shorter one- and three-hour cruises, as well as day-long and evening dinner cruises. The full galley provided meals.

Until about three weeks ago, there had been no ash in Hannibal, though the river had been affected. It was darker from ashfall that had washed downriver. The water was debris-laden, with plenty of flotsam. Uprooted trees and dead animals floated by.

Monty had decided to stay at dockside until things cleared up, not risking his boat, trying to avoid the new hazards. After the volcano erupted the second time, everything worsened. His two-man crew quit and headed south. Ash started to accumulate. Winds picked up. The river started running faster, carrying more debris. Now Monty was reconsidering his earlier decision to wait it out. Maybe he should head south to St. Louis. It would be tricky doing it alone, but his piloting experience should get him there. He decided to start tomorrow morning.

Day 93

He set out down the river as soon as he could see. An ash-darkened sky hid the sun and made the water opaque. It was impossible to see any snags hidden just below the water surface. The higher maneuverability of his sidewheeler was immediately put to the test dodging flotsam. Steering was very stressful and required his full concentration.

He passed through Lock 22, which had been left open. Then he passed under the bridge on U.S. Highway 54, and continued on to Lock 24. The current was fast, but he had to keep his speed low. *Ms Duchess* drew less than two feet, and the width of the hull helped with stability. By dragging or reversing the paddles as necessary, he could see surface hazards in time to avoid them. Dodging maneuvers are always tricky, though.

As he approached, he could see that a jam had formed along the dam between the Illinois side of the river and Lock 24. Tree trunks, root systems, dead animals, lumber, and wrecked boats obstructed his way. At best, it would be a tight squeeze, requiring all his skill and dexterity to navigate. He had been battling the river for hours now. It would be dark soon, and he was worn out. There was no way he could make this in one run. He would have to find a place to anchor for the night, then try to move on the next day.

Scanning the riverbanks, he saw that the Missouri side of the river was also backed up with debris. The Illinois side, however, had a wide stretch of sandy beach inside the curve of the tree-covered peninsula. If he could do this right, he'd be able to pull out of the current and drop anchor in the shallows close to shore. Then, when things cleared up a bit and he'd had some rest, he could pull back out and make a run for it through Lock 24.

At the last possible moment, he was caught up in a cross current that forced him toward the riverbank. Dragging and backing slowed him down, but the boat was pulled swiftly to shore. The best he could do was point toward the open space, the only tree-free location along the shoreline, and wait helplessly as the prow gently came to rest on land. He was grounded.

Monty walked forward to the bow and surveyed the deserted landscape. The narrow beach rose abruptly to a sand-covered, twenty-foot-tall levee that cut off his view of the land beyond. He smiled ironically, threw out his arms, and proclaimed,

"In the name of the Duchess of the Mississippi, I claim this new world!"

It could definitely have been worse. *Ms Duchess* was fully provisioned, so there was no danger that he would go hungry. A quick check assured him that the engines had suffered no damage and that the paddlewheels were intact. He was just grounded. There was no way one man could push the boat back offshore, but maybe the water level would rise and float him off. Monty was an optimist by nature.

"Oh, well," he sighed philosophically, shoving back his pilot's hat to scratch his head. "These things always happen for a reason. Might as well get some dinner."

Chapter 21

Dead Man's Boots

Day 93

Sunday, again? Ian started out early on his ten-mile journey. He decided not to steal a vehicle today. He didn't have a good feeling about it. There had been so much on his mind since Ashmore. He headed west down Thayer Road.

"Man, I'd give anything not to wear this mask again. Hell, I'd give anything to hear a damn bird again, or to see my kids and my wife again. God damn it!" Ian had stopped in the middle of the road and screamed so hard that he could feel the veins bulging in his head.

He pondered the fact that all he had were his thoughts… countless hours of thinking…countless hours of internal dialog. "My thoughts are like my best friend. They either keep me company or they drive me fucking crazy."

After his time with Ellen and Katie, a new level of frustration had set in. A combination of social, intellectual, and spiritual interaction was now lacking, and this weighed heavily on his being. That energy experience with Ellen. He wished he could have that feeling back right now. That feeling of being "One." That feeling of "touching souls." The real love and safety that exists when oneness is achieved. Nothing in this illusion had prepared him for that. He had heard his brother tell stories of "energy flows," but his only comprehension of the practice was on an intellectual level.

He had had a major life-changing episode in the middle of a major earth-changing event, which unforgivingly robbed him of the ability to process the experience. He needed time: time to digest it, to talk about it, to understand it. It had been two weeks since it happened, but he missed that feeling of having no earthly body, of floating above the ground. During the flow with Ellen, they had been perfectly safe, wrapped in a blanket of cosmic security. Now those feelings were gone.

Ian had been so "trance-fixed" by his thoughts that the ten-mile walk had seemed to take only minutes. The road had turned into a serpentine set of curves. The wind was picking up now, and he knew that the pressure was changing. His head started to pound with a sinus headache. The darkish sky ahead seemed even more ominous than usual. Ian realized that he might be heading into a storm.

There was a series of large farms on both sides of the road, but some had signs of active life. Ian would have to be careful in choosing a place to sleep. The land was as flat as a pancake in all directions. The vigilant farmers would surely see him. Now he would be watched until he was no longer deemed a threat.

Ian continued to walk west. Near Highway 111, he noticed a small house up ahead. As he got closer, he discovered that it was an old fieldstone farmhouse, much more modest than the other farms he had passed. Behind the house were numerous outbuildings and a large barn, even an old smokehouse with a metal roof. Ian approached the house cautiously but with an air of purpose, as if he were getting ready to sell the owner a set of encyclopedias. There was no car, no dog, and no glowing candlelight or visible burning oil lamps. There were also no recent tracks leading into or out of the driveway. Ian stepped up onto the front porch, knocked on the door, paused, and knocked again. There was no answer. He walked around to the back porch and repeated the sequence; again no answer. Ian tried the handle, and to his surprise the door opened up. He nervously poked his head in.

"Hello?"

Once inside, it was apparent that whoever lived here had left some time ago. The house had that soaked-in cold feeling, as if it hadn't seen heat in a while. The woodstove had no visible signs of a recent fire. The mantel clock had not been wound, and there was ice in the toilet. Ian walked around and checked each room. He knew he would not be able to start a fire because the smoke would attract the neighbors. He didn't want that!

He began his nightly ritual of going around the house looking for food, water, and blankets. In the basement Ian found some emergency candles, oil lamps, and a flashlight with dead batteries. His menu choices tonight consisted of canned ham, chicken noodle soup, whole yellow corn, large pitted black olives and a can of garbanzo beans. There was also an old semi-rusty can of poppy seed cake and pastry filling. Ian gathered the canned goods in a bucket to carry upstairs. He filled his canteen from the water heater tank. Then he spotted a little box with a picture of a radio on it. Upon further inspection the dusty box read:

RadioShack®

EMERGENCY CRANK RADIO

- Crank the generator rod just a couple of minutes to power the radio for more than an hour
- Receives AM, FM and shortwave bands 1 and 2
- Built-in light comes in handy during power outages at night

Internal generator provides power—
No batteries or electricity required!

Ian could not believe what he was seeing. He opened the box and, sure enough, there was the radio as advertised: small, lightweight, and sporty too. This was as good as gold. Ian could now listen to news and music and there was even a built-in flashlight.

Settling in for the night, he pulled the shades and drew the drapes to hide any light that he might produce. He prepared his dinner by lighting three emergency candles under a frying pan. After dinner he secured the doors against intruders. He lit an oil lamp and turned the wick to a dim light. He took the radio out of the box, sat down in the chair by the woodstove, and cranked the dynamo for a few minutes. Switching the lever to AM, he turned it on and adjusted the knob until he found a station that was broadcasting good old Southern gospel music.

Day 94

Ian was so excited. He had always wanted to see Arvo Pärt in concert, and here he was in Ann Arbor. It had been a while since Theresa and Ian had been on a "dress up" date. To show off his beautiful wife and to see his favorite contemporary composer perform.... Wow!

The concert began with his melodic piece, "Spiegel im Spiegel." Then, about eight minutes into it, the cymbal player began smashing the cymbals loud and violently. Ian was confused. The music was ethereal in nature; cymbals weren't even a part of his music. But why didn't the audience seem to notice? It was so obvious that it didn't fit in with the piece. Something was wrong. Not even Theresa noticed. She just sat there with a smile on her face, like the rest of the audience. Finally, Ian couldn't take it any more. He stood up and screamed—

"STOP!"

Ian immediately awoke to the sound of a ferocious wind, like a squadron of jet planes circling the house. Continuous rolling thunder shook everything. Flashes of lightning were obscured by the blowing ash and he couldn't tell where it was coming from. He could hear something smashing rhythmically into the metal roof of the smokehouse and realized that must have been the reason for the cymbal player in his dream. He got out of bed to look. He noticed his throat was extremely dry and he started to cough.

"The wind must be a hundred miles an hour out there," Ian said to himself. The whole house creaked. Ash pelted the windows. Branches snapped off, sounding like pistol shots, and trees crashed to the ground. Then he heard a large smash against the side of the house that startled the hell out of him.

Ian realized that he should probably not be hanging out upstairs anymore. Panic set in as he contemplated where he could go that was possibly safe. If he stayed up here he could be injured by flying glass and debris. If he went into the basement, he could easily be trapped if the roof collapsed. Every option seemed to be a bad one.

He decided to try his luck in the basement. He quickly cranked the radio for about a minute and turned on the flashlight. The air in the house was thick with ash. That explained the coughing. He rapidly collected his belongings and headed down into the basement. He briefly ran back upstairs to grab the oil lamps and matches.

In the safety of the basement, Ian lit the lamps. He cranked the radio, hoping to find out what was going on outside. Eventually he found a weather report announcing a tornado warning for portions of southern Illinois. Radar was tracking sustained winds of 360 miles an hour. It would affect all of Scott County southwest of Jacksonville.

"Take cover immediately!" the announcer warned. "We have never recorded a storm of this magnitude before. It will destroy everything in its path." Ian was stunned. He got out his maps and found that the area under the warning was only about twenty miles west of him and the storm was heading north; but the winds hitting the house were obviously connected to it.

Suddenly there was a loud crashing sound accompanied by glass breaking and falling to the floor. Ian knew that a window had been breached. Ash began flowing into the basement through the crack under the basement door. An ash storm now swirled through the room, and Ian regretfully put his mask on. This basement was neat and orderly and whoever lived here certainly wasn't a hoarder. It seemed hopeless that he would find anything to block the bottom of the door. Ian then looked up and noticed that the hot water lines were wrapped in foam insulation. He tore down about a four-foot section and stuffed it under the door. Voila! But too late; he would have to wear his mask the rest of the night.

It was a long night....

The storm lasted only about an hour, but with the chilly cellar temperature, the fear of the roof collapsing, and the dust-filled basement, sleep was out of the question. Morning sunlight started to appear through the basement windows as Ian headed upstairs to assess the damage. The interior of the house was surreal. The kitchen window had surrendered to the gale-force winds and ash now filled the house. The windows facing west had been etched by the blowing cinders. Every crack in the wall was outlined by a dusty buildup of ash.

Ian opened the back door and a two-foot pile of debris fell onto the floor in front of him. The outside looked like a war zone. Most of the trees in the yard had been uprooted. Those left standing were heavily damaged. The source of the loud crash was the huge oak tree directly behind house. Years of internal rot had weakened the tree so much that it could no longer hold its own against the storm. Debris was everywhere. Most of the metal roofing on the barn was gone. The top of a neighbor's silo lay smashed in the yard. Strips of vinyl siding were scattered about. Little pink tufts of insulation clung to the surviving tree limbs like floral growths.

Ash drifts were piled high against the windward side of the house and barn. As Ian walked around surveying the damage, he was shocked to discover that the ash had not only polished the stones on the house but had also eaten away two or three inches of the mortar between the stones. The wood on the house and barn that faced the wind was completely sandblasted and looked like old driftwood. The wind on its own would have been bad enough, but when combined with the ash it was devastating. If he had been out in that storm, his fragile flesh would have been stripped from his bones.

This twisted, alien landscape left him feeling totally disoriented. He was so dazed he almost couldn't function. The storm had spooked him badly. He couldn't just move on. But what now? After a short while, he decided to stay put for another day to let the confusion clear from his brain. His survival depended on his alertness and clarity.

Day 95

"On the road again…R.O.A.D. on the road again…" Ian sang out loud in his best southern drawl as he backtracked down to 111 heading north toward Waverly. Between Waverly and Franklin, devastation from the storm was fairly extensive: trees uprooted, homes obliterated, vehicles turned over, signposts bent in half. Ian saw a children's swing set turned onto its side, with all four legs embedded perfectly into a concrete wall as if it were planned that way.

Day 96

The morning of a new day, and Ian was still feeling somewhat depressed. All he had seen for the last two days was devastation; and he wasn't even at the point of impact, where the tornado had touched down. He packed up and headed out. About a mile down the road he stumbled upon a gruesome sight. The body of a man appeared to have been thrown at high velocity. He was wrapped around a speed limit sign like the dead ringer of a horseshoe around a stake. This corpse looked fresh, definitely a victim of the storm. It looked as if it had been dragged behind a car at high speeds. Layers of flesh were gone, flayed down to the bone. Parts of his clothes had melded into his skin. His head was cracked open like an egg, and brain matter was exposed to the air.

As Ian witnessed this horror, his eyes were drawn to the dead man's feet, for there was a brand new pair of boots. Ian's shoes were just about worn out, and he could sure use a new pair. He quickly removed the boots from the dead man. They were size 13.

"Holy Crap! These boots will be perfect," he exclaimed. Without hesitation, Ian sat down and changed his shoes. He jumped up and walked around in a circle, as if he were at a shoe store.

Ian continued on his way toward Woodson wondering who the dead guy was and what scenario led to his demise. He realized the cosmic threads that connect us and provide us with what we need. He broke out laughing at how twisted his life had become.

"Three months ago I was sitting at a faculty luncheon, and now I'm swiping shoes off of a mangled dead guy. That's some funny shit." But Ian's eyes welled up with tears and he started to cry uncontrollably. He sat down on the road and wept until his eyes could cry no longer. The stress had finally festered to the surface. How could he be so callous, so desensitized, so savage? What next? Ian sat for a while holding his pounding head, trying to re-center himself before moving on.

"You just did what you had to, man. It's all about survival now."

The conclusion of today's ten miles was just the icing on an already depressing cake. What used to be the town of Woodson was now a desolate wasteland of debris and destruction. Concrete wall sections jutted up around the landscape. There were mangled vehicles strewn around town. Twisted signs identified intersecting streets, and a single flag pole had managed to survive. What trees still stood were completely decimated. There wasn't even ash on the ground.

"Wow," Ian said out loud.

He walked around the empty streets realizing there was nothing there: no water, no shelter, no food. Instead of panicking, Ian thought, "This is a small town in an area of the country that regularly gets tornados. There must be homes with tornado shelters or root cellars, or even basement sections that are still intact. If there are undamaged basements, there could be useable water heater tanks and possibly even food." Changing his attitude to a positive outcome helped to refocus Ian. He got to work, determined to find such a place.

It didn't take long to find his first basement, but the force of the tornado had ripped the first floor completely off, leaving the space exposed to the elements. There was a water heater, apparently undamaged; but the stairs were broken and getting in and out of the basement could be tricky. Only one basement in town had a stairway that was intact. Ian went down and filled his canteen with water. It was starting to get late and he knew he had to find shelter soon or die.

On the outskirts of Woodson, Ian saw the roof of a school bus barely protruding above the ground. Further investigation revealed that someone had deliberately buried it there. Steel cellar doors covered a cinderblock wall built around the back of the bus. A ladder provided access down to the emergency door. Ian climbed down the ladder, opened the door, and peeked inside. Darkness permeated the interior. He dug out his radio and cranked up the flashlight.

The interior was clean and ash-free. Thick insulation foam covered all of the windows. A section of seats had been removed to make room for a table. Shelving units, installed in the area where the driver and front door used to exist, were filled with cans of food and bottled water. A couple of bare light bulbs hung from fixtures in the ceiling. The wires exited the wall and connected to a generator inside a large vented box.

"Holy shit!" Ian blurted.

Starting the generator brought instant light to the situation. Ian closed the door. Tonight he would eat, look over his maps, catch up on notching his staff, and listen to the radio. This had been a day filled with miracles, he marveled as he unlaced the dead man's boots. His old world, with all its ease and comfort, was gone; but the universe still provided for his needs. He was enormously grateful, but he did wonder why he was being singled out for protection. What made him so special?

Day 97

Ian awoke to the sound of a steady rain hitting the metal roof of the bus.

"Rain. That sucks." He stuck his head out and resigned himself to a wet day of walking. After rearranging his gear, Ian took the small blue nylon tarp he had pilfered from a house in Indiana and wrapped it around his backpack. This was the first time he had encountered rain on his trip.

There is nothing—absolutely nothing—worse than being in forty-degree temperatures and rain. The cold does more than chill you to the bone; it soaks into your soul. Now the ash had become even more slippery and disgusting to walk in. If it weren't for the fact that Ian had to walk harder and with more determination than usual, he would probably have serious hypothermia by now. He sang songs in pace with his stride so that he could remain focused on the mission of walking another ten miles. He thought about all of those camping trips when the kids were little, how they would go to the UP in August. Often the weather would change and the temperature would drop into the forties. They would huddle under their "tarp city" and shiver by the fire. The kids' hands would be wet and cold and filthy from the dirt. What really sucked was having to take down the tent and pack up all of the muddy gear. He laughed.

"Man, I'd give anything to be there right now."

Chapter 22

Easter Weekend in Detroit

Day 98

"What I wouldn't give for a pair of toenail clippers," Ian thought. His toenails had become long and thick. They rubbed against the front of his boots causing pressure and discomfort. A few of the nails on his smaller toes had broken, and their sharp edges caught on his socks creating painful little surprises when he least expected it. "I am so ready for this nightmare to be over," he said out loud.

Stepping outside, Ian was happy to see that it was no longer raining. He had stayed the night near the small town of Winchester, Illinois. The tornado had caused quite a bit of damage, knocking down trees and power lines and causing roof, siding, and window damage to most of the housing and store fronts. This morning he wove his way around the debris to get through town.

Heading west on 106, the monotony of flat acreage changed to a nice mixture of trees, rolling hills, and farmland. The area reminded Ian of the west side of Michigan. Eventually he found himself walking uphill in a heavily wooded area. The slightly steep incline proved to be difficult and time consuming with the slippery snow and ash mixture. He found himself having to shuffle slowly along the shoulder of the road to get a better foothold.

At the apex of the hill, the woods opened up into flat farmland again. A row of large hay rolls, heavily covered with snash, stretched at least a mile along the south side of the road. Something about their frozen visages reminded Ian of the dead man wrapped around the street sign. He wondered if humanity would ever recover from this, or would we all end up frozen in time by the side of the road?

After a much needed rest and water break, Ian continued heading west. Flat land as far as the eye can see—lifeless flat land. Strange Seussian clouds churned on the horizon to the north. The wind whipped across the barren landscape, stinging any skin exposed to its abuse. A few miles down the road Ian came across a sign with two motionless lights on top. The sign read, "Draw Bridge Up When Flashing." He knew from the maps that he had made it to the Illinois River. He recalled the warning from Father Adrian in Pana: the only way he was going to make it to the Mississippi was by crossing this bridge at Florence.

Approaching the bridge cautiously, Ian took the time to study its long expanse. The green-painted bridge appeared to be from the early 1900s. Its lattice-truss steel sections were riveted together like one big Erector Set project. The drawbridge segment sat high above the water waiting stoically for a boat to pass.

"STUPID LYING SIGN!" Ian yelled. "God damn it! Now what?" He stood there pissed off, hungry, cold, and desperately surveying his options. He took a long deep breath. "Why is nothing ever easy?"

After calming down, Ian noticed that on the north side of the bridge there was a stair system going up to a small metal platform. From there he could climb a caged ladder up to the catwalk, get onto the top of the hanging road section, cross the gap, and come back down the other side. There was only one problem. Ian was deathly afraid of heights. He stepped over the guardrail and onto the stairway. The climb to the first platform didn't seem that hard—until he stupidly looked down.

"Holy Crap! That's gotta be a hundred-foot drop," he exclaimed. Fear shot through his body, down his legs, and he instantly collapsed to his knees. Adrenaline coursed through his veins, and he began to panic. The strong wind buffeted his body and he worried about being blown into the river. Ian sat petrified by fear, eyes closed and head down. The wind blew up through the platform grate into his face as if to mock and taunt him, and every possible scenario played out in his head as to how he could resolve this dilemma.

Time seemed to be dragging, but Ian guessed that it was probably mid-afternoon. This meant that he had been on the platform for quite a while. He was now very cold from sitting stationary for hours exposed to the wind. He worried about the onset of night and hypothermia. With tears welling up in his eyes, Ian whispered a desperate plea while looking up to the sky.

"What am I going to do now, God?" Almost on cue, snow began to fall, slowly at first; but then rapidly it changed into a mixture of heavy snowfall and wind. Ian knew he was a dead man if he stayed where he was. He closed his eyes and pictured himself getting up, climbing the stairs, crossing the catwalk, and getting back down the other side fearlessly and without incident.

"Don't look down this time, asshole!" he reminded himself as he stood up and grabbed for the ladder. Looking up he began to climb.

"At least the cage will keep me from falling," he thought. The metal cage that surrounded the ladder gave Ian a false sense of security, but any security at this point was okay with him. The wet snow made the metal rungs slippery. Slowly he climbed, meticulously making sure that he had a positive foothold with every step before advancing further.

At the top of the ladder there was another small platform which opened onto the catwalk above the raised bridge. The wind and snow blew hard as Ian stepped onto the platform and looked across the long expanse to the pilot house that sat in the center. Panic again shot through his body and he dropped to his knees once more.

"What am I going to do?"

"I can't stay here!"

"I have to keep moving or die."

He tried to stand, but the fear was overwhelming. He grasped the steel grate with his hands and started crawling on his knees, slowly advancing across the cold metal gridwork.

Reaching the pilot house, Ian painfully stood up and tried the door. It opened. Stepping inside was a welcome change from the bitter cold wind that had blasted his body for the past few hours. His sore and battered knees needed a break. Ian sat on one of the chairs to rest. Looking around, he saw a control panel with all sorts of buttons and lights and levers and gauges. There were four television monitors attached to the ceiling, a CB radio on a shelf next to a speaker, lots of memos on magnetic clips stuck to the gray-green steel cabinets, and maps and charts hanging on the walls. He laughed at how the interior looked like a set from an old science fiction movie.

Swiveling his chair around, he noticed a small dorm-sized fridge behind him. Excited, he jumped up and opened the door to discover three unopened water bottles inside.

"Jackpot!"

Ian drank one bottle of water and put the rest in his backpack. He figured there was only about an hour of daylight left and he had to do everything he had just done all over again—only faster. He also had to travel safely, find shelter for the night, get warm, eat dinner, and get some much needed rest. If it wasn't so damned cold, he would stay here.

Looking at one of the bridge diagrams on the wall, he discovered that the pilot house sat in the middle of the 300 foot expanse of the drawbridge section. That meant he had another 150 feet to go, on sore knees, before he could make his way down and off this damn bridge. After ten minutes of mental preparation, Ian stood up, grabbed his stuff, and headed out the door.

Wincing from the discomfort on his kneecaps, Ian painfully crawled at a faster, more determined pace across the metal catwalk and onto the first platform at the caged stairway.

"Wow, that wasn't too bad!" Ian exclaimed. It had taken him only about fifteen minutes to get across this time. He stood up and grabbed the cage, slowly turned around, and started down the ladder like a horse heading for the barn at feeding time. Suddenly, Ian's foot skated off one of the slippery rungs. His chin slammed violently against the ladder, and he bit, deeply and painfully, into his tongue. Hanging with one arm he frantically scrambled to regain a safe hold as his heart pounded out of his chest and blood flooded his mouth. Grasping the ladder tightly while he calmed down, Ian warned himself between heavy breaths,

"Okay…slow down cowboy…just…get down…in one piece."

Approximately 45 minutes later, still spitting blood, Ian found himself safely on the other side. He took a few minutes to give thanks for making it across the gap safely, with only minor injuries. With darkness settling in, Ian quickly headed west again down 106 until he came to an abandoned farmhouse on the south side of the road. It appeared to be safe for occupancy, so he went around to the back to discover the best way in. A nice supply of dry wood, which once must have been neatly stacked, was now scattered about on the back porch. After carefully wading through the wood to get to the door, Ian took one of the log sections and broke out a window pane.

On the verge of hypothermia, Ian decided to throw caution to the wind and start a fire. He got the radio out of his pack and cranked it up to use the flashlight. Old newspapers and kindling were in a hammered copper bucket next to the woodstove and matches were on a small handmade shelf above. Ian's mouth was very tender now and he knew he would not be able to eat solid foods tonight. He got out one of the bottles of water he had found in the pilot house and opened it. A thick slush floated on top as Ian took a drink and let his swollen tongue drift amongst the frozen crystals.

Once the fire was going, Ian cranked up the radio to catch any news updates and hear the list of refugee names that was read every night. The announcer was already fast approaching the end of the alphabetized list. Disappointed, Ian opened the woodstove door to get light into the room. He sank back into his chair, took a deep breath, and stared at the fire. He was so exhausted he could easily fall asleep where he was. But he was also very hungry. He should probably get up and find something soft to eat.

Before Ian could stand up, a bulletin came over the radio: until further notice, all roads and bridges across the Mississippi River were to be shut down immediately. As the broadcast continued, a complete list of the affected states was read, and the announcement was repeated. Ian grabbed his backpack and pulled out the maps. Sitting closer to the fire so he could see better, he pored over each one to get a better understanding of how this latest news would modify his journey. Again.

The urgency of the situation weighed heavily on his soul. With his hands clasped together and resting against his face, he sat and stared into the woodstove. Exhaustion had become angst. Ian realized that by crossing the bridge at Florence he had effectively trapped himself. He couldn't go north because of the heavy ash. He had just crossed the Illinois River, so unless he wanted to cross that bridge again, he couldn't head east. The Mississippi River was to his west, and the Illinois and Mississippi funneled into each other, just south of his position. Ian was literally trapped in the middle of an island. Heading back east wasn't an option because he would have to cross major rivers like the Wabash and the Ohio. He would have to go 600 miles east to travel 600 miles west, only to arrive back at the Mississippi again. That wasn't even logical.

Ian thought about the 800 miles he had already traveled. The walking, stealing vehicles and food, breaking into houses: was this really the end of the road? Wasted time? An exercise in futility? Panic and depression began to set in. He wished he had access to a computer so he could pull up maps and get a better look at the area along the Mississippi. His maps just weren't detailed enough to be sure where to go next. He sat for a while and tried to center himself.

"What are my options?" he mused. "Death and uncertainty. Aren't those really the only options I've ever had?"

The words of the National Guard driver in Michigan resurfaced from the depths of his memory: *"...stay focused on the task at hand and hope it will be okay in the end."*

With a renewed sense of optimism, Ian turned back to his maps. He kept seeing locks along the Mississippi. Maybe they were like the locks up at the Soo, Ian thought. The ash-buried locks at Sault Ste. Marie had been the gateway between Lake Superior and Lake Huron. When they were closed, they basically became three-foot-wide walkways spanning the locks. Stirring the fire, Ian began talking out loud.

"Crossing at a lock is one option. Or I could find a boat. There must be boats at the houses along the river. Or I can hope for a miracle. I just have to stay north of St. Louis." The rest of the night was spent thinking and planning, pacing and worrying.

Day 99

By the early morning Ian was spent. His worry-filled all-nighter had only resigned him to the fact that his single option was to continue west to the Mississippi River. He packed his stuff, gathered what provisions he could from the house, and headed out the door to face another day.

"I'm so tired, I feel sick," he thought. That immediately made him laugh, thinking about the many Christmas mornings Theresa and he would make that very statement after staying up all night wrapping presents for the kids.

The morning was cold and it was still pretty dark outside, but Ian wanted to get an early start. He was now eager to get to the Mississippi. With every step he organized his thoughts into a cohesive game plan. He would continue west on 106 until it dead-ended into the river. Then he would head south looking for houses with boats. If he wasn't able to find a boat, he would continue on until he reached Lock and Dam No. 22. "That has to be crossable," he thought.

Still deep in thought, Ian passed a small green sign on the north side of the road which read "Detroit," Suddenly, he was startled by a high-pitched whizzing sound that raced past his left ear. Instantaneously a gun report resonated in front of him. Ian's neck snapped upward to alarmed attention. A big white barn sat by the road ahead, with a message painted in large red letters:

STAY OUT OF OUR TOWN!!
TRESPASSERS & LOOTERS WILL BE SHOT ON SITE
TURN AWAY NOW!!
SURVIVERS WILL BE CRUSIFIED!!

Almost immediately, a terrifying scene began to materialize before his eyes. Not more than five feet in front of him lay a pile of frozen, partially snow-covered bodies in the center of the road, each one with a gunshot wound to the head. Three bodies, arms stretched above their heads, were nailed to the telephone poles near the barn. Ian frantically tried to comprehend this disturbing sight as another gun shot rang out and a whizzing bullet entered the top left corner of the backpack next to his head.

Ian's mind seemed to shut down as he turned to run. He was now viewing each horrifying second in slow motion. The telephone pole to his immediate right had two bodies nailed to it. One body was hung upside down, her throat slit and her face and hair covered in blood. Now facing east, he could see that six of the other poles he had passed had similar gruesome displays. Additionally, each pole had a warning sign nailed to it. These messages announced certain doom, and Ian had been too exhausted and too deep into his thoughts to see them.

As the third shot echoed from the barn, Ian felt a slight tug on his right arm. Looking down, he saw that his coat was ripped just below the shoulder. He reached over with his left hand and pulled the jacket toward his eyes to get a better look. The bullet had grazed his deltoid muscle, leaving a small valley in his arm. As soon as he saw this, Ian's wound felt as if it were on fire, like being burned with a torch.

Fear switched to panic and he now experienced a floating sensation. The earth seemed to move rapidly below him and he no longer felt the awareness of his feet on the ground. Oblivious to the gunfire that continued to erupt behind him, Ian had switched to survival mode and his mind was now just a stunned passenger, witnessing the brutal carnage on every pole he passed and unaware of how he was moving his body.

Ian ran back to the dirt road at the curve on 106 and kept moving. Snaking his way south through the landscape, he came to the tiny town of Milton. Wounded and literally gun-shy, he warily edged through the fields around the town. About a half mile outside Milton, he found a nice house with plenty of food, supplies, and alcohol. Ian used the alcohol to clean his wound, then applied antibiotic cream from his medical kit. He still had a sore mouth from biting into his tongue but found some canned soup and had a good dinner. Then he got drunk and went to bed.

Day 100

Ian woke up with a hangover, vowing never to drink again. He tended to his wound but skipped breakfast.

He zigzagged south and west that day, putting another six miles between himself and the crucifying vigilantes of Detroit, Illinois.

Chapter 23

Lock 24

Day 101

Having to piss like a racehorse, Ian jumped out of his sleeping bag into the brisk Monday morning air and headed out to the back porch to relieve himself. His stomach growled as the steam from his urine rose up from the ground, and the ten-degree air made it uncomfortable to stand in his bare feet for very long. The grayish-green light reflecting off the snow created an eerie, almost horror-film-like atmosphere that made Ian wish he could just stay inside for the day.

Feeling as if his arm were on fire, he went back into the house and removed the dressing to check for infection. The wound was a little red and irritated but looked surprisingly good.

"I guess the booze and antibiotic cream combo really worked," Ian said out loud. Using more gauze and a liberal amount of ointment, he fashioned another compress to get him through to the next layover.

A lack of food in the house meant he would have to break into his emergency stash in order to have breakfast this morning. Putting on his coat, Ian realized the cold wind would take full advantage of the convenient entry point the bullet had created. He got out his sewing kit and took a few minutes to mend the rip.

"This last week has been a real bitch," Ian said to himself as he exited the house to continue down the road.

The road to Nebo was an unwelcome surprise: hills and curves and patches of dense forest. Rocky outcroppings appeared as the hills got steeper, and the area began to develop a very distinctive rural atmosphere.

"Well, this isn't a good combination," Ian blurted out as he began sliding uncontrollably down the steep incline. Slipping and falling on his butt, he slid his way over to the edge of the road where he could get better traction on the gravel. He took the flag off the staff and stood up. Now he could use the bayonet on his staff to keep from falling. He painstakingly navigated the hilly roadway until it became flat again just east of Nebo. A train track merged on the south side and ran parallel to the road into town. This place was spooky, and he wasn't about to get ambushed again. To avoid being seen, Ian got off the road and walked along the track behind the treeline.

After navigating the hilly terrain, Ian was ready to call it a day. On the western side of Nebo, a small river cut between him and the road. With darkness looming, he had to get off the desolate tracks and back on the road to find a place to stay. Luckily, about a mile out of town there was a small ranch-style house set back from the road. It had plenty of food in the pantry and even a partial case of beer. Ian spent the rest of the evening listening to the radio, worrying about how he was going to get across the Mississippi, and plotting out his next moves.

Day 102

A heavy wind rattled the house and startled Ian awake.

"Oh great," he muttered. "Now what?"

The temperature outside was much warmer this morning. The wind was blowing in from the south. The combination of trees, hills, farms, and farmland had Ian daydreaming about what a perfect area this must be in the late summer and early fall. He drifted so far into his thoughts that he could almost hear the symphony of crickets performing their evening sonatas and see the millions of lightning bugs rising slowly up from the fields. These thoughts, of course, led to missing his family and his home, which led to feelings of depression, worry and despair. Ian knew he had to snap out of it. He started singing.

Take me to the river…

Two hours down the road, the wind shifted and the temperature began to drop. Dark clouds were approaching from the north and Ian knew he had to move a little faster. As he passed a farm, he looked across the road into the pasture. There lay the ice-covered forms of five cows, their tongues hanging out of their mouths; frozen faces tortured from the lack of oxygen.

"Poor things," he thought. "What a crappy way to die."

Immediately after the farm the road became a large curve with a very steep hill. So much for trying to beat the storm. Slowly and carefully, Ian navigated the downhill ice-rink road until it dead-ended into 96, the Mississippi River Road. Turning northwest, he headed toward the small town of Pleasant Hill, which looked on the map to be the closest point of access to Lock & Dam No. 24.

In town, a sign directed Ian to the "Pleasant Hill Access Area." That had to be near Lock No. 24. This land was flat, open, and empty. It stretched for miles toward the unseen river. The dark clouds were now upon Ian and the sky opened up. A steady wind and cold rain made it hard to see and unpleasant for sure. A long walk across exposed fields in a cold driving rain is penetratingly unsympathetic to one's mortality, and Ian knew he had to find shelter soon. The empty road crisscrossed its way across a deep ditch and then made a sharp turn south, eventually aligning with a little forest. The road cut through the bottom of the forest and led to a tiny bridge over one of the incoming ditches. A sign at the bridge indicated that the road to the left would take Ian to the "U.S. Army Corp of Engineers Field Operations Station for Lock & Dam No. 24."

Assuming he had reached his destination, he excitedly followed the road, which paralleled the tributary. The wind and rain seemed to pick up in intensity and Ian was now walking face first into it. Within a mile, he came across an area with a circle drive, a small house, a metal Quonset hut, scattered pieces and parts, a bulldozer, and two large storage tanks. At the end of the tributary was what appeared to be a power station. But where was the Lock & Dam? Ian ran over to the house and saw a note on the door. The sign was a warning to any engineers that came down this way. It read:

WARNING

DO NOT

Attempt to Walk on Lock

Too Slippery!!

A heavy wave of depression washed over Ian. Tears welled up in his eyes as he thought, "How do I get across this fucking river?" Wounded, hungry, depressed, and tired, Ian found it easy to conclude that this desperate situation was the end of the line.

With the weather and nothing but empty fields between Pleasant Hill and the station house, he would have to call this home tonight. He smashed the window on the door so he could gain entry, and as he reached in he thought, "Oh, great! Now I've just broken into a federal facility!"

Once inside, he scanned the interior. The only items in the house were a small charcoal grill, fishing poles, a blue tarp, a fridge with Cokes, a five-gallon bucket, some bungee cords, and multiple filing cabinets full of documents.

He was drenched, shivering from the cold. The lack of a bed meant that Ian would have to sleep on the floor tonight. He needed a fire to dry out and warm up.

The grill had a half-empty bag of charcoal, along with a bottle of lighter fluid, and a box of wooden matches. He set the grill just outside the doorway on the porch. He went over to one of the filing cabinets and grabbed a handful of documents. Seizing the five-gallon bucket, he went back outside and found half a dozen softball size rocks. He then placed the stones around the perimeter of the grill. Ian rolled up the documents into "logs" as tight as he could, stacking them over the stones. He created a windbreak using the tarp and bungees to stop the wind and rain from interfering with his fire. Ian soaked the paper and stones with lighter fluid and struck a match to the pile.

While feeding the fire with documents, Ian suddenly realized what he was doing and burst out into laughter. "Destruction of official government documents added to my list of transgressions," he thought. "Can't get any better than this!"

The cold rain persisted in its assault, as the fire's glow danced in rhythm with the steady wind. Depression was weighing heavily on his shoulders and Ian sat wallowing in despair over his predicament. To lighten his mood he created a little story about how the government had taken all of the secret documents pertaining to global warming and hidden them in these filing cabinets in this little engineer's shack in the middle of nowhere.

"I just torched the proof that global warming exists so I could stay warm," he thought. "How funny is that?"

Darkness…he used to enjoy darkness and everything it represented; whether it was relief from the heat of a hot summer's day, or reading to his kids before bedtime, or sitting outside having a beer with his wife and friends. Darkness was now harshly focused on one thing: survival. After 102 days it had gotten old, and Ian needed it all to end. Soon!

He cranked up the radio for light, put the lid on the grill to hold the heat in, and got up to prepare a place to sleep. With the filing cabinets and the tarp, Ian created a makeshift shelter. Leaving just the hot stones in the center, he carried the covered grill into the house and set it inside his tent. He took more documents and spread them out to guard against sleeping on the cold floor. With his sleeping bag over the paper bed, he was ready to call it a night.

The hot rocks under the tarp made for a comfortable sleeping environment, and Ian lay, warm and dry, wondering why he had never tried this before. The heat combined with weeks of cumulative exhaustion found the weary traveler's eyes too heavy to hold open and Ian passed out within seconds. Three hours later he awoke in a panic, remembering where he was: being funneled into a dead end again, with seemingly no options. Now he was stuck between a lock and a hard place.

Day 103

The next few hours found Ian caught in a tussle between slumber and consciousness. The constant melee induced a state of nauseous confusion and disconnection, compounding Ian's already fragile mental condition. As he was beginning to doze off again, suddenly the room filled with a glow as if someone had entered with a dim flashlight. Shining through the tarp, it cast a certain eerie blueness.

"Take the boat, Dad. Take the boat." Ian was startled awake.

"Oh my God! Gabe?" He struggled to get up and out from under the tarp. "How did you find me?" He threw open the side of the tarp, revealing the dark and quiet room of the shack.

"What the…?" Ian stood up and looked around. "Was that for real?" he thought. He went outside on the porch to check for any signs of footprints or people. There was no evidence of life. His mind questioned what had just happened as he replayed what he had heard:

"Take the boat, Dad."

"What boat?" Ian thought. "Where?"

The sun was rising. Seeing its warm radiance swiftly elevated his mood. Since he was now awake and the day looked promising, Ian saw no value in staying at the shack any longer.

"No heat, no food, why stick around?" he thought as he gathered his things. "I've got me a boat to find!" And with that he was out the door, heading back up the road and to the intersection where the sign was. This time he turned left toward the river and the boat landing.

Captain Monty awoke early to find that the sun was rising. He made coffee, grabbed his favorite "Leprechaun pipe," and headed out on deck to sit and wait. For ten days he had paused in preparation for this day, when the sun would finally come out. As he lit his pipe and watched the hill, he couldn't help but feel excited. Everything was revealing itself just as it had been in his vision.

Heading down a tree-lined road, Ian came up on a 30-foot berm. He began slowly climbing, in hopes of getting a better vantage point from which to spot a boat along the river. Midway up the slippery hill he stopped to catch his breath for a second. As he looked up, he saw the unmistakable ornate smokestacks of a riverboat. Gabe's voice echoed in his head.

"Take the boat, Dad."

In total disbelief, he scrambled to the top as fast as his feet would take him. He stood dramatically posed in complete astonishment. This beautiful vessel had seemingly appeared as if it were a gift of manna for one so weary of his journey through the wilderness.

Captain Monty had just taken a sip of his coffee when the figure of a man appeared at the top of the berm. The captain's vision had been incredibly detailed: a tall man, backlit by the rising sun. He had a staff with a bayonet and a flag attached to it. A gas mask dangled around his neck. There was one thing missing from his vision, however. Captain Monty took a drag on his pipe, laughed nervously, and shouted out,

"Hey! Where's your stag?"

Chapter 24

Day 104

The boat rocked ever so gently, like a cradle, safely hidden in the impenetrable darkness. Ian awoke from a dream into this abyss, disoriented by the unfamiliar movement. Suspended somewhere or somewhen, his heart was racing. Where the hell was he?

Fifteen eternity seconds later the portable space heater clicked on, casting a soft orange glow, illuminating the twenty-three kachina dolls mounted on shelving above Captain Monty's bed. From an airbed set up on the floor, Ian observed this eerie montage. Adrenaline coursed through his body, assuring there would be no further sleep for him this night. The space heater eventually clicked off, plunging the room back into utter darkness.

Oblivious, Captain Monty slept peacefully on his beloved boat. Hyperalert, Ian's thoughts turned to yesterday. He had arrived at the bow of the riverboat, physically and psychologically exhausted. His options had run out! He needed to get across this damn River Styx, out of the ash and back into the land of the living.

Ian remembered coming out of a foggy sleep yesterday to find himself nestled under layers of emergency comforters. While Ian slept, Monty had prepared a sizeable feast from the well-provisioned galley. The meal concluded with fresh strong coffee and homemade chocolate chip cookies with walnuts. Lord, he hadn't had homemade cookies since before the volcano.

Out came Monty's best bottle of vintage sherry, followed by a toast to Ian. Monty toasted the "mystery man with the glowing stag." Confused, Ian asked how he knew about the stag. Monty told of four recurring visions he had had in the last ten days, each vision vividly detailed, each identical to the last. The tall mystery man in a gas mask stood at the top of the levee in front of the rising sun on a clear day. He held a staff affixed with a bayonet and flag. Behind him, somewhat obscured by the sunlight, stood a giant greenish-glowing stag.

Over the last week it had become obvious to Monty that somebody was trying to get his attention. The message was clear.

Even if the logjam broke at Lock 24, he must not leave. He must wait at *this* beach, below *this* levee, until the sun came out and the mystery man appeared with the stag. Captain Monty waited ten days for the sun to come out.

Ian told Monty about his dream at the nearby engineering house, how the room had filled with a bluish glow, and how he had heard his son Gabe telling him to "take the boat, Dad." Then darkness. Ian knew his son had come to guide him to safety.

Ian then told the story of his encounter with the gigantic stag with the greenish-white glow. He told Monty about how Veronica had also seen the glow and how she had saved his life. Excitement overcame Monty. His vision had been real. There was a stag!

Both men marveled at how absurd all of this must sound. Yet clearly, something was out there, pulling the strings, guiding the players to their marks.

Out there hidden behind the quantum veil of destiny, cause, effect, and coincidence are not easily discernible. Especially when post-apocalyptic evolution is afoot.

Ian lay on the airbed for what seemed like forever, waiting for Captain Monty to rouse from his slumber. He had recalled just about everything he could from yesterday and was now ready to discover what unplanned excitement today might bring.

Long before first light, Monty's alarm clock broke the silence, playing an authentic digital recording of a ship's bell marking the time. It was 6 a.m.

Despite decades of nautical habits, an early alarm was not necessary this morning. The continuing logjam at Lock 24 would delay their departure yet another day. Monty's cabin was warm and spacious. The coffee pot on his desk and some leftover chocolate chip cookies would provide life-affirming sustenance. Except for going out in the cold to piss off the upper deck, they were good until noon.

Ian drank his coffee in silence, watching the surrealistic theater play out above Monty's bed. White light from a single table lamp illuminated the kachina dolls. The slowly building, then diminishing, orange glow from the space heater interacted with the ambient light creating continually changing shadows and the illusion of motion. The kachinas seemed to be alive, to move, and their glow seemed to waver in the fluid light. The softly rocking boat enhanced this effect.

Ian thought about the first time he had seen a glowing kachina. He told Monty the story of the kachina on the mantel at the snowshoe class. Then he remembered the kachina who was haunting his dreams. Given Monty's predilection for "dreaming," Ian shared those dreams. However, he was not yet ready to share the vision he had in the grotto at Pana—of the Virgin Mary and the eagle kachina observing an intense birthing struggle. That still made no sense.

These stories kicked Monty into focused awareness. With one broad, sweeping hand motion, he introduced Ian to the collected minions positioned above his bed.

"Well, son, I know a thing or two about kachinas. For over twenty-five years I've studied the southwest Pueblo Indians, their customs, and the meaning of each of these elaborately decorated figurines. Are you familiar with Frank Waters' *Book of the Hopi*?"

"Oh, yeah. I love that book! During my college years, I worked off and on at a spiritual bookstore on Pearl Street in Boulder. The *Book of the Hopi* was very popular at that time. I've spent many a snowy afternoon with customers, delving into the alternative worldview of the Hopi."

Captain Monty was exuberant. Finally, someone who could understand! Obviously, the man with the spirit stag was a fellow spiritual traveler, capable of understanding the complexities of

Hopi belief. His guest was not like the dinner-cruise dimwits who had confronted him over the years about his kachina collection.

Monty continued, "The *Book of the Hopi* inspired frequent trips in the off season to the Hopi reservation. I purchased most of the kachinas you see here at that time. All twenty-three were mounted around the main dining room on the lower deck. That is, until the bible thumpers came in droves.

"You see, word spread quickly through the fundamentalist churches in the region that my boat displayed pagan Indian idols: the kachinas. A born-again Christian fatwa descended upon my boat.

"Well-intentioned but ill-informed people advised me I was headed straight to hell. They screamed at me and my crew. Calling the kachinas 'idols.' Calling me an idolater. Calling the Hopi 'pagan idolaters.' Some nights around here it took on the feel of a holy war. The dinner cruise became very unpleasant. Business began to suffer. I spent more time in the dining room acting as a referee than I spent steering the boat down the Mississippi.

"The fatwa continued for two seasons. Eventually it got so bad I had to move all of the kachinas here, to my private quarters. Slowly, then, things returned to normal."

Ian responded, "That explains how they got here, but it doesn't explain why. Of all the things you could have taken away from the *Book of the Hopi*, why did you focus on the kachinas?"

"Well, one summer in the late '70s, while I was still in college, I spent a couple of months bumming around Great Britain. I had been drawn to Scotland, to a small seacoast community called Findhorn. Several popular books at the time detailed the magical things that were happening there. Residents supposedly coexisted, co-farmed, and actively conversed with creation devas and sprites. In only four inches of topsoil, huge cabbages, monster carrots, and other gigantic vegetables thrived. It defied the laws of agriculture and physics. Scientists came from around the world."

Ian interrupted. "Monty, I was in Findhorn ten years later, in 1989. I witnessed what you're talking about. Several weird events happened to me there. But please, continue."

"You asked why the kachinas were so important to me. I had never heard of the Hopi Indians or kachinas until I went to Findhorn. I met a woman there who introduced me to the *Book of the Hopi*. She claimed that what was happening at Findhorn was identical to what had been happening to the Hopi over the last thousand years. Long before the white man arrived, the Hopi people chose to live at that harsh, uninhabitable place in the middle of the southwest desert. There were no streams or standing water. They never built ditches to irrigate their crops. Why would they choose to live in such an arid, godforsaken place? And yet, this place was not forsaken by God. They survived for centuries with abundant harvests of the Three Sisters—corn, squash, and beans."

"I'm certain they endured the hardships there solely to prove a point," Ian added, "to set an example for the rest of the world to follow. Look, during the great Hopi migration across most of the Americas, they could have permanently settled in many comfortable locations. But they refused to stop at any one place for long. Why? The Hopi elders claim that their ceremonies still depict the powerful evil that afflicted the entire world before the great flood." Ian was in full lecture mode now.

"For generations they kept moving in great circular patterns, working out the bad juju from the antediluvian Third World. The journey became the catharsis. The Hopi would never forget. They weren't going to fall back into the old bad habits. When people settle down and become too comfortable, they become spiritually lazy. Then they stop sending and receiving God energy out of the top of their heads. Sadly, billions of people—whole civilizations—have become so spiritually lazy they no longer even know what that means."

Monty chimed in. "That is exactly why I am so fascinated with the kachinas. The Hopi elders claim that because they have continually communicated with the Creator out of the top of their heads, they receive aid and direction from the kachinas. These spiritual beings sent from other worlds and other dimensions help the Hopi manifest the unseen forces of creation. Exactly like the Devas over at Findhorn, they defy the laws of agriculture and physics.

"Centuries later, the Hopi still sit there in that desert…waiting. Waiting for us to come to our senses, and come back home!"

This last statement triggered a download of memories buried deep within Ian. Images older than mind from an ancient lifetime. Ian stood at a landing site on a beach. The Guardian of this new fourth world issued a warning:

> **At the time of the Great Purification to come... unrelenting famine shall sweep across the face of the living Earth. Those last remaining remnants of the circular migrations will hear the *final urgent calls*...and travel west toward home.**
>
> **This *Journey to the West* will require the permanent suspension of all prior understanding. The next step in creation will demand that.**

Ian lingered briefly in the imprint of that ancient collective memory. Monty, however, had already moved on. This was his first chance to update Ian on a widespread apocalyptic movement sweeping through the Native peoples of the Americas. Ian rejoined the monologue as Monty described the cultural injustices that had inflamed this end-of-the-world movement.

With his reading glasses resting out at the end of his nose, Monty continued to explain that by 1877 Native peoples had been displaced and confined to reservation lands, to indigenous concentration camps. Federal laws and regulations had been specifically designed to destroy every part of Native culture. Young people were sent to Indian boarding schools to learn the white man's ways and religion. Within a generation Native languages, cultural memories, and spiritual practices had perished with the elders.This sociocide continued on for another sixty years, until the mid-1930s, when the federal government suddenly rescinded the repression.

"So how could Native tribes go about re-establishing forgotten, erased cultures? Fortunately, the answer sat way out in the middle of that godforsaken Hopi reservation. The remote, shifting desert terrain thwarted all government attempts to parcel out the Hopi land. Children could not be found to send to white schools. Finally the federal government just gave up and let the Hopi keep their language, religion, and complex culture.

"Because the ancient Hopi cosmology remained intact, their stories and practices found their way back into the spiritual beliefs of many other tribes. Now, since the eruption, almost all Native people believe the end of the Fourth World, our current world, has come. They anxiously await the return of the White Brother."

"Yes," Ian added. "The long lost White Brother from Hopi mythology, the Pahana."

Monty smiled. "The one who will return at the end of the Fourth World with the missing piece of the tablet. The one who will bring the white, red, yellow, and black races together to create a new spiritual brotherhood of man. So you see, Ian, while you

were slogging your way through the ash to get here, Indian tribes all over the Americas were desperately combing the countryside searching for the Pahana."

On the south side of lunch, the conversation continued back in the captain's quarters.

"One word: Koyaanisqatsi. The Hopi word meaning 'Life out of balance.' Do you remember the 1983 movie?"

"Yes, yes, I do!" Ian responded. "It was mesmerizing. I was just a teenager in Ann Arbor then, but I remember. When the movie ended—no one could move. Just total silence throughout the theater. We all understood the meaning of that profound spiritual message. Hopi prophecy was sung in the Hopi language. It struck every one of us at some very deep level."

"For me a spiritual alarm went off," said Monty. "*KOYAANISQATSI* hit the theaters shortly after I finished reading the *Book of the Hopi*. Clearly, the Hopi were sounding a warning. Something was desperately wrong here. They were finally revealing their ancient prophecy of impending extinction. But why now?"

For thousands of years, the Hopi had never revealed their secret sacred beliefs. Everyone from conquistadors to anthropologists had failed to comprehend their ceremonies or complex worldview. Then, in the early 1960s, more than thirty elders unexpectedly agreed to sit down with Frank Waters to record the complete oral history of the Hopi people and their prophecies. Why did those clan leaders suddenly end their silence? What had changed? What did the Hopi know that we did not?

After all, Westerners thought they had all the answers. Monty had fought that battle nightly on his dinner cruises. The technologically superior white culture valued nothing the poverty stricken, illiterate Hopi culture had to offer. This arrogant lack of respect and lack of curiosity would lead to the termination of the Fourth World. Monty was certain of that. Those who had enthroned technology as their god would soon perish from this earth. This was not the first creation to suffer that fate.

Long before the volcano erupted, the Hopi had warned that the end of the world was near. Monty feared for his survival. In the great flood, life on earth was terminated abruptly. Survivors, however, always appeared to be deliberately guided to their mark. What specific actions did they take that allowed them to live? The survivors held the clues. We have much to learn from the survivors.

What did the exterminated victims always do wrong? Why were they targeted? There appeared to be patterns, but this required time to ponder. Armed with single malt and Cuban cigars, our beached mariners had nowhere to go and nothing but time. They began to connect the dots, searching for clues.

The last mass extinction event occurred at the great flood. Ian and Monty began their inquiry there. For the Hopi, the time surrounding the flood is referred to as the Third World.

The *Book of the Hopi* describes life at that time: in big cities, in a large civilization somewhere near the Himalayas. As in preceding creations, great corruption, evil, and war came to this Third World. Their flying shields (saucers) inflicted massive aerial bombardments on other cities and countries. Those Hopi who could still open the kopavi at the top of their heads were being killed off in the destruction.

The Creator feared for their survival. The situation became so dire that the Creator evacuated them from the Himalayas to the coast of Southern China. He then unleashed the flood waters upon the earth. Keeping their kopavis open, a Hopi flotilla island hopped across the Pacific Ocean to Central America. Guided by God, they emerged out of the flood into this world, the newly created Fourth World.

Hindu sacred texts from the Himalayas corroborated much of the *Book of the Hopi* Third World story. Monty hauled out his collection of ancient Sanskrit texts. References to Vimanas or flying machines can be found throughout the Vedas and other Eastern literature.* They described their fuel, construction, size,

---

*See Appendix J

types of propulsion, and combat maneuverability. Everything from rockets to seven-story UFOs. They describe heat-seeking missiles, nuclear bombs, nuclear war, laser weapons, death rays, sound weapons, hypnotic weapons, and divine lightning.

Like the Hopi, the Hindu sacred texts also describe massive giants. The texts declare that the giants were destroyed by God, not for their sins but for their misuse of psychic powers. The giants psychically attacked those who could emit seventh chakra energy out of the top of their heads. The blossoming, evolving ones were facing extermination from these head pounders. Divine intercession and flood waters brought life back into balance.

Not many Westerners know of these ancient stories hidden in plain view. Their ignorance begat arrogance. And Captain Monty was damn sick and tired of their condescension toward the Hopi.

"The Hopi Air Force fought valiantly for air supremacy over the Himalayas. Meanwhile, the 'technologically superior' Western folks lived in crude tents, tended sheep and goats, and built primitive wooden boats. The Hopi were not the ignorant barbarians in this picture."

RUKMA VIMANA

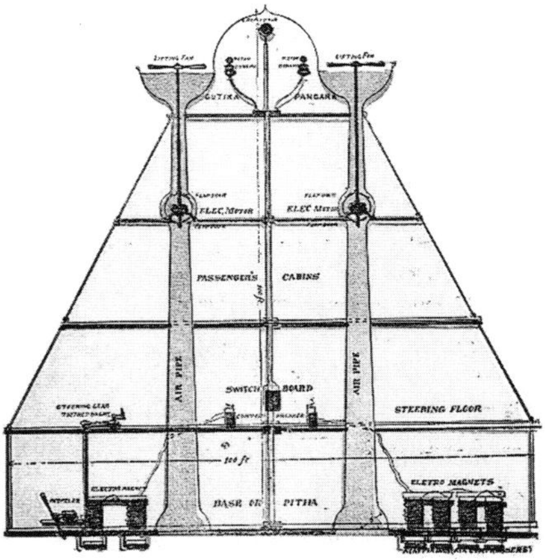

VERTICAL SECTION

Drawn by
T. K. ELLAPPA,
Bangalore.
2-12-1923.

Prepared under instruction of
Pandit SUBBARAYA SASTRY,
of Anekal, Bangalore

"And the Hindus were not dirty snake charmers who slept on beds of nails," Ian added.

Patterns of survival were forming, but it was still too early. The Noah's Ark Bible story offered other perspectives, and perhaps other clues.

"The Great Flood was an extreme punishment for the alleged crime. We recognize that. After all, there were not specific charges, just a handful of vague phrases: man's thoughts are only evil; earth filled with violence (unspecified); earth corrupt before God; wickedness was great (unspecified). That's it! For that we got 'termination with extreme prejudice'."

Puzzled, Ian reflected. "All we got was a pretty little rainbow and a promise that God would not do this again. What the hell did we do in the first place? This was all purposely vague. Clearly, the vibrational rate was different in that world filled with giants and angels and 900-year-old geezers. But something huge is missing here. We are not being told anything else! Why aren't we getting the real story here?"

It was then that Monty cracked a big smile but didn't move a muscle.

Ian continued, "Obviously, the Hopi and Hindu stories never made it into the final edit of the Bible. Instead, humans got blamed, and all that remained was an ego-based morality play of good vs. evil. Just corruption, wickedness, and sin. All ego crap. Not a single word about consciousness energy."

Monty stood, poured himself a stiff drink, and lit a cigar. That Cheshire cat smirk could not be contained.

"I let you go on to show you just how preposterous all that sounded. That morality play twaddle. We have been intentionally diverted from the truth for millennia. Ian, I found the smoking gun. The missing piece of the puzzle.

"You've never read *The Book of Enoch*, have you? I have it below decks in storage. You've got to see this! You won't believe it! It's way worse than the Hindu–Hopi version of the time before the flood. We'll spend some time with that tomorrow. But I can tell you now that *The Book of Enoch* is over 108 chapters long, describes flying vehicles, Enoch flying to heaven, massive monstrous giants, 199 fallen angels, and psychic attack. It never made it to the Bible, even though Enoch was Methuselah's father and Noah's great-grandfather. Clearly, the founders of Christianity and the Jewish rabbis did not want this shocking information revealed. History has been purposely perverted."

"So what you're saying," Ian added, "is that you can prove that reality has been inverted. The religious founders who were unable to experience altered states diverted our attention. Western Civilization moved toward a left-brain, victim, ego, sin-based model of reality. Consciousness energy in all its forms was branded as evil, to be avoided at all costs."

"Yes," Monty added, "and Enoch's direct communication with God was considered blasphemy. If your culture has been diverted away from consciousness energy, then no words were ever created to describe that energy. Without those words, it cannot be explained or examined or understood..."

Ian finished his sentence, "...and consciousness energy will not play any role at all in the culture! And this is a huge obstacle! Columbus, Captain Cook, and even Darwin encountered this problem. The explorers' large ships anchored just offshore were invisible to the island populations. They could see the small landing boats but had never encountered the larger mother ships. No words existed. No context existed. Thus, the big ships did not exist. This is a baffling glitch in human perception. That's exactly what we have now. You can see that this lack of a common vocabulary is a major obstacle for the Pahana to overcome!"

Monty nodded. "But then the *Star Wars* series created a vocabulary that explained ancient consciousness experiences. The description of the 'Force' gave Western Civilization a term for the energy the rest of the world already knew as chi, or ki, or Kundalini. This is the beginning of a universal shared terminology."

Up to this point Ian and Monty had explored only the Great Flood from the perspectives of three civilizations. To understand the dynamics of an apocalypse, they would need to examine several more near-extinction events. They needed to figure this out! This was more than just surviving some final apocalypse. Another message was emerging. The clues were with the survivors. It was about a way of life: not in an ego way, but in an energy way.

From the beginning, it had always been about the energy, the force, or God consciousness.

The *Book of the Hopi* revealed that the ones who had survived kept the kopavi open at the top of their heads—*at all times!* And not just during the final destruction, *but at every phase of existence*; at the emergence into the new world, then through the decline, and finally into the destruction. Their kopavi had led them where they needed to go. This was true in the First World, in the Second World, and in the Third World.

It also has been true in this, the Hopi Fourth World. From the emergence in Central America to today's volcanic "life out of balance," they have kept their kopavis open, waiting for us to figure this out. Meanwhile, the ancient training continues for Hopi initiates in the upper floors of their teaching kivas.

Monty and Ian stopped for the night, certain they had stumbled into major clues. Tomorrow they would tackle the perplexing Noah story and the larger looming problem: What's a poor Pahana to do?

Day 105

Logs and debris continued to pile along the length of Lock 24. Travel through the impassible lock would be impossible again today. However, these obstacles begat opportunity. *The Book of Enoch* waited patiently on a table, behind fresh cinnamon rolls and very strong coffee. The *Book of the Hopi* sat next in line, and finally there was a little blue book yet to be introduced. A philosophical logjam; but at least this one came with cinnamon rolls.

Captain Monty began to pace vigorously. He put on the Beatles' *White Album* and played "While My Guitar Gently Weeps." He replayed the song five times. Monty shared George Harrison's bitter frustration. Transcendental experiences with the Maharishi in India in 1968 had awakened Harrison's God Consciousness. *This energy is a fundamental part of existence. In fact, it's our primary reason for being.* How did Western folk miss something this huge? How come we were not alerted? Harrison struggled with the anguish throughout the song, and sadly, throughout the rest of his life. This severely pissed Monty off!

Monty was frustrated. "No one alerted us! But this was always about the battle between God Consciousness and the psychic 'dark side of the force.' God had no other choice. There were giants so massive they needed to be exterminated under very deep water. These were not those puny giants like the eleven-foot tall Goliath, or the twenty-foot tall giants that Moses annihilated. Not to mention the 199 angels that taught incantations, sorcery, and psychic attack—or those flying disks. God was fighting his own fallen angels.

"Oh, and that story about the rainbow. Humans got the blame for the flood, but maybe we were never the intended target. Maybe we were just the collateral damage in that flood. The unintended dead villagers.

"Other civilizations weren't afraid to tell this story. Enoch's story was the Hopi story, was the Hindu story. But Western civilization wasn't even on the same page. Left-brained priests and rabbis covered this up, lied to us, and sent us down the wrong track, plummeting toward eternal separation—away from our true connection with God."

"And you wonder why there aren't any white teachers of consciousness," Ian commented. "Monty, there's something else I can't figure out in this puzzle. Why Noah? Every rabbi in the world now accepts that the Jews pilfered the ark–Gilgamesh story while in captivity. And every five-year-old can calculate that three million different species and all their food can't fit onto that one little boat. What is it? Like Dr. Who's Tardis? Bigger on the inside than it is on the outside?"

Monty picked up the little blue book and waved it under Ian's nose. "It's exactly like Dr. Who's Tardis! This is *The Gnostic Gospels*.* Read this verse from *The Apocalypse of the Great Power*."

Ian's eyes grew large as he read. "'Noah decided to rescue the gods and angels and their spiritual power and their manna. He

---

*See Appendix K

moved them from that aeon and fed them in eternal realms.' My God, Monty! The ark was an energy portal!" He paused for a moment, awestruck. "Holy shit! This changes everything! This is profoundly different from what we were taught. This will take a while to process. I guess the next question is, 'Why Noah?'."

Monty grabbed his Bible off the shelf. "It says that Noah walked with God. He talked with God."

"But Monty, those left-brained priests don't do consciousness. They don't understand that divine communication is not usually verbal. Entire sets of instructions are downloaded. These Bible translators were talking out of their left-brained asses here, trying to control the masses!

"But communicating with God…now that's interesting," Ian mused. "To do what he did, Noah had to have had his kopavi open. That's why he was chosen. That's why he was a survivor. He could 'speak' to God through his chakras or kopavi. That's why his family made it out, too. It's genetic. The whole damn family, his whole damn lineage, past and present, had wiring."

"Look," Monty interrupted, "Enoch, his great grandfather, 'walked and talked' with God, and eventually disappeared into heaven. Why Noah? Okay, that's why it was Noah!"

"I've been watching this for ages," Ian continued. "There appears to be a direct relationship between higher consciousness and evolutionary changes. Consciousness people do things that humans can't do. Most of these evolutionary changes look like they occur in particular families. Along 'selected' lineages. It says in the Bible that 'Noah was perfect in his generations'."

"So it turns out that this is the same story as the Hopi," Monty added. "Noah represents the Spider Woman, who protects and leads humanity through the flood to a safe new world. Noah thereby preserved and insured the survival of his own genetic lineage. Enoch's lineage that had the wiring. *An evolutionary lineage.*"

WHAT'S A POOR PAHANA TO DO?

"Monty, all I can tell you is, I wouldn't want to be that poor bastard. The Hopi say that this guy is supposed to bring the white, yellow, red, and black races together in a spiritual fellowship of man. Supposedly, he will forge an agreement between the races. Good luck with that! The Hopi trust that the Pahana will come to the table and figure out this problem. Oh, and he'll also show up with that missing piece of the stone tablet.

"I just don't see how any of this can be successful! There are just too many obstacles. For starters, how can he get the white people to cooperate, to participate? If this one white guy who can open his kopavi comes to the table, is he the 'token' white guy, the lone representative for all the other white people?

"And then there's no way to discuss consciousness with white culture. There aren't words. Nothing can be expressed. There is no cultural history of consciousness. Worst of all, there is no cultural history of real spirituality. Just astral-demonic-ghost spiritualism—and the dogma of religion."

Monty and Ian hashed this out for hours. The academics attack consciousness as delusional mumbo jumbo. The Western Abrahamic religions consider it blasphemy. God lives in Heaven, sitting on a throne, judging you. Ego reigns supreme. Yoga meditation is satanic. There is no vehicle to teach consciousness techniques in Western civilization. Instead the piggies just go around pissing everybody off. In the immortal words of the Beatles, "What they need's a damn good whacking."

Exhausted and famished, Monty could just shake his head in displeasure.

"We know the Pahana is sitting there right now, watching all of this unfold. He's working through all of this, just like we are. He knows the score. He knows the odds against him. The only thing I can ask is…WWPD. What would the Pahana do? What could he possibly do here?"

After a late dinner, the two men settled back with sherry. Monty lit his pipe.

"You know," he said, exhaling his first satisfying puff, "when

I was on the rez with the Hopi, this was something that really bothered them. How could they find the Pahana? They needed him to fulfill the prophecy, but he was nowhere in sight."

"That explains Banyacya then," Ian murmured.

"Huh?"

"When I was living in Boulder, a Hopi elder named Thomas Banyacya came to town. He gave a lecture at the university in the spring of 1992, and we all went. My brother, his wife, me, and several of his friends all sat together to hear what the man had to say. He explained the Hopi prophecy and warned us that we were perilously close to the start of the final purification. He handed out a letter he had written to the United Nations, asking to speak to the General Assembly.* The U.S. had blocked his invitation three times, he said, and if they did it one more time, there would be no turning back. We were doomed.

"Then he told us he had been sent to Boulder by the other Hopi elders to find the Pahana. They had a vision that told them the Pahana was in Boulder, and they even described him. Banyacya began to plead with us, begging the Pahana to make himself known. The Hopi desperately needed him, he said. 'If you are here, please, step forward now!' he urged.

"Nobody moved. I don't think anybody in our group even breathed. I remember how disappointed Banyacya looked. His shoulders slumped and he seemed to cave in on himself. It was heartbreaking to watch."

Monty hummed sympathetically, but before he could get a word out, Ian continued.

"You know, the really weird thing is that he wasn't the only one looking for the Pahana. The day before his lecture, one of my brother's friends, Cherokee Dave, ran into a Kiowa medicine man who had just arrived in Boulder. He had also been sent by his elders after they had a vision. I remember Dave squinting at my brother and saying, 'Ya know, that description sounded a lot like you. You might want to keep a low profile for a while.'

---

*See Appendix L

"Cherokee Dave was a hell of a good friend. He diverted the Kiowa by lending him his truck and giving him a case of beer. The Kiowa disappeared for three days. By that time, Banyacya was gone, and the two never had a chance to team up."

"Wait a minute!" Monty exclaimed. "Why'd y'all block it? What the hell was that all about?"

Ian shrugged. "I was just a kid," he said. "The others told me that sometimes the fruit has to ripen on the tree longer. That's all the explanation I got. I have no idea what they meant by that."

Monty looked puzzled, then thoughtful, and then he figured it out.

"Unless...that was twenty-five, thirty years ago, wasn't it? I bet you look like your brother did then, don't you? That's what they meant! You're the Pahana, not your brother. I knew it! Damn it, Ian, you're the Pahana!"

"No, I'm not," Ian protested. "No superheroes here, Monty, just an art professor trying to find his wife and kids."

Monty completely ignored that nonsense.

"You've got to get to the Hopi rez! And I'm gonna get you there. *Ms Duchess* and I will take you all the way to the I-40 bridge at Memphis. That'll save you a big chunk of time, and it's a whole lot easier than walking through ash. Damn, I've been studying this for thirty years, and now I'm going to be part of it! I'm going to be part of history!"

Day 106

The two men had planned to sleep late following their long discussions of the previous days; but the Mississippi had other plans for them. Shortly after dawn a long, low groan brought both of them wide-eyed and alert. Ian, sleep dazed, was confused and alarmed. Captain Monty, however, broke into a huge grin.

"At last!" he exclaimed. "I thought that damned logjam would never move. Get up, Ian. If we want to get out of here, we've got work to do and not much time to do it."

Ramming his cap down onto his head, Monty clamped his pipe between his teeth and filled the coffee pot.

"First things first," he stated firmly. "Without coffee, we'll hate ourselves in a couple of hours."

Ian, still groggy, watched this alert bustling with bemusement. To him, there was no explaining morning people. How on earth could anyone be that awake at this hour of the day? He himself could barely make his fingers grip the mug of steaming coffee the captain thrust into his hands.

A few sips later Ian began to feel his head clearing.

"Okay," he croaked. Clearing his throat, he repeated himself, then added, "What do we have to do?"

"Well, if we want to head for Memphis, now's the time. I'll run my usual diagnostics, then we'll shove off this beach and head south. By the time I get the engines going, the jam that's blocking the lock should have cleared itself. Sound good?"

"But you haven't even looked outside yet," Ian protested. "How can you know the debris is clearing?"

"Sorry, I forgot," Monty apologized. "You don't know the river, do you? Well, when you've been up and down her whole length for a few decades, you get to know every sound and exactly what it means. That groan we heard? That was the river putting pressure on the logjam, pushing that sucker right out of the way. It'll be clear within the hour. Not only that, it'll be moving fast. If we can get ourselves into the flow, we'll get a push downriver."

Ian felt a leap of hope. It was happening!

"What do I have to do to help?"

Monty pointed to the railing on the beach side of the boat.

"See that long pole there? When I get the engines going, you're going to use that pole to push us off the shore. Then you're going to haul it back in, lay it down, and hold on for dear life."

And that's exactly what happened. As Ian clutched the railing, Monty gunned his engines in reverse. The *Ms Duchess* tore herself free from the land and took her rightful place in the swift flow of the Mississippi. Once back in her natural element, the *Duchess*, which had looked like a barge pretending to be a wedding cake, regained her grace and dignity.

Her captain was likewise transformed. Gone was the earnest, sometimes comical gnome with reading glasses. In his place stood a confident, highly competent riverboat captain, posture ramrod straight and steely gaze fixed on the rapidly moving waters ahead. Ian marveled at the changes.

As the boat settled into the current, Ian made his way up to the pilothouse. Monty handed him a set of binoculars and instructed him in scanning the waters ahead for hazards. Ian focused intently on the scenery around them.

Even as devastated as the river and its shoreline were, the views were spectacular in their post-apocalyptic starkness. The current was fierce but flowed straight through the lock, forcing debris out of its way with its own brute strength. *Ms Duchess* passed through and continued south, past Clarksville Island on the left. The Clarksville light sat on the Missouri shoreline off to the right. Here the Army Corps of Engineers had put up an off-bank protection system of underwater dikes, wing dams, and a thousand-foot-long revetment. It seemed to be holding well even against the current, the rising waters, and the battering of the flotsam.

Everything was gray. The sky, the water, the shoreline, the islands—all uniformly gray. Ian strained to differentiate land from river, snags from islands, sky from water. He found his eyes tired and stinging after just a couple of miles; but the gray seemed to stretch on forever. It was going to be a long way to Memphis.

"How fast are we going?" Ian asked. "And give it to me in miles per hour if you can, okay?"

"Okay," Monty returned. "We're going about three miles an hour right now. I'm trying to hold to the speed of the current so we don't overrun any drifting snags. It's enough of a problem dodging the ones that have piled up."

Ms Duchess continued her careful way south, staying close to the Missouri shore. They passed the end of Clarksville Island. After another agonizing mile they reached the northern end of Carroll Island and painstakingly inched past the Amaranth Island light on the Missouri side. Their progress was steady but mind-numbingly slow and tedious. The concentration required to steer a safe course was excruciating for both men. Ian was exhausted already.

"How far have we come?" Ian asked after an eternity had passed.

"'Bout six miles," Monty replied. "And, no, we're not there yet. In fact, this has been the easy part. We're gonna hit some real snake track navigating just up ahead. Keep your eyes peeled for the next half hour or so. Look for the Mulheron Field Light on Slim Island. That's where we cross back over to the Illinois side of the river."

Ian rubbed at his tired eyes and squinted down the river. "God, Monty, my eyes feel as if they've been worked with a scouring pad."

"Oh, stop griping. We've got a long way to go yet. If you use up all your complaints now, you'll have nothing to bitch about later. How about a sandwich?"

That was a welcome diversion. Ian dug into the large cooler Monty had hefted up to the pilothouse before they set out. Sure enough, there were a variety of sandwiches, a couple of thermos bottles of coffee, some cans of cola, packages of cookies and cakes. There were even a few apples.

"A feast fit for a king," Ian exclaimed happily. "What kind of sandwich do you want?"

Somehow, eating made even his eyes feel better. Maybe it was just that he was doing something other than just staring down that damned river.

"Hey, Monty, what are we going to do when it gets dark?" It said a lot for Ian's confidence in his new friend that it had taken him this long to come up with that question. But now that he had realized how slowly they were moving and how very far they had to go, the issue was urgent. There was no way he'd be able to see in the dark, especially since he could barely see in what passed for full daylight.

"Took you long enough to figure that out," Monty grinned. "Not to worry—there's a marina about a mile south of Hamburg. It has a river dock we can tie up to for the night. I've even got a friend who lives there. With any luck, he's still around and we might be able to get a good meal out of him."

Ian puffed out a sigh of relief.

"Man, you do think of everything," he said admiringly. "It's a good thing I'm not in charge of this trip."

At Slim Island, Monty eased *Ms Duchess* back toward the Illinois shoreline and gently curved his way past a series of islands: Grimes Island, McCoy Island, and the ominous-sounding Dead Mans Island. As they neared the southern tip of McCoy Island, Ian heard Monty mutter to himself,

"Oh, crap. Do I bear right or left at Tisdel Towhead? I can never remember."

Ian shot a panicked look at the pilot, only to find Monty watching him from the corner of his eye, a tiny grin on his face. "Gotcha!" he chortled. "Sorry, but it gets damned stressful, steering through this mess. I needed some comic relief. Don't worry, I know this river like the back of my hand."

Back to the Missouri side of the river they went. Then, a bit more than a mile further, it was back to the Illinois side, tucking between the shoreline and Mosier Island.

"Not too far now," Monty noted. "We're about three miles away from the marina. Give it another hour or so and we'll be docking. Don't know about you, but I'm about ready to get back on land." Ian's agreement could not have been more fervent.

Hugging the Illinois side of the river, they made their way south. They were about halfway down the length of Mosier Island when they heard the worst sound in the world.

Ms Duchess coughed.

Ian and Monty stared at each other in horror. That sound meant the death of an ash-suffocated engine. Ian had heard it before, on tractors and riding mowers across the Midwest. It had always meant he had about another mile, maybe two, of riding before the engine gave in to the choking ash.

"How far out are we now?" he croaked.

"Couple of miles," Monty managed to return.

"Can we make it?"

"We'd better. If the engine goes, we lose the steering and we smash into whatever the river throws at us. And if we go down, we'll be dead from hypothermia in three minutes."

Grimly clenching his pipe between his teeth, Captain Monty began playing with the engine controls. He reduced speed, then revved the engines, then reduced again. *Ms Duchess* hiccupped, coughed, and smoothed out. Another mile passed. The village of Hamburg came into sight on the Illinois bank. On the Missouri side of the river a wide concrete ramp rose from the water and headed onto shore.

"What's that?" Ian asked. Monty squinted at the ramp.

"Oh, yeah. That's the old Hamburg ferry ramp. Used to be a river ferry ran across the river here. It's long gone now, but the access is still in place. I figured if things really went south on us, we could ground ourselves there. I think we're going to make it all the way though. Less than a mile to go. Keep your fingers crossed."

It was the longest twenty minutes of their lives. Both men were taut as drawn bows until the dock of the marina came into view on the Missouri side of the river.

Stuttering and choking, *Ms Duchess* lurched toward the dock. Monty fought the controls, trying to bring her in smoothly. Ian left the pilothouse and headed down to the main deck. With a final jerk, the bow crunched against the rubber dock buffers. While Monty killed the engines, Ian grabbed the bow line, jumped to the dock, and began tying the boat down. Monty threw him the rope from the stern, and *Ms Duchess* came to rest. They had made it.

Chapter 25

The Calling

Day 107

The air was uncomfortably chilly. Ian recognized the faint smell of moth balls as he pulled the wool blanket up over his head for warmth and just a tiny bit more sleep. The kitchen floor creaked with early morning movement, and the aroma of coffee drifted from room to room.

The house belonged to Captain Monty's friend Tom. He now managed the Timberlake Marina and lived nearby along the river. After the first eruption, Tom decided he didn't want to get caught up in the mass exodus that was heading south. Instead, he decided to hunker down and watch the ash and debris drift by. He figured the river would let him know when it was time to leave.

A short while later, Ian awoke to the side door slamming and the voices of Tom and Monty. Apparently, these two had gotten up early to go down to the boat and assess what could be done to fix her. Ian listened as they deliberated over the options. The tone of the conversation was not at all optimistic.

"Monty, I'm afraid you're lookin' at at least two or three weeks, or maybe even a month before she's up and running again. This one's gonna take some time!"

Tom's assessment was met with an angry retort. Ian could tell from his tone, however, that Monty respected his friend's opinion. The debate over what should be done was still going on when Ian entered the room.

"I've been listening to your discussions," he interrupted, "and I've decided to keep moving. I don't have two or three weeks, or even a month to wait. Hell, by that time I could be below the ash line and clear into Oklahoma! No, I think I'm going to continue on foot from here."

"Wait a minute!" Captain Monty protested, "You can't do that to me! What about our plans? We're supposed to go downriver to the I-40 bridge. It's a straight shot to Albuquerque from there!"

With a confused countenance, Ian looked at Monty for a few seconds before responding.

"Monty, I'm not doing anything to you. This isn't about you."

Captain Monty stumbled over his words as he attempted to respond.

"Well, I just…I thought it was…I just thought it would make your life easier if you could get to I-40 quicker and have someone with you for added protection."

Monty paused for a second and concluded, "I just want to be a part of this historical event!"

Ian looked down at the floor, and with a big sigh, he slowly raised his head in response,

"Captain Monty, you have already been a major part of my journey. I'm not convinced it's historical, but you are the reason I'm even able to continue. If it is, as you say, 'historical'," Ian said with a grin, "then it's you, who will most certainly go down in history as the Ferryman."

Monty's smile filled the room. Ian's allusion to Siddhartha's Ferryman and the River Styx ferryman was not lost on him. With his ego now placated, Monty's agenda quickly shifted.

"Since you're adamant about walking alone, then you're gonna need some assistance."

Tom sat with Ian at the table and went over plans for the next phase of Ian's journey. Monty made breakfast, listened, and added his two cents' worth when he thought it was appropriate. The consensus around the table seemed to be to go west for a while before turning south. There was too much turmoil and danger around St. Louis. Tom discussed the route in detail, drew a small map, and pushed it over to Ian.

"This'll steer you clear of St. Louis. Now if you can just avoid Mr. Death, you should make it!"

As soon as breakfast was finished, Tom and Monty wasted no time gathering food, water, and clean clothes to support Ian. It was still morning, so there was plenty of time to walk the ten miles and get to his next destination before dark.

As the three men said their goodbyes, Monty got a bit emotional and hugged Ian.

"Damn, Monty!" Tom chortled. "Maybe you two should get a room."

"Fuck you, Tom." Monty replied.

At the end of the street, Ian laughed. He could hear Monty grumbling profusely about missed opportunities and having to stay behind. Some of Captain Monty's more colorful words still managed to reach Ian's ears as he walked around the corner and out of sight.

Spending the last three and a half days with the Captain was a nice break, but it was also good to get back on the road. It was becoming clear to Ian that long breaks made him feel anxious, and he worried about the long-term psychological effects this trip would have.

Thank God for Tom's map. To navigate the back roads without it would have been difficult. Winding his way along, he finally ended up on MO79, which paralleled a set of railroad tracks to the east. On the tracks were abandoned hopper cars frozen in time. They almost looked lonely, Ian thought, like they were waiting to fulfill their purpose.

Out of boredom, he started counting each car as he walked along, trying not to get too far ahead of himself. Almost all of the cars were gray, but a few were brown, and many of them sported vividly painted graffiti and tags. When he reached the last, he had counted 118 cars, all connected together to two brightly colored, orange, yellow and black engines; large bold black letters, BNSF, adorned their sides.

As he continued down the road past the railcars, Ian felt surprisingly joyful. The exercise of counting each one, combined with the stimulation of color and graphics, created a welcome diversion from the lifeless, grayscale mundanity he had now become accustomed to.

Just west of Paynesville, Ian found a house sitting far back from the road. Tibetan prayer flags adorned the porch, and a sign that read "Namaste" was hung above the door. "Niiice!" he announced as he stepped up onto the porch.

It was apparent that whoever lived here was spiritual in nature and practiced living simply. Inside, there were very few material possessions and the rooms echoed with every footstep on the hardwood floors. Incense, sage, cardamom, and ginger—these aromas permeated the air and calmed the spirit. An ancient familiarity washed over Ian.

A stone fireplace was built into the east wall of the living room, and a large Persian rug adorned the floor. Two upholstered wing-backed chairs flanked the hearth. A small, humble wooden table nestled against the south wall. In front of the table sat a large square pillow with a small round pillow on top. In the center of the small table were candles, an incense burner, and some crystals. There was also a smudge stick, some hawk feathers, and a rattle. On the wall behind this altar was a framed 8x10 picture of Yogananda, whose piercing eyes and half-smiling face followed Ian's every step.

In the kitchen was a gas stove. Ian smiled. He found brown rice and barley in the cupboards, along with spices and teas. He gathered water in multiple pots and started them boiling. A hot beverage would warm him up and a healthy dinner would keep him sustained.

After dinner, he lit a small fire in the fireplace to take the chill off of the room. He then lit the candles and a stick of incense at the altar. The dancing smoke and light animated Yogananda's face, and his eyes were now like beacons signaling a safe harbor. Intrigued, Ian sat down on the cushions. It had been a while since he had practiced meditation, but having such an inviting space, how could he pass it up?

He sat with his back straight, legs crossed, and his hands lying open across his lap. He closed his eyes, took a few deep breaths, centered himself, and slowly opened his eyes. Ian's mind raced, but he had learned long ago just to allow the internal noise and dialog to happen. The candle flickered hypnotically, shifting his point of consciousness. The room was now slowly disappearing into a white, cloud-like space. Ian's breathing became shallower, his spine straightened, and his throat opened up. He felt high and could feel a fluttering below his chest. When the energy reached his chest, he began to feel his heart opening and expanding outward, filling the room, moving beyond the borders of the house and out into the world.

Suddenly, out of nowhere, a voice. A distant singing. A woman...calling the Pahana to return to the Hopi people. She beckoned unceasingly, with egoless intent. The blast of energy was so intense that Ian responded verbally.

"Wow!"

And immediately, he was back. The intrusion of ego into his consciousness had abruptly ended his experience. He sat for a moment, overwhelmed. Ian stood up. He could not continue his meditation. He would need time to process this.

Energy coursed through his body. Sleep would elude him. Too many questions. Where did that voice come from, and who was it? Was Captain Monty right? Ian's whisper broke the silence.

"Am I the Pahana?"

Day 108

Preparing to leave, Ian thought about his experience with Ellen, his talks with Monty, and what happened last night.

"This energetic work is a trip," he quipped as he closed the front door to the meditation house.

A gentle snow greeted the morning, but inside Ian's mind a blizzard raged: confusion, questions, considerations, anxiety. "Why me?" he thought. "I wonder if anyone else can hear this Hopi woman. Did I accidentally tap into a telepathic message? Was she calling in the last remnants of the great migration, or just the Pahana? On the other hand, maybe I'm just crazy and I'm hearing voices."

Ian was deeply engrossed in thought. His mind raced with questions. What does all this mean? He wondered about the future. What would happen when he found his wife and kids? Different scenarios played out in his head. Where would they end up? Would life ever be normal again? What am I supposed to do? It's not like I can just give up on my family. It was pretty clear, however, that he had to continue his journey west—but for what? Would visions, and voices, and assumptions from others cause him to make irrational decisions? His choices could destroy his family, his way of life, everything he knew and loved.

Cold, hunger, and fatigue compelled Ian to stop. He had spent the whole day obsessively consumed by his thoughts, completely oblivious to space and time. He had covered a lot of miles, both physically and mentally.

The Antioch church came into view as Ian rounded a curve that circumvented a small patch of forest. The structure was tucked into the wooded area and it seemed like a safe place to stay for the night. That unmistakable church smell greeted Ian as he broke in through the back door.

"Forgive us our trespasses," he jokingly announced.

Ian investigated each room of the church to ensure that he was indeed alone. While in the basement, he noticed a six-foot-tall framed canvas leaning with its image facing the wall. Flipping it around, revealed an unexpected depiction. The painting was of a large white horse with puppets on both hooves. One puppet was a fiery red devil, smiling defiantly with a real gold cross earring in his ear. The other puppet was Jesus. His eyes glazed in horror, as fresh blood dripped from his crown of Christmas lights and his brutal crucifixion wounds. The white horse's eyes were the same black void as the ambiguous background, and tears flowed from one of them. The frame was painted as well. On the bottom, in big bold letters was the title: *ISAIAH 45:7*

And around each side of the frame was painted:

I form the light, and create darkness:
I make peace, and create evil:
I the Lord do all these things.

Ian sat down on the floor. This work was raw. It had an outsider-art quality to it, but with the stability of a Renaissance painting. He stared up at it for a while as the words played over and over in his mind. It was almost as if it was in response to the whole of his experiences, a blunt reminder that nothing was as it seemed.

Upstairs, Ian made his way to the front row pews. He chuckled as he set his gear down and looked up at the giant wooden crucified Jesus.

"Back to back altars, huh? Are you trying to tell me something?"

Lighting the candles behind the podium created a warm comforting glow. Ian broke out some provisions and gazed around the church as he ate. I must have found this place for a reason, he speculated.

Ian pulled out his sleeping bag and unzipped it all the way. He wrapped himself up and sat cross-legged on the pew. Looking up at the crucifix he smiled. He closed his eyes and took a few deep breaths to center himself.

The wind actively kicked dust up into Ian's face as he stared down the road. The sun's warmth barely made it tolerable to withstand the chilling effects of the mountain zephyr. In the distance something white was coming, but it was hard to identify. Unexpectedly, the voice of the Hopi woman softly blended in with the breeze. Suddenly, time stopped as the object abruptly appeared within a few hundred feet of where Ian stood. A beautiful Conestoga wagon with its brilliant white canvas top, blue sides, and red wheels rolled down the road led by a team of muscular white quarterhorses. The Hopi woman's calling now resonated fervently as the wagon approached. As it got closer, Ian could see that the pregnant woman sitting on the seat was his wife, Theresa. She was looking straight into his eyes

> *as she called to the Pahana to return to the Hopi people. The power of her song captivated his heart, and as the wagon rolled up, a white light with the intensity of a billion suns blazed forth from her pregnant belly.*

The blast of energy jolted Ian back to awareness. His attempt to meditate had apparently been sidetracked by overwhelming fatigue. Questions surged through his mind. Was that a dream or a vision? Why my wife? Why my pregnant wife? The Hopi woman's call seemed so real. Was it? What was the source of that energy? He spent the remainder of the night perplexed, trying desperately to make sense of this and its confusing cast of characters.

Days 109–110

The candles had burnt down to the sconces as the first hint of morning gray shone through the windows. Ian packed his things and headed down the road. His mind was full. He used the hours of monotonous walking to examine what had recently transpired, and he reached conclusions that he thought made sense. He decided to skirt Bowling Green to the north and spent the night just east of Curryville.

The next day he headed toward Vandalia. The sound of his own breathing melded into the sound of the Hopi woman calling. Her voice was clear and now filled his head with her insistent request. His logical conclusions from the prior day were no longer valid. He thought he could easily write these events off as hallucinations or dreams, but he wasn't meditating or asleep now. He was walking down the road! He feared that he was losing his mind. Perhaps he had become psychotic. Ian's heart rate accelerated as anxiety harbored. The woman's calling eventually faded, But he would spend the rest of the night in an agitated state of concern, inquiry, and doubt.

Days 111–113

The next three days were spent walking in a constant state of contemplation. Whatever this was, it was very disconcerting. His conversations with Monty replayed in his mind. Now it was just getting weird. This was not some one-time strange event. No, it was obvious that this person was really calling, which meant that the situation was getting serious.

Ian was still reluctant to buy into Monty's story that he was the Pahana. It was just too farfetched to be real. He chose instead to believe that he had telepathically tapped into this calling. Perhaps the energy work had somehow heightened his awareness, almost like an antenna, and he was now picking up signals that were being broadcast. This explanation seemed to give him a thin veil of solace. But even the slightest amount of relief from his anxiety was worth it.

Ian had traveled thirty miles since hearing her voice last. He felt numb and tired. He was hopeful that sleep would not elude him tonight.

Days 114–115

It was hard to get out of bed. Ian felt achy and cold. The unwelcome sound of sleet pelting the roof caused an audible response,

"Oh, crap!"

It was a slow, wet, and miserable walk. The sleet and ash combination created a slippery mud that clung heavily to his boots. Shortly out of Mexico, Missouri, Ian passed a golf cart manufacturer. Hundreds of golf carts sat idle and he wished he could just use one to get out of the sloppy mess he was in. He sluggishly made his way down West 22, passing farms and light industrial buildings. A short distance beyond the Dawson's Country Store, Ian walked up on a billboard that seemed to mock his very predicament. A picture of a woodstove with a raging fire adorned the sign.

The sleet was turning into a heavy driving rain, and as it increased, so too did his misery. As slushy water dripped down his mask, all he could do was shake his head and laugh.

Without warning, the Hopi woman's call shattered Ian's thoughts with an intensity that he had not yet experienced. This powerful outburst startled him. His visceral reaction was a jump of fear. He had walked all day in the cold, in the rain, and now... the Hopi woman again. Enough was enough. Ian walked another quarter mile and was done for the day.

These experiences were very disruptive to his system. He knew that he would not sleep tonight, which meant arduous travel tomorrow. He decided to take a break. He would take a day to rest at this house near Centralia.

Chapter 26

Days 116–120

Four days went by filled with monotonous walking, with nothing to do but think. Ian kept his path above I-70, avoiding cities; but this meant an unvarying diet of gray landscape. He brooded his way through Missouri, pondering the changes he had come through in what seemed like a very short time.

Less than four months ago, he had been discontented with his comfortable, pedestrian lifestyle. He had been berating himself for being a walking cliché, a middle-aged art professor at a second-tier university in the Midwest. He remembered thinking. he needed a major change. But not a major, worldwide catastrophe.

This had become an existential crisis: the agony of the ecstasy. He'd been hit hard by a series of consciousness experiences—with Ellen, with Monty, with the calling of the Hopi woman. These had jarred him out of the mundane reality he had occupied for decades, throwing him back to the spiritual ecstasy he had once known. Now he faced an agonizing decision. Family or spirituality? Buddha, when confronted with this dilemma, chose to abandon his family. Most others stayed. Which reality should he embrace?

Beating himself up mentally every step of the way, he headed west from Centralia to Fayette, then south toward Boonville and Syracuse. The ash gradually diminished and he was able to cover more ground every day. As the ash was reduced, population began to increase again. This meant his overnight accommodations became more and more primitive; back to outbuildings and sheds.

On Saturday night, Ian's Motel 6 was a semi-trailer parked on a side road just north of Boonville. Peering at his maps in the fading light, he noticed that he was now almost directly south of Minneapolis. He did a quick calculation of distance. Just as he had thought: he was almost exactly 500 miles south of there now. Staring off into space, he realized how far he had come. He started out 500 miles east of Minneapolis and a couple of hundred miles north. That meant he had covered about 1200 miles since the first volcanic eruption. No wonder he was so worn out.

Ian's meager meal was a can of beans he had been carrying since he left the marina. Provisions were getting low and his constant companion, hunger, was making itself known again. It was hard to sleep with a rumbling gut, even after a long day's slog. Finally, though, he fell into a restless slumber and began to dream vividly.

He was in his hovel again, sitting at a wooden table, hard at work on writing his memoirs. His shirt sleeves were rolled up and a lock of hair fell into his eyes as he concentrated intensely.

Suddenly there was a knock at the door. Ian looked up, startled even in his dream. He walked across the small room and opened the door.

There stood Officer Obie from Monon.

"Son," he said, shaking his head sadly, "You lied to me."

Ian was overwhelmed with guilt. Obie began listing Ian's transgressions, looking more and more like the old cartoon character Deputy Dog as the list grew. At least 87 cases of breaking and entering; over 300 thefts of food, clothing, vehicles, supplies.

"And then there's the gun," Obie concluded. "A dead man's gun. You took it right off his body. Did you kill him, son?"

Obie's eyes grew stony and accusing.

"I'm going to have to take you in."

Ian felt himself begin to panic. Then a small voice at the back of his mind whispered. "Wake up!"

Ian blinked rapidly, shook his head, and expelled a puff of air. Wow! What a dream! Why would he dream something like that? Okay, he was tired and hungry and he had been walking through terrain that held absolutely no mental stimulation for several days now. "But still," he thought. "Why that?"

Ian began to worry. Could the police really be looking for him? The list Obie had recited wasn't that far from true. There could be an arrest warrant waiting for him in the next town. Unlikely, he reasoned. Nothing he had done would warrant an all-out search; he wouldn't have made the "most wanted" list. Besides, the police had enough on their hands at the moment.

"I'm probably safe," he reassured himself. A low profile would be a good idea, though. With that thought, Ian drifted back to sleep.

Day 121

Ian woke to another gray Sunday. Time to notch his walking stick again. Seventeen weeks since the first eruption. God, he was tired of this. With a deep, heartfelt sigh, Ian left the shelter of the semi-trailer and continued his journey. At least the ash was reduced. He was making better time than before.

Ian was a lot tougher than he had been at the beginning of this odyssey and in a lot better shape than he had been since he was a kid. He'd lost at least 30 pounds by this time, and the weight that remained had long since converted to muscle.

Oddly enough, the strange dream had been cathartic for Ian. His mood lightened considerably. "Maybe I just needed to say it all out loud, even in a dream," he thought. "I can't keep pretending that I haven't done anything against the law. So, okay. I have bent as many rules as I could and broken a lot of other ones. And I'm just going to have to get used to that. It happened."

Ian picked up his pace. He crossed the quarter-mile wide Missouri River on a pedestrian walkway and entered the unexpectedly large town of Boonville. Low brick buildings lined the streets. Most of them looked tired, as if they had seen other centuries. It was very typical small-town America, Ian mused as he ambled contentedly along the sidewalk. The few people he encountered ignored him, intent on their own business.

He left the town behind and continued south through the open countryside. It was only about three miles to Interstate 70 from the middle of Boonville. Ian crossed it via an overpass, looking down as he had at I-65 in Indiana. Here, too, there was no traffic along the highway. The road stretched empty to the horizon in both directions.

"But it's beginning to settle down," he thought hopefully. "Maybe things will be back to normal soon." He built a picture in his mind of hundreds of cars and trucks hurrying along the busy interstate, drivers intent on reaching some destination and completing some important personal business. The thought of returning to ordinary life was comforting.

Days 122–124

Three more days of walking brought Ian through the low-standing town of Syracuse and on to Sedalia, a fairly bustling population center. Food was definitely becoming an issue now, and his water supply was down to a few swallows. Ian knew he had to find somewhere to resupply. Still wary of the authorities, he began looking for a vacant house.

Because the ash accumulation here was small, vacant houses were at a premium. Ian was about two miles south of Sedalia before he saw the faded, battered "For Sale" sign at a driveway to his right. He drifted casually in that direction. Even though he had not seen another person or vehicle in this area, caution was a habit he had no intention of breaking. Ian examined the driveway for signs of activity.

Ash lay undisturbed on the graveled drive. It was obvious no one had been up that way for quite some time. Ian glanced around surreptitiously, then hurried toward the empty brick ranch house. The house looked forlorn and abandoned.

The attached garage's door was unlocked, and the side door entering the house had no more than a flimsy lock on the knob. Ian, backed by months of experience in housebreaking, was undeterred. He was inside the house within a minute.

"Ah," he thought, pausing to survey his surroundings, "an old couple lived here." The interior, although covered with a coating of dust, was meticulously neat. He had entered into the kitchen and found himself looking at evidence of an elderly woman's pride in her domain, a 1950s scene frozen in time. Canisters on the counter sported gingham-checked covers, crocheted potholders hung on hooks near the stove, and a lacy tablecloth covered a wooden table in the exact center of the room. There was even a cross-stitched homily hanging on the wall, asking God's blessings on this happy home.

This was the type of household where he would have expected to find an abundance of food. But the cupboards were not generous in this respect. Aside from a box of teabags and the molded or crystallized contents of the canisters, there was nothing. It puzzled Ian. "What's wrong with this picture?" he asked himself.

A door on the northwest side of the kitchen opened to reveal a stairway down into a basement tornado shelter. Flashlight in hand, Ian gingerly descended to the lower level. A quick check confirmed that there was still water available in the hot water tank.

And there it was, abundance—a whole shelving unit filled with neatly labeled canning jars: tomatoes, green beans, pickles; peaches, applesauce, plums; jams and jellies of all varieties; even a couple of canned chickens. Bonanza! Ian couldn't wipe the grin off his face. His deprived salivary glands leaped into action. With the utmost care, Ian began to carry his treasure back up to the kitchen. Tonight, he would feast.

He took the time to prepare a civilized table setting for himself, complete with a cup of tea and a cheerful little candle. All that was missing was dinner music, so he cranked up his radio. Nothing but static greeted his efforts to find a station. With a shrug, Ian conceded that he couldn't have everything and began to eat his chicken and vegetables with great enjoyment. It was pure bliss. Ian sent his heartfelt blessings to the old woman who had prepared dinner for a guest she would never meet.

Day 125

When Ian awoke the next day, he felt groggy. There had been so many nights of broken sleep. Rest had been snatched in short stretches as he shivered with the cold and came alert at every sound. A full night's sleep in a real bed was always a luxury. He stretched to his full length and snuggled into the warmth of the handmade quilt that covered his body, sending another wave of gratitude to the former resident of the house.

"I wish I could stay here," he thought. Then with a regretful sigh, he pulled himself out of bed. Dressed again in his dirty clothes, he returned to the kitchen, planning breakfast as he went.

The sight that greeted him through the kitchen window came as a complete shock. Yesterday's clear sky was gone. Swirling gray ash filled the air, thick as fog.

"What the…."

Ian was so astounded he spoke out loud. He rubbed his eyes and blinked in disbelief, but the ugly vision persisted. However much he might have wished it, this was no hallucination. The ash was back in full strength.

"Noooo!" he wailed in betrayed protest. "No more! No more! Not again!" The lump of anguish in his throat was too big to swallow. Tears sprang to his eyes. Ian slid down the wall and crouched like a cornered animal making its last desperate stand against fate. His head shook slowly in denial as he stared vacantly at the ash-filled sky. This was the last straw; he was a broken man.

Later, Ian was never able to reconstruct how many minutes or hours he spent pressed against the kitchen wall. His mind refused to remember that traumatic event; but when he surfaced again, nothing had changed. Ash still hung heavy in the air. The world was a monochromatic gray again. Even the cheerful kitchen seemed to huddle in on itself. Suddenly feeling old and tired far beyond his years, Ian pushed himself back to a standing position and shuffled to the table. He lowered himself into a chair, never taking his eyes away from the dismal sight outside the window.

His brain finally began to function again. Well, at least that explained the static on the radio last night. The damned volcano must have gone off again. Ian's mouth tightened in a bleak line. He snorted derisively at himself, remembering that he had wished he could stay here. "Be careful what you ask for," he thought.

Though he spent all day surfing the dial on the radio, he never did find a station clear enough to give him the information he needed. Ian passed a gloom-filled day. At least he had food, water, and shelter. He reminded himself to be grateful.

Days 126–127

The following morning found the ash settling out of the air. As Ian closed up the little house and bid it a final farewell, he noted that the ash came to the top of his ankles again, about six inches deep. He snugged his gas mask tight to his face and set forth once more.

Two more days of grueling southward travel brought him to a point just west of Cole Camp. The heavy ash continued to swirl around him. Wind again became a factor, gusting unexpectedly and pushing him sideways more than once. Ian struggled on, his mind numb with the effort of staying on his feet and moving ahead.

On the evening of the second day, he made camp inside a tractor shed set back from the road and finished off the last of his canned chicken. Then he curled up in his sleeping bag and drifted into an exhausted sleep.

Chapter 27

1261 A.D.

Western central Missouri, about two miles south of what will become the town of Cole Camp, Missouri. High prairie—open rolling grasslands. A major river winding out of Lake of the Ozarks is about ten miles south of this location.

Open land spread from horizon to horizon. There were some hills in the area, but these sat low to the ground. The world appeared to be a sea of golden grass, about waist high on a six-foot man. Endless blue sky, with only a few high clouds, capped the undulating, open prairie. A light wind blew across it at all times, creating waves in the grassy sea. The day was clear, but in the distance there was a brownish haze that seemed to be moving across the landscape. It was coming toward the hunters who crouched in the grass. They listened to a steady rumble and tested the ground as the tremor increased. The hunters were Wah Zha Zhe, whose name the French would later corrupt to Osage.

The rumbling was clearly not thunder, the tremor was not an earthquake, and the haze in the distance was not rain. Instead, it was a herd of bison. Thousands of the huge animals headed south toward the river. The ground trembled for miles around as they passed. They were just one of many herds that migrated up and down the spine of the Rockies, radiating out into the plains and prairies as far east as the western slopes of the Appalachians.

The hunters scouting this herd were the most competent and the bravest of their band. They had to be, since hunting bison was a highly skilled and extremely dangerous activity. There were no horses at this time: the hunt was on foot. In this part of the country, running a herd off a cliff or into a corral was not feasible. They weighed up to a ton apiece, stood about six feet

tall at the shoulder, and could jump six feet in the air. Because bison hide is thick and very tough, there was no way to kill from a distance, either. The force needed to penetrate even the most vulnerable areas of the animal was considerable. Ideally, a hunter should drive a spear under the shoulder and into the heart. Needless to say, "ideal" conditions were rare.

The huge size of an individual animal and the size of the herd made them virtually invulnerable. In addition, their curved horns were up to two feet long and were used as defensive weapons. But even that wasn't the whole story. Bison are intensely vigilant to any potential threat. They are also very bad-tempered and aggressive. They are not the preferred prey of anything—except wolf packs and humans.

If they have a weakness at all, it is vision. Bison are myopic. This was the sole advantage available to the hunters, and it was exploited creatively. If the hunters could disguise themselves, they could get close enough to stragglers at the edge of the herd to make a kill possible.

These hunters had disguised themselves as wolves. Wearing full wolf skins over their heads and backs, carrying their bows and spears, they crawled on hands and knees to the edge of the herd.

Bison are not threatened by small numbers of predators near the herd, even if those predators might be dangerous in larger groups. The hunters were noticed by the bison, but the level of alarm was low. They appeared to be too small and insignificant to be a threat.

The three camouflaged hunters, tense and vigilant, crept cautiously forward through the haze of dust. Then they froze: something was very wrong here.

Deep inside the herd, they saw a strange sight. A white banner covered with strange symbols fluttered in the breeze over the backs of the bison. Below the banner appeared to be the head of a man, moving at a leisurely pace toward the hunters' location. But it could not be true. No one can walk among the bison like that! They would surely kill any human who dared come too close. The hunters exchanged glances full of trepidation. What on earth was this?

Cautiously, they began to crawl backward, away from the herd and away from this strange apparition. They didn't even disturb the grasses with their careful retreat, but the stranger still followed their direction, still headed directly for them. The hunters increased their pace as they got farther from the herd.

On a low hill just a few yards away, a medicine man had been praying to the spirits for good hunting. He had also seen the approaching apparition. His low-level chant had increased in urgency, and it no longer had anything to do with bison. But the strange figure kept coming.

As he got closer, the hunters and medicine man could see him more clearly. He was tall and light-haired. The clothing he wore was unremarkable, tanned buckskin shirt and leggings like those of the Wah Zha Zhe. But he could not be a man like them. His face was covered with hair, like an animal. And his eyes! They were the color of the sky. What demon was this? The medicine man continued to chant desperately, his voice beginning to quaver.

The demon stopped a few feet away from the huddled hunters. With the tall staff he carried, he gestured for the medicine man to come to him.

It was now that the Wah Zha Zhe spiritual leader earned his place in the oral history of his people. Though his fear was obvious, he stepped toward the white demon, head high and back straight. He and the stranger moved away from the hunters, whose eyes remained glued to the threatening intruder.

As the hunters watched, the demon began to speak. The hunters could not hear what was being said, but it was clear that the medicine man understood. The conversation continued for several minutes.

The fear in the man's posture disappeared as the stranger talked, replaced by fascinated attention. He nodded at something the stranger said. The stranger reached into a pouch he carried and produced a small leather bag. The medicine man took it reverently and bowed his head.

The stranger turned away and walked back into the herd of bison. The hunters watched in amazement as the herd ignored his presence. One young bull even moved aside to let him pass. Eventually he disappeared back into the haze from which he had emerged.

When the medicine man returned to the hunting group, the other men eagerly asked what had happened. He just shook his head.

"It belongs to the sacred," he said. "I can tell no one. You must tell no one what you saw here today. The future of the Wah Zha Zhe depends on it."

Chapter 28

Day 128

Ian woke to another gray day under an ash-laden sky. With a sigh, he shook off his depression and prepared to trudge onward.

There was always a wind blowing with a dreary, cold monotony. Ian lowered his head and walked into it, watching his feet as they imprinted, however impermanently, the six inches of ash swirling around him. It depressed him even more to know that all signs of his passing would be erased by the wind within minutes.

Ian walked on. The road continued west, and so did he.

Ahead, he began to see signs of storm damage. At first, it was just some tree limbs scattered helter-skelter along the roadway; but it quickly escalated, and he saw whole trees ripped from the ground. Bits of roofing and boards, either whole or in tattered pieces, littered the roadway.

Eventually, he saw signs of civilization ahead. It wasn't much, just a couple of large free-standing buildings that looked like factories or warehouses. Beyond them, though, he saw roofs through the few trees still standing. Virtually every house showed evidence of storm damage.

It was starting to get late when he reached the center of the town of Windsor. Buildings here were old, made of brick, and low to the ground. Even here there was evidence of a disaster greater than the gray film of ash coating this small world. Ian saw a number of buildings with missing roofs and open-air second floors. The stubs of light poles and telephone poles marched down the sides of the road.

Ian spotted a miraculously undamaged brick kiosk, with an American flag flying bravely from its roof. The incongruous structure actually sat in the middle of the street, surrounded by traffic lanes. This was worth investigating, Ian thought. He walked to the kiosk and discovered that it served as a post office as well as a message board. Most interesting. It was the first time he had ever seen this arrangement.

A tattered poster for a school bake sale gave him a moment of nostalgic sadness, but he was scanning for something far more urgent: a place to spend the night. He found that an emergency shelter had been set up by the Red Cross at the United Methodist Church. Ian breathed a sigh of relief and continued through town.

The church had a steep pitched roof, almost an A-frame, which probably helped it avoid the worst damage inflicted on its neighbors. A wide brick column ran up the front of the church, with a simple cross adorning it. The building appeared intact.

Figuring he knew the drill by now, Ian entered the side door of the church, ready to register for a night's lodging. He spent that night in the church basement on a cot that he thought might have been designed for children. Even so, he slept deeply and peacefully.

Day 129

The next morning, he was packing up his things when the minister stopped by his temporary quarters.

"Leaving us so soon?" he asked. Ian nodded.

"I'd like to make another ten miles before I sleep tonight," he replied.

The minister's eyebrows shot up to his nonexistent hairline. "I rather doubt you'll be able to do that," he said. "You're going to have to cross the actual path of the tornado to go any further west, and you haven't seen what it left behind. It's a moonscape out there. You might want to scout it out before you try crossing."

"It's that bad?" Ian asked with a touch of apprehension. The minister grimaced in reply. "Maybe you're right, then. How far away from here did it pass?"

"Only about a mile to the edge of it. You could check it out and be back for lunch."

Ian set out. The storm damage increased as he headed further west from the church. Roughly a mile down Route 52, he arrived at a heavily damaged truck stop. The roof had disappeared, the signage was twisted and bent. Three gas pumps were missing from their concrete pods. Two others had been ripped out and smashed to the ground. A single pair of pumps appeared to have been completely untouched. Chunks of concrete littered the asphalt drive, along with cracked and splintered boards.

The truck stop originally sat on a small rise, so Ian climbed the gentle grade to its apex and looked out at the countryside to his west.

"'Moonscape' is right," he muttered to himself, gazing at the devastated panorama spreading before him. It was a bleak scene that met his eyes, a tortured landscape smothered by a heavy coat of ash. A few weird, twisted silhouettes rose up through the dismal gray, stretching toward the sky like the survivors of a holocaust beseeching their god for mercy. A trail of debris reached as far as he could see, broken by inexplicable areas of absolute, sanitized tidiness.

A clean line marked the border of the tornado's path. It looked as if someone came through with a snow blower, sharply slicing through the edge and removing everything in its way to a depth of about three inches.

Thoroughly daunted, Ian retraced his steps to the church to spend another night and think this over. He knew he had to keep going; he just didn't know quite how.

Day 130

As Ian left Windsor the next morning, it grew eerily quiet. It was a dreary day to begin with. Same old, same old: there was no motion; no birds dotted the sky, no small animals scurried along the roadside. No grass or leaves waved or rustled in the breeze, but the closer he got to the devastated area, the stranger his surroundings became. He was presented with a surrealistic landscape, broken only by broken things.

Wind-swept ash lay deceptively smooth ahead of him. The road he wanted to follow had been obliterated under this blanket of gray, and all obstacles and pitfalls were hidden from view. He would be forced to rely heavily on his compass and take precautions before every step into this minefield laid down by nature.

His previous day's survey of the area helped. At least he knew what to expect, as far as that was possible. Before he left the warm comfort of the church in Windsor, Ian had removed his peace flag from the bayonet attached to his walking stick. He would now use the resulting tool to sweep the ground ahead of him, probing for uneven surfaces or buried pieces of metal. One slash from a jagged piece of steel, one rusted nail through his boot—that is all it would take to end his journey permanently.

Any observer would be struck by Ian's resemblance to an astronaut about to begin exploration of the moon's surface. With his gas mask, his puffy down jacket, a pair of work gloves, and boots he certainly looked the part.

Ian took a reading from his compass. His direction would take him right to the first pile of debris he could see. Sighting on the heap, he tucked the compass into his coat pocket and firmly gripped his walking stick, sweeping the bayonet across the barren path ahead of him. "That's one step for a man...."

Progress was at a snail's pace. Every step had to tested, and even then taken cautiously. The monotonous view didn't seem to change as he crept onward. Piles of debris, many of them taller than he was, blocked his path as ordained by the compass. Circumventing them was an agonizing affair; the ragged edges of branches ripped from their mother trees clawed at him as he struggled past. Bent strips of chrome, torn from cars and trucks; sharpened scraps of lumber ripped off buildings, their bent nails protruding like malevolent fangs dripping tetanus; unidentifiable rubble—all of this seemed to be maliciously intent on devouring him, whole or in pieces. It was a nerve-wracking process that required every bit of concentration he could bring to bear.

Hours passed. Ian paused to eat the generous lunch packed for him by the minister's wife, silently blessing the good-hearted woman, who had provided food and water, "just in case," as she insisted.

He leaned cautiously against the bark-bare trunk of a blasted, twisted tree and looked around. There were no reference points here. No treelines marked the horizon, no road wound its way ahead; no sign of civilization marred the perfect sameness all around him.

Ian had never felt so isolated, so alone. His body was a symphony of tension-induced aches and quivers; neck, back, thighs, even his eyes hurt from their intensely concentrated focus on the unending gray expanses. He had wandered into limbo.

Ian pushed himself away from the tree trunk and continued his tortuous journey onward. Hours crept by. Though he couldn't see the sun, Ian realized that it must be late afternoon by now, and he began to grow anxious about losing what little light there was. The tornado was supposed to be three miles wide. Surely he had traveled more than that. He checked his compas again shook it to be sure it hadn't got stuck. All he would need would be to find that ash had infiltrated the compass and frozen the needle. But the needle quivered, then readjusted itself to point faithfully north.

Ian slogged on, grimly determined to reach the end of this wasteland, and finally his persistence was rewarded. A thin shadow lying diagonally across his path far ahead marked the western edge of the swath cut by the tornado. Ian was so exhilarated by the sight that he nearly forgot to scan his next step—and narrowly avoided disaster when his bayonet clanged off a sharp-edged piece of steel girder half buried in the earth beneath the ash.

The harsh sound quickly returned him to reality. What irony it would be to get so close to the end and mess up now. He returned his concentration to the task at hand and finished his cautious navigation of the tornado war zone successfully.

The three-inch-deep gouge in the earth left by the tornado was a clear demarcation of its passage. The debris continued as far as the eye could see, though, scattered across the barren landscape.

His compass navigation had been excellent. He had arrived at a point where he could again see the road ahead of him. It was getting late, however. He needed to find a place to spend the night, and it didn't look promising.

Ahead to his left he saw a still-standing tree. Wrapped around its trunk was a Ford Focus, the car bent into a U-shape. The front end of a minivan had been driven into the driver's side of the car. The minivan was so totally destroyed that the make and model were indecipherable.

The third part of this artistic metal sculpture was an old pickup truck. The truck bed had been forced halfway through the back end of the minivan, leaving the cab facing outward and apparently undamaged. "Amazing," thought Ian.

He scanned the horizon, looking for an intact structure where he could spend the night. Standing against the empty skyline was a lonely fireplace, its chimney pointing at the darkening sky like an accusing finger. Ian allowed himself a wistful moment, imagining a crackling fire in a cozy room with a leather recliner. He pictured a pair of slippers, a good book, and a snifter of brandy. Wouldn't that be a wonderful way to end the day? If only....

"Ah, well," he sighed. There was no room surrounding the fireplace; in fact, there was no sign of the house that had contained the room. Ian brought his eyes back to the tortured vehicle sculpture.

Still carefully feeling his way through the ash, Ian approached the pickup truck. The front end was remarkably undamaged, except for one thing: the paint had been scoured off completely, leaving a polished metal surface shining dully in the fading light.

Ian mused to himself about the sturdy truck. They sure knew how to make them in the old days, back when cars were actually made from metal, rather than the twisted shards of plastic that marked the remains of the other two vehicles. He missed his own truck, abandoned in upper Michigan and probably buried under several feet of ash by now.

"For old times' sake," he murmured to himself as he opened the passenger-side door. This was where he would spend the night. However cramped and crowded it would be, however hard to wriggle into his sleeping bag, however uncomfortable sleeping while sitting upright, the truck would protect him from the wind and whatever marauding predators lurked in the dark.

Day 131

Ian was startled awake by the distant crack of a rifle, followed immediately by a high-pitched scream. Jesus! What was that? Still sleep confused, he peered through the windshield at the empty early-morning landscape. Nothing moved. Did he dream those sounds? As if to answer his doubt, another rifle shot rang out. Another scream followed. The hair rose on the back of Ian's neck.

He crouched on the floor, heart hammering, still tangled in his sleeping bag. Cursing quietly, he clumsily struggled free of his nighttime cocoon, quivering like a newly hatched butterfly. He waited there, body tense, ears straining.

For a long time, there was nothing. Finally, he heard another gunshot, much more distant than the earlier two. Even so, he waited ten minutes, counting the seconds in his head.

When the silence continued, Ian cautiously raised his head and scanned the horizon. It was perfectly motionless, a frozen tableau laid out for his inspection. His search for movement was futile.

Finally, satisfied that the threat had passed, Ian stepped out of the truck to continue his journey. Today, he would try to get to the little town of Clinton.

It was a slow, painful trek. Not only was he sweeping the ground ahead of him before every step, but now he also scanned the skyline compulsively. Threats were everywhere. The weather did not add further complications. It was simply gray and still. Somehow, this only added to his unease. He felt as if every breath he took must be audible for miles. If anyone—any *thing*—was stalking him, what pitifully easy prey he was. His skin crawled at the thought of an all-too-easily imagined malevolent pursuer.

Twice more during the day he heard rifle shots in the distance. He was almost certain that there was more than one gunman. Each time, he also heard the screams, full of pain and fear and rage. Why did they sound so familiar? He knew he had heard that sound before, but he could not remember when.

Progress was excruciatingly slow, but eventually he reached the outskirts of Clinton. This area, too, was heavily damaged, but

Ian found a barn with only half the roof ripped off and three walls still standing. There was even hay in an undamaged stall. Ian made himself a mattress, then buried himself in the sweet smelling, insulating stalks.

Days 132–134

The next three days were uneventful, though he continued to hear periodic gunshots and screams.

He finally remembered where he had heard that sound before: Kendallville. Those were the same screams he had heard back in Indiana. Then, he had detoured around what he thought was a riot or rampaging looters. But he still didn't know the source of the screams.

On the third day, he saw in the distance a small herd of animals, low to the ground, moving fast against the horizon. There were about a dozen of them. They were too far away for him to identify what they were.

Day 135

It was Sunday again, time to notch his walking stick to mark the start of the twentieth week on the road. He looked at his map and discovered he was only about thirty miles from the Kansas border. With a decisive nod, he started walking briskly into the gray morning.

The day passed slowly as Ian slogged along. Twice the quiet was broken by the sound of gunshots and screams. Every time it happened, Ian shivered. What was that? Who or what was being hunted with such determination? And who were the hunters?

Again he saw a small group of animals in the distance. They were moving quickly, in apparent flight from something.

That evening Ian found a deserted house. He broke a small window in the door, cleared the glass, and reached in to unlock the back door. Inside, he found cardboard and tape to cover the broken window. The gunshots and screams had left him feeling spooked. He jammed the door closed and slid a portable dishwasher in front of it, locking the legs in place.

Ian's food and water supply was low. The minister's wife's generosity and concern had proved to be valid. There had been no place to resupply during the past few days. He scoured the kitchen of his new abode; but there was little to be found here, just a few canned vegetables and a box of pasta.

Day 136

It was still dark when Ian was awakened by strange noises outside the house.

The sounds were muffled, but there were thumps and thuds and low-voiced murmurs that brought him to instant alertness.

He slid silently out of his sleeping bag and moved stealthily to the room's only window. He cracked the curtains and peered outside. The sky was just beginning to lighten; he could see shapes and shadows, but nothing was defined.

Off to his right, he saw three shadowy forms. They were definitely animals, moving on four feet, low to the ground; but they were big, bulky. They appeared to be sniffing at the ground. They moved toward the back door. What were they, anyway?

Ian's hair stood on end. Were they scenting him, following his trail? He left the bedroom window and moved swiftly through the house, heading toward the kitchen and the door he entered last night. What if they tried to break in the way he did? Would that dishwasher be enough to keep them out?

The kitchen window at the back of the house was uncurtained. Ian crept closer, careful to stay hidden from the view of whatever was outside, and peeked at the back porch.

It was getting lighter by the moment. As he watched, the three unwelcome visitors rounded the side of the house and headed for the porch. Ian stared in pop-eyed amazement. They were pigs.

The three pigs grunted and jostled each other at the steps leading to the back porch. Their trotters clattered against the wooden stairs as they clambered up. They snuffled at the doorsill for a minute. Then the largest of the three, probably about 300 pounds, pushed against the door.

Ian held his breath; but the dishwasher didn't budge. Outside, the pig pushed harder. Still nothing happened. Ian, watching, could swear the pig looked frustrated. It backed up a step and hurled itself at the door. Thank God it couldn't get a running start! The door shuddered a little but stood firm.

Ian quickly reviewed everything he knew about pigs. "Well, they're big, they're strong, they're mean, and they're smart. They're omnivores—ohmigod, they're omnivores! And these guys look hungry." Ian broke into a sweat.

Over the next hour, the other two pigs each tried to break through the wooden barricade. Ian was frozen in place, his eyes moving only from the ground assault being mounted by the pigs to his last line of defense, the door and the dishwasher.

Then other pigs started to arrive. Soon there were a dozen of them milling around the yard, squealing and grunting. Periodically one would climb the steps and attack the door.

Meanwhile, Ian had brought up reinforcements. The door was now barricaded with everything he could move in the kitchen. He had also blocked the front door, moving a heavy sofa and a big entertainment console to close off that access point.

As he cowered in the kitchen, it occurred to him that, while the pigs were being kept out, he was trapped inside. It was a siege. Was he prepared to withstand it?

Ian inventoried his supplies. He still had some crackers and hard sausage left from the minister's wife's food. Here in the house there were two cans of peas, one of corn, one of green beans, and one box of pasta bowties. Water would not be an issue for days.

Defensive weapons? Ian had his walking stick with its attached bayonet. That was it. There was no way it was enough to fight his way free, and the pigs certainly weren't going to honor the peace flag.

Hours passed as Ian considered his fate. The sky was darkening again. He had not eaten all day, so he opened one of the cans of peas. His meal was punctuated by repeated thuds as the persistent animals threw themselves against the door.

That night Ian barricaded himself in the bedroom and tried to rest. It did eventually get quiet outside the house. Even pigs need sleep.

Day 137

Dawn was announced by another pig battering ram. Ian stumbled to the kitchen, wondering how much more the door could take. He looked outside with a forlorn hope that at least some of his attackers would have gotten discouraged and given up. No, all were present and accounted for.

He examined the door, or as much as he could see of it through the piled kitchen appliances. It was sturdy oak, still standing proud. The problem he discovered was the door frame. It was beginning to buckle. He could see where it had pulled away from the interior wall of the room.

With no time or materials to fix the door, he began moving his supplies into the bedroom. If the pigs broke through, he would make a last stand there. The bed and dresser would reinforce the flimsy interior door at least for a while.

Now the pigs had discovered the front door. The pounding was coming in stereo as they threw themselves at both doors. The front door frame began to splinter. Ian eyed it warily, then retreated toward the bedroom.

An explosion startled him into a three-foot vertical leap. It was followed immediately by four more. Then the screams began, the same screams that had followed him for days: pain, fear, fury. And gunshots. Blessed rifle fire! Hope flared in Ian's heart.

The battle raged on for several minutes. The doors had been abandoned, and Ian heard the sounds of retreat. The rifle volley continued. So did the screams.

Finally it was silent. Ian moved cautiously toward the front door, just as he heard a firm knock. "Anybody in there?" a voice called tentatively.

"Yes! I'm here! Just a minute," Ian shouted back. He rushed to the door and frantically began moving furniture. When the doorway was clear, he flung the door open.

Two heavily bearded men stood on the front porch, rifles in hand. A third could be seen coming toward the house, while a small cloud of ash dust announced the location of the fleeing pigs.

Ian collapsed against the door frame in relief. "Man, am I glad to see you. Thank you! You just saved my ass. That door was about to give." With great effort, he stood straight and struggled to contain his emotions.

Ian introduced himself and learned that the three men had been hunting these pigs for several days. They looked with some gratification at the five corpses littering the porch and front yard. "Five down, and—what did you say?—seven to go," the leader commented in satisfaction.

"Where did these damned pigs come from?" Ian asked.

"Well, we already had a problem with wild pigs," replied the leader. "Then the ash storms started. What with the winds and the weight of the snow and ash on the roofs, the barns started collapsing. We've got a lot of hog farms around here, and the pigs got loose. You ever try to catch a pig?" Ian shook his head. "You can't," the leader said flatly. "They're fast and slick and strong, and they can turn on a dime. They all took off, and they've been causing nothing but problems since. They tear down the fences. They've been killing livestock. Now they're chasing people." He shook his head in dismay.

"How many are we talking about?" Ian asked.

The second man shrugged. "Dunno," he said. "A lot. We've shot maybe a couple hundred, and we haven't made a dent."

"Then that must have been you I've been hearing over the past few days," said Ian.

"Could be. There are a bunch of us, though. If you keep going, you'll probably hear more." He shrugged again and fell silent. After a few minutes, the leader pushed his weary body away from the porch railing. "Guess it's time to get moving," he said. "Are you going to be all right now?"

Ian assured the men that he was fine. He thanked them again, and the three men slouched off in the direction taken by the fugitive pigs.

Ian returned to the house and put his barricade back against the front door. Only now did the physical reaction set in. He began to shake uncontrollably. His legs gave out, and he fell onto the sofa in front of the door. Breathing became a labor and his heart hammered painfully in his chest. "Oh, my God," he kept repeating to himself as his mind raced over how close he came to dying here.

Eventually, the fear was replaced by anger. Damn those pigs! He had an almost overwhelming urge to take revenge. Lifting his walking stick, he removed the bayonet, then pulled his makeshift barrier away from the front door.

The dead pig on the porch must have weighed close to 400 pounds. Ian looked at the body with pure hatred. Raising the bayonet over his head, he stabbed the corpse again and again until his breath came in sobs and his arms ached and trembled.

It still wasn't enough. Ian stumbled into the yard and began collecting whatever wood he could find. There were matches in the kitchen cabinet. He built a fire.

Returning to the mangled hog, Ian sliced a large slab from the ham of the animal. He put this in a cast-iron frying pan and set the pan directly on the fire. "Turn about is fair play," he muttered. "You were sure planning to eat me." The meat sizzled. He turned it over with his bayonet, then retrieved a plate and the can of corn from the house. Tonight, he would feast in triumph over his enemy.

Days 138–139

For the next two days, Ian walked steadily through the countryside. He was constantly alert, scanning the horizon for movement, listening intently for gunshots and screams.

Only once did he hear anything, and the sounds were distant and muffled.

He spent his first night in the partly-destroyed hayloft of a barn. It was not the most comfortable of accommodations, but the ladder access made it very attractive to Ian. Pigs can't climb ladders.

By the end of the second day, he reached State Line Road at the border between Missouri and Kansas. Just west of the boundary sat a lone outbuilding, long and low. Approaching it with relief, Ian pictured himself entering the lobby of a fine hotel. "Single with a view, please," he murmured as he ducked into the dark, quiet shed. Three crackers and two thin slices of sausage comprised his dinner. Dreaming of a fourteen-ounce prime rib with all the fixings, Ian unrolled his sleeping bag and called it a day.

Chapter 29

Days 140–141

Not so bad, Ian thought to himself as he entered Kansas. There was only about four inches of ash on the ground. The sun was beginning to give a hazy light to the landscape, and Ian could even trace its haloed outline in the sky. It was pretty flat and open, but there were groves of trees along the road and very precise, neat fields. A few farmhouses with attendant outbuildings sat back from the road. Along the highway it was quite heavily forested, especially on the west side, all the way to the tiny town of Trading Post.

The area appeared to be somewhat populated, which led him to re-evaluate his situation. Obviously, he couldn't break into houses any more. People were home, and they could be hostile. Other than the farms, there were few buildings along the road and no sources of potable water. He needed a new strategy: no water from water heaters, no abandoned pantries were available around here. It almost made him nostalgic. At least when he had to slog through a foot of ash, he got a hot meal and a bath at the end of the day.

"And it's just going to get worse from here on," he reminded himself. As the ash decreased, there would be more and more population. There would be less and less water, too. Especially when he got to New Mexico. That's 300 miles of desolate desert! Clearly, he would have to revise his plan again.

He reviewed his experiences so far. Interactions with law enforcement had been negative: he had been arrested in Monon and looters had been strung up in Illinois. Even the militia thought they were enforcing the law. Churches, so far, had been good to him. He decided he would keep that in mind.

On the first night he managed to find an empty corn crib on the west side of the road. Two cups of stray corn kernels hid in a far corner. He found two rocks and ground them into cornmeal, mixing it with a little of his last water. He ate some as cornmeal mush. It tasted like an unsalted taco shell, but it was food. He put the rest inside a baggie he had been carrying, with a little water to moisten it.

That night he listened to his radio. He learned that eight weeks ago there was no ash on the ground here. Only health-related evacuations had occurred.

It was mid-May now, but it felt like late March. Still, with his sleeping bag he was able to make do.

The second day took him south of Pleasanton and west through little Mound City. He spent that night in an unlocked storage unit in a small complex about two miles east of Blue Mound. Here he ate his ground corn and drank the last of his water.

He was starting to feel grimy. He hadn't been able to clean up for days, and the gas mask was beginning to chafe the skin on his dirty face.

Day 142

Ian walked south through the small town of Blue Mound, all six blocks of it, and continued west. The area was flat and open, with occasional stands of trees. Roads were laid out in a regular grid pattern. He crossed a north–south road every mile. It was easy to time his walk.

Off the road to his north, Ian saw a barn with an ash-collapsed roof. Three men were struggling to move timbers, trying to rescue trapped cows. Their terrified bellows could be heard for miles. Taking a chance, Ian approached and offered to help, and the men gratefully accepted. They worked together to pull a dozen dairy cows from the barn. Three of them were mortally injured. Crushed legs and hips from the roof collapse meant they must be put down.

To thank Ian, the men gave him two quarts of water and a sandwich. Ian thought this was a great return for his help.

He passed Kinkaid on its southern end. Just west of town was a large farm that appeared to be occupied. He was still skittish about approaching houses, but then he saw a long, low outbuilding sitting close to the road. Ian waited until just after dark. Then he sneaked in, hoping there was water to be found inside.

It was a chicken coop—occupied by a flock of hens and a white rooster, who wasn't particularly territorial. He didn't challenge Ian's presence.

Ian spotted a hose, but when he opened it, there was no water. He remembered Leesburg: without electricity to run the water pump, they ran the backup gas generator only when they had to. The people in the house had water and weren't likely to turn the generator on tonight. He found a bale of straw and made himself a bed.

Days 143–144

Early the next morning Ian stole four eggs and ate them raw. They were still warm from the nest, but Ian found it hard to overcome his gag reflex as he swallowed the slimy things. He sneaked out of the coop before dawn and continued west.

Ian was thirsty, stiff, sore, and grumpy. He was running out of water again. With no way to clean up, his skin was irritated and abraded by the gritty ash. He was down to his last few mouthfuls of water and had no food.

This area was very flat and open with cultivated fields covered in ash as far as he could see. There were no buildings of any kind for miles on end. He spent his nights in abandoned outbuildings.

Day 145

Ian woke up just north of Carlyle. "Looks like another grim day," he thought. "I have to find food and water now, today!"

He walked slowly at first, until his muscles loosened and he could pick up a little speed. He noticed that the ash seemed to be less than even the day before.

By late morning he was approaching a large town—Iola. As he got closer, he saw something truly exciting, something he hadn't seen for a long time. The road was plowed! His pace picked up as he reached bare pavement once again.

At Route 54, Ian headed into Iola. Even the sidewalks were cleared. It felt wonderful not to slog through snash, not to fear slipping and falling with each step. Ian began to whistle as he walked.

Oh, what a beautiful morning
Oh, what a beautiful day…

He had to stop; his mouth was too dry to whistle.

In Iola, he saw a level of activity that had been missing from his life for months. People were actually outside, moving around. The vehicles on the streets were pretty much all four-wheel-drives or pickup trucks; but still, there were vehicles on the street. There were stores and gas stations and even a bank—all open for business. He'd been waiting for this day for months! There was even a guy walking away from an ATM, putting his wallet into his back pocket.

Ian stopped dead cold as a light bulb went off over his head. A functioning ATM? Really? Could it be possible to access his own bank account after all this time? Excited, with shaky fingers, he inserted his card into the machine. He entered "Withdraw" and "200." There was a welcome "whirr" and muted clunk before ten twenty-dollar bills popped out of the slot. It worked! The university must have automatically deposited his pay at the end of December.

Hoping for even more good news, he went into the bank to ask the teller if there was a library with computers so he could email his wife. However, once inside, his eyes fell greedily on a coffee urn set out for bank customers. Oh, what a beautiful morning, indeed! Ian grabbed a cup, downed it in one searing gulp, and refilled it before approaching the teller with his question. The teller shook her head.

"Internet access is sporadic at best these days," she said. "When the system shuts down, we shut down. Banks have been given priority to use the satellites, to keep the economy flowing. Today's the first day we could reopen the ATM because the road to Wichita is clear and we can get real money to stock the thing! We actually ran out of cash. It's been tough around here for the last couple of weeks."

Ian smiled and walked out of the bank with one more cup of coffee for the road. "Couple of weeks! Hah! Try five months," he thought wryly. Lots of useful information there, though. The road to Wichita was plowed. That was his route. That meant he should be able to make time if he got moving. Maybe he could even catch a ride.

But that wasn't going to happen. What Ian didn't know was that, while he had been struggling to survive under the ashdome, the rest of the world had altered in ways he hadn't imagined. FEMA hadn't told him about the structural and cultural changes to society.

It was the 20th of May, but the cherry trees in Washington, DC, still hadn't blossomed. Average temperatures in Florida were under 50 degrees. Planted crops weren't growing; it was too cold. Dramatic temperature drops were affecting the northern hemisphere. Acid rain defined the boundaries of the jet stream. Panic was beginning to set in worldwide.

In the U.S. alone, 80 million people, a quarter of the population, were either displaced or assumed dead. Over 55 million refugees had clogged the system, creating bottlenecks in food and gas distribution. Housing had reached a crisis point. Where do you put 55 million people?

Bureaucrats scrambled frantically to meet the needs of this unexpected influx of population. Issues of jurisdiction arose. Whose responsibility was it: federal, state, or local? The lines of authority weren't clear, and this had been a daily battle for five months.

Ian walked across Iola. At the west end of town, he came to an open gas station convenience store. He decided to get food and continue.

After hearing from the clerk that mandatory gas rationing was in effect and that twenty-six refineries had shut down in twelve states under the ashdome, Ian was not shocked that gas had risen to $40 a gallon. The price was twice what it had been even two months ago at Ellen's. These prices would certainly discourage unnecessary travel.

He ate two hot dogs at the store and had his first Coke in months while he chomped through a bag of Fritos. Grabbing a few power bars for the road and another cup of hot coffee to go, he headed out toward Wichita feeling full, warm, and optimistic.

He continued west on Route 54. After a couple of hours, the wind picked up again. It started getting colder and the sky became menacing. Ian began to get a little anxious about finding a place to stay before the weather got worse. He figured he had already made about twelve miles today, so stopping now still put him ahead of his normal pace. He started looking for shelter.

About another mile down the road, Ian came to Piqua. He could see a towering collection of silvery grain silos to his right along the divided highway. He turned toward the town, heading north. After walking about two blocks, he saw an American flag flying on the corner a block away. The flag marked the location of a U.S. Post Office. He went inside to ask about a place to stay for the night.

Only one person was there, an older woman behind the counter. Posted prominently on the wall was an old "Mr. Zip" poster. Ian hadn't seen one of these since he was a kid.

She looked at Ian with undisguised curiosity. He realized that she must recognize everyone in town and knew he was a stranger.

"Can I help you?" the woman asked. She gestured toward his staff. "Nice flag, by the way."

"I'm just passing through," Ian replied, "and I wondered if there's anywhere nearby to spend the night. A motel, a cabin, something like that?"

"Well, there are places in Iola," the woman offered.

Ian shook his head. "I'm headed west," he explained.

The woman gave a brief snort of laughter. "Then you're pretty much out of luck until Yates Center. That's another ten, twelve miles down the 54."

That would be another full day's walk. Ian's face fell in disappointment. "How about a rooming house or somebody who'd be willing to rent me a room for the night? I'm walking, you see, and there's no way I could make it that far today."

The woman asked where he was going, and Ian introduced himself, giving her the short version of his story. When he finished, she nodded sympathetically.

"College professor, huh? I've got a couple of kids in college—or at least they were, until all the schools shut down because of the ash. They're home now, bored out of their skulls. Maybe we could put you up for the night and you could give them something to think about so they'll stop complaining for a while. What do you think? Is meatloaf okay with you?"

"Sounds wonderful. But could I ask a favor first? Does your phone work? Could I call my family?"

She shook her head. "I'm sorry. The phone lines are down right now, and we don't have any cell service."

He spent the night with Postmistress Kathy Howard, her husband, and two college-age kids. Ian found it wonderfully warm to be with a family again.

At dinner, they asked about his plans. He told them he was headed for Wichita, then south on I-35 to I-40, headed for Albuquerque and his family. Kathy and her husband both shook their heads at this.

"You don't want to go to Wichita right now," Kathy said. "With all the refugees flooding in there, they're having a lot of trouble. Last we heard, there were food riots and a lot of looting. Besides, we just found out that the Texas riots ten days ago were caused by flash mobs. This may be going on in Wichita, too. Anarchy is breaking out. It's gotten really dangerous out there."

"What can I do?" Ian asked.

"Try cutting south on 99 instead," Kathy's husband offered. "It will take you down to 160. Go west on that, and you'll come out south of Wichita." Everybody at the table nodded approval of this route.

Days 146–147

Before leaving the next morning, Ian wrote letters to Theresa in Albuquerque and his brother in Boulder. These letters were Ian's first opportunity to communicate with anyone in his family in almost five months. The last time he talked with his wife was on January 3rd, eight days after the eruption of the behemoth.

He had not heard from them since. No one in his family knew he had journeyed almost 1300 miles from St. Ignace; or that now he was sitting at a kitchen table in Piqua, Kansas, desperately trying to bridge the catastrophic gulf rendered by space and time and ash.

Ian was now hundreds of miles south of the primary spray pattern and kill zone of the volcano. Within another 100 miles he would be totally out of the ashfall and onto dry pavement. Daily walking distances would increase dramatically. At least, he hoped so. But how many times had he hoped that would happen?

The letters he was mailing today would alert family in Albuquerque and Boulder to his estimated time of arrival. After he got around the south side of Wichita, he would be only about 600 miles from Albuquerque. At 20 miles a day, it would take only about a month to get to Theresa and the kids. From this very kitchen table, the whole rest of the journey should take only 40 days. Ian would be to safety by July 4th. What a celebration they would have! He had not felt this optimistic in months.

Ian gave the letters to Kathy, who explained that it might take a while to get them delivered. No east–west rail lines or roads were open into Denver. All mail had to go southwest to Albuquerque, then be transported north by army trucks up I-25 across the Raton Pass into Colorado. Mail could take up to eight weeks to arrive in Denver. Besides, Wichita was battened down and she didn't know for sure when the next pickup would be. Ian told her he understood.

Ian left the family standing at their doorway, all waving goodbye and calling out their good wishes as he walked away. The road was plowed, so walking was easier, and his high spirits added a spring to his step.

Ian spent the next two nights along the road in his sleeping bag. Fortunately, the convenience stores were all open.

Days 148–149

He was covering good distances now. By late afternoon he came to Neal, Kansas, another tiny town just two blocks wide.

Ian spent the night with a minister who offered him a ride as far as the turnoff to 99 south the next day. He was headed into Wichita to help out at a soup kitchen. He agreed with Kathy's family's assessment that Ian should head south and skirt the larger city.

Up early, Ian found himself on the road in the minister's car as the sun was rising. He was well fed and carrying plenty of water. Ian marveled at the feeling of being a passenger in a car again. It felt almost normal: cars working, roads plowed, sun out. He reflected that his last ride was outside Pana, with the Catholic Social Services rescue team. By 9 a.m. Ian had said farewell to the minister and set off down Route 99.

The road went south with a couple of jogs, and Ian set a good pace even though this road was not plowed. Ash no longer even covered his shoes. He estimated it was less than two inches deep. Compared to what he had been through, this was a piece of cake.

By about 5:00, he was just south of the town of Severy. It had been a great day. He figured he had covered about 25 miles, when he included his ride.

Days 150–151

Two days of easy, uneventful walking followed. Weather was good, ash was now only an inch deep, and terrain was open and flat. With no place to shelter for the night, darkness and bitter cold forced Ian to huddle in his sleeping bag by the side of the road. This meant he missed the president's Memorial Day speech.

On May 25, the president of the United States declared an extreme federal state of emergency, bordering on martial law. The FBI had confirmed that all food and gas riots over the past two weeks were flash-mob riots orchestrated by texts, calls, social media, and email. In an effort to contain them, all personal cell phone usage was suspended until further notice. All personal computer-based communication systems were also suspended. The president reassured the business community that their activities would not be affected. Essential business services would be maintained.

"We will continue to protect public health and safety and maintain vital activities: food, shelter, and fuel," he concluded.

Day 152

After three nights along the road, he was tired, dirty, and starting to feel the need for human contact again. He decided to take the road south into Grenola. Ian still had money left from raiding the ATM in Iola, and he was hungry.

The tiny town of Grenola consisted of one main street with just a few businesses, including—oh, wow—the Grenola Bar and Grill. The name raised a grin, and Ian entered the quiet restaurant.

Three men, obviously farmers, sat at a table eating breakfast. One other sat at the counter drinking coffee. All four looked at him suspiciously, then deliberately looked away. There was no real welcome in their faces; strangers were clearly not the norm here.

Ian approached the counter. A tired-looking woman, probably somewhere in her late 30s, gave him a perfunctory smile.

"What can I get you?" she asked, showing no curiosity about who he was or why he was there.

He ordered coffee, eggs, bacon, pancakes, then sat alone to eat them. There was a low murmur of desultory conversation from the other table, nothing he could really hear. No one approached him or even looked at him again, though he knew they were very aware of his presence. Breakfast was most uncomfortable.

Ian ordered a "Grenola Special" sandwich to go. It turned out to be ham and cheese on white bread, not an alfalfa sprout in sight. Oh, well.

He left Grenola heading south until he came to a tree-lined creek. Suddenly, a large German shepherd raced toward him, snarling and barking fiercely. Ian dove to the far side of the road. He stumbled, tripping over a deadfall branch, and came up with a yell of pain. A sharp splinter of wood had sliced into his hand. He sucked hard at the wound, glaring back at the dog, who had come to a halt in the middle of the road. The dog was now simply watching him. Ian cursed prolifically.

Still distracted by the dog and the pain in his hand, Ian moved down to the creek. Carefully watching the German shepherd, he washed the free-flowing blood from the ragged cut in his palm.

To keep the dog from pursuing matters, Ian waited until it finally got bored and wandered off. Then he moved back onto the pavement and continued walking toward the endless horizon. He was a quarter of a mile south, still muttering under his breath about people who don't control their animals, when it hit him. He had put an open wound in the water! He flashed back to the NPR programs about the effects of ashfall on open water, the vicious bacteria that kills. What monster had he just invited into his body?

There was really nothing he could do about it now. He kept walking south, then turned west again. It was getting late in the day, time to seek shelter for the night.

The road was wide open. You could see for miles in any direction, not that there was much to see. Just fields and a sparse scatter of trees. Farmhouses sat about a mile apart, and all appeared to be occupied.

Finally Ian spotted a corn crib sitting back from the road on his right at the end of a long tractor road. It was dusk by now and there was no apparent human activity anywhere around him. He crept down the drive and entered the crib through its small access door.

"Darker than the hubs of Hades," he murmured to himself, "and just about as cold." It would be an uncomfortable night, but at least he would be out of the wind and ash.

It was a long night. He guessed he'd been settled about two hours when the dog pack arrived. He could hear them outside the corn crib, grunting and scratching at the door. They knew he was in there, and clearly they wanted a piece of the action. He spent most of the night in wide-eyed fear, holding the door shut and listening to the scrabbling dog claws as they tried to breach his sanctuary. Thank God this dog pack hadn't discovered him the last few nights while he slept by the side of the road.

Chapter 30

Day 153

Ian lay cold and cramped in his sleeping bag inside the corn crib. The dogs had stopped scratching and growling outside. He could hear in the distance the chugging of a tractor, an early rising farmer out harrowing ash into his fields. He choked down the stale remains of his "Grenola Bar Special," chasing it with a spare sip of water, and stealthily left the corn crib into the hazy morning sunlight. He was in luck: the tractor was heading in the opposite direction as Ian made his way back to the road.

"Not too cold or windy today," he thought; "good walking weather." The road seemed to stretch out forever as he followed his shadow west.

Hours passed. There was no sign of life anywhere. The road was empty, the fields were empty, there were no houses or buildings of any kind. It was desolate and lonely beyond belief.

As the afternoon wore on, he began to sweat. It wasn't that warm and he hadn't been walking that fast. Worried, he paused, took off the gas mask, and felt his forehead with his uninjured hand. He was feverish. This could be serious trouble. Glancing at the cut on his hand, he noted that the surrounding area was swelling and inflamed. What now? He had very little water—the corn crib didn't have running water, so he couldn't refill his water bottle. There were only a couple of swigs left. All he could do was keep walking and hope for the best.

He started moving more slowly. The fever was rising rapidly. He was now sweating profusely and beginning to feel weak. The farther he went the more pronounced these symptoms became. By late afternoon he was beginning to weave and stagger like a drunk, but there was still no sign of any place to stop or anyone to help him. He kept going.

Evening fell on the same lonely scenery he had passed through the entire day. By now he was seeing everything through a haze, sometimes two "everythings" at the same time. He realized he was becoming delirious. Squinting, he turned slowly in a full circle, looking for shelter, any shelter. There was nothing in any direction.

He was too sick to go on. Ian dropped his backpack off the side of the road under the only tree in sight. He rolled out his sleeping bag and crawled inside. As soon as he stopped moving, he started shivering and his teeth began to chatter. "Maybe this is it," he thought. "But I can't go any farther."

Darkness fell in silence. Ian's eyelids drooped and he fell into an exhausted sleep.

Day 154

Throughout the night as Ian tossed feverishly in his sleeping bag, he drifted in and out of consciousness. Periodically he thought he could hear the high-pitched yipping of a coyote pack on the hunt. Then a greenish-white luminescence would surround him, but he'd lose consciousness again before he could begin to react.

By the time he regained awareness, the sun was high in the sky. Ian had had no food since the previous morning, and his precious water was down to two small sips. He carefully wetted his mouth, trying desperately not to spill any. His hands were shaking so badly that this was a real challenge, requiring all the focus he could bring to bear. The fever was raging through his body now. His vision was clouded and uncertain.

"Must keep moving." It was all he could think. With painful slowness he began to repack his sleeping bag. As he stood up, he saw what appeared to be deer hoof prints in the ash all around his sleeping place, but he discounted that as a hallucination. The prints were bigger than his hand. "That would be one big fucking deer! Like the one in the UP? Nah...."

Ian began to stagger down the left side of westbound KS 28. Unable to see clearly, he decided to keep his feet at the edge of the road to keep himself from wandering off in his delirium. He lurched along, watching his feet.

As a result, he did not see the actual intersection at southbound KS 15. This intersection, unlike any other he had encountered so far, is a curved "Y" instead of a "T". Ian followed the gentle curve south, instead of continuing along KS 28. His feverish focus on his feet and the clouds covering the sun meant he had no idea he hadn't kept going west.

He was making terrible time now. Dehydrated, hungry, and fevered, he could walk for only very short distances between rest stops. The road continued to be devoid of life. With what little thought he could muster, he wondered if he'd have to spend another night out in the open.

It was early evening when he looked ahead and saw a wonderfully welcome sight: a driveway! He staggered toward it, feeling his first surge of hope in the past two days.

Ian arrived at a parking lot near a set of buildings. Two 24-foot long trucks were parked in the lot. There were two outbuildings on one side of the lot, a larger building across the way from him. The building was dark, but there was a sign out front. Ian went closer and squinted to clear his vision. "Am I completely crazy?" he wondered. The sign seemed to say

Maude's Candy Co.
Hand Made Candies

Ian peered through the window. Sure enough, he saw long tables, big steel bowls, candy molds, and taffy-making paddles. He walked around the building, holding himself up against the walls, looking for an entry point. This place looked as if it might be on an alarm system, so he didn't want to try to break in. All the doors were locked.

At the back of the building he found a lone delivery van. The driver's-side door wouldn't open. Neither would the passenger door. In despair, he tugged at the rear doors—and it opened. He crawled into the closed van, leaving the door open for the little remaining daylight. There was room to lay out his sleeping bag. Even more marvelous, there was a single box marked "Maude's Favorites." Inside were candy bars—a whole box of them. Maybe caramel fudge, peanuts, and milk chocolate aren't recommended to treat fever, but they certainly treat hunger. Ian ate four of the candy bars and finished his last drink of water before lying down to sleep. "Got to be out of here early," he reminded himself. "Don't want to go to jail for stealing candy!"

Day 155

Despite his intentions, Ian slept heavily. When he awoke, the sun was actually shining, although a bit murkily.

It was still quiet outside the van. He pushed himself up, groggy with sleep and fever, and leaned forward to look out the window. There was no sign of movement, so he cautiously opened the rear door of the van and poked his head out. The parking lot was still empty.

He could barely move, but he knew he must get out of there; so he forced himself onto his hands and knees to repack his sleeping bag. Not exactly shipshape, but it fit back onto the frame of his backpack. Staggering, he went around the building, hoping for an outdoor water spigot. Surely someone watered the lawns. He was rewarded for his persistence. The water was brackish, a little brown; but it helped with the fever thirst. He filled his water bottle and wobbled out of the parking lot.

He had gone only a few yards down the road when he stepped into a pothole and severely twisted his ankle. Walking became painful. He traveled very short distances between collapses to rest, frequently lapsing into unconsciousness. Finally, as evening began to fall, he fell as well and, in his infected delirium, couldn't get up. He lay there, feeling awareness slip away.

"Ash…there's no ash…."

Darlene Pritchard and her husband Jim had just finished dinner in their farmhouse on Route 15. She was in the kitchen, finishing up the dishes. The sky was darkening early because of all the ash in the atmosphere.

Darlene was an Osage woman. Small and slender, she had dark hair, eyes, and skin. She had been raised on the reservation just south of her current home in Dexter, Kansas. Her brother, an ex-Marine medic, still lived on the rez.

Jim, her husband, was a big, quiet man; a farmer to the core. He supplied organic food to the reservation. He loved his wife devotedly, but he didn't even pretend to understand her.

As she rinsed the last pot, Darlene glimpsed a greenish-white glow through the kitchen window. It seemed to be on the road. She called her husband to look, but neither could tell the source of the light.

They decided to look from their front windows. Outside, standing a little north of the gate to the yard, was a gigantic, glowing stag. It was magnificent, breathtaking. They stared in awe.

"What the hell is that?" Jim wondered.

Darlene was transfixed, mesmerized by the sight. Her mind flashed to the winter nights when her grandmother would sit the children down by the fireplace and weave the old stories of her people. She could hear her grandmother's voice explaining:

"It's a spirit guide. Sacred, holy." She didn't realize she had said this out loud until Jim reacted.

"But what does it want? Why is it here? Where did it come from?"

Darlene simply opened the front door and walked out onto the porch. Jim followed anxiously. Darlene offered a mental prayer to the spirits, remembering her grandmother's teaching.

"What do you want from me?" she asked silently. With her whole being, she felt the response:

"Follow."

She started down the walk to the gate. Jim, fearful for her, grabbed her arm and held her back.

"It wants us to follow," Darlene explained, as if it were the most normal thing in the world to traipse off into the darkness behind a glowing, greenish-white stag.

"No!" said Jim.

"Yes," said Darlene.

Jim persuaded her to wait while he got the rifle. Even he didn't think bullets would be effective against this vision, but coyotes were singing in the distance.

They followed the stag. Darlene was confident; Jim, tentative but determined to protect her, whatever it took. The stag moved with gentle fluidity in front of them, northward down Route 15. The coyotes were beginning to yip now; they had found something.

The road curved gently about half a mile from the house. As they rounded the curve, the stag came to a halt. Its glow illuminated a crumpled form lying at the side of the road.

"Ah," said Darlene.

Jim was now galvanized to action.

"Take the rifle. Hold off the coyotes. Wait here. I'll bring the truck." Gazing at the stag, Darlene replied,

"I won't need the rifle. The sacred stag will protect us." Reluctantly, Jim nodded and turned back toward home.

Chapter 31

Day 157

Ian regained consciousness with the smells of brewing coffee and frying bacon teasing his nose. He heard a frying pan being shifted over the flame; soft but heavy footsteps, and the low murmur of voices. He was warm and comfortable, drifting up out of sleep.

Sudden realization popped his eyes wide. Where the hell was he? The last thing he remembered was pushing himself down a desolate road, one step at a time. How did he end up in a bed? In fearful confusion he looked around him.

He was in a small room, maybe ten by twelve, with a single east-facing window through which blessed sunlight was pouring. The walls were a smooth cream color, as were the curtains. He lay in a twin bed, covered by a crazy quilt. An oak dresser sat along the wall to his right. On a straight-backed chair beside the dresser were his clothes, neatly folded. His shoes were tucked under the chair. His eye was caught by a medicine wheel hanging on the wall next to the window. Hmmm?

His gaze traveled to the door on the west side of the room just as a bearded face appeared near the top of the doorframe. "My God!" Ian thought, "This guy's a giant!" The face smiled at him and disappeared.

"Hey, Darlene," Ian heard a basso profundo voice boom. "Our guest is awake." Moments later the door was pushed open to allow the bustling entry of a small, compact woman followed by a very large man. Both were smiling cheerfully.

"Welcome back," the woman sang. Ian smiled uncertainly. Did he know these people? In his befogged state, he wasn't sure of anything.

"Uh, hello," he offered tentatively. "Um, where am I? How did I get here?"

"You're about two miles north of Dexter," the woman replied. "We found you lying by the road two days ago with a raging fever and this awful, infected gash on your hand."

Now Ian was even more confused. He lived three miles north of Dexter. Had this all been a dream? What happened to him? Where was his wife? Ian tried to sit up and gasped at a sharp pain in his left leg.

"What happened? Did I get hit by a car or something? Is Theresa here?"

Looks of puzzled concern crossed the faces of his two observers.

"Who's Theresa?" asked the woman.

"My wife," Ian answered. The woman shook her head.

"You were alone when we found you," she responded sympathetically. "Maybe she went for help? Though there aren't a lot of places around here. She'd have found us, wouldn't she, Jim? Oh, my God, do you think there's someone else lost out there?"

Panic surged through Ian, but a small part of his consciousness was waving a red flag: something was not right. "How could she be lost a mile from home?" he thought.

"Wait," he said. "I'm just north of Dexter, right? On Mast Road?"

"Mast Road?" the man asked in a confused tone. "No, we're on Route 15. Where is Mast Road?" Ian felt the onset of despair. Not a dream, after all.

"I'm not in Michigan any more, am I?"

"Good grief, no! We're in Kansas."

Ian's head fell back against the pillow. Kansas. Memory came rushing back, replaying everything to the moment he lost consciousness and sank to the road. He smiled wearily at the couple.

"I should introduce myself, at least," he said. Even that exhausted him, and he fell back into a deep sleep for several hours.

By the time he resurfaced, it was dinnertime. Darlene brought him a cup of beef broth with a few soda crackers. He managed to keep this much down.

"Let me clear away these dishes. Then we'll take a look at your ankle, okay?" A few minutes later, she returned and turned back the quilt covering Ian's legs. He winced as he looked at his left ankle. It was swollen to the size of a grapefruit. "Looks like I swallowed something whole and that's where it ended up," he thought. And suddenly that struck him as hilariously funny. He started to chuckle, and it built to a full-blown laugh. Dimly, he realized it wasn't that humorous, but he couldn't seem to stop laughing. Darlene and Jim exchanged a concerned look.

"It's okay," said Darlene soothingly. "Really. It's a pretty bad sprain, but it will be all right." Ian choked back the laughter. He pulled away from the edge of hysteria but felt himself fading again. He lost consciousness.

Day 158

Ian was in and out of consciousness all day. Darlene fed him broth and medicine, and wiped away his fever sweat. He didn't remember much else about it.

Day 159

Because he was still weak and had to rest frequently, it took most of the day for him to tell his story to the increasingly astonished couple.

"Wow," said Darlene, "That's just amazing. I can hardly believe you made it out, but I'm really glad you're here." Jim just nodded in agreement. After a pause, Darlene declared, "Well, it's getting late and you must be wiped out. We'll be right across the way, so if you need anything in the night, just give a holler. See you in the morning." And with that, she and Jim left Ian to his own thoughts.

Ian tried to absorb what he had learned. "Dexter, Kansas," he snorted to himself. "Dexter, Michigan. Paradise, Michigan. Paradise, Illinois. Detroit, Michigan. Detroit, Illinois." Everything was coming in sets. What did that mean? He had no idea, but the idea was intriguing, so he played with it for a while. He knew he was just putting off thinking about his real situation, but he was so tired, so worn out. He didn't want to grapple with it.

Day 160

"How did you find me?" Ian asked.

Darlene recounted the evening a few days ago. She described the glowing stag, the message it gave her; how the two of them followed the apparition down the road and discovered Ian's crumpled form; how she waited with the stag while Jim fetched the truck to carry him back to the farm; how the stag simply disappeared as soon as it was clear that Ian was safe.

"I knew you were special," she said firmly. "A spirit guide that powerful doesn't waste time on just anyone."

"So they've seen the stag, too," Ian thought. "And now it's a spirit guide?"

"You're on a vision quest, aren't you?" Darlene asked. Ian hesitated, remembering Captain Monty.

"Well, maybe. What made you ask that?"

"Your whole story sounds like a vision quest," she said. Darlene explained the concept, as it was told to her by her grandmother. During a vision quest, a person would go into the wilderness alone, without food, water, clothing, or weapons. After he went through days of hunger, thirst, and no shelter from the weather, suffering and praying with intense sincerity, the spirits might answer. One of them would agree to become a protector to the vision quester as long as he continued to live a righteous life, seeking truth and honor.

"Grandma was a storyteller. She went to the Gathering of Nations in Albuquerque every year for as long as I can remember, collecting stories from all the nations," she told him. "She said that our own histories and traditions had been so badly fractured and fragmented by the whites that we now had to patch things together like this quilt. It isn't seamless and the colors don't all match, but at least there is a pattern you can follow. I don't really know where the idea of spirit guides came from. The stories she told came from everywhere in Indian Country. It could have been any of a hundred different traditions." She paused, briefly brooding. "Still, having a spirit guide that strong means you are important. I had to help you, and I will help you any way I can. Right, Jim?" The bearded giant, clearly a man of few words, nodded again.

Darlene glanced at the shadows beginning to fill the room and declared it time to make dinner. She went out to the kitchen, Jim trailing along behind her.

Darlene brought dinner to his bedside. She had made a beef roast with potatoes, gravy, home-canned green beans, and freshly baked bread. Ian devoured it like the starving man he was, and she beamed with pleasure at his appetite and appreciation.

"That's more like it. We were really worried about you, weren't we, Jim?" Jim, looking solemn, nodded and grunted an affirmative. Darlene was gone for several minutes. When she returned, it was as if a whirlwind had entered the room.

"I called Mitch," she said to Jim. "Susan said he's in the middle of a ceremony and won't be back for a couple of days, but she'll let us know as soon as he returns."

Ian heard just one word: "called."

"My God! You have phone service?" he asked eagerly. "Can I call my wife?"

"Well, not really," Darlene replied sadly. "We have two-way radios. They reach as far as Mitch and Susan's place in Pawhuska, but not a whole lot farther. That's a little over 40 miles as the crow flies," she explained, seeing Ian's look of incomprehension. We haven't had cell phone service since the flash-mob riots. The president shut the whole system down."

"Oh," Ian's sigh seemed to deflate his entire body.

"Mitch is my brother," she said, back in full spate. "I called him for advice about your ankle. He was a medic with the Marines in Afghanistan, so he really knows his stuff when it comes to patching people up on the fly in the worst possible circumstances. Our people have come to depend on him for emergencies ever since he got back. But don't ask him about the war. He doesn't like to talk about it. I don't know what happened to him over there, but when he got home he had changed completely. He was studying law at Oklahoma State, but he dropped out and got real traditional, went back to the old ways big time. Even changed his last name to 'One Feather.' He studied with an old Kiowa medicine man. He's deep in the movement now, waiting for the purification of the earth. But he's still a really good medic, and if anyone can fix you up, it's Mitch." Ian nodded his thanks. "Oh, by the way, I told Susan about the stag. Even if he has other things on his plate, Mitch won't miss a chance to talk to you about *that!*" Darlene shook her head in wonder. "Man, I still can't believe it, and I saw it myself. It *talked* to me, and I *still* can't believe it."

Days 161–162

Ian was still sleeping a lot, but he was starting to notice patterns in the household. He could now sit up and talk for longer periods of time.

Jim was usually gone during the main part of the day, caring for the large farm he operated. Ian learned that Jim had created an unusual three-story greenhouse, with a fish pond on the lowest level, a wealth of vegetables growing in the middle, and composting on the top. He provided much of the produce for Pawhuska's main grocer. Because he was married to an Osage woman, he was able to land the lucrative contract; but it was his own considerable farming skill that had maintained his position. He took it very seriously. Ian heard him leave the house quietly before the sun rose and rarely saw him until evening. Then the big man, clearly exhausted and quiet as ever, came to visit Ian. The two men developed a friendship based on smiles and nods and peaceful silence.

Darlene, on the other hand, never seemed to stop: moving, talking, a constant whirlwind of activity. She filled Ian's days with breezy conversation and highly competent care. Her limited first aid kit provided him with an NSAID to reduce his pain, fever, and ankle swelling.

When they realized how bad Ian's infection was, she explained, Jim went in to Dexter to see old Doc Peabody. He provided an incredibly strong antibiotic to clear up the massive infection Ian contracted when he washed his cut in the water at Grenola. The doctor told Jim he had just received the drugs from the CDC. They were specifically developed to combat bacteria found in ash-contaminated water and had been targeted to communities on the edge of the volcanic ash. He also made a house call to give Ian an intramuscular shot of the antibiotic to start attacking the infection. The next day, Ian regained consciousness.

At some point, Ian noticed that his gas mask was missing. He asked Darlene about it, but she professed total ignorance. Somewhere during his feverish trek from Grenola to Dexter, it had simply disappeared.

Sometimes he could hear the murmur of television from the living room, and the evening news filtered into his room. Still too weak to go out and watch, he heard fragments. Almost nobody was coming out of the affected area now. Anyone still inside was considered "missing, presumed dead." The war in Syria was effectively over: all troops were called home to deal with the emergency here. The area covered by volcanic ash was referred to as the "ashdome," and it covered most of the nation's food-producing territory. The U.N. was coordinating emergency food relief efforts, with donations from South America, Australia, and the Philippines. Ian figured he'd have to find out more when he was feeling better. Now, just listening for a few minutes was exhausting.

Darlene didn't talk much about current events, worried that she might overtax him and impede his healing. She would, though, talk about the millenarian movement in which her brother was so active. She told him that she didn't completely buy into what Mitch believed so fervently, but she'd picked up the main outlines of what that belief was. She explained the basic ideas behind the movement, which originated with the Hopi in Arizona.

The volcanic eruptions were to be a great cleansing of the earth. All who have violated the wishes of the Creator and despoiled the planet would be destroyed. When the earth had been scoured, it would be renewed, restored to its previous pristine state. Those who survived would be rewarded with stewardship of the bounty of the earth. Hopi prophecy stated that Masaw would return to lead them from the Fourth World to the Fifth. Ian smiled fleetingly, warmly remembering Captain Monty, reading glasses perched on his nose, earnestly reading that prophecy from the *Book of the Hopi*.

A return to the old ways was the way to achieve the Creator's will. This meant limited use of modern technologies and an emphasis on self-sufficiency for communities of believers. The goal was simplification, maintaining harmony with the earth.

Ian absorbed as much of this information as his fevered brain would hold. He was still bedbound, and even after a week, his ankle was swollen and painful. There was no question of putting weight on it. If he so much as wiggled his toes he was rewarded with shooting pain. Darlene kept cool cloths on the swelling and piled pillows under his leg to help reduce the buildup of toxins, but it was obvious this was no minor injury that would clear up in a few days.

After dinner that evening, Darlene burst into his room beaming happily.

"Mitch is back. He just called and said to bring you to his place. He'll take a look at your ankle and you can stay with him until you're healed. We can head over there day after tomorrow. He has meetings all day Saturday, or we could go right away."

Ian's face lit up so brightly that Darlene had to laugh.

"It's okay," she said. "I know how frustrating this is for you. We're going to miss you, but we really understand. You have a quest to finish."

Day 163

Early in the afternoon, when Jim had finished his chores, he carried Ian out to the pickup truck and laid him down on a bedding of straw and quilts in the truck bed. Ian was eager to move on, but still…

"Are you sure you can do this? Do you have enough gas to take me all the way there?" he asked anxiously. For the first time, he was treated to Jim's booming laugh.

"You've been inside the ashdome for a long time. You don't know much about how things are running now, do you?" Jim asked. "Okay, long story short. I'm a farmer. Even with gas rationing, I have priority so I can get food in the ground and then take the harvest into town. I also have my own tank, which is pretty close to full. No problem, my friend."

To Ian's surprise, Jim kept talking. With considerable enthusiasm, he explained that his modern tractor could handle even the ash in the atmosphere. It had a very efficient two-stage air cleaner element, as well as heating and air conditioning in the cab.

Ian's mouth fell open. "Son of a bitch! I could have stolen one of those. I didn't have to walk a thousand miles."

The trip to Pawhuska was uneventful. They traveled on paved roads through open farmland, going south for a little under twenty miles to the Oklahoma border. Jim drove slowly and carefully, stopping every few miles to check on Ian. Darlene plied him with water and fried chicken. At the stop just inside Oklahoma, Ian waved a chicken leg and called out, "Hey, Darlene. I guess we're not in Kansas anymore, are we?"

Darlene laughed. "And me without my ruby red slippers! How will I ever get home?"

They continued south through the small farming communities of Grainola and Shidler. After another twenty miles or so they reached US 60 and turned east for the final twenty-mile leg into Pawhuska. It was late afternoon by the time they reached the outskirts.

Pawhuska was a good-sized town. As they rolled down Main Street, Ian was treated to the view of a very neat, clean, and well-maintained place. Many of the buildings showed signs of having been built over a century ago—squared off, brick edifices mixed with more recent additions like fast-food joints. City Hall looked like something from the 1880s. Ian marveled at how normal everything seemed. People were walking down the sidewalks, just going about their business. There was even a small amount of traffic on the streets.

A thought came to Ian. His existence had been normal for 45 years. Then, for six months, every step had been life-altering… life-threatening. Now life was suddenly normal again, and that seemed weird.

Jim and Darlene brought him to her brother's small frame home in an old part of Pawhuska. As soon as the truck stopped moving, Darlene burst out of the passenger side and barreled up to the porch, nearly knocking over the man who had just turned to close the screen door.

"Mitch!" she squealed. Staggering under the weight of her onslaught and looking extremely embarrassed, the man muttered, "Hey, Darlene."

Ian and Jim got out of the truck. With Jim's help, Ian hobbled painfully toward the porch, leaning heavily on his walking stick. The peace sign fluttered its intent to the breeze.

Introductions allowed Ian the time to size up Darlene's brother. Mitch was a small, wiry man, probably about five years younger than Ian. He seemed to be reserved and quiet, very different from his sister in this way. While she chattered on, he assessed Ian quite thoroughly. Ian felt a little self-conscious. It was clear that Mitch wasn't just looking at the surface. Apparently having made up his mind, Mitch nodded to himself and invited them inside to meet his family.

Waiting in a small living room were Susan and their two children. Susan was a large, comfortable-looking woman who responded to Darlene's flying hug with a rich laugh and a warm hug of her own. The two little boys both started tugging on Darlene's skirt, crying "Aunt Darlene! Aunt Darlene!" vying for the attention of a clearly favorite relative. Ian found himself staring at the children and realized this was the first time in months he'd seen any kids who weren't terrified, bewildered, and starving.

Susan took Darlene and the boys to the kitchen, calling over her shoulder that she'd be right back with coffee and cake. Jim, looking after them with affection in his eyes, murmured to Ian, "That Susan. You can't ever come here without getting something to eat. She's *so* Osage."

Mitch, Ian, and Jim sat in the living room. The silence stretched out. Ian was just thinking, "Great. Now I have two men who won't talk," when Mitch cleared his throat and said, "Darlene tells me you have a spirit guide."

"Wow," thought Ian, "no small talk for this guy." He explained the history of his experiences with the stag, emphasizing that he himself had seen it clearly only once, just before his truck ran into that tree in the UP. Jim broke in here.

"I've seen it, Mitch," is all he said; but that seemed to be enough for Mitch.

"With Darlene," Mitch sighed, "you can never be too sure. She got a lot of the storytelling from Grandma, and sometimes she embellishes things. You, though," he nodded at Jim, then shook his head. "If you saw it, it was there." The silence returned, but now it had a different flavor, wonder mixed with uncertainty.

Finally Susan and Darlene returned, talking and laughing as they carried trays of coffee and food. The mood lightened substantially. Talk turned to the family, friends, what was happening on the rez.

"Did you hear Mary is pregnant again?" Susan asked Darlene.

"No! When did you hear that?"

"Oh, just this morning. She found out yesterday afternoon."

Jim, seeming more relaxed here than at his own home, grinned at Ian. "That's called the moccasin telegraph," he explained. "Anything that happens here spreads like wildfire. No secrets."

After dinner, Darlene and Jim were preparing to leave. The last week with Ian had been life-changing for Darlene. Something awoke within her, and having to separate from him now was going to be difficult.

"You know," she told Ian, "Grandma always said I'd do something really important for the people. She said the spirits would let me know when I had to start. Well, that stag sure let me know. Guess I'll be waiting to see what I have to do next."

Darlene and Jim headed back to their farm. Susan took the children off to bed. Ian felt his own eyelids drooping, and Mitch was quick to notice.

"Why don't we call it a night?" he suggested. "We can talk in the morning." With that, he helped Ian to his room. The house grew very quiet, and Ian fell into a deep, dreamless sleep.

Chapter 32

Day 164

Ian awoke to the sound of birdsong outside his window. Great joy flooded his heart as he realized these were the first birds he'd heard since before the volcano.

Sun streamed into the room, highlighting the medicine wheel on the wall opposite the bed. For a moment, he thought he was still at Jim and Darlene's house; but the walls were a soft yellow and the medicine wheel was different, larger and somehow more stark and demanding of his attention.

As consciousness returned, he realized where he was and remembered how he got here. Now awake, Ian heard quiet talk coming from the kitchen. The kids were clearly trying to be considerate. He got up, dressed quickly, and hobbled out into the main part of the house, leaning heavily on his walking stick.

Mitch was walking toward him, carrying an eagle feather fan and a stick of burning sage. He was using the fan to waft sage smoke throughout the house. Ian came to a halt and stood with his eyes closed as Mitch bathed him in the pungent smoke. He felt a deep sense of peace come over him as he inhaled. Mitch nodded and walked on.

Ian continued into the kitchen, where Susan was making breakfast. He admired her deft work at the wood cook stove as she moved the iron frying pans from hotter areas to cooler ones, keeping the eggs from scorching as bacon was frying. "That's pretty much a lost art," he thought. "It takes real skill and a lot of practice to cook on a wood-burning stove!"

Mitch now wandered back into the kitchen, saging the room as well as his wife and two sons. Everyone paused as he gently waved the smoke over their bodies. Even though it was already very comfortable, the kitchen took on a new serenity. The day would begin from the proper spiritual place.

After a pleasant breakfast, Mitch took Ian to the living room to examine his ankle. The diagnosis was a very bad sprain, with torn ligaments.

"You'll never be able to rely on that ankle again," Mitch told him briskly. "Be prepared for it to give way on you at the most unexpected times. I've actually seen people with this kind of injury go flat on their faces on perfectly level ground. Your tendons are stretched, and they do not repair themselves. Just be careful, okay?" Mitch wrapped the ankle tightly, telling Ian to take off the pressure only when he slept. Meanwhile, he should keep using his walking stick and start to walk on the foot as much as was comfortable. "Not the best news," Ian thought, "but it could be worse." At least this wasn't a fatal injury.

"How long until I can travel?" Ian asked.

"I'd give it a month, more or less," said Mitch. "Depends on how well you follow instructions and how quick you heal. You're going to be pretty sore for at least a couple of weeks. Then it should start feeling better pretty quickly. After that, we'll see.

"Meanwhile," Mitch continued with a small smile, "we should be able to keep your mind occupied. I think you have a lot to tell us, and we have a lot to tell you."

"'We?'" asked Ian. Mitch nodded.

"There are some people you need to meet. Let's give you a few days to get settled. Then I'll invite them over."

Days 165–171

Ian stayed at the house. He was still in bed most of the time, but he was steadily getting more mobile as the days passed.

He soaked his ankle daily, kept it wrapped tightly, and removed the bandage only at night. He could feel his strength returning as the infection in his hand reduced.

Day 172

A sage ceremony and breakfast began another day, with Ian feeling more coherent. After breakfast, Mitch asked Ian about any other experiences he had had that were more spiritual in nature. Ian told him about the glowing Eagle Kachina at the snowshoe workshop and the strange calling he heard in Missouri. He felt reluctant to talk about the calling. He still didn't know what to make of it himself. Mitch had been fascinated throughout the narrative, but his eyes widened at the last item.

"When was this?" he asked with barely suppressed excitement. Ian referred to his well-notched walking stick.

"Let's see....I'd been on the road for over a hundred days. It was my first Sunday in Missouri. I remember I notched my walking stick that day. So it must have been the second Sunday in April? What date was that?"

Mitch looked stunned. "It was April 12th."

"That was quick," Ian replied in surprise. "How did you know the date so fast?"

"Because," said Mitch, "that's the first time I heard it too."

The two men stared at each other in amazement.

"Could you tell who it was?" asked Mitch. Ian shook his head.

"I don't know. She didn't send her name. In fact, there weren't any words at all, just energy. But I had this sense of urgency, that whoever she was calling needed to get to her now."

"It was a woman's energy, then," Mitch confirmed. "Me, too. And the message was the same for me. That's when I got serious about the movement. I still don't know who she is, but she's Hopi. She's calling the People home. And she's calling the Pahana."

Ian flashed again to Captain Monty. "The white brother?"

Mitch nodded. "He has to rejoin the Hopi before the Fifth World can begin. He has a critical piece of the prophecy. Without that, nothing can happen."

Ian thought about this for a few minutes. "So," he asked slowly, "how many people are hearing this calling?"

"Well, you're the first white person I know of," Mitch said quietly. The silence returned, and this time it settled in for a long visit as the two men sat lost in their thoughts. Finally they met each other's eyes and both smiled ruefully.

"It's going to take me a while to process this," said Ian.

"Yeah," Mitch agreed. "Let's call it a day."

The rest of the afternoon and evening passed quietly. Susan and the boys were clearly used to having Mitch go silent and abstracted. Susan glanced curiously at Ian, recognized the symptoms, and took the boys into the living room. When Ian looked in a little later, all three were curled up on the couch with books. No TV or radio in this house. He was grateful for the space he'd been given to think about his conversation with Mitch. He worked on trying to find a meaning for the rest of the evening.

Day 173

After breakfast, Susan announced that she and the boys had finished their books. It was time to run into town.

"We go once a week," she told Ian. "That's when we get groceries, go to the post office, pay bills, and go to the library. Want to come?" Ian eagerly accepted. He'd been confined to bed for almost three weeks, and he was going a little stir crazy. The idea of feeling the sun on his face, breathing fresh air, and getting out into an actual, fully functioning town drew him like a magnet. He badly needed news of the outside world.

As Susan, Mitch, and the boys got ready to go, Ian had the chance to ask Mitch how he felt about the family reading books.

"I mean, you've gotten rid of a lot of the outside influences in your life, even though it's only been a few months since things got really serious with the movement," he explained. "Are you going to keep the library in your life?" Mitch looked a little sheepish.

"Well, I've got to draw the line somewhere," he muttered. "The boys do go to school, after all, and they can't just run wild and play all the time. I want their minds to be as strong as their bodies. Anyway," he added, just a bit defensively, "going back to the old ways has never really been complete. Even in the old days, men usually got to keep their rifles and God help the man who tried to take away his wife's iron cooking pot!" Ian laughed and gently slapped Mitch on the shoulder.

"Yeah, there are limits," he agreed.

First stop was the library, just two blocks away. This was a low, modern building with a blue metal roof. Susan and the boys made a beeline for the books. Ian lagged behind, winded and fatigued by just that short walk. Then he realized that there were computers here. Email! He could contact his wife! He signed up for a computer, only to find that he couldn't log on to his email account. Puzzled, he approached a librarian for an explanation.

"I'm having trouble accessing my email account," he told the woman apologetically. "Am I doing something wrong?" The librarian looked at him in disbelief.

"We haven't had internet access for three weeks. Not since all the servers were nationalized, anyway. Where have you been?"

"Under the ashdome," Ian replied. "I just got here a few days ago. Sorry, I really didn't know." The librarian's jaw literally dropped.

"How long were you in there?"

"From the beginning. I got caught in northern Michigan." Ian's bleak smile hinted at months of gray ash covering a blighted landscape.

"My Lord," the librarian breathed. "How did you get here?"

"Mostly, I walked."

"You...walked? That's got to be almost a thousand miles!"

"Sure felt like it," Ian agreed. He smiled again, and the librarian responded a little uncertainly, with respect and awe in her eyes.

"So, what now? How do people communicate?"

The woman chuckled. "Well, mostly the way we're doing now. The landlines are all so overstressed that getting a call through is next to impossible. Mail is really iffy—no mail planes with all the gas rationing and no trucks to deliver it anyway. Everything goes by train now, and official communications and business have priority. You can try to send a letter, but heaven knows when or even if it will arrive." She shrugged. "All we can do, really, is wait for things to get back to normal."

Ian explained his desperate need to contact his wife.

"Is there any way to find her?" he asked. She suggested that he try the Government Refugee Registration Center.

“The GRRC is about the only thing we can get online,” she told him, and gave him the appropriate website to search.

Ian eagerly entered the site and typed in his wife’s name. The search engine was slow to respond, and Ian was on pins and needles waiting. Finally, a list popped up with Theresa’s name highlighted. Gabe and Claire were there, too.

“Oh, thank God!” Ian exclaimed. Where are they? He checked for location and discovered they signed in at Champaign-Urbana, Illinois. What? That made no sense to Ian. They should have been far south of there. Why would they be heading west in Illinois? What the hell was she doing, driving into the teeth of the ash? Gabe’s lungs couldn’t take that. It wasn’t what they had agreed upon.

He remembered standing on the overpass, looking down on the bumper-to-bumper traffic on I-74. But his family had been there too, headed west toward Champaign-Urbana on January 5. Ian didn’t pass through that area until two months later.

Reluctant to give up even this tenuous connection to his family, Ian stared at the screen for several minutes, but there were no other listings. Finally, he logged out and returned to Mitch and Susan, who were waiting near the door.

“Any luck?” Mitch asked. Ian told them what he had found.

“I’m not going to be very good company for the rest of the day,” he apologized. “Got a lot to think about.” Mitch and Susan nodded their understanding and gave him the space he needed.

Day 174

At breakfast the next day, Ian turned to Mitch.

“So,” he said, “tell me more about this movement you’re involved in. What’s it about?”

Mitch brightened visibly. He began to fill Ian in on the millenarian movement that had gained power and momentum after the first eruption of the volcano.

“The Hopi have always believed this was coming,” he explained, “but the rest of us took a little convincing. The caldera was definitely convincing. We really are at the end of the Fourth World, and if we want to be part of the Fifth World, we'd better clean up our act."

Volcanic eruptions are a sign of anger by the Creator, Mitch said. As he went on, Ian realized that all of this was just a repetition of what Darlene had told him. Ian nodded, partly to encourage Mitch to continue, and partly in approval of Mitch's sister. He loved her ability to summarize something she wasn't even sure she believed.

To be part of this transition, people must return to the old ways. This meant limited use of modern technologies and an emphasis on self-sufficiency for communities of believers. Exceptions would be allowed in some cases. Modern medicine could blend with herbal and spiritual healing techniques. Some use of communication devices was acceptable. Electricity could be used to power food freezers. Metal tools were considered okay, and, of course, they had rifles. But wherever possible, people gave up modern technologies. The goal was simplification, maintaining harmony with the earth.

In Mitch and Susan's case, she chose to go back to a wood cook stove. It is always the women, though, who have to make the biggest sacrifices. They're the ones who would have to wash clothes by hand, or heat water to bathe the kids in a washtub, or give up their kitchen appliances.

"If we purify ourselves, become part of nature again instead of trying to conquer it, we can survive the end of this world. Now that we have learned what our mistakes here were, we won't make them again. Our children's children's children will still be doing the will of the Creator, and the world will be a much better place. No more violence, no more pollution, no more disease—everything will be in balance again." Mitch leaned forward, intense and deeply sincere as he said this. Ian couldn't help responding to Mitch's fervent hopefulness.

"That's beautiful. It would be just wonderful," Ian said wistfully.

"Not 'would'," Mitch replied vehemently. "'Will!'"

Ian smiled back. "May it be so."

"Do you think you're ready to meet some of the others? I've been holding them off to let you get more comfortable, but they're really eager to meet you. And they may be able to answer some of your questions better than I can." Ian considered the question seriously. Was he really ready for this? Darlene's voice echoed in his head.

"You're on a vision quest, aren't you?" And for someone on a vision quest, there was really only one answer to Mitch's question.

"Okay," Ian replied. "When do you want to do it?"

Mitch exhaled noisily—apparently he was actually holding his breath waiting for Ian's response.

"Would this evening be too soon?" he asked. Ian's eyes widened in surprise.

"You mean people are really that eager?"

"You have nooo idea!" Mitch laughed.

After dinner that evening, men began arriving. The first to arrive was a very tall, quiet man with a beautiful smile. He welcomed Ian to Pawhuska.

"Well, you've already been here a while, but better late than never," he commented. Two more men followed quickly. One was grinning with excitement. The other appeared to be a bit skeptical. He nodded politely but said nothing. Both newcomers were at least as tall as Ian. If these three men were typical, then the Osage were a handsome people. Three others gradually filtered into Mitch's living room and seated themselves. Two of them were cut from the same mold as the others, but the third was different. For one thing, he was much older. Silver strands shot through his black hair. He was also much smaller, only a bit taller than Mitch, and his features were not nearly as close to perfect. He appeared hawk-like, with a sharp nose bisecting two piercing, hooded eyes. He reminded Ian of Kiowa people he had met in Colorado.

The quiet conversation dropped into silence as they all watched Ian. He noticed that after their greetings, they seemed reluctant to make direct eye contact. Instead, they watched him from under lowered eyelids or from the corners of their eyes. It made him a bit uneasy, as if he weren't already nervous enough. Finally, Mitch broke the stalemate.

"I know you guys have all been waiting to meet our friend from the ashdome," he said. Then he lifted his chin toward the guest of honor. "This is Ian. He had some interesting experiences in there. You're going to want to hear what he has to say. Ian, can you start off by telling us about the stag?"

"Well, it all started with a Christmas present from my family," he began. He explained about the snowshoe workshop, marveling to himself how distant it seemed to him, as if it had occurred during another lifetime rather than just six months ago. He relived the sheer terror that overtook everyone after the first big eruption, how he himself felt the frantic need to get back to his family, the tense drive toward St. Ignace.

"Then I came around a sharp curve, and there it was, standing in the middle of the road. It was a stag, but not just any old deer—it was about eight feet tall and it was glowing. There was a greenish-white light all around it. No, that's not right—the glow was coming from inside it. In my shock, I automatically hit the brakes. The truck spun out on the ash. The last thing I remember was seeing those trees coming at me."

His audience barely seemed to breathe. No one moved a muscle throughout his description, but their eyes were riveted on his face.

"That's the only time I actually saw it," Ian continued, "but several other people have told me they encountered it. The woman who found me after I wrecked the truck told me she saw this eerie glow just before she came around the curve, and that's why she had slowed down to a crawl. If she'd been moving any faster, she'd have run into me and I probably wouldn't have lived through the crash. Then I got to the Mississippi and was looking for a way across, but all the bridges were closed. Finally, I met a riverboat captain who greeted me like a long-lost friend and asked me where the stag was. He'd dreamed about me coming up over the top of the levee with this big, glowing stag right behind me.

When he said that, I whirled around to look, but—no stag. Captain Monty was convinced the dream was real, though. He was so convinced that he waited for me for ten days. If he hadn't waited, I might never have gotten across the river.

"There was no more sign of the stag as I traveled through Missouri. And I'm not really sure about the next time, whether it was real or just a fever dream. You see, I got an infection from the water in Kansas. I was so sick I was hallucinating; and the second night I had it, I just collapsed and had to sleep by the side of the road. I could hear coyotes all around me, but I just couldn't go any farther. During the night, I kept waking up and seeing this greenish glow all around me. The next morning, I was still pretty sick; but I thought I saw huge hoof prints all around my sleeping bag. But don't forget, I was really, really out of it.

"I kept walking for another couple of days. Finally, though, I just fell down in the middle of the road. That's when Mitch's sister, Darlene, and her husband Jim found me. Darlene and Jim said a giant glowing stag came to their door and led them back to me. Darlene said it talked to her, and it stayed with her and me until Jim could bring back the truck. Then it just disappeared. Jim and Darlene took me in. They brought me back from death's door, and I owe them more than I can ever repay. And here I am," Ian concluded, smiling at the men.

Then the quiet, skeptical Osage asked Ian, "Just one thing, man. With all that crap in the air, how did you breathe?"

"Well, I did have a gas mask, all the way from northern Michigan through Kansas; but I guess I lost it when I was sick," Ian replied. "It was gone when I got to Jim and Darlene's house."

The skeptic raised an eyebrow but didn't say any more. There was a long moment of silence, then a collective stirring among the men.

Susan, as if she'd been waiting for her cue, brought in a tray filled with coffee and cake. She quietly offered food and drink to the eight people in the room and, just as quietly, left.

While they were eating, Mitch opened discussion.

"Well, obviously the stag is a spirit guide, but. . . ." The other men nodded agreement.

"But what does it mean?" Ian asked urgently. "Why is it following me? What does it want?" He looked desperately from face to sympathetic face, but no one answered.

Instead, all eyes turned to focus on the quiet old man, who was calmly eating his cake. He took a drink of his coffee and set the cup down deliberately.

"This is out of order. Usually people go on a vision quest to find a spirit guide. Your guide found you, and then you began your vision quest. The question is, why?"

His dark eyes transfixed Ian. "When there is great need, Power calls on people of energy. You have energy. I can feel the strength of it. You don't know how to use it yet, but Power will show you the way. You have drawn the attention of Power. Now you must listen!" Ian stared back in helpless confusion.

"To what?" he asked. The old man shook his head.

"Just listen," he repeated

After a moment of silence, Ian asked the old man, "Okay, then. There's one other thing I want to ask about. It happened before I ever saw the stag, but I know it's all part of the same thing. When I was in my snowshoe workshop, there were these two-foot tall beautifully carved wooden statues of kachinas on the fireplace mantel. One in particular just drew me to it. When I got closer, it started to glow, the same color as the stag. And it was at the very instant that the big eruption happened. Was it trying to tell me about the volcano? Or that the stag was coming? Or both?"

"Which kachina was it?" the old man asked intently.

"There was a brass plaque that labeled it as the Great Spirit Eagle Dancer."

"Ah," the old man nodded. "The messenger. Of course." Ian waited, but there was nothing more.

"So what did that mean?" Ian insisted.

"I will have to ask," the Kiowa murmured cryptically. "You will have to wait."

Tight-lipped, Ian realized he had no choice. He was frustrated. He didn't want to stop here. Things were just starting to make some kind of sense; the pieces of the puzzle were beginning to come together. But clearly, the old man was unwilling to go any further tonight.

Mitch cleared his throat, breaking the tension with an offer of more coffee. The other men took the hint and said their farewells. As the old Kiowa reached the door, he paused to look back at Ian.

"We will meet again soon. I will have answers for you then."

Day 176

Luther Black Bull, senior Osage medicine man, shuffled up the sidewalk to Mitch One Feather's house behind Lone Wolf, his Kiowa counterpart. Black Bull took his responsibility to his people and to the new movement very seriously, but at age 79, he was old and tired. He resented being dragged out for this but felt obligated to check out a possible Pahana.

The door opened. He entered Mitch's house and saw Ian for the first time. It was like being slammed against a wall. There he was—tall as an Osage, with a beard and very blue eyes, leaning on a notched walking stick topped with a white peace flag. It's the man in the prophecy! And, he remembered, there's even a stag involved—just as it was foretold. It's been hundreds of years since the prophet appeared to the Osage bison hunters during the great drought. "Is it time?" Black Bull wondered. "Is it time to fulfill the prophecy?"

As these thoughts rushed through his head, he was introduced to Ian. He managed to acknowledge the introduction, even to shake hands. His mind continued to race as they went into the living room. Susan brought coffee and left. Ian, Mitch, and the Kiowa kept up a conversation, but the old medicine man wasn't paying much attention as Ian retold the stories of the stag and kachina.

His abstraction did not go unnoticed. Mitch and the Kiowa both were aware that he had lost focus. They cast uneasy glances his way, clearly worried.

Black Bull finally became aware that he had been silent too long.

"So," he said to Ian, "How long have you been following this stag?"

"It's more like the stag is following me," Ian laughed.

"Are you sure?" Black Bull asked seriously. Ian's smile faded. Mitch and the Kiowa looked at each other, disconcerted. Ian's intent gaze now focused on the old Osage.

"No," Ian said quietly. "Now let me ask you, what about the glowing kachina? What did that mean?"

The old medicine man paused. This could be the Pahana. It could be the man in the Osage prophecy. But why was he acting as if he were ignorant of the meaning of what had happened? How should he handle this? Mustering all his years of teaching and learning about spirit, he began.

"What do you think it meant? Consider: it happened at the very moment the volcano erupted. The glow was the same as the stag's. Of course they're all connected! The clues are all there. The kachina, the stag, and you are in a dance right now, and this is bigger than you can imagine. We've been waiting for hundreds of years for this. The buffalo prophet told us—" he stopped abruptly. "Well, maybe we'll speak of that another time."

Chapter 33

Day 177

After the old Osage medicine man had left the previous evening, Ian and Mitch sat talking for a long time, trying to figure out what was going on. They ended up baffled, unable to put together any coherent picture. There just wasn't enough information—too many blanks in the puzzle, and no clues that fit.

"Is anybody ever going to answer my questions?" Ian finally asked. "Whenever I ask something, their faces just snap shut. They become completely blank, like a stone carving. Then I get 'We'll talk about it later' or 'I'll get back to you on that,' except nobody ever does. How am I supposed to make any sense out of this?"

Mitch just looked back helplessly. "I don't know. I don't have a clue about what they're thinking. Those two old men are the strongest medicine men I've ever met. What they know between them is scary. But I don't know why they aren't helping more now. All I can say is they must have their reasons."

"That doesn't help me much either," Ian said sadly.

Day 178

"Okay," Ian thought the next morning. "So what do I do now? It looks like I'm on my own again. These guys are just giving me the run around."

He took stock of the situation. His ankle was getting steadily better. With the heavy wrap, he could stand and walk for quite a while without feeling the hot ache that warned he was overdoing it. If he used his walking stick, he could go a considerable distance. He still couldn't wear his boots, so he had taken to wearing soft moccasins. They were so comfortable he was thinking of giving up hard-soled shoes, but given the country he still had to cross, he decided regretfully that it wasn't very practical.

To be safe, he decided to give it another week; but then it would be time to go. He still had a lot of ground to cover to get to Albuquerque, and it was already past the middle of June.

At breakfast, he was ready to tell Mitch and Susan his decision; but Mitch beat him to the punch. Black Bull had sent a boy with a message for Ian, asking if they could meet again this evening. Ian felt a surge of hope and agreed immediately.

The day passed uneventfully and much too slowly for Ian, who was impatient for answers. Maybe, finally, someone would tell him something he didn't already know.

That evening, Luther Black Bull arrived shortly after dinner. He, Mitch, and Ian settled down in the living room. Mitch and Ian gave their full attention to the old medicine man, and he began.

"You told us of hearing the calling when you were in Missouri. It reminded me of the history of our people. We, the Wah Zha Zhe people, once lived far to the east of here, in the valley of the great Ohio River. It was a land of plenty and a time of happiness for us. But then came the fierce Iroquois. They wanted our land, and though we fought them, they were strong and could not be defeated. We were pushed west, across the Mississippi. Then President Jackson became your leader." Black Bull paused to dry-spit at the floor in contempt. "He pushed us even farther west. We lived in Missouri for many generations. You were not the first to wander through that land. We learned to hunt the buffalo and to live on the Plains in Missouri. The stories of our great buffalo hunts are still told."

"Funny you should mention buffalo in Missouri," said Ian. "I didn't even know they ranged that far east, but Mitch has told me they showed up even in Indiana in the old days. It helps explain a dream I had while I was just north of Lake of the Ozarks."

"A dream?" queried Black Bull. "Tell me about it."

"Well, it was really strange. I dreamed I was walking through a herd of buffalo. They were pretty much ignoring me, and I was completely calm about it, as if it were the most normal thing in the world to be wandering among these huge, aggressive animals. Then I came out of the herd and suddenly I was surrounded by wolves. That's when I woke up." Ian shook his head in bemusement. "Pretty odd, huh?"

Black Bull sat silent, but his dark eyes gleamed with a disturbing light. A sense of triumph was beginning to build inside him. Yes, this is the man! But he wanted further confirmation, just to be certain.

"That was an important dream," Black Bull told Ian. "Very important."

"Really?" asked Ian, puzzled. "Why?"

Black Bull shook his head. "I can't tell you yet."

Ian sighed to himself. Same old, same old. Ah, well.

"Let's talk about the calling. Can you hear it now?" asked Black Bull.

"I've had to shut it out in order to focus on everything else. Yes, I can hear it whenever it broadcasts, but I didn't hear it when I was sick. In fact, I haven't heard it for a couple of months. Anyway, it's not exactly like you can hear it. There are no words or sounds. I just have to open my mind to the energy of the calling. Sometimes it resonates intensely with my heart chakra. There is a great sense of urgency: 'Get here now'. However, there is no fear, no ego in this call. This is not ego telepathic. It's almost like someone has begun an intense call to join."

Mitch nodded in agreement. "I do the same thing. But I open the door at the top of my head and resonate with it."

"That's kópavi, right?" Ian asked.

Mitch looked surprised.

"Captain Monty again." Ian explained. "He reminded me of that when we were talking about Waters' book."

Black Bull gave the two others a small smile. This exchange confirmed two things for him. First, Ian could very well be the Pahana. Second, in Mitch, he might have found his successor as head medicine man of the Osage. For Black Bull, this had been a very successful meeting.

He sensed Ian's dissatisfaction though. The poor guy must feel really frustrated. He asks questions and keeps getting stonewalled. Black Bull decided he had to offer something to keep Ian engaged and cooperative.

"There is something I would ask of you, Ian. Would you be willing to undergo a sweat lodge ceremony? It will give you some of the information you need. The spirits will tell you things that even I can't tell you. They will guide you if you will let them."

"Hmm," thought Ian, intrigued. "That could be interesting."

"Okay," he responded. "What should I do?"

Black Bull smiled warmly. "Let Mitch help you prepare. I'll make all the arrangements. We should be able to hold the ceremony in a few days. Thank you, Ian. I know this has been hard for you, but you have told me many things that are more important than I can say right now. Have patience. Soon you will have your answers."

Ian visibly relaxed. Just having someone acknowledge the situation had really made him feel better. "No wonder he's the head medicine man," Ian thought. "This guy's good."

Day 179

Ian and Mitch returned from their daily walk to strengthen Ian's injured ankle. Ian's rehab was proving quite successful with steady improvement. All healing was now directed at surviving the next 600 miles of this impossible vision quest.

Ian's near-fatal infection was also finally subsiding. He couldn't believe that almost a month had passed since Darlene had found him unconscious near her farm in Kansas. In the last few days his mental state had improved dramatically. His thoughts were once again clear and lucid.

Ian stated, "Now that I'm thinking clearly again, I realize that I haven't said anything about my past spiritual experiences. In fact, I've only shared what happened after the eruptions began. Now we're about to do a sweat lodge ceremony. Power may kick up and anything might happen. I just wanted to give you a heads up in case something weird happens."

Standing on the front porch in the hazy solstice week sunshine, both men concurred that they had light and time on their side. They retreated to the lawn chairs in the back yard to talk.

Susan saw them sitting outside and suddenly appeared with a pitcher of iced tea with lemon slices and a plate of crackers and cheese. She also brought news. While they were out walking the president of the United States had addressed the nation. News of the speech had spread quickly down the moccasin telegraph, and Susan summarized what she had heard.

The Memorial Day crackdown on cell phones and personal email communication had not been effective. Flash mobs had resorted to using other communication devices like CB radios and walkie-talkies. Looting had intensified. In the last four weeks counties across the U.S. had declared posse comitatus. Now, National Guard and federal troops would enforce dusk-to-dawn curfews. Commodities would be transported at night. Travel restrictions were being considered. Ian's trek had just become even more complicated.

Ian and Mitch spent considerable time into the afternoon sorting through this unexpected turn of events. They finally gave up trying to interpret the incomplete reports and decided to discuss Ian's early spiritual experiences instead.

Ian told Mitch that by age 16 he had "stopped the world" and had experienced seventh chakra energy flows. Meditation, shifting point of consciousness, and mindfulness techniques were all part of his daily explorations.

Ian was white and could do the kópavi energy release, which are both characteristics of the Pahana. He wanted to make it crystal clear, however, that he didn't really want groupies following him around, declaring that he was the Pahana. He felt there were too many questions left unanswered. They would discuss his "Pahana problem" tomorrow.

Day 180

Gentle rain fell through the night and into the next morning. Wet, slippery sidewalks aborted the daily rehab walk. Slightly warmer temperatures and rain coming in from the Gulf of Mexico moved today's discussion onto Mitch's dry and spacious front porch.

"I've been grappling with this Pahana problem since I left Captain Monty's riverboat ten weeks ago," Ian said. "People around the world are so frightened for their survival that everyone is searching for a messiah. Someone to rescue them from the apocalypse. Now some solitary white guy who can open his kópavi is supposed to unite all the races into a universal brotherhood of man.

"It just doesn't make sense to me! I know a substantial number of white people who know the kópavi exists…and can actually open the portal. But most white folks don't give a rat's ass about your Pahana. They have their own savior. I've been fighting this battle my whole life! I doubt that Western civilization is coming to the spiritual table, when all you've got is one token white guy."

Ian continued, "Look, bathing in streams and cooking with firewood isn't going to make the Creator happy. Humans have done that since the beginning of time, and it has never worked. Just making things simpler isn't the answer. There is something else going on here. A return to the old ways is not the way to achieve the Creator's will. The Creator told you what is required. But everyone is so damned anxious to get their butts into the Fifth World where everything will be 'okay.' Hah!" Ian looked square into Mitch's eyes.

"How is getting to the Fifth World going to change anything? There are very real problems here that have been going on for far too many creations. **JUST WHEN DID WE PLAN ON STARTING TO SOLVE THESE PROBLEMS?** Were we just planning to kick this can down the road once again?"

"What's been going on for far too many creations?" Mitch asked. "Which problems are you talking about? Are you referring to how creations deteriorate? To how people get spiritually lazy and resort back to ego, greed, and attack?"

"Well, that's part of it, but it's way bigger than that!" Ian explained. "I don't fully understand it yet, but I think I found a major structural glitch in the system. It appears that ego is the primary operating system for all of creation. However, only the seventh chakra kópavi people can override the ego operating system. Was this override intentionally inserted into our DNA for survival?

"We know that the Creator creates all good and all evil—and thus, all ego. And he lets the ego harass our energy channels unmercifully. Yet you can override the ego. It just makes no sense that the Creator would assemble such an elaborate, all-pervasive operating system that could then be overridden. The glitch is there for a reason! But what?

"All those Hindu, Buddhist, and Chinese holy saints, they all used this glitch to circumvent the ego. They understood the great wiring chasm that separated them from other humans.

"Everybody on the planet knows that Buddha was up to something. They just don't know what. This evolved species does things that other humans can't do. There is a reason they got as far into the mountains and remote deserts as they could.

"They have journeyed to the far *right* brain and on to the One. They know that they are already home, that there never was a journey. They know that all of this has always been a dream, but they vowed to do whatever must be done. The rest of the world has always ignored them, sweeping them under the carpet of the 'mysterious'."

Ian had held the metaphorical talking stick for a considerable time, but Mitch did not object. He used this monologue to piece together a more complete picture of his friend.

Ian continued, "Except for the Hopi, most native spiritual practitioners have done the opposite. They moved their points of consciousness to the far *left* brain and on to the astral. Working with a Yaqui sorcerer, Castaneda described this process in great detail. Moving the assemblage point to the far left accumulated great personal power. But all of that comes at a great personal and cultural cost."

Ian and Mitch then spent hours deconstructing astral, ego spirituality. They observed that over the centuries hardscrabble survival had altered the focus of talented shamans. Focused conscious intent can manipulate the environment around you, bending reality. But is focused earth magic the proper use of your intent? Levitation, shape-shifting, dematerialization, and a host of other powers are very real, but they're all ego-based. And they are in the toolbox of every shaman, medicine man, witch, and sorcerer across the planet. The spiritual shaping of reality is a very powerful *ego* experience. It seduces people to take themselves far too seriously and believe they possess unparalleled personal power. They see no need to spend years of contemplative focus on their navels like the yogis of the East. They gain their enlightenment from the astral spirits. Everyday survival demands immediate attention. Service to the Creator then rapidly diminishes.

Public opinion had assigned all those spiritual manifestations of personal power to the tribal, native, first peoples of the world. Mitch and Ian found that the Hopi seemed to be the only exception to this rule. Like their comrades of the "mysterious Orient," the Hopi were also a kópavi seventh chakra culture.

The Hopi still remembered and understood the great misuse of psychic supernatural power in the collapse of the previous Third World. Mitch recounted a story from the *Book of the Hopi* that expressed this deep concern. When clans finally returned to the desert after their great circular migrations, any clan that used supernatural power wrongly and failed to act in a humble manner was denied admission to the mesa.

Ian remembered an old Buddhist story. One day while Buddha was teaching, his very best student came levitating in over the top of the class. Buddha admonished the student for trying to distract everyone with useless siddhis (powers) that weren't even relevant to enlightenment.

The Creator's message and actions have been very clear here. Open that damned kópavi! Don't take shortcuts. Strong personal power exists only in a petri dish of ego. Enlightenment exists entirely outside of ego.

Sadly, however, most religions do not put in the work to achieve spiritual enlightenment. Some even believe that to merge with God is blasphemy. With no direct contact with God, their religions rely on dogma and blind repetition of ritual—only mindlessness based on empty ego prayer.

Christians, for example, totally ignore Jesus' statement that "If thine eye be single, thy whole body shall be full of light." Sorry. No seventh chakra experiences allowed, despite having Jesus hand them the answer.

Spiritual teachers of the East consider whites to be "wannabes" and spiritually inferior. Annoyed, they create diversions to keep the silly whites occupied. Eastern condescension toward the West creates impossible barriers for shared spiritual enlightenment.

Native peoples of the world are even more hostile and unforgiving. A biting, sarcastic "not bad for a white guy." A condescending "I didn't bring my pipe bag because there are no spiritual people here." Both reflect centuries of suppressed, explosive anger. And it gets way worse. Usually spitting is involved. And loud shouting. Christian terrorists inflicted centuries of devastation on the Eastern and native populations of the world. Good luck healing those wounds.

"We need to look at this differently." Ian spoke into the gathering gloom. "Look, you're native and you can also use the seventh chakra, and I'm white and I can use the kópavi. We aren't following any of society's rules here. According to public opinion and the prejudices of organized religions, neither of us should be able to open the kópavi. Maybe all of humanity needs to be sorted differently. You know, like that sorting hat thing in Harry Potter. Where would you and I end up?"

Day 181

The storm had continued through the night. In fact, it had gotten stronger and now blew straight onto the front porch. The back porch, just off the kitchen, was on the leeward side of the storm, however, so the two men headed there to carry on with their discussion. Both had mugs of coffee in hand. Mitch also carried a large seashell and a braid of sweet grass. Susan watched them leave as she stood at the sink with a dishpan full of breakfast dishes. Sage smoke from Mitch's earlier blessing ceremony wafted out the door behind them.

"Sweet grass," Susan observed. "Things are getting serious if Mitch wants to draw in the spirits." She decided to take her time with the dishes and see what else she could find to do in the kitchen. This could be interesting.

Ian began. "Last night I stayed up late and just couldn't get to sleep. We were talking about how we needed to look at things differently. And how the ancient patterns needed to change. But I hit a brick wall. Nothing new or different appeared.

"It's pretty hard to ignore what's going on in the world. The devastation caused by the volcano: the millions of dead and displaced people, the spreading world-wide famine, the impending world economic crisis. These things have overwhelmed the human spirit. Everyone is absolutely certain the end is near.

"Even though everything points to the end, something just doesn't seem right. We've missed some important piece of the puzzle. We've dissected this from every angle, but it still doesn't make sense to me."

Then both men were startled by a loud voice from the kitchen.

"But the ancient patterns have already changed. That's what you missed!"

Ian's mouth dropped open.

Mitch laughed. "How long have you been listening in there?" he called out.

"Long enough," Susan replied, peering through the screen door.

"Then bring the coffeepot and join us," Ian invited. Susan was there in an instant.

"Okay," Mitch said. "So talk to us! What do you mean?"

"Well, every day for months now, groups of frightened people have been traipsing through my house, sounding the alarm that it's all over. The Pahana's coming! The famine's coming! We're all gonna die unless we do something right now. But what? I've been beside myself wondering if our family or our people will survive.

And all this is scaring the crap out of the kids.

"Then about two weeks ago at breakfast, Ian was talking about how, in the Third World, the left-brained astral sorcerers psychically attacked and destroyed the kópavi people. It got so violent and desperate that the Creator had to step in and evacuate the kópavi people. It got me to thinking that I'm not seeing anything like that going on now in our disaster. I may not know a lot about these things, but I've never heard of anything like that going on in this Fourth World. It appears to me that the Creator has made some major improvements here! Progress has been made!"

Ian stood up, walked over, and clasped Susan's hands. "That's brilliant, Susan. I've been looking at this Pahana thing for decades, and this never crossed my mind." Ian shook his head slowly. "How the hell did I miss that?

"You see, I bought into the hype back in April of 1992, when a Hopi elder came to Boulder to find the Pahana. He said the Hopi needed to tell their story to the United Nations by August 22 of that year. If not, the final purification would begin the following day. The United Nations refused.* Then, the next day, on August 23, Hurricane Andrew devastated south Florida. That got my undivided attention! Apparently, the final purification had begun. I became a believer in the Hopi message.

"After that Hopi elder came to Boulder, I never examined the progress made in this Fourth World. But we need to look at this in a new light. After all, we survived the Cold War. We survived Y2K. We survived the Second Coming at the beginning of the new millennium. The Mayan calendar ended in 2012, but the world didn't end. We're still here."

Mitch chimed in, "And I'm going to dare to suggest something radical: volcanoes happen. Daily. All over the world. At any given moment, there's a volcano going off somewhere. They don't usually signal The End."

"Yeah, good point. Well, okay, then...let's see," Ian said. "So what do we already know? We know that, creation after creation,

---

*See Appendix L

the ego operating system reigned supreme. But some humans were able to open their kópavi and transcend to higher consciousness. Other humans manipulated energy within the operating system to gain personal power and control. The vast majority of humans just sat there, living their lives in the crossfire between earth magic and transcendence.

"Then, in response to this stalemate, the Creator, apparently without notice—except to Susan—decided to bring these raging conflicts under control. The last world, before the flood, was a disaster. How could this be fixed? We know that the Creator has always rescued and supported the kópavi people. But it appears that, this time, to ensure the peace, both warring factions were confined and suppressed. They would have no power in the Fourth World.

"This is interesting. You can watch the Creator trying to bring this riot under control. The left-brained villagers with their pitchforks rose up from the sidelines and took over the world! Look at history. It's really clear. They established tight, left-brained control. They made sure it wasn't going to get out of control again. They created large, strong empires that covered most of the world: Greek, Roman, Egyptian, Chinese, Mayan, and all the others. Large-scale organized religions and powerful militaries dominated the world. Apparently the Creator wasn't taking any chances.

"Both the earth magic and the transcendence people were relegated to remote areas of the Fourth World. Worldwide, neither group would be honored, respected, or admired—and both were treated with skepticism, great suspicion, and fear. They never got any traction in this world. Only the dogma and ritual survived."

Suddenly Susan exclaimed, "I want to learn to open my kópavi, damn it! How do I learn this? Who's going to teach me? Will you *let* me learn this?"

"Ah, that's the most important question, isn't it?" Ian replied. "In this Fourth World, no matter which tradition you followed, too many people weren't allowed to learn what they all needed to know.

But the Creator's message has always been the same, and it has always been clear. The only right way to live is to learn to open your kópavi. In the end, you have to let *yourself* learn this.

"It appears that the Creator wants us to continue to open the tops of our heads. Because if enough of us can do it, we'll know we aren't separate beings with separate roles to play. We're all one. We've got a long way to go. A lot to unlearn before the learning can begin.

"I discovered something else. In 1975, *A Course in Miracles* was downloaded and published. It is a 1000-page manual for understanding and overriding the ego. Suddenly, for the very first time, God is pushing for the '*Joining*'! It comes up hundreds of times in the *Course*. Override the ego, open up the chakras, and then the joining can begin. Why would God be pushing for that now? This is very advanced energy work. Obviously, the Creator is finally ready for the next stage. An advanced stage of evolution. But it happens in the context of this world, not the next world. Something's happening right here! What do we do with this? Where do we go from here?"

Susan responded with subdued excitement in her voice. "This is a great message of hope, Ian! Why leave the Fourth World now, when we're making such great progress? We need to follow this blueprint."

Ian chuckled. "You know, ironically, this is an anti-apocalyptic message in a post-apocalyptic setting. How cool is that?"

"It appears that we kópavi people now have the Creator's approval to go forward with sharing the 'Joining' message," Mitch declared, his face glowing with enthusiasm.

"But I ask once again, how do I go about learning this? Who's going to teach me?" Susan asked.

"Well, it looks like we're going to have to develop a new way of teaching," Mitch replied.

"Neutral ground. We need neutral ground, where everyone is equal before the Creator," Susan emphatically declared. A silence ensued as all three pondered this idea and tried to visualize how it could be done.

"Oh, my God. My brother's kiva. That's what we were building there!" Ian turned to the others, his face alive with excitement. "My brother told me the kiva would be open to everyone! It would be the teacher! The energy of the kiva would decide who could stay and who was not ready yet. He always said it wasn't his call. '**JUST OPEN THE DOORS AND LET GOD SORT IT OUT**,' he told me. 'It's an accelerator to help create the *Joining*!'

"But it's not the only accelerator. This volcanic apocalypse is most likely also accelerating evolution. There's this thing that scientists call junk DNA. It waits patiently and springs into action, potentially unleashing significant evolutionary changes. But what would those changes look like?

"The wiring. Is that what would change? Yogananda and the old yogis always talked about the special 'chakra wiring' that could carry a billion volts of energy. That damned behemoth is triggering the crisis and stress that is altering human wiring. A *new* wired species will appear to join the other wired ones already here.

"Now I understand. That explains the three girls that appeared in the hologram at Katie's house in Illinois. Three sisters in the Great Kiva in the Fourth World. Accelerated beings in an accelerator kiva. Damn it, that proves it. We're not done here! It's not over yet!"

"I guess we need to learn how to teach this new message," said Mitch.

"And we've got a kiva to build," added Ian.

Chapter 34

Day 182

"So, Ian," said Mitch at breakfast the next morning, "have you recovered from our spiritual marathon of yesterday? Ready to learn about sweat lodges?"

"I don't know much about them," Ian confessed. "Once, when I was in grad school in Boulder, I considered going to one. But my brother suggested I check it out further before I signed up. Turned out to be run by some New Age white guy from back east, and he was charging people for an 'authentic Native American' experience. When I told my brother this, he just snorted; and my sister-in-law's lip curled before she could stop herself. They didn't have any problem with his being white. It was the whole 'profiting from spirituality' aspect that bothered them. I gave it a pass."

"Good call," said Mitch. "You sure wouldn't have gotten much out of that. And it makes this much easier for me, since you don't have any negative experiences to get rid of."

Mitch outlined the preparations for a sweat. "Since this is your first one, we'll take that into account. And because you're white, we'll coat you with bear grease to protect your skin from the heat. Otherwise, you will have blisters you wouldn't believe!"

"Well," Ian interjected, "I have done saunas. And aren't they pretty similar? I remember reading once that saunas and sweat lodges started out in the same place, in Central Asia. When some of the people migrated west, they became saunas; and when they went east, all the way to North America, they became sweat lodges."

"Okay," said Mitch. "I won't argue that. It helps that you have some experience; but even so, sweat lodges are different. Somewhere along the way, saunas became almost purely physical experiences. Sweat lodges are at least *intended* to be primarily spiritual.

"Normally, preparing takes four days; but you aren't ready for that, so we'll cut it down. The day before you enter the lodge, we will purify your body and your mind and your spirit. That means we cleanse everything. You'll take an emetic and fast for the day—"

Ian interrupted: "An emetic? To make me vomit? Isn't that a bit extreme?"

Mitch shook his head in sharp disagreement. "No. You must be completely empty to be filled with spirit. We will empty your mind by praying—or meditating, if you prefer that term—and open your spirit by focusing your intent. Remember Castaneda? We're going to move your assemblage point so that, by the time you enter the sweat lodge, you will be ready to hear and see and understand."

"Okay," said Ian uneasily. "I don't have any problem with the mental and spiritual part. That's just the left-to-right-brain process we talked about a couple of days ago. The physical part is a lot more than I expected, but I guess it makes sense. I'll do it."

"I'm glad you agreed, because Black Bull has arranged the ceremony for two days from now. Better get some rest today," Mitch commented. "Tomorrow's going to be a busy day."

Day 183

With Mitch's help, Ian purged, fasted, and worked to center himself for his entry into the sweat lodge.

Day 184

In a field outside Pawhuska, a stand of trees lay at the west side of the field and a small stream ran just inside the treeline. The sweat lodge was backed up to the trees, its opening facing east. It was simply an inverted bowl made of piled-up brush covered with blankets and pelts. An animal hide hung over the opening.

In front of the sweat lodge was a roaring fire. A sturdy forked branch lay near a pile of rocks close to the fire. Black Bull sat cross-legged at the opening.

Ian and Mitch approached and sat quietly. Black Bull performed the now-familiar sage ceremony. He asked the spirits for a blessing, informing them that Ian had come with a pure heart and mind to seek their guidance.

Black Bull held aside the hide that covered the entry to the sweat lodge. Ian entered the dark interior and seated himself at the back of the lodge. Then Black Bull entered, carrying a hollowed gourd dipper. Mitch came behind him, carrying a red-hot rock balanced on the forked branch. He placed the rock in the center of the lodge, then repeated the process until there were several hot stones piled together.

Black Bull began to pray in the Osage language. He filled the gourd dipper from a hide bag full of water and slowly sprinkled the water onto the hot stones. Steam rose, rapidly filling the dark, enclosed lodge. Black Bull continued to chant and Mitch brought in more stones. Between them, they would hold the sacred space.

Ian began to move into right brain. His unblinking eyes lost focus on the present as his consciousness shifted. His breathing became inaudible. He was absolutely still. Soon he was completely unaware of his surroundings. He was elsewhere…elsewhen. Time and space had lost all meaning for him. At last, Ian returned from elsewhen. He blinked softly and inhaled a sudden deep breath. The hot steam seared his lungs and he immediately began to choke and cough.

Black Bull sat silent near him, waiting patiently. After a while, Black Bull sensed that Ian was totally back with them and, without a word, he stood and moved to open the hide door covering. Ian, equally quiet, followed him outside into the early evening air. Black Bull led Ian to the stream, where both of them splashed cool water over their steam-heated, dehydrated bodies. Refreshed and reoriented to the here and now, the two men returned to the fire where Mitch was waiting.

"How do you feel?" Mitch asked Ian, handing him a large cup of herbal tea.

"Wonderful," Ian replied with a beatific smile. "Wonderful." He wanted to say more, but language failed him. There was no way he could describe his experience or his state of being. Wordlessly, he marveled at this; but he remembered from his training that this pattern was normal. He simply noticed, without judging.

Black Bull nodded in satisfaction, and the three men sat silently watching the fire as it danced in the evening breeze. Lost in thought, Ian was abstracted, distant. The other two men sat silent and patient. Finally, Ian stirred. He looked up slowly into the quiet, expectant gazes of Mitch and Black Bull.

"That was amazing," said Ian. "I saw so much. There was a time when I just was. No, it wasn't really 'time' as we usually talk about it—it could have been a nanosecond or a millennium, I have no way of measuring it. I mean, I existed, but I was part of something else.... Bliss. That's what it was," he nodded to himself. "Sheer bliss. Then my consciousness brushed that away...my mind became still and I was absorbed into the void. I wasn't even aware of myself. Awareness of things ceased altogether.

"Then, when I emerged from that deep total absorption I was back within that dream from Missouri. I could see myself walking through the buffalo herd. I could hear them breathing, snorting; feel the ground tremble as they walked. I could even smell them! Damn, that's one strong smell! Then I came to the edge of the herd, and there were the wolves again. This time, though, when I walked into the middle of the wolf pack, they all stood up on their hind legs and turned into men." He gave an apologetic smile. "I know that sounds crazy."

Black Bull shook his head vigorously, and his eyes gleamed. "No. It is not crazy at all. It is as it should be. What else did you see?"

"Well, that was about it for that one. But, Mitch, remember the dream I told you about my little hut in the wilderness? I was there again. This time I was in my garden, looking at my corn and beans and squash. In the vision, I remember thinking that I had planted the Three Sisters, and they were all healthy and growing tall and strong. I felt really happy and satisfied. I was fulfilled—that's what it was. I had the sense that I had completed a mission."

"That's enough for me," exclaimed Black Bull. "You. You are the man in our prophecy."

"What prophecy? What are you talking about?" asked Ian, astonished.

"I have something important to give you, something that has been passed down from head medicine man to head medicine man for many generations," Black Bull said. "We were told to expect your arrival. And now you're here!" He looked at Ian with excitement in his dark eyes. "I must prepare to carry out the rest of the prophecy. At last, the prophecy can be revealed to all the Wah Zha Zhe. We must have a ceremony!

"Please forgive me if I don't explain any more tonight. It will all be clear to you very soon, but now," he rose to his feet with great agility for such an old man, "I have to go. Thank you, Ian. Thank you."

Without another word, Black Bull rushed off into the darkness, leaving Ian and Mitch staring, open-mouthed, after him.

"Before you even ask," Mitch said, shaking his head, "not a clue. I'm as much in the dark as you are."

Ian smiled gently. "It's okay," he said.

Day 185

Ian woke feeling deeply content. Everything was as it should be.

He dressed and, for the first time in several weeks, put on his hiking boots. It was a tight fit over the support bandage on his ankle, but the boots were not uncomfortable. Still leaning on his staff, he joined the family for breakfast.

"Ankle's better, I see," Mitch commented.

"Yeah, I figure I'd better start getting used to the boots again. I should be able to head out pretty soon and let you have your house back to yourself. I've put you guys out for far too long."

Mitch's jaw dropped. "Are you kidding me?" he asked incredulously. Ian just looked confused and a little apologetic. Mitch continued, "You have no idea who you are, do you? You have fulfilled one of our ancient prophecies, and I believe you may be the Pahana as well. It has been my honor to have you share my home!"

Ian was taken aback by the vehemence of Mitch's outburst. "Me? No, man. I'm not who you think I am. I'm just a middle-aged art professor trying to find his wife and kids." But even as he said this, he knew something had changed for him. His face betrayed his inner knowledge of the difference, and Mitch was quick to notice.

"Hah!" he exclaimed. "Right." There was a long moment of silence. The two men stared at each other, Mitch's expression daring Ian to face up to the reality of his situation. Ian stared back defiantly, but he was the first to drop his eyes.

"Right," Mitch muttered again. He shook out his napkin with a flourish, then said in a normal tone of voice, "So, when do you figure you'll head out?"

"I'll stay for Black Bull's ceremony," Ian replied. "I could tell it was really important to him. I still don't know what it's all about, but I'll stick around. He's been good to me, and I wouldn't want to disappoint him. But I've got to get back on the road soon if I want to get to Albuquerque before winter. I've still got about 700 miles to go, and I have no idea what's waiting for me between here and there."

Mitch looked thoughtful. "You still have some rugged country to cross, and things are not normal out there. Can I make a suggestion? I think you might have an easier time of it if you took someone with you, someone who knows the country and could show you the shortcuts, maybe. What do you think?"

Ian smiled at Mitch. "Great idea," he said. "I must admit, I wasn't looking forward to being alone again. Did you have anyone in mind?"

"How about a naval intelligence officer? Trained with the Seals, served two tours in Afghanistan, then came home, got a teaching degree, and teaches fourth grade. Everything's been so screwed up that school isn't starting until October this year, so there'd be no problem there. Sound okay?"

"Yeah!" Ian responded enthusiastically. "Tell me more about this guy. How did you meet him?"

Mitch grinned. "She's my niece," he said. "Annie's my older brother's daughter. Her mom died when she was born, and my brother was killed in a wreck a couple of years later. Darlene and

I pretty much raised her, so I know her all the way through. She's solid. Strong, smart, and very capable. I think you'll like her."

Ian tried very hard not to react, but his consternation was written all over his expressive face. Mitch doubled over laughing. "Gotcha!" he said.

Wiping tears from his eyes, Mitch added, "I'd like the two of you to meet as soon as possible. We could do a pipe ceremony to ask blessings on your trip together, if you wouldn't mind." He shot Ian a quizzical look.

"Oh, sure," Ian replied hastily. "Whatever you think, Mitch. When do you want to do it?"

"How about tomorrow?" Mitch suggested.

Day 186

It was a beautiful day, the last day of June. The sky was clear, with just a few wispy cirrus clouds. There was a gentle breeze from the southwest. It carried warmer air that made it possible to go outside with only a light jacket.

Ian sat on the front porch steps in the late morning sun, savoring the weather. He remembered the months of darkness and snash, the cold, biting winds howling past his frozen ears as he waded or skidded down ash-slick, empty roadways. Thank God that was over! The rest of the journey would have to be better than that. Wouldn't it?

Mitch's niece was due to arrive in a couple of hours. Ian wondered what she'd be like. He thought fondly of Darlene. Maybe her niece would be like her. That would be nice. He wandered back into the house at Susan's call to lunch.

Mitch and Ian were sitting in the living room after lunch when there was a knock at the door.

"That'll be Annie," Mitch noted. "Hi, Annie. Come on in," he called.

Ian looked up with a polite smile—and froze in place. Standing in the doorway to the living room was a woman who took his breath away. She was a good six feet tall, with a lithe, athletic build and long, shapely legs. Black hair hung loose to her waist, and her skin was the color of old gold. Her high cheekbones accentuated her exotically slanted dark eyes. A wide, mobile mouth smiled at him, exposing impossibly white teeth.

"You must be Ian," she said in a warm, melodious voice. She crossed the room in three long strides, hand outstretched, as Ian stood. "Annie St. Cloud. Good to meet you."

"Ian Cameron," he responded, sharing a firm handshake. "Your Uncle Mitch tells me we have something in common. I'm a teacher, too."

Annie laughed. "There's a bit of difference between fourth grade and the university," she said.

"Sometimes not as much as you'd hope," Ian replied with a grin. He had already decided he liked this woman. There was a basic honesty to her that was very appealing.

Ian, Mitch, and Annie talked late into the afternoon. Conversation was easy. A beaming Susan invited Annie to stay for dinner, and the talk continued, getting even more comfortable as they found more things in common.

Annie left well after dark. By that time, it had been agreed that she would travel with Ian at least through Oklahoma. Mitch, looking pleased with himself, suggested they meet again in a couple of days to finalize plans. He offered to conduct a pipe ceremony to bless their journey.

The two men returned to the living room. Mitch turned a quizzical look on Ian. "Do you know anything about pipe ceremonies?" he asked.

Ian nodded. "Yeah, my sister-in-law in Boulder is Chippewa. When I lived up there, she opened the pipe for us many times. She said it wasn't traditional for a woman to do this, but she was the only one who was there, so what the hell?"

Mitch chuckled. "My feelings exactly. I've never been able to understand how we can pretend that half the human race has no power. Do men think that Spirit travels on the Y chromosome or something?" He shook his head. "Take Annie, for example. She's a warrior, but that's not the only reason I wanted her to travel with you. She *knows*. You can talk to her and she'll understand at every level."

Day 188

Annie arrived late in the afternoon. The three retired to Mitch's back yard, where they sat cross-legged on the ground in a triangle facing each other. Mitch held his pipe bag with quiet reverence.

Opening the bag, he took out a piece of red flannel and laid it on the ground. On the flannel, he began unloading the contents of the bag: a large clam shell, a carved wooden pipe stem, a red pipestone pipe bowl, smudge sticks of cedar and sage, a braid of sweetgrass, and a pouch of tobacco.

Ian and Annie sat silently attentive as Mitch began the ceremony. He lit the cedar smudge stick and bathed himself in the smoke before passing it to Ian and Annie. "Let any evil spirits depart now." Next, he lit the sage stick and repeated the process. "Let us be purified," he said. Finally, lighting the sweetgrass, he asked that all good spirits approach them.

Mitch filled the pipe bowl with tobacco. He held the separated bowl and pipe stem above his head for a moment of silent prayer before he joined them and brought the unified pipe down to his chest.

To open the pipe, Mitch lit the tobacco and inhaled. He exhaled smoke to the six directions (above, below, and the four cardinal directions), invoking the spirits of these points to hear and grant the requests of the smokers. He offered a prayer of thanksgiving for the blessings of the spirits, then passed the pipe to Ian.

Ian accepted the pipe respectfully. He exhaled smoke, offered thanks, then asked a blessing on his journey to find his family. Everyone sat silent for a few minutes. Then Ian passed the pipe to Annie.

Annie's request was to be worthy of the task she had been given, to be a good companion and guide for Ian as they traveled.

She also asked blessings on her family, particularly Uncle Mitch and Aunt Darlene.

When Mitch received the pipe, he asked again for the blessing of the spirits on the journey Ian and Annie would undertake and offered another prayer of gratitude. He then raised the pipe above his head again and solemnly disconnected the bowl from the stem.

He emptied the ashes into the open clamshell, rewrapped the stem and bowl in pieces of leather, and returned the items one by one to the pipe bag. The ceremony was complete.

Ian, Mitch, and Annie returned to the house, where Susan had prepared a light meal "to feed the spirits." There was little conversation, and Annie left soon after the meal was finished.

Day 189–190

On this quiet day, Ian began packing up for his journey.

Late in the day, Black Bull sent a boy with a message. He had arranged a full tribal ceremony to honor Ian two days from now. Ian must undergo a purifying sweat tomorrow. Ian and Mitch spent the rest of the day preparing for Ian's departure. Mitch contacted Annie to let her know she and Ian would leave right after Black Bull's ceremony.

Ian spent the day fasting and quietly contemplating what was to come. He only wished he knew what that was.

Day 191

Ian and Mitch met Black Bull at the sweat lodge late in the morning. Black Bull had spent the night there, praying and preparing the rocks for today's use.

Ian entered the sweat lodge for the second time. He stayed inside for the rest of the day, emerging at sunset.

By this time, his state of consciousness was incredibly high. His perceptions were crystalline. He felt complete peace and benevolence toward the world, but he realized that he had no sense of attachment to anything he saw.

This altered state remained intact through the night.

Chapter 35

Day 192

Ian opened his eyes to a beautiful day. The sun was shining warmly through his window. Birdsong provided the background to his gradual awareness of his surroundings. He could hear low voices and the bustle of Susan making breakfast. All was right with the world.

Realization washed over him. This would be a red-letter day. Today he would take part in Black Bull's honor ceremony—though he still did not know why he was being honored—and this was the day he and Annie would leave Pawhuska to continue his search for his family. Suddenly fully awake and alert, Ian sprang out of bed and dressed hastily.

At breakfast, it dawned on him that this was the last time he would sit at this table, the last time he would see these now-familiar faces in what had come to feel like home. Looking around with warm affection at Mitch, Susan, and the two boys, for a moment Ian doubted his decision to continue his odyssey. He had felt so welcome here. And he was tired. He reminded himself that he was now 45, not 25. The thought of walking another 700 miles over rough terrain and desert no longer sounded like an adventure; it sounded like an endurance test. Maybe he should just wait here and keep trying to contact his family by phone and letter. Things were bound to get back to normal sometime, and he could drive the distance in a day instead of walking it in three months.

Then Theresa's face appeared in his mind's eye, with Gabe and Claire close behind her. He felt a pang of longing that overcame all his rational arguments. No, this was the way it must be, however much he would regret leaving Pawhuska.

The honor ceremony was set for early afternoon. Ian spent the morning repacking his backpack with his few possessions. Finally, dressed in his traveling clothes, Ian collected his well-notched walking stick and left his room for the last time.

It was quite a walk to the open field at the edge of town. Ian and Mitch's family made their way together in silence. Ian was pleased to note that his foot and ankle held up well; he now could walk for some distance without even a twinge.

When they arrived at the ceremony site, Ian was taken aback. There was a large crowd gathered, almost all recognizably Osage. A circle had been formed around an open area. Elders held comfortable front-row seats in lawn chairs. Groups of men and women stood talking and laughing, while children chased each other through the crowd. Ian noticed, though, that even the smallest child did not venture into the open area at the center of the circle.

"Good grief," he said to Mitch, "there must be a thousand people here!"

"Yup," agreed Mitch calmly. "Just about everybody within walking distance. Black Bull sent out the call by moccasin telegraph, telling everyone it was really important to the tribe for them to be here, even if it is a Monday. And a few even managed to get here by car," he added, grinning at a small woman who was waving frantically to attract his attention. Ian focused on her and recognized Darlene, with Jim at her side. A smile burst out as Ian waved happily back.

Susan and the boys turned aside, greeting friends and joining Jim and Darlene. Mitch led the way forward, toward the center of the circle, with Ian following uncertainly behind. Ian looked anxiously around for Black Bull.

Black Bull was almost unrecognizable. He stood at the edge of the inner circle talking to another older man. It was the other man Ian recognized first: the Kiowa shaman, Lone Wolf. Lone Wolf actually appeared to be a bit uneasy, as if he were out of place and knew it.

Black Bull, on the other hand, appeared serenely confident. He wore traditional nineteenth-century Osage clothing: a ribbon shirt, leggings, and a vest. A blanket was wrapped around his waist. Low, beaded moccasins covered his feet, a scarf was tied around his neck, and he wore an odd head covering that looked like a brimless top hat. An eagle wing fan was held in his right hand. He looked regal, authoritative, commanding. Glancing up, he saw Ian and Mitch and motioned to them to approach.

"Welcome," he greeted them. Ian suddenly found himself feeling awkward and even a bit embarrassed.

"I seem to be seriously underdressed for the occasion," he offered, looking down at his worn jeans and boots. Black Bull did not smile; he merely nodded.

"No," he replied, "It is as it should be. Come, we can begin now."

With that, Black Bull strode to the center of the circle. After a nudge from Mitch, Ian hesitantly followed. Mitch remained at the edge of the crowd.

The noise level began to drop. Children were caught up in their parents' arms or held protectively at their sides. All attention moved to the two men standing in the center of the circle.

Black Bull extended his arms toward his people. A total hush fell, and the old man began to speak in a language Ian did not know. Even so, it was clear that this was a prayer, a seeking of blessing. Peace and reverence fell like a protective blanket over the assembled Osage.

Black Bull completed his invocation and paused.

"It is not usual for me to conduct ceremony in any language but that of the Wah Zha Zhe," he began, "but this day we honor Ian Cameron, he whose coming has been foretold by our ancestors. For that reason, I will speak his language." He nodded respectfully toward Ian.

Ian nodded back, but his brain was whirling. "Foretold by our ancestors? Who, me? There's got to be some kind of mistake. What's going on here?"

Black Bull drew himself up to his full height. Turning back toward the now very alert crowd, he lifted his arms and his voice and began.

"In the days of our ancestors, we hunted the buffalo. In those long-ago times, the buffalo were as many as blades of grass on the plains. Our hunters went on foot, stealing close to the herds and bravely fighting to the death to bring us our food, our clothing, our shelter, our tools—all of these gifts of the buffalo." Ian saw heads nodding in agreement among the onlookers.

"In the days of our many-times grandfathers' grandfathers, one day a hunting party came upon a small herd of buffalo. To disguise themselves from the buffalo, the hunters wore the skins of wolves over their heads and backs. This allowed them to come close to the herd, because a few wolves were no threat to the huge buffalo.

"Their medicine man was with them, bringing good luck through his presence and his prayers for their success. He stood praying on a small rise nearby.

"As the hunters stalked closer through the tall grass, they looked up to see a man walking toward them, right through the middle of the herd. To their amazement, the buffalo did not attack this man; they simply let him pass.

"The stranger was not like anyone the hunters had ever seen before. He was as tall as an Osage. He wore hide leggings and a hide shirt. His hair was a light color and his eyes were the color of the sky. His face was also covered with hair, something that was most peculiar to the hunters. He carried a long stick, and at the top of the stick was a banner with a strange symbol on it.

"Though the hunters were concealed in the tall grasses, the stranger walked straight up to them. He greeted them in the Wah Zha Zhe language and asked to be taken to their medicine man. Though they were frightened that he might be a demon instead of a man, the hunters led the stranger to the medicine man. This man, Many Bears, was strong in his heart. He did not flee or show his fear, but met the threat knowing that he would be protected by the spirits. He greeted the stranger with courtesy, and the two went aside to talk.

"Through all the generations since that time, what was said there has been passed down from one head medicine man to the next. Many Bears passed the stranger's secret message to his successor, Night Stalker, who passed it to Friend of the Wolves.

And so it came down, man after man, to my own teacher, Day Weaver, then to me. The names of the other medicine men who held this trust are known to us. Their 27 names will be learned for the future by Mitch One Feather so the story will not be forgotten."

At this, the crowd stirred in a quiet excitement. Black Bull had just named his successor, the next head medicine man of the Osage. Mitch, at the edge of the circle, humbly bowed his head.

"We were given a sacred and secret responsibility by the stranger, one that must be completed for the very survival of the Wah Zha Zhe. Today I will have the honor of fulfilling that duty for our people." Black Bull's voice broke and he stopped, visibly overcome and fighting for self-control.

He continued in a husky voice. "The stranger told Many Bears that in the time of darkness he, the stranger, would come again. When the skies filled with dust like the passing of a buffalo herd, he would appear out of the blackness."

"We, the medicine men, were to watch for him, however long it took, from generation to generation," Black Bull explained to the raptly attentive audience. "He would look much the same, tall as an Osage with light hair and sky-eyes, and he would carry his staff with its strange banner. He would remember walking with the buffalo."

Black Bull paused dramatically, then turned to point with his chin at Ian. "This is the man!" he cried. The Osage crowd reacted with murmurs of surprise and slight shiftings. Everyone stared at Ian, who was as astonished as they were.

"Consider!" demanded Black Bull. "He came to us out of the darkness of the ashfall. This stranger was led to the very door of the Wah Zha Zhe by a glowing spirit stag. The spirit spoke to a woman of the Wah Zha Zhe, commanding that she save and protect the special one the stag guided.

"Look at him! Is he not the very image of the light-haired, bearded man who came to our ancestors? Is he not tall as an Osage? Are his eyes not the color of the sky? Does he not carry the strange banner our ancestors described?

"When we took this man, Ian Cameron, to the sweat lodge, he had a vision. He saw the plains black with buffalo. He walked among the buffalo until he was surrounded by wolves—and the wolves turned into men! Just so would our hunters have appeared to the stranger!" Black Bull gazed intently at his mesmerized listeners.

"Now it is time to fulfill the prophecy," Black Bull continued. Reaching into his shirt, he pulled out a small, well-worn leather bag. He held it out to Ian in both hands and said, "This belongs to you."

Hesitantly, Ian accepted the bag. "What is it?" he asked softly.

"The bag is a gift from the stranger from long ago," Black Bull declared. "It holds seeds of the squash plant, one of the sacred Three Sisters who have fed our peoples through the ages. The stranger left these for you. He also left you a message:

Plant your seeds carefully. The Three Sisters will nourish the world in times to come. And you must follow the stag!

Black Bull bowed his head. "The prophecy is fulfilled. It is finished," he said.

The crowd sat in stunned silence. No one had had any idea of what to expect when Black Bull summoned them to this gathering, but the wildest speculations fell far short of this. A 750-year-old prophecy that had been faithfully passed down in complete secrecy was almost beyond belief. It would take a while to absorb this.

Ian stared in wonder at the worn bag in his hand. He found that he had no words to respond to this unprecedented gift. He simply nodded solemnly to Black Bull. Ian's brain was spinning more than ever. There's that damned stag again, he thought in confusion. What *is* it with that stag?

Black Bull raised his arms once more and began to pray with great intensity and fervor. The collected Osage followed his every word breathlessly, and Ian was caught in the emotional depths of the moment. At last, Black Bull came to a conclusion and dropped his hands and his head. It was still for what seemed an eternity.

A slight movement at the edge of the circle: it was Mitch, who stepped just away from the other observers. He announced, "This is an honor song for Ian Cameron."

He started to beat softly on a hand drum, using a drumstick with a padded leather tip. He began singing in the Wah Zha Zhe language, softly at first, then gaining in strength and volume. He chanted with the rhythm of the drum, standing straight and tall as he sang. The song was soothingly repetitive to Ian. Mitch continued singing for several minutes, then simply stopped. Switching to English, Mitch called out, "Ian, this is what it means.

"He came to us out of the darkness, this man
A glowing stag led him to us
He walks with power
He walks in honor
This man."

Ian smiled his heartfelt gratitude to his friend. He was almost overcome with emotion at the depth of his feelings. His heart swelled with love for these people who had accepted him so completely. He wished he had a song to return, a way to express how he felt; but he could think of nothing that would be adequate.

After another moment's silence, the crowd began to awaken from its trance, drifting away from the edges of the circle.

"What now?" Ian asked Black Bull.

"Now we eat," the old medicine man replied. "It's time to feed the spirits." And with that, he, too, wandered away.

Mitch, taking pity on Ian's obvious bewilderment, led him toward the new center of attention. A long plank table had been set up at the edge of the field, behind which several women were busy dishing up plates of steaming beef stew. Chunks of beef, potato, carrot, and onion simmered in the hearty gravy. On the table were towers of fry bread, pitchers of iced tea and lemonade, and a huge coffee urn.

Groups of people stood or sat, all talking animatedly. Some conversations appeared serious, with people talking about what they had just experienced. However, there was also laughter and obvious pleasure in each other's company. As Ian and Mitch passed each group, people nodded a friendly greeting then returned to their conversations.

Ian was not the slightest bit surprised to see Susan behind the table, dishing out stew with lightning speed. She flashed a smile and told Mitch and Ian where they should sit.

"Jim and Darlene are over there," she said, waving the stew ladle off to her right. "They've got the boys. Annie and Black Bull and Lone Wolf are with them, too." Then she handed over two heavily laden plates and moved on to the next in line.

Darlene scooted over to make room for Ian at the table, almost pushing a startled Jim off the end of the picnic bench. "Sit here," she ordered. Mitch, grinning, fit himself in next to his two sons.

"So, you're really leaving today?" Darlene asked Ian.

"Yep. I still have to find my family," Ian replied. "They were headed for Albuquerque, so that's my destination too. God, I hope they made it there safe!"

Darlene patted the back of his hand sympathetically. "Don't worry, Ian. Everything will work out the way it's supposed to. It always does."

"There goes Aunt Darlene getting all metaphysical again," Annie called from down the table. Darlene giggled and turned back to her stew.

Ian suddenly realized just how hungry he was. For the next few minutes he let conversation wash over him as he devoured a very good stew and two whole rounds of fry bread.

Once he had taken the edge off his hunger, he began to pay more attention to his companions. They were relaxed, comfortable with each other—and with him. There were three separate conversations going on. Meanwhile, Mitch and one of his boys were completely focused on the food. It was such a warm, pleasant scene that Ian felt a lump rise in his throat.

"Dang, I'm going to miss you guys!" he blurted out. Everyone paused and looked toward him. They were all smiling, even the old medicine men.

Then Black Bull, with a faraway look in his eye, said, "You will miss us; but you will be back. Your spirit will not abandon the Wah Zha Zhe."

Ian felt a slight chill at these words, though he didn't know why. Still, he smiled back at Black Bull and thanked him for the reassurance—if that's what it was.

Finally, everyone had eaten as much as any stomach could hold. There was no excuse to linger any longer, however reluctant the diners were to end this companionable time. With a sigh, Ian stood and looked down the table to Annie.

"Well, I guess we'd better get started if we want to cover any ground today. I'd like to make ten miles before we stop for the night, and that's going to take some fast walking. It's getting late."

Ian was astonished when everybody started to laugh at him. "What?" he asked, surprised.

"We have a little going away present for you, Ian," Mitch said. "Jim and Darlene aren't here just to say goodbye. Jim has a truck, remember? And a gas allowance? He's been saving up, a gallon here, a gallon there. We've got it all set up to take you and Annie about a hundred miles west. One of our tribal members has a ranch out that way, and he's going to loan you some horses, too. Things are about to get a lot easier, brother."

Ian's jaw dropped. "You guys are the best friends I've ever had," he managed to say.

The people at Ian's table stood to leave. As if prearranged, the people at the other tables also rose to their feet. The crowd followed as Ian and his friends headed toward the parking area at the edge of the field. And there was Jim's truck.

It was time to say farewell. Ian turned to his friends.

"Thank you," he said. "You have all been so good to me, I have no words to say how grateful I truly am."

Black Bull smiled at him. He stepped forward, and Ian impulsively grabbed the old man in a bear hug. Black Bull stiffened in astonishment, then relaxed and patted Ian gently on the back. "Safe journey, Ian. Remember, you must fulfill the prophecy."

Lone Wolf stepped forward next, with his hand carefully extended to prevent the indignity just suffered by his colleague. "Don't forget the Hopi, Ian. The prophecies are connected. You are the Pahana, the White Brother returned after all this time. Follow the stag, and it will lead you to the Hopi."

Susan appeared at the edge of the group, a bit sweaty and disheveled but still, as always, smiling warmly. She took her sons by the hand and led them forward to say their goodbyes. Then she hugged Ian, who stammered his deep thanks for her care and her caring.

Ian turned to Mitch. "I can't say goodbye to you—I just can't," he said.

"That's okay, my friend. I'm going to ride with you as far as the ranch, anyway," Mitch replied with a gentle smile.

Jim and Darlene were already in the truck by this time. Ian turned to Annie.

"Would you like to ride up front with your aunt and uncle?" he asked. "Mitch and I can ride in the back. It's only fitting. I came to Pawhuska in the bed of this truck, and I'm going to leave the same way."

Annie laughed and climbed into the front seat. Jim started the engine and pulled away. Ian waved and watched as the Osage grew smaller with the distance.

Then he noticed that there were three other vehicles pulling out from the parking area and falling into line behind them.

"What's up with that?" Ian asked Mitch.

"Oh, just some spiritual groupies," Mitch responded. "They'll follow us as far as their gas will take them. After all, how many times does a person get a chance to hang out with somebody who fulfills a 750-year-old prophecy and is the Pahana to boot?"

"Geez, Mitch! Do you really believe that?" Ian exclaimed.

Mitch nodded soberly. "It's a little hard not to believe it, Ian. Too many coincidences. I don't believe in coincidence."

The truck was now on paved road, headed west out of Pawhuska. For a few minutes Ian and Mitch sat in silence, lost in their thoughts.

"You know," Ian said at last, "I've been thinking about coincidence. And I just realized that the key to this whole thing is Darlene. Without her, none of this happens." He looked earnestly at Mitch. "Think about it. She's the one the stag went to, she's the one who could hear it and the one who would do what it wanted. Then she called you, her brother, and made sure I got to Pawhuska. If she weren't married to Jim, there'd have been no way to get there—or to be where we are right now, for that matter. And she raised Annie. Everywhere you look, there's Darlene. Quite a woman, your sister."

"Yeah, she is," Mitch agreed quietly, "but you don't know everything. Remember when Black Bull said you were in a dance with the stag and the kachina? And that this is bigger than you can imagine? Actually, there may be another in the dance.

"Let me tell you what the stag told Darlene while you were unconscious."

APPENDICES

Appendix A

See page 145, Chapter 16

During the two-year period between 1966 and 1968, until the Beatles went to India, there was a dearth of information about Eastern religious thought and experiences. Having an altered state of consciousness experience and trying to find information about it was impossible. There was no vocabulary, no words to define the experiences we were going through. However, 5000 plus years of definitions did exist throughout the world. But we had no knowledge of their existence, and thus no starting point of reference.

It's easy to forget that in 1966 certain things were not in existence yet. There were no "spiritual books," no spiritual book stores, and no "new age movement." Authors like Castaneda, Ram Dass, and Lilly did not publish their works until after 1968. *Psychology Today* would not be available until 1970. Groups like The Beatles, The Moody Blues, The Incredible String Band, and Jefferson Airplane had not yet begun to sing consciousness-related songs.

There were no personal computers, no Internet, no Google, and no cellphones. Information was not easily retrievable.

What did exist in 1966 was veiled. Spiritual books like *Autobiography of a Yogi, Siddhartha, The Razor's Edge,* and the *Book of the Hopi* existed, but they were not readily available to the general population, unless you were an English or religious studies major. Science fiction books like *More Than Human, Childhood's End,* and *Stranger in a Strange Land* used fantasy to expose fact, but the culture did not yet respect science fiction. *The Twilight Zone, The Outer Limits,* and *Star Trek* utilized television to begin to shift that cultural perception.

Bible verses, such as Matthew 6:22—"The light of the body is the eye: if therefore thine eye be single, thy whole body shall be full of light"—revealed major clues. But if one doesn't understand the Eastern concept of the sixth chakra "third eye" and the seventh chakra "single eye," then this phrase has no meaning.

The years from 1966 to 1968 were a unique time...a limbo time. Our minds were being altered and expanded to other dimensions and realities, yet we had no model to describe it or understand it. Multiple forms of cultural platforms—books, songs, television shows, movies—overlapped and layered to create a bridge to 1968 and beyond. This bridge led us to understanding consciousness, to remembering our connections with ourselves and our planet. Mindfulness, yoga, meditation, and Gaia have now forcefully interwoven their way into the fabric of our culture. This was *not* the case in 1966.

Appendix B

See page 154, Chapter 17

"But these guys were all Explorers of a new frontier."

In Appendix A, we noted that there was a dearth of spiritual/consciousness information between 1966 and 1968. With this dearth, how could you go about exploring and understanding your experiences? Especially without keywords or a known vocabulary to go by. Again, there was no starting point of reference, no Internet, no Google.

As you can imagine, experiencing an altered state of reality created confusion. The Explorers then questioned all of reality and their now-fragile sanity. Was it real? How could it be described?

They sought answers from "professionals," clergy and professors. This exercise revealed nothing but more grief, confusion, and anger. And anger is a great motivator.

The Explorers began by making up words, giving them definitions, and creating a new vocabulary to define their experiences. Their academic backgrounds gave them a starting point. Look at the data, follow the clues. So they treated their experiences like data. They threw as much as possible up onto the wall to see what stuck. When all of the variables were seen together, they might start to make sense.

After the data was assembled it became clear that this was a new form of energy. Drugs were not needed to get high or to access this energy. What the hell was this?

An intriguing question led them to look at physics. If you can levitate a cup, what forces make that happen? Dead end. Science hasn't gotten here yet.

They looked into documented information on abnormal psychology: psychosis, schizophrenia, delusions. Dead end. They knew they did not fall into this category because they had witnesses. If other people could see you levitate a cup, then clearly you are not insane! Woo hoo! But now where should they go? There's almost nothing left.

Then they wondered if anyone in their families had had these experiences. Family histories, grandmothers' stories, oral histories revealed people in the family tree with unusual abilities, including some in 1692 Salem, Massachusetts. A new realization emerged. If you levitate in the convent of the church, you become a saint. But, if you levitate one block down the street at the pub, you get burned at the stake! Who is making up the rules here?

After working through these issues, only two things stuck to the wall that they could research: witches and saints. The church has 25,000 plus saints. Surely, they must have pretty good documentation? A visit to the

University of Michigan Graduate Library in 1966 gave overwhelming proof of this. Stack after stack, floor to ceiling, the lives of the saints were recorded here.

The European and North American courts generated thousands of pages of transcripts relating to hundreds of years of witchcraft trials. These were the unfortunate ones who had demonstrated their powers outside the protection of the church.

No other categories existed in Western thought to explain these "superhuman" abilities. Such things could only be good or evil, saintly or satanic. The very concept of evolution did not come to public attention until Darwin's work in the 1850s, and the idea of applying this to humanity is still controversial.

In 1968, when the Beatles went to India, the floodgates opened to reveal all those well-kept Hindu and Buddhist secrets about altered states of consciousness. Now finally there were answers.

Appendix C

See page 156, Chapter 17

*"Egoless, the **<u>God Gates</u>** in very far right brain could now open...to accept you home."*

The information we have included in this appendix is not well understood by even the most ardent of seekers or "practitioners." From our extensive experience, a majority of spiritual teachers—from all corners of the world—cannot differentiate between chi (prana) energy and shakti (higher kundalini energy). If you are at all interested in spiritual growth, it is **imperative** to understand this distinction. To put it in "Western speak," the one with the blue light saber does not use the same energy as the one with the red light saber. Do you know the difference?

Buddha did. When his best student distracted everyone by levitating in over the class, Buddha admonished him for enticing the others with **useless** powers that weren't relevant to enlightenment.

The blue saber people use shakti (God consciousness) energy—the white light that pours in from the heavens. The shakti enters the human body at a very specific point in the head—and exits through very specific portals in the upper body. This is the energy of God enlightenment.

The red saber people use chi/pran/prana energy that permeates and binds the illusion. Shaman, sorcerers, chi masters, and other people with great personal power focus the chi to manipulate the world around them. Levitation, dematerialization, and shape shifting are just a few of the tools in a medicine man's toolbox. These powers are very real, but they're all ego-based. Those kung fu fighters flying across the screen use focused ego attack. Balanced chi is essential for "right" living in this dream, but most are seduced by this ego astral power.

Now, here's where it gets really interesting. Ego lives primarily in the left brain of humans. Carlos Castaneda in one of his many books on sorcery spent the entire book discussing the technique for shifting his assemblage point from the right over to the left side of his brain/body. Enlightenment never came up in his many books. Just sorcerer's intent—different energy, different release, different species. Humans can't fly. Buddha won't fly.

The Buddha/Christ consciousness beings move their point of consciousness to the **right** side of their brain. Ego is reduced the farther right-brained you move. Your heart rate drops, your hertz rate drops—while portions of the brain shut down, turning off the ego squirrel cage.

You cannot mix ego with the shakti white light. You are **not** allowed into this sacred space with **any** ego baggage. If you can shift your point of consciousness to the very far right brain, you arrive at a "stopping the world" space. Without ego baggage, you are allowed entry into the cosmic light. Cosmic circuits are opened and the brain becomes an energy reception device—conducting focused cosmic energy.

Appendix D

See page 158, Chapter 17

Hertz Wave Frequencies

Delta	0.5-4 Hz	Deep sleep
Theta	4-8 Hz	Meditation
Alpha	8-13 Hz	Relaxation
Beta	13-40 Hz	Solving problems/sorting out issues
Gamma	40-100 Hz	Normal functioning activity

Gamma and High Beta are the everyday normal activity states of a functioning adult. If your brain waves are in a Gamma/Beta state you will not be able to enter into the subconscious mind which is only accessible through the lower Alpha and Theta states. You can't stop the squirrel-cage chatter if you can't shift your assemblage point into these lower states. This is why people have trouble with meditation. Meditation is not contemplation.

And then there is the ADD/ADHD issue. There is an interesting phenomenon that occurs in children and adults with ADD/ADHD. They have high amounts of Theta activity in their frontal lobes. What does this mean? Well, the slow 4–8 Hz Theta waves flood the frontal lobe preventing effective communication with the rest of the brain. That means that these people function in a constant meditative state. This has a **HIGH EVOLUTIONARY VALUE!**

Unfortunately, Western society does not value meditation or consciousness or evolution. Instead, children are sedated with pharmaceuticals in the hopes of bringing them back into a "normal" functioning state. Evolution will be suppressed one way or another. It could be argued that the "normal" evolutionary functioning state might very well be ADD/ADHD.

For more information on hertz rates and brainwave activity see:

- Beauregard, Mario. *Brain Wars: The Scientific Battle Over the Existence of the Mind and the Proof That Will Change the Way We Live Our Lives.* New York: HarperOne, 2012.
- Dispenza, Dr. Joe. *Breaking the Habit of Being Yourself: How to Lose Your Mind and Create a New One.* Carlsbad, CA: Hay Horse, 2012.

Appendix E

See page 159, Chapter 17

"Ancient languages like Sanskrit even had words that could alter your state of consciousness."

We created an appendix for this one sentence in the hope that the reader might pause and take the time to ponder the implications of this concept.

Written Sanskrit emerged out of the fog of oral prehistory almost 5000 years ago. Imagine…at that moment ancient teachers already understood that particular sounds could awaken the spiritual chakra centers. Sanskrit was developed as a language of consciousness. Roadmaps for understanding the intricacies of altered consciousness were already in existence **prior** to the development of this language. Ancient Upanishads detail and confirm these roadmaps.

Explore the ancient use of "mantras" among Hindus, Buddhists, Jains, and many other Eastern traditions. This may alter your perceptions of remote prehistory. These concepts require our attention.

Appendix F

See page 165, Chapter 17

This is the original advertisement for Jacob's Ladder Gallery that appeared in *The Periodical Lunch* in the summer of 1974.

Appendix G

See page 165, Chapter 17

The experience of a 6th chakra energy flow is at once divinely powerful yet existentially disturbing. What just happened here? There are no words to describe this—organs and wiring you never knew existed are activated in your body. Your perception of reality is forever altered.

First, a word of caution. Hundreds of thousands of "new agers" practice open-eyed work worldwide. This 6th chakra energy exchange between two people is **not** a staring contest. And it is **not** related to chi energy. It is far more powerful than that! This is shakti energy that stimulates internal Kundalini energy. Please do not be misled by uninformed teachers that claim to teach Kundalini—yet unnecessarily stress manipulating the first three chakras. Never do this. Run from any teacher who tries to rile up the lower chakras. Our own near-fatal experiences and the wisdom of the ancient rishis advise against this.

Our detailed description of the 6th chakra energy flow in Chapter 17 is based on the many energy flows we the authors have experienced over the decades. We learned that a good upper chakra flow is similar to a rocket launch. They come in two phases—a pre-launch preparation phase...and a launch + ride phase.

The pre-launch phase can, and in most cases, should take years of preparation. Learn to meditate correctly. To do this you must first learn to shift your point of consciousness rapidly and "at will" into the right brain. This could take years. Eventually you will be able to get to far right brain (see Appendix C). Your heart rate and your electrical brain activity will drop dramatically (see Appendix D)—shutting down most of your brain—shutting down the ego. You are now sitting on the launch pad—all systems "go," ready for "ignition."

"Stopping the world" allows for final system checks. If all systems are "go" and you are cleared for liftoff, then "ignition" occurs. At this moment it is exactly like a rocket sitting on the pad with all engines "firing"...but waiting that final five seconds to gather the power for liftoff.

At this moment you enter the **second** phase of the 6th chakra energy flow—"liftoff." The "all clear" ignition command triggers the medulla oblongata to open the heavenly gate at the base of the skull. Shakti God energy pours in—igniting the pineal gland (internal vestigial third eye). The shakti activates the dormant Kundalini. Then, through the fiercely-tingling third eye in the center of the forehead—the slingshot is released...liftoff has occurred! A cosmic circuit is opened between the two participants. A concentrated blast of Kundalini energy blows out from their foreheads. Their energy flows merge in the dance of joining. Hours pass locked in this powerful gaze.

Appendix H

See page 171, Chapter 18

The full moon in May of 1999 provided the wondrous strange circumstances described here. For some time, we had been struggling unsuccessfully to discover the exact dimensions of this Great Kiva. What diameter? How many rows of seating? It was exhausting and discouraging. One night, about two weeks into the process, we took a break and repaired to the back yard—and there a miracle awaited.

A thin veil of cloud had been pulled across the face of the moon. It was remarkable in itself: a wispy parallelogram with clearly defined edges. The light of the moon diffracted through it in expanding haloes of different colored light, as though someone had dropped a pebble into a reflection of the moon.

The proportions were perfect. With this design, the kiva would measure 300 feet across. It would have twelve ascending rows of comfortable seating overlooking a central performance area. At the very top, above the rows of seating, a wider path around the circumference of the kiva would provide a second performance level.

Following the downloaded diagram, we began construction of the model in June. The Great Kiva slowly took shape over the next three months. On an afternoon in early September, as we were putting the finishing touches on the model, the kiva activated. It sent a blast of energy right through Lani, who was innocently gluing carpet to the stairs. She yelped, jumped straight up in the air, and landed about three feet away from the kiva. Any questions we may have had about how effective our kiva would be as a spiritual energy accelerator were answered.

When the model was completed, we got the final confirmation. We learned about the crop circle at Morcott, England—a two-dimensional, full-scale replica of our kiva.

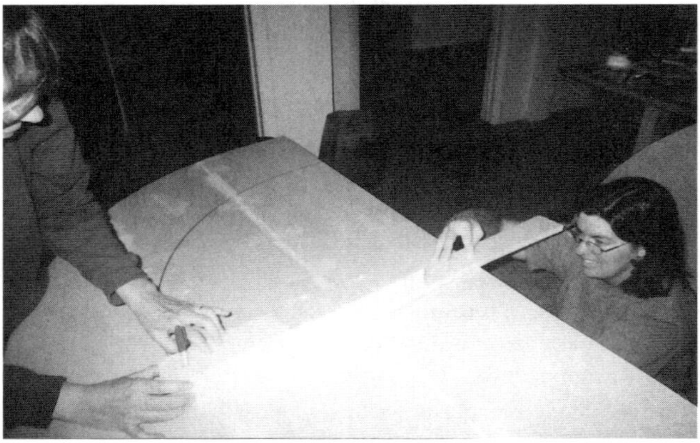

Lani (left) and Karina (right) measure an early level of the kiva model

Literally seconds before the kiva zapped Lani

Appendix I

See page 195, Chapter 19

"Desperately, he clung to his memories of his family and the more recent, even more important, connection to Ellen."

Hmm. Interesting statement.

Given the unique information included in this book—in a variety of spiritual areas not typically found in Western literature…we asked 20 readers to evaluate our manuscript. We chose a carefully constructed sample of readers with a broad range of lifestyles, beliefs, and backgrounds.

Interesting responses to that statement.

Those readers who are more family-oriented, living a life without spiritual experiences and more enculturated into Western civilization, responded to that sentence with almost hostile disbelief. How could anyone—particularly Ellen (just an acquaintance along the road)—be more important than his family? What were we thinking? Many felt we should delete chapters 16 to 18 because they made no sense as part of Ian's epic adventure.

Our readers with considerable spiritual understanding and experience asked us to expand the "Ellen" chapters to include much more spiritual information. Same sentence. Entirely different response.

If you have had an intense, reality-bending experience, you understand that the illusion we perceive is, in fact, not real. When you reach out and touch the hand of God, it's a little hard to come back to this reality. For example, those who have had a 6th chakra energy flow (like Ian and Ellen) understand that they did not come here to get a job, own a home, and raise children. Billions of others, still caught in the illusion—still caught in the matrix—do not understand that they have a choice. Buddha understood. He left his home and family forever to live a life devoted to spiritual enlightenment. The phony narrative we have about family and school and community is totally false. Something else is going on here.

Explorers of altered consciousness need to discover what that "something else" is. How does this affect our definition of reality?

So, yes, even more important, Ian desperately clung to his recent connection to Ellen.

Appendix J

See page 233, Chapter 24

Vedas are ancient Hindu texts that form the basis of the Hindu religion. There are four Vedas: the Rigveda, Samaveda, Yajurveda, and the Atharvaveda. The Vedas vastly influenced Buddhism, Sikhism, and Jainism. The Vedas are the most ancient texts still in existence. They cover religion, spirituality, and secular life in India 5000 years ago.

List of Indian literature where information about ancient flying machines (Vimanas) is available:

- *Mahabharata* (the Indian national epic)
  - *Drona Parva* (section of the Mahabharata)
- *Ramayana* (one of the two epic Hindu poems, the other being the Mahabharata)
- *Bhagatava Purana* (one of India's great histories)
- *Samarangana Sutradhara* (a work on classical Indian architecture and warfare)
- *Rigveda* (Veda)
- *Yajurveda* (Veda)

Questionable Text:

Vaimanika Sastra (20th century text): Many books and television programs reference this writing. In researching the *Vaimanika Sastra* we found the validity of the material questionable and therefore did not include it.

Appendix K

See page 238, Chapter 24

The Gnostic Gospels are a compendium of about 54 ancient texts, written in Early Coptic, that were discovered in Egypt at Nag Hammadi between 1896 and 1955. The word "gnostic" comes from the Greek word *gnosis* which means "knowledge." These gospels are the sayings of Christ and the disciples that were not included in the New Testament.

The texts demonstrate the underpinnings of gnostic cosmology—that the answers to spiritual questions are to be found within...not without.

NOTE: "The little blue book" is *The Gnostic Gospels,* translated by Alan Jacobs. This edition was first produced in 2006 for Sacred Wisdom, an imprint of Watkins Publishing, London

Appendix L

See page 241, Chapter 24 and page 337, Chapter 33

These are copies of the original handouts that were distributed publically in Boulder, Colorado, on April 6, 1992. Ancient Hopi prophecy foretold the arrival of the white race and their takeover of Turtle Island (North America). At the end times, an inverted gourd (nuclear bomb) would appear over Hopi land. The prophecy stated that shortly thereafter a Great House of Mica (glass) would be built on the eastern shore of Turtle Island, a place where nations would come together and solve world problems and create peace.

Prophecy stated that Hopi elders would go to the House of Mica four times to promote their message of peace and cooperation. The Hopi elders went to the United Nations four times between 1948 and 1992, requesting an audience. Prophecy stated that they would be refused all four times.

The letter attached in this appendix is a copy from Thomas Banyacya of the final 1991 letter from the Hopi to the U.N. Secretary General. Banyacya came to Boulder in April of 1992 to issue a final warning of impending purification and apocalypse. He stated that the U.N. had until August 22, 1992, to respond to the Hopi request for an audience.

Ultimately, the United States vetoed the Hopi request to present their message of peace.

So, on August 23, 1992, a massive hurricane, Andrew, devastated south Florida. Apparently, the purification had begun.

Also attached is a copy of the Hopi Declaration of Peace. This Declaration was originally copied onto the back of the United Nations letter that Banyacya distributed.

Banyacya
Hopi Traditional Elder
P.O. Box [redacted]
Kykotsmovi, AZ 86039
October 22, 1991

The Honorable Perez de Cuellar,
Secretary General of the United Nations
New York, NY

Dear Secretary de Cuellar:

I, Banyacya, made a commitment in 1948 to the Kikmongwis (leaders) and other religious elders of the assembled Hopi clans to take the Hopi Prophecy and its message of peace to the United Nations, known to them from the ancient prophecy as the Great House of Mica on the Eastern shore where the nations come together to solve world problems without war. This house is built on the original native peoples' land, yet it has not permitted native peoples to speak in its General Assembly.

Since 1948, I and other Hopi Elders have made several pilgrimages to the United Nations and although we have not been permitted to address the General Assembly, we have been warmly received by several personages including Robert Muller, the former Assistant Secretary General, and most recently, on December 29, 1990, by John L. Washburn, Director of the Executive Office of the Secretary General. In that meeting with Oren Lyons (Faithkeeper of the Onondaga Nation), Lewis Jarvis and me, Mr. Washburn indicated there would be several ways that the Hopi Elders could be received in the General Assembly to present the Hopi message which warns against war and promotes peaceful cooperation among nations and peoples of the world.

Such an opening of the doors of the Great House of Mica would fulfill the instructions of the Kikmongwis and other Hopi Elders given in 1948. Today I am making the fourth and final pilgrimage on their behalf because this is the time of year when the Hopi Women's Societies hold their sacred ceremonies for Mother Earth.

As Mother Earth cries out in the pain of abuse, so I, of the Coyote Clan, add my desperate cry on her behalf, in the hope that the United Nations will soon extend an invitation to Hopi Elders and traditional leaders of the four directions. If this invitation is extended, the traditional Hopi societies and traditional leaders of the four directions will meet together to choose the appropriate representatives to be sent to the United Nations where they will be given the opportunity to present their oral message of peace to the world leaders assembled there.

The Hopi and many other native nations have struggled continually to maintain harmony with Mother Earth and all the universe through our way of life. The foundation of our way of life is the sacredness of the land on which we dwell. If that land continues to be abused, the sacredness of all life will disappear along with most of humanity in a great purification by Mother Earth and the Great Spirit.

This is my fourth and final attempt to open the door of the Great House of Mica. If it is not opened as we humbly request so that the red, white, yellow and black peoples might work together for a peaceful world, then we will return to await the inevitable time of purification.

Yours respectfully,

Banyacya

Banyacya
Hopi Traditional Elder

Hopi Declaration of Peace

It is in the Power of the True Hopi People to unify the minds and spirits of all true peace seeking peoples of the earth . . .

"Hopi" means "Peaceful People" . . . and the truest and greatest power is the strength of Peace . . . because Peace is the Will Of The Great Spirit . . .

But do not think that just because the True Hopi People have been told by the Great Spirit never to take up arms . . . that the True Hopi People will not fight . . . even die for what we know to be the right way of Life.

The True Hopi People Know how to fight without killing or hurting . . .

The True Hopi People Know how to fight with Truth and Positive Force In The Light Of The Great Spirit . . .

The True Hopi People Know how to Educate by clear thoughts . . . good pictures . . . and by carefully chosen words . . .

The True Hopi People Know how to show to all the world's Children the True Way of Life by setting an example . . . by working and communicating in a way that reaches the minds and hearts of all people who are truly seeking the methods of a simple and spiritual Life which is the only Life that will survive . . .

THE TRUE HOPI PEOPLE PRESERVE THE SACRED KNOWLEDGE ABOUT THE WAY OF THE EARTH BECAUSE THE TRUE HOPI PEOPLE KNOW THAT THE EARTH IS A LIVING . . . GROWING PERSON . . . AND ALL THINGS ON IT ARE HER CHILDREN . . .

The True Hopi People Know how to show the Right Way of Life to all the world's people who have ears to listen . . . who have eyes to see . . . and who have hearts to understand these things . . .

The True Hopi People Know how to generate enough Power to link up the forces of the Minds and Spirits of all the True Children of the Earth . . . and to Unify them with the Positive Force of the Great Spirit so that they may put an end to affliction and persecution in all afflicted places in this world . . .

THE TRUE HOPI PEOPLE DECLARE THAT HOPI POWER BE A FORCE WHICH WILL BRING ABOUT WORLD CHANGE.

Banyacya
P.O. Box [redacted]
Kykotsmovi, Arizona 86039

ATTRIBUTIONS

3 MPH Publishing Company would like to acknowledge the following individuals for their contributions to this book:

Graphics Credits

- Rukma Vimana T. K. ELLAPA (Ramayana) [CC BY-SA 3.0 (https://creativecommons.org/licenses/by-sa/3.0)], via Wikimedia Commons
- Maps by AAA, 2017, modified by Kurt Parfitt and Jon Van Eck
- Graphics for Peace Flag, Riverboat, Kokopellis, Broken Tablets, Kurt Parfitt and Jon Van Eck

Photographic Credits

- Camp 33 mantel/Kachina photo, Bill Daniels
- Kiva photos, Peter Van Eck
- Florence Bridge photo, Calvin K. Lunny
- Isaiah 45:7 painting and photo, Jon Van Eck
- Bison photo, Jon Van Eck
- Book design, illustrations and portraits, Kurt Parfitt

Song Lyrics

Title	**Composer** Nature's	**Year**	**Page**
Way	Randy California (Spirit)	1970	69
The Lumberjack Song	T. Jones/M. Palin/F. Tomlinson	1969	93
Ol' Man River	Jerome Kern	1927	112
On the Road Again	Willie Nelson	1980	205
Take Me to the River	Al Green	1974	219
Little Piggies	Lennon/McCartney	1968	240
Oh, What a Beautiful Mornin'	Rodger & Hammerstein	1943	287

Please note: Use of any graphics or song lyrics in this book does not imply endorsement or use of the work by the creators of said materials.

Authors

Van Eck is the pen name of a family of authors

Peter Van Eck created Jacob's Ladder Gallery, a consciousness art and book store in 1970s Ann Arbor. A prolonged "chance" encounter with Yogananda (author of *Autobiography of a Yogi*) on a California beach when he was a small child activated Peter's spiritual mission. He started work on this book in 1966 while he was a student at the University of Michigan.

Dr. Lani Van Eck taught for 30 years at universities as an anthropologist specializing in Native America. She cofounded Wounded Knee: the Museum in Wall, South Dakota. She is contributing editor to *Sitting Bull: His Life and Legacy* (2009: Gibbs Smith), an oral history written by Sitting Bull's only surviving great-grandson.

Jon Van Eck, BFA, has been a professional potter for over 35 years and is a former member of the Ann Arbor Potters Guild. He is also a painter, sculptor, and woodworker. As an MFA candidate in the early 2000s, he was a graduate teaching assistant in the fine arts program at Eastern Michigan University. When he's not working he loves hanging out with his wife and five kids.

N. DAK.
S. DAK.
Ellendale
Wahpeton
Breckenridge
Falls
Wadena
Brainerd
Aitkin
Mobridge
Selby
Aberdeen
Bowdle
Sisseton
Alexandria
Mille Lacs Lake
Little Falls
Sandstone
Faulkton
Gettysburg
Webster
Graceville
Sauk Centre
Glenwood
Milaca
Pine City
Spooner
Ortonville
Benson
St. Cloud
St. Croix Falls
Milbank
Watertown
Redfield
Miller
Willmar
Litchfield
Montevideo
Anoka
MINNEAPOLIS
St. Paul
MINN.
S. DAK.
De Smet
Arlington
Huron
Granite Falls
Redwood Falls
Marshall
Presho
Brookings
Madison
New Ulm
Red Wing
Durand
Lake City
Chamberlain
Woonsocket
Howard
PIPESTONE NAT'L MON.
Pipestone
Faribault
Mitchell
Salem
Winner
Platte
Gregory
Lake Andes
Dell Rapids
Windom
Worthington
Mankato
Owatonna
Winona
Rochester
Sioux Falls
Jackson
Albert Lea
La Crescent
Rock Rapids
Fairmont
Blue Earth
Austin
S. DAK.
NEB.
Wagner
Canton
Spirit Lake
Sheldon
Estherville
MINN.
IOWA
Missouri
Bassett
Yankton
Spencer
Emmetsburg
Mason City
Osage
Decorah
O'Neill
Vermillion
Le Mars
Algona
Charles City
EFFIGY MOUNDS NAT'L MON.
Postville
Cherokee
W. Union
Plainview
Laurel
Sioux City
Storm Lake
Sac City
Fort Dodge
Humboldt
Hampton
Waverly
Waterloo
Taylor
Norfolk
Mapleton
Iowa Falls
Cedar Falls
Manchester
Madison
Onawa
Webster City
Carroll
Boone
Marshalltown
Cedar Rapids
Anamosa
West Point
Oakland
Denison
Ames
Tama
Ansley
Columbus
St. Paul
Blair
Missouri Valley
Harlan
Des Moines
Newton
Adel
Fremont
Wahoo
Council Bluffs
Iowa City
Grand Island
Kearney
Omaha
Winterset
Knoxville
Muscatine
York
Greenfield
Indianola
Sigourney
Plattsmouth
Creston
Oskaloosa
Chariton
Hastings
Minden
Lincoln
Glenwood
Shenandoah
Osceola
Ottumwa
Fairfield
Mt. Pleasant
Nebraska City
Mt. Ayr
Leon
Corydon
Bloomfield
Alma
Red Cloud
HOMESTEAD NAT'L MON. OF AMERICA
Hebron
Auburn
MO.
IOWA
Phillipsburg
Superior
Beatrice
Maryville
Princeton
Lancaster
Memphis
Keokuk
NEB.
KAN.
Marysville
Bethany
Unionville
Craig
Falls City
Smith Center
Mankato
Seneca
Belleville
Kirksville
Hiawatha
St. Joseph
Trenton
Canton
Concordia
Chillicothe
Brookfield
Beloit
Osborne
Cameron
Holton
Monroe City
Macon
Atchison
Leavenworth
Manhattan
Carrollton
Brunswick
Paris
Russell
Lincoln
Junction City
Excelsior Springs
Moberly
Hannibal
Ellsworth
Salina
Abilene
Kansas City
Topeka
Independence
Waverly
Marshall
Great Bend
Lawrence
KANSAS CITY
Mexico
Lyons
McPherson
Ottawa
Columbia
Emporia
Harrisonville
Warrensburg
Fulton
Warrenton
Hutchinson
Florence
TURNPIKE
Garnett
Sedalia
ST. LOUIS
Newton
Burlington
Warsaw
Jefferson City
Lake of the Ozarks
Eldon
Wichita
Yates Center
Iola
El Dorado Springs
El Dorado
Augusta
Chanute
Fort Scott
Nevada
Camdenton
Harper
Wellington
Stockton Res.
Lamar
Bolivar
Rolla
Winfield
Independence
Pittsburg
Buffalo
Lebanon
KAN.
OKLA.
Parsons
G.W. CARVER NAT'L MON.
Springfield
Arkansas City
Cherokee
Joplin
Carthage
Mountain Grove
Ponca City
Bartlesville
Coffeyville
Miami
Monett
Willow Springs
Enid
Pawhuska
Vinita
Neosho
Cassville
Ava
Mansfield
Table Rock Lake
Fairview
Pawnee
Cleveland
Claremore
Branson
West Plains
Hennessey
Perry
Tulsa
Gainesville
Alton

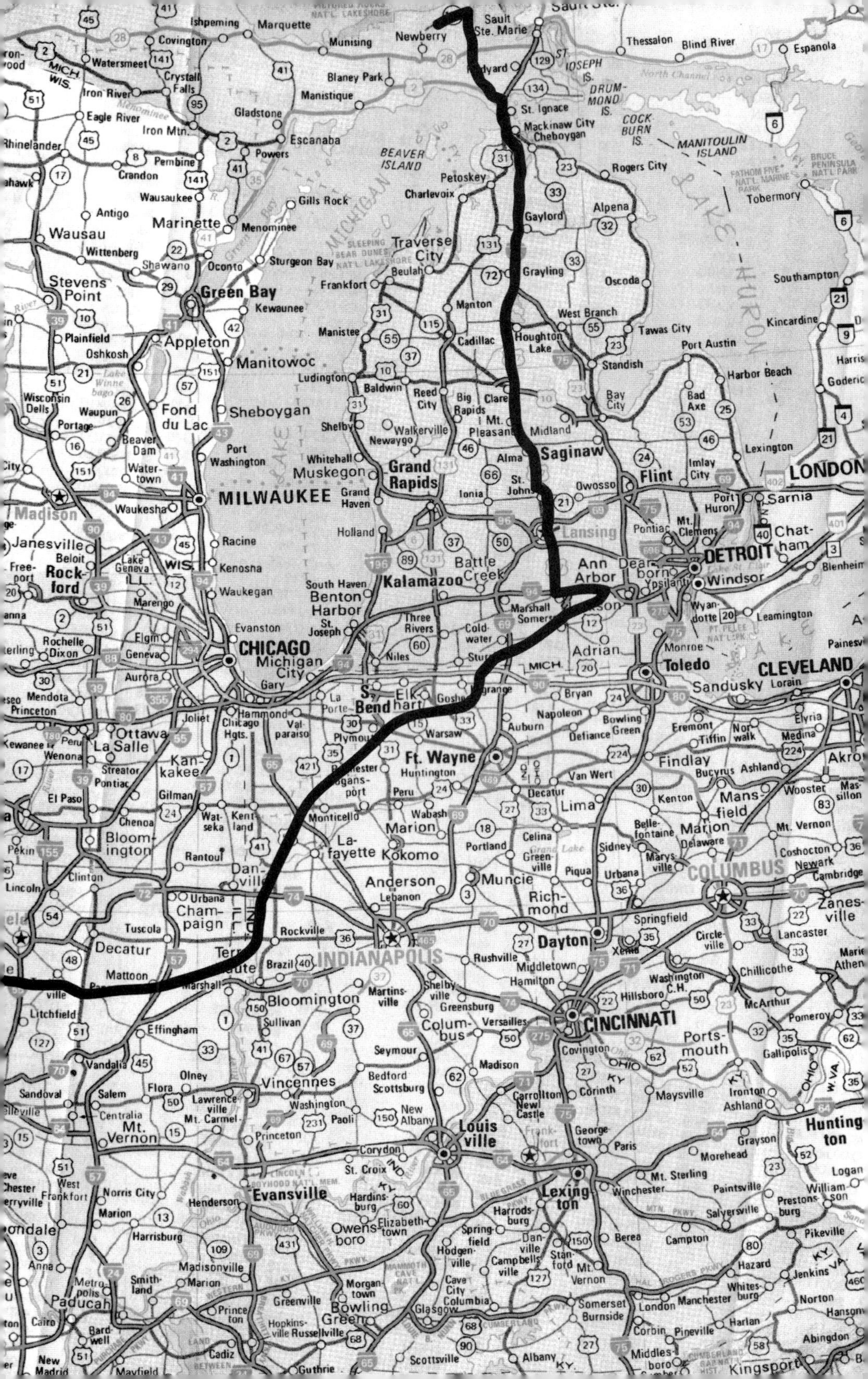
Ishpeming
Marquette
Sault Ste. Marie
Munising
Newberry
Thessalon
Blind River
Espanola
Covington
Watersmeet
Blaney Park
Manistique
Iron River
Crystal Falls
Gladstone
St. Ignace
Mackinaw City
Cheboygan
Eagle River
Iron Mtn.
Escanaba
Rhinelander
Powers
Pembine
Crandon
BEAVER ISLAND
Petoskey
Rogers City
MANITOULIN ISLAND
Tobermory
Wausaukee
Gills Rock
Charlevoix
Alpena
Antigo
Marinette
Menominee
Gaylord
Wausau
Wittenberg
Traverse City
Shawano
Oconto
Sturgeon Bay
Grayling
Oscoda
Southampton
Stevens Point
Green Bay
Frankfort
Beulah
Kewaunee
Manton
West Branch
Plainfield
Appleton
Manistee
Cadillac
Houghton Lake
Tawas City
Port Austin
Kincardine
Oshkosh
Manitowoc
Ludington
Standish
Harbor Beach
Baldwin
Reed City
Big Rapids
Clare
Wisconsin Dells
Fond du Lac
Sheboygan
Mt. Pleasant
Midland
Bay City
Bad Axe
Waupun
Portage
Shelby
Walkerville
Newaygo
Beaver Dam
Port Washington
Saginaw
Lexington
Whitehall
Muskegon
Grand Rapids
Alma
Flint
Imlay City
LONDON
Watertown
St. Johns
MILWAUKEE
Grand Haven
Ionia
Owosso
Port Huron
Sarnia
Madison
Waukesha
Holland
Lansing
Pontiac
Mt. Clemens
Chatham
Janesville
Racine
Beloit
Battle Creek
Ann Arbor
DETROIT
Freeport
Rockford
Lake Geneva
Kenosha
Dearborn
Windsor
Waukegan
South Haven
Kalamazoo
Ypsilanti
Benton Harbor
Marengo
Marshall
Wyandotte
Leamington
Evanston
St. Joseph
Three Rivers
Coldwater
Rochelle
Dixon
Elgin
CHICAGO
Adrian
Monroe
Geneva
Michigan City
Niles
Toledo
CLEVELAND
Aurora
Gary
Sandusky
Lorain
Mendota
Princeton
Hammond
La Porte
S. Bend
Elkhart
Goshen
Bryan
Joliet
Ottawa
Chicago Hgts.
Valparaiso
Plymouth
Napoleon
Bowling Green
Elyria
La Salle
Warsaw
Auburn
Defiance
Fremont
Tiffin
Norwalk
Medina
Peru
Streator
Kankakee
Rochester
Logansport
Ft. Wayne
Findlay
Ashland
Pontiac
Huntington
Van Wert
Bucyrus
El Paso
Gilman
Decatur
Lima
Kenton
Mansfield
Wooster
Massillon
Chenoa
Watseka
Kentland
Monticello
Wabash
Marion
Bellefontaine
Marion
Mt. Vernon
Pekin
Bloomington
Lafayette
Kokomo
Portland
Celina
Sidney
Delaware
Coshocton
Rantoul
Greenville
Marysville
Newark
Clinton
Danville
Anderson
Muncie
Piqua
Urbana
COLUMBUS
Cambridge
Lincoln
Urbana
Champaign
Lebanon
Richmond
Zanesville
Tuscola
Springfield
Decatur
Rockville
INDIANAPOLIS
Dayton
Xenia
Circleville
Lancaster
Terre Haute
Brazil
Rushville
Middletown
Mattoon
Marshall
Martinsville
Shelbyville
Hamilton
Washington C.H.
Chillicothe
Athens
Bloomington
Greensburg
Hillsboro
McArthur
Litchfield
Sullivan
Columbus
Versailles
CINCINNATI
Pomeroy
Effingham
Portsmouth
Covington
Seymour
Madison
Gallipolis
Vandalia
Olney
Bedford
Scottsburg
Vincennes
Carrollton
Corinth
Maysville
Ironton
Ashland
Sandoval
Salem
Flora
Lawrenceville
Washington
New Castle
Huntington
Centralia
Mt. Carmel
Paoli
New Albany
Louisville
Frankfort
Georgetown
Paris
Grayson
Mt. Vernon
Princeton
Corydon
Morehead
St. Croix
Mt. Sterling
Logan
West Frankfort
Norris City
Evansville
Lexington
Winchester
Paintsville
Williamson
Henderson
Hardinsburg
Harrodsburg
Salyersville
Prestonsburg
Marion
Elizabethtown
Owensboro
Springfield
Danville
Berea
Campton
Pikeville
Harrisburg
Hodgenville
Stanford
Anna
Madisonville
Campbellsville
Mt. Vernon
Hazard
Jenkins
Smithland
Marion
Metropolis
Paducah
Morgantown
Cave City
Columbia
Manchester
Whitesburg
Norton
Greenville
Bowling Green
Glasgow
Somerset
Burnside
London
Cairo
Princeton
Hopkinsville
Russellville
Harlan
Bardwell
Corbin
Pineville
Abingdon
New Madrid
Cadiz
Scottsville
Albany
Middlesboro
Kingsport
Mayfield
Guthrie